Moths
TO A FLAME

Moths
TO A FLAME

Sarah Ash

MILLENNIUM

An Orion Book
LONDON

This edition first published
in Great Britain in 1995 by
Millennium
An imprint of Orion Books Ltd
Orion House, 5 Upper St Martin's Lane
London WC2H 9EA

A CIP catalogue record for this book is available
from the British Library

ISBN: (Csd) 1 85798 272 X
(Ppr) 1 85798 292 4

Millennium

Typeset at The Spartan Press Ltd,
Lymington, Hants
Printed and bound in Great Britain by
Clays Ltd, St Ives plc

For Michael

ACKNOWLEDGEMENTS

With especial thanks to my editors at Millennium: Deborah Beale, Charon Wood and Caroline Oakley; Tad Williams for early insights; Alison Sinclair for much-valued moral support; David Pringle and Lee Montgomerie of INTERZONE for first publishing 'Mothmusic'.

The Land of Ar-Khendye

The seven cantons of Ar-Khendye have been ruled for centuries by the House of Memizhon which claims direct descent from the god Mithiel.

The Court of the House of Memizhon

The Arkhan Melmeth	Ruler of the Seven Cantons known collectively as Ar-Khendye, and head of the House of Memizhon
The Arkhys Clodolë	His consort
The Haute Zhudiciar Jhafir	Prime Minister with responsibility for justice in Ar-Khendye
The Torella Sarilla	Noblewoman
Torella/Torellan	Noblewoman/man owning estates in the Seven Cantons

NB – the Arkhan is given the honorary title of Haute Torellan of the palace of Myn-Dhiel.

The Tarkhas Memizhon (The Blues)

The Arkhan's bodyguard – also known as his 'Clan' – are a select band of chosen men.

The Tarkhas Zhudiciar (The Reds)

The bodyguard of the Haute Zhudiciar, with special responsibility for law-enforcement throughout Ar-Khendye.

Tarkhas Officers

Razhirrakh	Champion bladesman
Tarrakh	Officer in charge of the training of tarkhastars and fighting slaves

PROLOGUE

Springtide on Ael Lahi.
  Dusktide washing the pale sands.
  Moontide.

Lai Dhar scanned the twilit bay. The seashore was, as he had hoped, empty. No one would hear him here if he sneaked one last practice before the new moon rose.

He sat down, bare toes wriggling through the warm sand to the damp sediment below, so deliciously cool after the day's heat.

Lifting the flute to his lips, he took a breath and began to weave the intricacies of the Spring Invocation.

A lock of wayward hair flopped forwards over his face; he shook it out of his eyes and carried on.

He had been practising the invocation for moons beyond counting – and still he couldn't get it right! And tonight it was vital he should get it right; tonight was the night of the moonmoths. And as youngest adept of the Sacred Grove, he had been chosen to play, to charm the moths to the Goddess's shrine. The knowledge that his partner in the invocation would be his twin sister Laili did not improve his mood; she was so much more accomplished a flute-player than he – and he did not want to let her down. If she was nervous about tonight's ceremony – their first as newly initiated adepts of the Sacred Grove – she would be able to conceal it. Whereas he had hardly slept, tossing and turning all night beneath the stars.

Even now he was not sure what had persuaded Aela, Eldest One, that he was ready to participate in the moon mysteries. This morning when she had commanded him to play to her, she had soon stopped him with one tap of her staff; gentle, yet firm.

'Patience, patience. Don't rush at it so impulsively. Let the notes flow. They can only flow when you can forget what your fingers are doing . . . and that means—'

1

'More practice.' Lai nodded his head, sighing. 'It's just – the music in my head, Aela. It sings, it soars, and when I try to capture it—'

'You can only let the music fly when your body and mind work together in partnership. Music in the head is all very well, but you cannot express it when your fingers are tripping over each other.'

'You mean – I'm not ready?' He could not bear to think he might have to wait another year to be admitted to the mysteries.

Her gnarled fingers cupped his chin, tipping his face up to hers.

'Lai and Laili – so alike in looks – and yet so different in temperament. How could I separate you tonight of all nights?'

Body and mind working together . . .

His fingers moved more fluently over the holes in the flute, repeating the wreathing patterns of the invocation. Better – it was getting better –

There was not a cloud in the dusky sky . . . and yet Lai's skin suddenly chilled as if drenching monsoon rain were about to fall.

A warning?

He glanced uneasily behind him, but only the fragrant leaves of the balsam trees stirred slightly.

Just a breeze off the waves, nothing more sinister.

And yet . . .

He returned to his practice. Now the notes began to flow, to soar, to wing out over the waves . . .

A hoarse squeak suddenly marred the flowing purity of line; in a fury, he took the flute and flung it from him across the silvered sands.

'Tsk, tsk!' Laili was standing behind him, her moongauze robes stirring in the light evening breeze. She wagged her finger at him in imitation of old Aela. 'Still so impatient, Lai Dhar! Your temper will be the undoing of you one day!'

Lai made a grab for her but she slipped out of his reach and snatched his flute, waving it over her head. Her laughter, light as the evening breeze, teasing, tantalising him.

'Give it back!' He chased down the beach after her, feet slithering over the sand.

Danger . . .

He stopped, gazing out over the misted sea.

'You sensed it too,' she said softly.

'It's nerves – nothing more.' Lai forced a laugh.

'Then why are you watching the sea?'

He shrugged. All day this faint sense of unease had been troubling him. He could hide nothing from her. They might be opposite in temperament but each had always known the other's feelings without a word passing between them.

The purple skies were already peppered with stardust; soon the new moon would rise. A waft of frangipani flowers, cardamom-sweet, drifted across the strand.

'Come.' Laili touched his hand, her fingertips soft and cool. 'It's time.'

'Wait—'

There was a shadow on the horizon, the ghost of a ship where there had been nothing but a misted expanse of sea.

Danger . . .

Lai's body chilled again with a sudden inexplicable shiver of fear.

'Probably a spice barque,' Laili said.

'But what spice barque could move so fast on a calm sea?'

From the darkness of the moonhaunted glades an eerie shimmer of sound arose to greet the moon. A sound to ravish the heart. To make the heart ache almost to breaking.

'Listen,' Laili whispered. 'It has already begun.'

Aela, the Eldest One, stood, supported by her sisters, in the heart of the Grove. Sweet-burning incense candles lit her gnarled face. She beckoned Lai and Laili close . . . and as they knelt before her, she touched each in turn upon the forehead where the white crescent, moonmark of the Goddess, gleamed pearl-pale against their brown skin. Then she handed them each a ceremonial weirdflute, carved from sea-bleached bone.

Lai moistened his dry lips with his tongue and raised the flute to his mouth; Laili did the same. He took a breath – and began to play. To echo, to embellish the glittering sounds emitted by the moths.

Moonmoths. Sacred to the Goddess, the moonmoths of Ael Lahi emerged gauze-winged from their chrysalises on this one night of the year to sing, to mate, lay their eggs – and die. With the Goddess's blessing, the moonmoths would be drawn to the flute-music and the glowing incense candles . . . and would sanctify the Grove with their presence.

Lai's flute sent spirals of notes curling upwards like the incense fumes to intertwine and mingle with the notes rising from Laili's flute in perfect unity of purpose. A drowsed spell of drifting music enwreathed the Sanctuary. Lai raised his eyes as he played and saw the moonmoths come floating down from the black sky—

Voices. Men's voices, shouting, sharp as smashed glass in the Grove's stillness.

'What's happening?' The flute dropped from Laili's fingers.

A scream seared the air. Men came running into the Sanctuary, adepts scattering in front of them like wind-blown petals. Lai saw a blur of crimson in the torch flares.

'Slavers!' he whispered.

Aela stepped forward, her hand upraised.

'This is a sanctuary, sacred to the Goddess. Go now and leave our hallowed places undefiled. Or the Goddess will strike you down!'

For a heart's beat, the strangers stopped to stare at the frail old woman. And then one of them began to laugh.

'You don't frighten me, old woman, with your mumbo-jumbo. Curse away!' His words were in the common tongue – but harshly, oddly accented. 'We want young ones, healthy ones. Tell us where to find them – and we will spare your Sacred Grove.'

Aela drew her robes about her and proudly raising her head, spat in the stranger's face.

He stared back at her, the spittle wet on his cheeks. Even the insect-whirr had ceased, the moist air hung silent, still, empty of sound.

'You're very foolish, old woman. We could have reached an agreement. But now—'

One of his men moved behind the Eldest One; the blade gleamed, slashing downwards towards the silvered head. Aela fell without a sound. Scarlet, redder than spilt wine, stained the silver.

Lai shuddered. The pale lifeflame was snuffed out, in a breath of a passing breeze, leaving a cold desolation in his soul. He heard Laili's sharp indrawn breath, felt her stunned shock, her disbelief.

'Aela—' she began, starting out across the clearing towards the crumpled body.

And Lai came to his senses.

'No!' He caught hold of her, pulling her back. 'Run, Laili!'

'I – I can't—' Her ornate robes slowed her down, winding themselves tighter about knees and ankles.

'Faster!'

She lost hold of his hand and fell. Lai turned back, bending to scoop her up, only to see two of the slavers coming straight towards them.

'Lai!' Laili screamed aloud. One caught hold of her by the other arm, jerking her away from him.

4

'Let her go!' Lai flung himself onto her abductor, thumping both fists against the man's broad back.

A blow to the side of the head sent him reeling. Glancing dizzily up, he saw a drawn blade glinting in the darkness.

'Tarrakh-zhan! Look at this one!'

The point of the blade pierced the skin of Lai's throat. In the torch flares he could see a cluster of crimson-clad men around Laili. They had ripped her gauze robes open, baring her arms, her small breasts, tender and pink as guava-flesh.

'Take her.' A curt voice cut across the others. 'She'll do.'

'Lai!' Laili cried out sobbingly. 'Help me!'

Lai reared up only to be slapped down again.

'And the boy?'

'He's young. Sturdy. Take him too.'

Ducking under the blade, Lai clamped his arms around the man's legs, tugging with all his strength.

'Laili!'

The man kicked out. His foot caught Lai in the chest.

Lai fell. Flat on his back. Too winded to roll out of the way.

The blade came whistling through the moist air, striking him full on the forehead.

White lightflash.

Then dark, dark of the moon . . .

Void.

Herded together like animals, golden Aelahim, pale Mynezhilim, dark-skinned tattooed Enhirrans, they crouched in the darkness of the slave galley, men separated from women by a slatted wooden partition.

Lai opened his eyes; pain flashed through his skull, dazzlebright.

He could remember nothing. Only that white flash of pain; slowly the dazzle was dimming and fragments of memory returning. The stench of the hold, the sickening roll and pitch of the vessel, the ache in his skull, all centred on the dizzy lurch of his stomach; he retched until his throat burned but only a thin slime came up.

The pain had become a jagged slash across his blurred vision; his hand rose, shakily, to touch his forehead and came away caked in half-congealed blood.

Blood. Scarlet seeping through silver. The reek of choking smoke . . . Confused fragments of memory amongst the cindered firesparks.

'Lai . . . li?'

'Here, Lai.'

A glint of russet caught his eye in the distant shadows.

Lai began to crawl slowly, painfully towards a chink in the partition until the bite of metal into his ankle told him he was shackled to the bulkhead. Stretching his full length, he extended his arm until they could just touch fingertips . . .

'They haven't – harmed you?'

'No. Not yet. If I am forced against my will, it will be a crime against the Goddess. A desecration of her name. But I will never be able to serve her again . . .'

Now he remembered. And groaned aloud, letting his head sink into his hands. Intruders in the Grove. The sacred vessels smashed, the Sanctuary violated. The smirch of smoke and flames—

'Aela. I should have protected Aela. But I just stood there.' The ache of remembering was worse than the throbbing pain in his bruised head.

'What could you have done against them? They were armed. They would have killed you too.' Her fingertips pressed against his, reassuring, comforting.

'What will they do to us?' he whispered, raising his head.

'What do they do with slaves? They are barbarians. They worship Mithiel, Wielder of the Undying Flame. They do not understand the ways of the Goddess.'

He felt her fingers begin to tremble against his; her head drooped. Unable to bear the unspoken accusation of her silent tears, he whispered fiercely through the partition, 'I'll get us back to the Island, Laili. Somehow.'

She did not reply.

6

CHAPTER 1

Melmeth, Arkhan of Ar-Khendye, Lord of the Seven Cantons, last scion of the House of Memizhon and Guardian of the Undying Flame, gazed down over the great city of Perysse. He could not sleep. The dream had returned again, he had woken clutching at darkness, trying in vain to hold her back . . .

Who was she?

Night after sleepless night he had climbed the winding stair to the dizzy belvedere atop the Eidolon Tower to stare out over the crowded rooftops to the silver, silken ribbon of the river Yssil far below. Was she there, somewhere, the elusive woman of his dream? If he were to disguise himself as a commoner and slip out into the narrow lanes of the city, would he find her in some humble wine-shop or laundry?

But even if he found her, she would like as not prove to be just as compliant, as vacuous as all the others . . . Diverting, doubtless, for a day or two . . . An arkhan could have anyone he wanted, just snap the fingers . . . What was the point of it all? A few hours' pleasure, gone in the blink of an eye. Beneath the tower lay the royal mausoleum; the glorious relics of the House of Memizhon quietly mouldering to dust beneath their jewelled funeral robes. Even his warrior father Sardion lay there, even Sardion the Invincible had sickened and died . . .

'And now this is all mine,' whispered Melmeth.

The star-trail in the sky made him blink. A pale bright fire blazed across the darkness.

A comet.

The starry tail extinguished itself in the utter darkness beyond the rim of the distant heights.

An omen. But what did it signify? Was it a portent? A portent of impending disaster?

Melmeth felt a sudden chill, cold as a splash of rain water.

The night sky seemed all the more black now that the dazzling trail of fire had vanished.

An omen. ·

Perysse, capital city of the Seven Cantons of Ar-Khendye, had grown rich on two thriving trades: silk – and slaves. The wide river Yssil was crowded with merchant ships, slave galleys, spice barques, all seeking a mooring to offload their precious cargoes. But Lai and Laili, ankles and hands shackled, saw only the towering buildings, the sky dwindling to a pale slit glimpsed between overhanging roofs, the gutter-dirt slimy beneath their bare feet as they shuffled forwards in a straggling line, goaded onwards by the harsh voices of their captors.

Legs cramped and weak from confinement in the hold of the galley, the captives stumbled, grasping at each other to stay aright. Knocked off-balance, Laili lost her footing. Lai put out an arm to support her – only to cower away under the sharp sting of a slaver's flail.

'Keep moving!'

The slave-market was held every day except holy days in the Square of the Ylliri Fountain, gift to the people of Perysse from the Arkhans of Ar-Khendye. Lai gazed with desperate longing towards the fountain, its milky marble bowl stained green by the gushing water; his dry tongue licked his cracked lips.

'Me too,' whispered Laili. Her fingers curled around his. 'Very thirsty. If only—'

'Silence!' A slaver wheeled around, flail raised.

'Don't touch her!' Lai hissed.

A gong drum began to batter out an incessant, strident tattoo. The raised flail slowly dropped. People were gathering, milling at the foot of the steps for a closer view of the day's merchandise. Ragged lazars, begging for alms, were kicked and whipped away as the gong drum beat louder. Laili's fingers clutched Lai's more tightly.

'I think it's beginning.'

'I said silence!' The slaver tore the stained white robe from Laili's shoulders.

The shame of it. Stripped, chained like herd beasts. So many eyes staring at them, at their nakedness. Nowhere to hide. So many lascivious, lustful thoughts burning the air, heady as incense fumes.

Lai tried to place himself in front of Laili to shield her – but the slaver tugged roughly at his chain and he fell to his knees.

Voices were raised, numbers shouted. Bartering, Lai thought, barely understanding the unfamiliar accent. The language was the common tongue they shared . . . but the Perysse inflections were quite alien, rendering them almost incomprehensible to a foreign ear.

'They make a pretty pair, those two . . .'

A silk-draped palanquin was set down at the steps; a woman drew aside the curtains and pointed languidly with her feathered fan. The slave trader was instantly at her side, bowing and offering her his hand.

'Esteemed Torella, I welcome you. Would you honour me by inspecting my merchandise?'

The Torella beckoned with one taloned fingernail.

Lai reluctantly edged down the steps, Laili clutching more tightly at his hand. The ringed hand beckoned him closer still until it touched his head.

'Such hair, such an exquisite colour . . . fire flickering on strands of coppered silk.'

The fingers stroked his cheek, tilting his face upwards.

Beautiful boy . . .

Images, soft as drifting feathers, floated past. Lewd images, stirrings of lust . . . Lai tried to conceal a shudder of loathing. Not that, no please, not that—

'They're blemished.' The soft-fleshed finger-tip pressed the moonmark on Lai's brow.

'No, Torella, that mark is a guarantee of their true worth, I assure you.'

The Torella's plucked and painted eyebrows quirked inquisitively upwards.

'Please ask them yourself.'

'What does this signify?' Her breath was sweet, over-sweet with violet-perfumed cachous, as her finger pressed against the sacred moonmark. Lai shook his head.

'Speak!' The trader tugged at the chain.

'Perhaps the handsome young savage does not understand?' The Torella smiled into Lai's face.

'It means,' Lai said haltingly, 'that we are servants of the Goddess. We have vowed our lives to Her service.'

'I know nothing of this Goddess.'

The slave merchant whispered in the Torella's ear and Lai saw a slow smile spread across the powdered, painted face.

'And no one's interfered with them on the voyage?'

'Oh no, Torella, my men know better than to spoil the goods.'

Lai strained to decipher the stream of words, knowing that they held the key to their fate.

'Untouched . . . and with red hair. He has a predilection for red hair . . .'

'The Torella will take them?' The trader was rubbing his hands in anticipation of a good sale.

'Tell me your price.'

'A thousand gold eniths apiece.'

'Ridiculous.' The Torella raised her fan and turned away.

'Wait. Wait. One and a half thousand for the pair.'

'Extortionate!'

'The Pleasure House of Black Khassia is very interested in them. Virgins are much in demand—'

'They can have them.'

The palanquin curtain dropped, veiling the Torella from sight.

'Twelve hundred, Torella. A special price for you, my most esteemed customer—'

The silk curtain twitched. Lai saw the Torella's eyes, dark as jet beads, glittering with satisfaction.

'Have them brought to my rooms at Myn-Dhiel.'

Lai heard the clink of coins; a purse was tossed from the palanquin and the trader caught it in both hands.

'Those two. To the Torella Sarilla at the palace.'

The slavers pushed in between Lai and Laili and knelt to unchain them. The locks were rusted; one placed his scimitar on the step as he strained to turn the key. Laili's eyes met Lai's above the bowed heads of their captors.

Our last chance.

I'll make a break for it. They'll go after me – you slip away in the confusion.

She nodded, a slight movement, almost imperceptible. She had understood.

Lai drew in a breath, held it – then as the shackles dropped from his ankles, kicked the slaver in the groin, grabbed the scimitar and took off down the steps.

'Runaway!' The shout went up from the fountain steps; a warning bell began to clamour. Lai dived in amongst the crowd for cover, scrabbling his way through the onlookers who ducked hastily away from the shining blade, darting left, then right, like a fast-fleeing deer.

Now, Laili. Hurry!

Crimson jackets appeared in the crowd. Soldiers.

A girl screamed, sharp as a knife drawn across glass. Lai froze.

'Looking for this, were you?'

They were hauling someone between them. Lai caught a glimpse of the tumbled hair, flame-red as his own.

'Don't spoil the goods,' the trader said nervously. 'She's for Myn-Dhiel.'

'Myn-Dhiel! Why should the Arkhan get all the choicest titbits?' An arrogant voice rang out, well-used to command; obviously an officer. 'You won't mind giving us a sample, will you, sweeting?'

Lai heard Laili whimper some incoherent denial. There was something in the defeated sob that suddenly sent him mad, wild-crazed. And when he saw the officer twist her averted face towards him, forcing his mouth down onto hers—

'Let her go.' Lai's hand tightened about the scimitar hilt. Glint of steel in the cloud-veiled sunlight. 'I said – let her go!'

'Another runaway. Drop your weapon, slave!'

The officer's blade came stabbing in under his guard. Sheer instinct made Lai parry, striking it wide. Sheer instinct made him carry the blow through, slashing upwards—

The tip caught the officer at the base of the neck; Lai felt the shock as the honed metal sliced through the crimson jacket, jarred through flesh against bone.

The officer stared at Lai. His blade dropped to the cobbles with a clang. A crimson snake seemed to uncoil around his throat, his hands rose to tear it away. Slowly, he began to pitch forwards. A hideous half-human gargling, gasping sound issued from his gaping mouth.

'Lai – run!' screamed Laili as the slavers bundled her into the palanquin.

Lai just stood there. The man's glazed face stared up at him, drained of all colour. Yet still the coils of the crimson snake unravelled from his gashed throat onto the cobbles.

'I – I didn't mean to—' he whispered.

It had been his first vow to the Goddess.

I will harm no living creature. I will not kill.

He hardly felt the other soldiers prise the sword from his shaking hand, hardly noticed the jeers of the ragged crowd that had gathered about them. Hardly noticed that Laili's palanquin had disappeared from sight.

'Bind his hands!' ordered one of the soldiers.

Lai wanted to run. But his knees trembled so much he could not move. They forced his hands behind his back, the rope bit into his skin as they pulled it tight about his wrists, tugged him across the cobbles.

'Wh–where are you taking me?'

'Hold your tongue, slave!' One hit him across the mouth. He tasted blood, hot and salt on his swelling lip. 'You've killed an officer of the Tarkhas Zhudiciar. The punishment is death.'

Deep in the foetid hold of the slave barque, one of the slavers stumbled over a tumbled bundle of old rags. Cursing, he kicked at it – and then recoiled as, in the lantern light, the festering bundle opened . . . releasing an overwhelming stench of putrefaction.

Not every slave imprisoned in the airless hold survived the journey to Perysse. And by the smell of this one, he had been dead some while. Yet beneath the mouldering sacking, the slaver thought he saw a sudden convulsive stir of movement.

'Maistre – Maistre—'

'What's this racket?'

By the light of the Maistre's lanthorn, the slaver pointed out the corpse.

'Something's – *alive* in there.'

'Maggots,' said the Maistre impassively. With the tip of his staff he flicked aside the rags . . .

'What in all Ar-Khendye—' One hand clamped over nose and mouth, he held the lanthorn closer over the emaciated body.

'Dead leaves?'

'Mithiel knows!' The Maistre backed away.

Out of the folds of cloth came fluttering something with ragged wings. The slaver flapped his hands in front of his face, batting the sluggish creatures away.

'Afraid of a few moths?' jeered the Maistre, recovering himself. 'Get this carrion off my ship. And swab the hold down till it smells sweet as a spice barque. We don't want the Zhudiciar's men poking around in here, asking questions.'

The midden heap where the slavers slung the rotting sacks was already noisy with blowflies. They piled rubbish on top until the slave's corpse sank slowly down out of sight. Then they set off for the nearest tavern on the quay. After a glass or two of spiced khassafri, the incident was forgotten, blurred by a stupor of drink and dreamweed . . .

CHAPTER 2

The woman with hair of red-gold, spinning, spinning until her hair is like delicate fluttering wings, wings of a moth floating through dark woods, drifting on a night breeze towards a pale flame, hundreds upon hundreds of translucent wings drifting like snow, drawn towards the flame in the grove, the Sacred Grove where the flame of Memizhon burns palely, flickering paler, paler as the fanning of the smothering mothwings threatens to extinguish its dying light . . . And the floating hair of red-gold still spinning, spinning amidst the myriad mothwings, the glimmer of a naked white body changing in the festering flame, the woman's face, deathly white yet deathly fair—

Melmeth's hands reached out – only to clutch the empty air.

The dream again. The elusive dream-dancer, the flame-haired mystic, spinning in her shaman-trance . . .

'Who are you?' he whispered into the darkness. A sleep-laden sigh; the recumbent form beside him shifted, then lapsed back into slumber. He had forgotten the tattooed Enhirran slave, skilled in the erotic arts, Sarilla's latest discovery. He had even forgotten her name. She had been diverting enough for an hour or two's pleasure . . . but no more than diverting. Painfully eager to please, she had dutifully performed her rehearsed role and now she slept soundly . . . and he was awake.

On the outer rim of the city a gaunt black tower loured above the Temple of Mithiel, its slit windows barred with spiked iron, a star-gazer's glass belvedere at its dizzy top. This was the Tower of Perpetuity where Ophar, Augur and High Priest of Mithiel, charted the movement of the constellations and their influence upon the ruling House of Memizhon.

As last of the bloodline descended from the godking Mithiel, Melmeth had been reared to revere and worship his deified ancestor. He had been instructed from childhood in the secret rites of the temple. His earliest memories were of his father Sardion, robed in gold and flame, extending his hand to him. Convinced that this gilded warrior was the god come to consume him in fire, he had burst into terrified sobs and buried his head in his mother's skirts. He could still hear his father's scornful words issuing from behind the golden godmask.

'Take this crybaby away and don't bring him into my presence again until he knows how to behave like a man.'

Now it was he who put on the golden godmask and officiated at the rites. But he had not lost his dread of the temple . . . or the underlying suspicion that in praying to Mithiel, he was only praying to the memory of his tyrannical father. He had read and re-read the holy texts, hoping to centre his uncertain faith on the ancient prayers and psalms. But lately, even these had failed to comfort him. There was an emptiness inside his soul, an aching void. He longed to find a new meaning to his existence, a new peace to balm his doubts . . .

Melmeth had no need to cross the city to consult the priests of Mithiel; a warren of tunnels built by his ancestors allowed the Arkhan to pass beneath the city, unnoticed by the common people. Escape routes, constructed in more violent times, the labyrinthine under-ways facilitated secret journeys . . . and clandestine encounters.

Two dark-robed hierophants greeted the Arkhan with silent obeisances and led him up the winding obsidian stair, passing doorway after doorway as they climbed. Each dim room Melmeth glimpsed was filled with stacks of ancient black-bound, chained volumes. The air was dry and musty as if no window had ever been opened to let in the sun.

The hierophants stopped before an archway with the name 'Myn-Dhiel' emblazoned in gold across the lintel: the scarlet device of the flame curled like fire-tongues around the deep-cut letters.

'Welcome, Lord Arkhan. I have been expecting you.' Ophar came towards Melmeth out of the shadows, a gaunt old man with brows and beard as grey as dust. As a child Melmeth had been terrified of him; now that he was Arkhan, he still felt a tremor of unease in the High Priest's austere presence.

'The comet,' Melmeth said. 'What does it mean?'

Ophar beckoned. Melmeth followed him into a chamber whose walls and ceiling were painted black as night; stars and constellations, pricked out in gold and silver, glowed dully in the gloom.

'Sit, Lord Arkhan.'

The table between them was round, a disc of polished metal, dimly reflecting the painted sky above. Melmeth stared into it, seeing his own face drowned in stars.

'What do you see?' breathed Ophar's voice in the gloom.

Melmeth squeezed his eyes shut, opened them again. The stars flickered . . . Danced . . . Now they seemed to form a pulsating diadem across his brow.

'A crown . . . A crown of stars . . .'

Ophar drew a cloth across the disc, dark velvet fringed with scarlet.

'The comet comes as a warning.'

Melmeth started, jolted out of the trance.

'A warning? Of what?'

'You neglect your duties. You neglect your consort, the Arkhys Clodolë. Your court is renowned throughout the Seven Cantons for its excesses. You surround yourself with fawning exquisites who flatter you . . . And all the time your kingdom is crumbling into disorder . . .'

Melmeth stared at the old man's accusing eyes, taken aback by the vehemence of his words.

'But . . . The mirror . . .'

'Your vision betrays you. A crown of stars! Your people need a real king, not a dreamer with his head in the clouds.'

'I came to you for advice – not abuse.'

'My lord has become so glutted with gilded compliments that he is incapable of digesting the truth.'

'I could have you thrown from the top of this tower for insolence!'

'You could, lord. You are Arkhan.' Ophar stared back at Melmeth, challenging him. 'Your father would have done as much.'

'I am not my father!' Melmeth cried. 'Why should I be? The warrior's way is not the only way. Why must I always be compared with him?'

'You are unhappy, lord,' Ophar said softly.

Melmeth rose and went pacing over to the rail to gaze down over the mist-gauzed city.

'Not unhappy. But searching. Searching for—'

A dancer with hair of red-gold . . . A dream-dancer . . . A dream . . . Nothing but a dream . . .

'Sarilla! What is this? A new purchase?'

A white-haired gallant strode across the garden courtyard to help Torella Sarilla alight from her palanquin. Laili saw them exchange

16

exaggerated kisses, first one cheek then the other; dazedly she wondered if this could be the Torella's consort . . .

'Such a performance at the market, Ymarys, you would not believe it! I bought a pair, a perfectly exquisite pair – and just as I was leaving, the boy went berserk. A firebrand! He attacked a tarkhastar of the watch – seized a blade – I thought I was at the arena. It was so exciting!'

'So where is this slave bladesman?'

'On his way to the donjon.'

'A firebrand, hm? Intriguing. And the other?'

'Examine her for yourself.'

'Oho. Red hair.'

'Tell me what you think.'

Ymarys reached into the palanquin to draw Laili out into the open. Laili tried to turn her head away but Ymarys tipped her chin gently upwards until she was obliged to look directly into his eyes. And saw that he was not an old man as she had assumed, that the sleek pale hair was blonde-white and the eyes looking curiously into her own were eerily light, silver-grey, like sun breaking low over storm-waves.

'Hm.' Ymarys walked around Laili, critically eyeing her up and down. 'Maybe . . . Bathed and properly clothed . . . With that unusual hair, she might . . .' He began to drift away. 'My angel, your taste is impeccable as always.' He blew a little kiss from the tips of his fingers to the Torella and vanished, leaving only a waft of bergamot from his perfumed hair.

'You've passed your first test,' the Torella said. 'That gallant was Ymarys, the Arkhan's champion.'

Laili just stood shivering, her arms still clasped about her.

'Why are you weeping, child? Think of those other poor minxes bought by the House of Black Khassia, sent to the stews of Perysse, think yourself lucky you are not one of them.'

Laili shook her head, unable to contain the shuddering tears that racked her body.

'Stupid little hussy!' The Torella turned away from her in irritation. 'You will ruin your complexion with this constant crying. I should be crying – throwing away six hundred eniths on that madman brother of yours! If that pig of a trader doesn't give me all my monies back, I—'

'Lai,' whispered Laili, turning away. 'Oh, Lai . . .'

An oil cresset sent up a smirch of smoke-tainted flame into the frowsty

17

darkness; Lai sat slumped on the filthy straw, staring at the wavering light. All around him others slept, he could hear the wheeze and snore of rotting lungs, air-starved lungs, confined too long underground. He had almost become accustomed to the foetid stench of the place; the human detritus of Perysse had been swept in here and left shackled to the dripping walls. He was only glad that Laili was not here with him, condemned to this airless, lightless life-in-death.

His skin burned in an agony of louse-bites. But he had hardly the strength to lift one manacled hand to scratch any more. The meagre slops of watery gruel they were given left him so hungry that his stomach cramped with emptiness. Once there had been a whole loaf of black bread; the others had scrapped viciously over it like pyedogs and he had listlessly hung back and left them to it. Next time, he feared, he would be driven by hunger to join the fight.

What he could not understand was why there were so few of his own age in the donjon vault; most of the inmates were grey-haired, gap-toothed . . . Several had stared at him, nudging and whispering when the tarkhastars first kicked him inside. He had tried to ask them how long he might stay here, would there be a trial, what punishment might be given—

They had shaken their grizzled heads and turned away from him.

In the darkness, he tried to remember the sacred words of invocation, of praise, of thanks. The chants for the morning, for the noon, for the coming of dusk.

Goddess, forgive me. I have broken my vow to you, I have taken another's life. I am no better than these heathens, I struck out in anger and killed. I am no longer worthy to be called your initiate.

Lai blinked furiously, feeling tears prickling his eyelids.

Laili . . . ?

Not even a whisper of an answer.

They had never been apart before. What were they doing to her? She was resilient, level-headed, so much more so than he – and yet vulnerable beneath her seeming calm.

He had tried to save her. And now he could not even save himself. He would never know what had become of her. He would never see her – or the whispering balsam groves of Ael Lahi again. And suddenly the hot tears were rolling silently down his bruised cheeks and he could not check the flood, bitterly ashamed to be weeping, yet so tired, so achingly tired and alone that he could not stop.

Oh Laili, where are you?

*

18

The Torella's courtyard garden was surrounded on three sides by an arched walkway. Laili sat alone, staring at her reflection in the reed-shaded pool. The Torella had sent her outside to gather the last pale roses . . . but they were dying, their bruised petals tumbling one by one into the glassy water. Laili trailed her fingers listlessly in the pool.

Where are you, Lai? I know you are not dead, if you were dead, I would have felt the link that binds us together – severed.

She knelt up, pressing her fingertips tightly to the moonmark on her forehead, trying to centre herself, her mind, in meditation.

'Goddess?' she whispered. Perhaps in this rare moment's solitude she could rediscover the solace of that eternal stillness . . . but whenever she closed her eyes, she saw blood, blood coursing down Aela's wrinkled face, blood trickling from the slashed throat of the soldier, blood on the blade in Lai's trembling hand . . .

'He did it to save me. Let me take the blame upon myself, let me atone for his crime . . .'

Petals, pale as moonflecks, came drifting down about her head to float on the dark water.

At this hour, close to dusk, the adepts gathered on Ael Lahi to welcome the first stars. As a child she had heard the voices rising from the Sacred Grove and she had believed them to be spirit voices. She had always longed to join with them, to spiral upwards into the twilit skies, lost in an endless trance of music.

The melody of the invocation wreathed into her mind, her lips began to move, her fingers reached upwards . . . and haltingly, she began to sing.

There was a dreaming kind of comfort in the familiar ritual; almost unconsciously she let herself sway to the rhythms of the eternal dance, her fingers uncurling gracefully to form the sacred gestures: moonbirds flying, moonlily buds slowly opening . . .

Only gradually did she become aware that she was no longer alone. She was being watched. A shadowed figure stood in the furthest archway, silently observing her.

The song dried to silence on her lips. She stopped, hands trembling.

'Wh–who's there?'

'Don't stop.' A man's voice from the gloom-shrouded archway. A cultured voice, soft and pleading. 'Please don't stop.' What was he doing, trespassing in the Torella's gardens so close to nightfall, spying on her?

Terrified, she turned and ran indoors, scattering petals as she went.

They hauled Lai along endless tunnels to a bare room; a sudden shock of cold daylight made him screw his eyes up tight.

'Next!'

A balding man in robes of crimson velvet was seated at a desk, scribbling with a scratchy nib; he had barely bothered to glance up from his ledger.

'Name?' he said disinterestedly.

'L–Lai D–Dhar.' Lai was shivering with cold; how soft the crimson velvet looked and how luxuriously warm. The last day and night he had been gripped with a bloody flux and now he felt so weak he could hardly stand.

'Ah yes. A grievous crime. Wounding an officer of the Arkhan—'

'He's not dead?' cried Lai. A kick silenced him.

'Luckily for you – or you would have been condemned to the spikes without hope of reprieve. The usual practice in cases such as yours is to have the miscreant gelded and put to work in the dye works.'

Lai heard the words of his sentence through a blur of nausea; his bowels still churned and rolled, although they had expelled the last of their contents earlier and his breechclout was slimed with his own excrement.

One of the tarkhastars moved forwards and whispered in the man's ear.

'It looks as though it may have been decided for you; the Tarkhas Memizhon are short of one bladesman for the rites. If their trainer judges you suitable, you will be handed over to him. If not . . . then the dye works and the gelding knife . . .'

Pains griped his empty belly; he rolled over in the foetid straw, drawing his knees up to his chest to try to soothe the ache. If he closed his eyes and tried to remember Ael Lahi, he could force the pains to recede to the edge of consciousness, to where they were almost bearable . . .

Remember the shore at sunset . . . So many times he and Laili had walked barefoot along the soft saltsands to watch the drifts of silvered seabirds wheel up into the dying light . . .

Voices murmuring . . . The twilit strand dwindled as the voices penetrated his dreams . . .

Hunger gnawed, sharp as a wolf's fang, as consciousness returned.

'Leave me alone . . .' he groaned, turning on his other side, trying to recapture the dream.

On Ael Lahi's deserted shore night had cloaked the sea; the sky faded from mauve to indigo, jewelled by one bright star. Duskstar. A child's wishing star.

'This one? The red-head?'

Faces loomed over him. Nightmare faces. Spirit masks, lemur-striped, moonwhite and shadowblack. They had come to suck out his soul.

'G–g–go away! Let me alone!'

Lai cowered on the straw, manacled hands over his head, the chains clanking cold against his face.

'He's sick!'

'He's foreign. He's not used to the water.'

'Your water's polluted. It's not fit for dogs to drink.'

A lantern-flame flickered, the light falling hot on Lai's closed lids; he tried to open his eyes, screwing them up as the light dazzled.

'Here's five eniths for you. Give him powdered arrowroot and poppy to bind his bowels. Prepared with clean boiled springwater. Another five eniths for you when I hear that he's cured.'

Physic? Na . . . Must be dreaming . . . Who would care one enith whether he lived or died in this human cesspit – let alone ten?

Lai's eyes slid open: a receding lantern flame wavered through the darkness like a corpselight over marshland. Two men were picking their way over the sleeping prisoners. As one bent with a jangle of keys to unlock the door, the other turned and glanced back over his shoulder at Lai.

The leaping shadows, the golden lantern-flame lit the man's face for the space of a missed heartbeat.

Daemon mask, one side smooth, olive-skinned, the other a mockery of perfection, hideously pitted and scarred.

Lai rubbed his eyes and looked again. There was no one there.

Na . . . It must have been another dream . . .

'Wake up!'

A sharp kick in the ribs brought Lai to his senses. Blinking in the bright torchlight, he could see a tarkhastar holding high a torch which dripped gouts of fire onto the piss-soaked straw.

'On your feet!' The tarkhaster jerked hard on the chain about his neck; he staggered to his feet, half-choked by the metal collar. '*Djhë!* You stink like a midden!'

21

'Wh–where are you taking me?' gasped Lai.

The tarkhastar tugged on the chain viciously, making him gag.

'Have you forgotten your manners? How do you address your masters?'

'Zhan,' said Lai in a choked whisper.

'Like it or not you're going to the Tarkhas Memizhon to be trained as a bladesman for the arena.'

Lai stared at him in dulled incredulity.

'I suppose that wherever it is you come from you haven't heard of the arena? I thought not. Once every year, the Arkhan holds a contest to celebrate Mithiel's Day. Memizhon bladesmen against Zhudiciar. All Perysse crowds into the arena to see the bladesmen fight. If you fight – and win – the Arkhan grants you your freedom.'

'Freedom?' Lai repeated dazedly.

'You fight if – and only if – you complete your training to the Arkhan's satisfaction. If you are not satisfactory then we return you to the donjon. And the gelding knife.'

A brazier of coal glowed in one corner of the subterranean chamber, tainting the air with its thin acrid fumes.

'Memizhon or Zhudiciar?' A wizened old man in a leathern apron hobbled forwards to squint up into Lai's face.

'Memizhon.'

The old man spat and turned his back on Lai, hobbling back to the brazier.

'Give him a mouthful of the draught.'

'Here. Drink.' The tarkhastar thrust a dusty bottle between Lai's lips, tipping it until a wash of burning liquid spilt into his mouth, his throat, splashing down his unshaven chin until he choked.

Fierce spirit on an empty stomach; suddenly Lai's head was light, swimmingly, dizzyingly light. He no longer cared what they did to him. When the tarkhastar gripped hold of his arms behind him, forced him back on the couch, strapping him down, he did not resist. What was the point. What was the—

The old man's face loomed in front of his, the stained needle jutting towards his naked eyes. Mazily he realised what he was about. The obliteration of the Goddess's sacred moonmark.

'Don't – d–don't do this to me—'

And then the needle seared into Lai's forehead, drilling into his brain where the pain raged with incinerating wildfire. His body went rigid; the tarkhastar pinned him down as he tried to master enough self-control not to cry his pain out aloud.

'Now you belong to the House of Memizhon.' Lai half-heard the words through the singing whiteness of the pain . . .

And the wildfire was dying, cooling to a more bearable emberglow. Lai opened his eyes and saw through the painglaze the old man shuffling back with a crystal phial and a pad of soft cloth. He poured drops of an opaque blue liquid onto the cloth, dark, indigo blue, pressing it to Lai's forehead.

Lai flinched at the first cold kiss of the liquid – then sagged back as it seeped soothing balm into the pierced skin.

Tattooed. A slave, condemned to bear the mark of his servitude, etched into his forehead, for life. His head drooped, his rats' tails of filthy hair hiding his face, his brimming eyes.

'Head up!' The tarkhastar forced Lai's head back so far that Lai feared his neck would snap. The old man bent over him to scrutinize the tattoo, his breath as fustily stale as the stifling air of the claustrophobic chamber.

'It's taken well . . .'

Lai stood in the donjon courtyard, hunched against the wind in a threadbare jacket several sizes too large, screwing his eyes up against the glare of daylight. The tarkhastars had struck away the collar from his neck and wrists; his skin was chafed raw from the bite of the metal.

'Move!'

One of the tarkhastars gave him a shove in the back; he stumbled, his legs so wasted from lack of use that he fell to his knees.

'Is *this* the boy?'

Lai slowly raised his glare-dazzled eyes. A dark-skinned man towered over him.

'He'll never make it up the hill,' the giant said scornfully.

'That's your problem, Orthandor!' The tarkhastar walked away, laughing.

'Do you know who I am, boy?' demanded Orthandor.

'N–no, zhan,' said Lai. He tried to hold his head high but the cold of leaf-fall made him shiver, clutching his ragged coat closer to him.

'I am Orthandor. The Arkhan's slave-trainer. The Tarrakh. From now on you answer to me and me alone.' Ivory teeth gleamed in a tattooed face the rich brown of burnished chestnuts. 'You've a long climb ahead of you. And just so's you realise how lucky you are to be chosen, we'll take Dyer's Lane. Straight past the dye works. You'll smell them before you see them . . .'

The pungent odour of dye, blown on the wind, tainted the air long before they had reached the lane.

'*Faugh!*' said Orthandor. 'Imagine. To spend the rest of your days in this hellstench. What are they boiling up in there? Rotten eggs? Cat's piss?'

They passed the low-roofed sheds lining the river bank. Lai caught a glimpse of vast vats of bubbling dye stirred by toiling, sweating workers, their bare arms, flesh stained weirdly unnatural hues of purple, bright blue, green . . .

'Over there,' Orthandor said, pointing.

Shaven-headed, emaciated, shuffling along, chained by the ankles, they were carrying a steaming tub of some vile-smelling liquid. An overseer cracked a leathern flail over their thin shoulders, snarling orders at them. Liquid slopped onto the ground; the flail lashed down mercilessly again onto bent, wasted bodies. Lai turned away, sickened with anger.

'Once they've been cut,' Orthandor said dispassionately, 'they lose all strength in the arms. And some grow fat. Obscenely fat. The good-looking ones are lucky . . . They might be picked as stewards by rich families. A handsome eunuch makes a pleasing ornament to a torellan's household – and a suitable companion for his consort. No threat. Or so they say . . . But I've heard . . .'

The dyers had taken advantage of the brisk morning breeze, and skeins of drying silk dangled from every crumbling window ledge, broken roof and dilapidated balcony like the trails of old man's beard garlanding the autumn hedgerows.

They began to climb. The air grew cleaner, sharper, sweeter, free of the foul taint of dye. Lai gazed upwards; far above them he could see the Palace of Myn-Dhiel, rising out of the river mists, its gilded roofs glittering in the brittle leaf-fall sunshine.

'We're going to – to Myn-Dhiel?'

Myn-Dhiel. The Torella's tasselled palanquin had taken Laili to Myn-Dhiel. Was she still there? Might he even catch a glimpse of her? Might—

'Don't you understand anything? You belong to the Tarkhas Memizhon now. The Arkhan's bodyguard.'

The barracks of the Tarkhas Memizhon, the Arkhan's bodyguard, was situated beneath the terraced pleasure gardens of the Palace of Myn-Dhiel. As Orthandor and Lai approached, two tarkhastars on guard at the high-arched gateway, their azure coats like sun-rippled water, saluted Orthandor and drew back their blue-tasselled halberds to let them pass.

'See?' Orthandor gestured towards the grey-stone Tarkhas House with its fluttering pennants, argent, gold and azure. 'That's what every slave aspires to. The Tarkhas Memizhon. The Arkhan's fighting clan.' He struck his broad chest with his fist. 'But first you have to prove yourself in the Arena – first we have to make a bladesman of you.'

They passed a broad parade ground on which a troop of tarkhastars were at manoeuvres and came to a separate compound, dour and bleak, on the windy side of the heights. Slavering watch-hounds bayed and strained at the leash as they approached: Lai recoiled from their snapping fangs but Orthandor threw back his head and bellowed with laughter.

'That's right! Get a good scent of him!' He turned to Lai. 'This is my night patrol. I let them loose at nightfall in case any slave is rash enough to try to escape. Not that my troop have the energy to make a run for it. They want their sleep. And so will you after a day in the pit.' He gestured to Lai to follow him.

In a sheer-sided pit far below, men were wrestling on the dusty ground in unarmed combat; Lai could hear them grunting and gasping for breath with the exertion of the struggle.

'Jhered-nai,' Orthandor said, 'an essential discipline for a fighter. You'll join them tomorrow.'

'I am no fighter, I—' Lai began but Orthandor interrupted him.

'You will get up before dawnwatch, you will go to bed at sundip. They'll tell you I'm a hard taskmaster. Hard, yes – I've no time for shirkers. But fair; let no one say Orthandor is biased in his treatment of his men. And don't try to escape. With that mark on your forehead, you won't get far. There'll be no second chance. All who run from the Tarkhas Memizhon are sent straight back to the donjon . . . if my dogs don't get them first.'

The tiles of the domed bath house were shinily moist with steam; Lai lay back, closing his eyes as the mineral waters, hot from under-ground springs, bubbled about his body, suffusing the damp air with their pungent aromatic odours. Green pine resin . . . Blue terebinth . . . He could almost feel the layers of grime peeling away. Before they had let him near the waters he had been forced to undergo a humiliating dousing in some foul-smelling unguent; it had given him a perverse kind of pleasure to see the lice dropping off him to the damp floor.

'Time's up!'

Lai climbed out and began to rub himself down with one of the rough towels provided until his skin tingled. Orthandor reappeared with clean clothes: a coarse linen shirt, linen breeches and plain jacket the blue of lapis lazuli. Memizhon blue.

'And shave off that stubble. You're a disgrace to the Tarkhas.'

Lai took up the razor stone and slapped on the shaving-paste. Orthandor had left a small round bronze mirror; Lai pulled his face into the requisite grimaces to reach the most inaccessible copper bristles. When he had finished he took up the mirror and with a trembling hand pushed back his hair to inspect the indigo slavebrand. As he had feared, there was no trace left of the silvered moonmark; the tattooing needle had destroyed all sign of the Goddess's gift. Only his green-blue, deep-set, dreamer's eyes looked gravely back at him, unchanged, blue as the waters of the bay on Ael Lahi. Laili's eyes—

'You've had time enough to admire yourself.' Orthandor took back the bronze mirror and slipped it into his sleeve. 'Come.'

Lai followed him across the wind-blown courtyard and entered a low-roofed hall.

'This is where you sleep.' Orthandor gestured to the nearest pallet in the long, bare chamber. The windows were barred. 'You take your meals in the adjacent hall. You'll be well-clothed, well-fed and all at the Arkhan's expense. Never forget that.'

Lai sank down on the pallet and buried his face in his hands.

'What did they get you for?'

Lai looked up. A group of brandslaves ringed his pallet, all staring at him in the flickering lanthorn light. And he had thought he was alone.

'Well?' The spokesman was a sour-eyed man, slouching against the wall, arms folded.

'I was in a fight.'

The sour-eyed man let out a snort of derision.

'We've all been in fights.'

'Does it matter?' Lai said levelly. 'I got caught.'

The man leaned forwards and grabbed hold of Lai by the collar, pulling Lai's face close to his until Lai could see the red broken veins spidering his nose, the hairs bristling from his nostrils.

'Listen well and listen good. I don't like you. I don't like your accent, I don't like the colour of your hair and I don't like your insolence. You'll be nice to me, pretty boy. Be nice to Wadhir. Or you'll find yourself wishing you'd stayed in the donjon. Understand?'

Lai nodded. He could hardly breathe for the tight hold Wadhir was keeping on his collar, twisting it tighter each time for emphasis.

'Lights out!' Orthandor's voice echoed to the rafters of the sleeping-hall.

Wadhir slowly released his hold about Lai's throat as the others drifted back to their pallets. His eyes, sour as vinegar, still burned into Lai's.

'Don't forget. I'm watching you. Even when you're asleep.'

The single lanthorn was taken away and Lai heard the doors of the sleeping-hall slam to, the heavy bolts outside grinding shut, the key creaking in the lock.

In the darkness, he lay awake, listening to the distant baying of the watch-hounds as they prowled the compound.

A thin silverlight penetrated the bars of the hall, striping the sleeping forms.

Days without number since he had last seen Her sacred light.

Lai's lips silently framed the words of salutation . . . but other words soon overrode them, a plea, a desperate supplication.

I know I must atone. But how? These men are trained fighters. Killers. My only way out of here is to become as they are. Brutalised.

The faint silverlight wavered . . .

Is there no other way?

A cloud crossed the face of the moon . . . The light faded and went out.

Don't abandon me, Goddess! Don't leave me without any hope!

The hall was drowned in black. And in the blackness all Lai could hear was the howling of Orthandor's hounds as they pawed and snuffled at the locked doors.

CHAPTER 3

Voices in the ante-chamber, Laili started; it was late, too late for visitors, surely . . . She had dozed off on the couch of her mistress's dressing-room and now she was suddenly awake, recognising the soft, cultured tones she had heard in the garden that afternoon.

'Who *is* she, Sarilla? I must know.'

'So she intrigues you?' Coquettish delight in Sarilla's cooing voice. 'I thought she might.'

'Don't torment me! Tell me her name.'

'Her name is . . . Laili.'

'Such an evocative name. Laili. Distant shores . . .'

Laili sat up, clutching her gossamer shawl about her shoulders. She had begun to shiver.

'Far distant shores. She's from Ael Lahi.'

'Ael Lahi? Beyond the Spice Islands? I thought they were all painted savages there . . .'

'See for yourself, lord.'

The door opened; Sarilla's long nails beckoned.

Laili pulled her shawl more tightly about her.

'Come, child. You have a visitor.'

Laili came blinking into the Torella's living chamber. A man was seated by the fireside, the dying flames casting flickers of blue and red across his robes of heavy brocade. A Mhaell lord. She bowed, touching her forehead in obeisance, as Sarilla had taught her, aware that her mistress's sharp eyes were watching for the slightest mistake in etiquette.

'Sing for me, Laili. I want to hear you sing.'

'I – I do not know the art-songs that the courtesans perform, lord. And I have no instrument—'

He waved one hand, silencing her.

'I have heard enough florid court music to last a lifetime. It has no heart, no soul, it is all ornamentation and meaningless

28

embellishment. Sing me a song I have never heard. Sing to me one of the songs of Ael Lahi.'

Laili nodded. Then, hesitantly at first, she sang him one of the first songs her mother had taught her, the lament of the girl waiting in vain on the shore for her man to come home from the sea, the sighing refrain, 'Ai, lilua, luali . . .'

And when she had finished, the silence hung in the candlelit room like a veil between them. She was afraid that his silence implied he had found her singing displeasing . . . But after a while she saw him draw his hand across his eyes . . . wiping away tears.

'You are different from the others, Laili,' he said, gazing at her so piercingly, so intently that she felt as if he were looking into her very soul. She did not know what to say, how to reply; she was trembling at the sound of his voice at once soft and low, yet burningly incandescent. His hand moved out to touch her hair, threading the strands between his fingers.

'Red . . . as a flame.'

She had expected force. She had expected violation. She had not expected this . . . gentleness.

The brandslaves were roused every day before dawn with the jangling of a coarse-tongued metal bell. Firstmeal consisted of hunks of coarse bread washed down with hot malted ale. Then, no matter how cold the weather, they were made to strip down to loincloths and spend all morning practising the thirteen falls in Jhered-nai. After a short midday meal, it was practice of basic footwork and bladestrokes with wooden foils. When that session ended, Orthandor made them run the circuit of the barracks three times before allowing them into the bath house to soak away the day's grime and sweat.

Each night Lai fell into dreamless sleep the instant his head touched the pallet – but no sooner had he sunk into oblivion than Orthandor was standing in the doorway, bellowing that it was time to wake up, time to move, get out of bed . . .

'Red hair . . . Blue eyes . . . Honey skin . . .'

The Torella drew out robe after robe in dazzling silks, holding each one up to Laili's skin.

'This dark azure with the spangles – "dragonmoon" – looks delicious with your hair. Or the shot silk . . .'

'No.' Laili pointed to the white silk gown, plain as an adept's robe.

29

'That one.'

'Of course. How fitting. White for my little virgin.'

Laili looked at the Torella coldly. She did not like to hear her pronounce it in that way; her lascivious tone somehow implied that she was some choice morsel to be prepared for the Arkhan's consumption.

'So much to teach you, my innocence. And so little time.'

The Torella's opulent perfume was beginning to make Laili feel queasy; purple musk-orchids mingled with sharp patchouli.

'What is there to learn?' she said angrily. 'I am not entirely ignorant.'

The Torella pinched her cheek in a seemingly affectionate gesture – but the painted nail left a sharp scratch.

'First you must learn when it is prudent to keep your thoughts to yourself. And second – you must learn how to please. He will not be enchanted if his little virgin merely lies meekly back on the sheets and closes her eyes tight, grits her teeth, waiting for it all to be over! He will expect some effort at participation.'

'I'm still hungry.' Wadhir let out a belch; Lai stared studiously down at his bowl of soup, trying to take no notice. 'Well, Aelahim. Didn't you hear me? I said I'm still hungry.'

Lai slowly looked up.

'So?'

'I thought I made myself plain the other night. Short memory, huh?' He reached for Lai's bowl of lentil soup. 'I said I was still hungry.'

'Wait!' Lai grabbed at the bowl; soup slopped onto the scrubbed trestle.

'What a waste of good food,' said Wadhir. 'You'd better not let that go to waste, pretty boy.'

'You said you were hungry—' flared Lai.

The next instant, he found his face slammed down into the congealing pool, Wadhir's hands pressing on his head and neck.

'Lick it up, Aelahim filth. Go on!' hissed Wadhir.

Lai gasped for air, his bruised nose squashed into the glutinous liquid, hands flailing ineffectually.

'I told you to be nice to me. Or else,' Wadhir snarled in his ear. With one last tug at his hair, he threw him aside; Lai went tumbling onto the floor, blood dripping from his damaged nose. The other slaves watched in silence. No one moved to help him. Yet no one laughed. Wadhir noisily drained the last of Lai's soup and wiped the bowl with Lai's hunk of barley bread.

Lai pulled himself to his feet, one hand pressed to his nose; he could taste the warm blood leaking down the back of his throat. Anger almost blinded him; he wanted to pick up the soup-bowl and smash it over Wadhir's head. But he could hear Orthandor's firm tread outside: to retaliate now would be enough to condemn himself to the dye works and Wadhir knew it.

Lai turned on his heel and walked slowly, with as much dignity as he could muster, out of the hall. In the bath house he washed away the clots of blood with splashes of the icy water.

That night, long after the others had fallen asleep, filling the hall with the ebb and flow of their breathing, Lai lay awake, staring into the darkness, starting at every snore.

Run away, a voice whispered at the back of his mind. *Run away before Wadhir traps you alone in some dark corner. You'll never get on the right side of Wadhir.*

Lai turned restlessly onto his side. His eyes ached with sleeplessness.

But what was the point in running away? He was marked for life, the Memizhon tattoo still raw on his forehead. Wherever he ran, people would know him for a fugitive, a runaway slave. And if he ran he would lose his only chance of finding Laili . . .

Lai pulled the coarse blanket up over him, huddling down, seeking warmth. It was already colder than the coldest winter night on Ael Lahi; he was unaccustomed to these autumn frosts and chill winds.

Ael Lahi. Such a surge of homesickness washed over him that he felt himself drowning, hopelessly submerged.

Two russet-haired children wandering the warm white strands barefoot, searching the rock pools . . .

'Listen.' Laili cups a speckled cowrie shell over his ear. 'Aela says that if you can hear the sighing of tides on far distant shores, it means you're going on a journey.'

Distant shores. Chilling premonition. How could they have known that their childish wishing game would come so violently true?

At first the Torella spent hours painting Laili's face and nails. Laili found it easy enough to copy her; playing the apt and dutiful pupil seemed to keep her instructress content. After the art of cosmetics came the arts of perfumery and incense-making.

'The exquisites of the court like to hold contests to see who can devise the most fragrant incense.'

Soon Laili's little room became as sweet as the Goddess's shrine with the mingled scents of sweet pine, sandalwood, tulip and aloes.

And now the Torella began to ply her with books.

'This is a rare and precious manuscript from his library, it was commissioned by one of his ancestors.'

Laili could not decipher the ancient writing but she had no need, the drawings were explicit enough.

'Study it carefully. I will bring another text tomorrow.'

The Torella read to Laili from the text the next day without a single blush or faltering of the voice; most of the instructions were couched in obscure metaphor so that anyone listening casually would have heard only of jade branches and fragrant terraces. Laili sat, hands in her lap, seeming to pay attention but letting her mind loose, trying to recall the Grove at dusk, the rising of the springtide moon, the music of the moonmoths . . .

A sharp rap on her arm brought her back to the narrow tower room; she stared at the Torella, confused, her eyes suddenly blurred with tears.

'You haven't heard a word! I don't know why I'm wasting my time with you. He's coming tonight. Yes, you heard me then, didn't you! Tonight, sweeting.'

Flash of emotion, so vivid Laili could almost taste its acidity on her tongue. Jealousy. Resentment. The last flare of an old love that had almost died to embers . . . a love that she had not chosen to end herself. Laili looked at her closely and saw the fine lines of age at the corners of eyes and mouth, hairline cracks in fine porcelain.

The Torella unbound Laili's hair and began to comb it until it crackled with blue fire. Laili endured her ministrations in silence though all the while she was mutely praying to the Goddess of the Sacred Grove.

What do you want of me? Should I throw myself from the tower window rather than submit to him? I have sworn to protect the sanctity of life – even my own. You know I have not chosen this path . . . but they are forcing me to break my vow.

But the Goddess gave no answer.

The Torella was twisting fresh-picked winter asfodyl in Laili's hair, its poignant pale perfume moist as dark glades at twilight.

'I wish you joy,' she said, smiling with her perfect coralled mouth, although her eyes did not smile. 'And I leave you with some advice you would do well to bear in mind. Myn-Dhiel is a snare of whispered intrigues. You are safe here in your tower room. But do not play your part too well. I have prepared other concubines . . . others prettier than you . . . and where are they now? Beware the charming gift that comes unannounced, unmarked. Beware the embroidered gloves, the enticing sweetmeats, the jewelled fillet. The apothecaries of Perysse are skilled in devising new perfumes – they are also skilled in making poisons.'

He came very late, so late that the perfumed oils had almost burned out in the silver lamp. Laili was so terrified that she could scarcely enunciate the words of welcome she had been taught to say. But her training in the Grove had taught her to contain her fear, to hide it in courtesies. She offered him spiced wine, little cinnamon cakes; he waved them aside.

'Come, sit by me,' he said. 'I want you to tell me about Ael Lahi.'

It was not what she had expected. And he was not as she had expected, either, with his quiet voice, his expressive hands, his calm, easy manner. She began to talk. And as she talked she felt her hostility towards him slowly easing, evaporating like the scented fumes into the air. He seemed more disposed to talk than to use her for the purposes for which she had been prepared.

He raised one hand and gently touched the moonmark on her forehead.

'I have never seen this sign before. What does it mean?'

She swallowed hard.

'I am an adept of the Sacred Grove.'

'I know nothing of this Sacred Grove. Was that where you learned to sing?'

'To sing . . . and to play the flute.'

'The flute? I am not overfond of the flute. It can be shrill on the ears.'

'Maybe your Arkendym flutes are different from ours. We blow across the mouth-hole . . . like so.' She mimed, placing her lips to her hand. 'It makes a softer, sweeter tone. But I am so out of practice, I fear I would make a shrill sound now.'

'If your fluting is as accomplished as your singing, I should like to hear you play. Tell me more of your Grove.'

'It is a holy place. A place of mysteries.'

A frown shadowed his smooth brow.

'I hope you are not going to try to convert me?'

'Oh no. I have not the skill – or the power – to do that. The Goddess calls whom She pleases—'

'So what sets an adept of your Sacred Grove apart from ordinary mortals?'

This was the moment. Even though she detected a hint of mockery in his question, this was her chance to slip Lai into the conversation.

'I – I cannot easily explain. I – we – were Chosen. We endured the initiation and we were admitted to the mysteries—'

'We?'

Laili took a deep breath.

'I have a brother. He was arrested trying to protect me. Please – lord Arkhan – please spare his life. I will do anything – anything you want – but please—'

His eyes no longer looked so kindly on her.

'I do not concern myself with such matters. The servants of the Haute Zhudiciar deal with criminals.'

'I did not mean to presume—' Terror gripped her; she had been too presumptuous – and now she had offended him. In her desperation to save Lai, she had thrown away her only chance.

'What is his name?'

'Lai. Lai Dhar.'

'And what would you give me in exchange for his life?'

'I – I have nothing. Except . . .' She could not meet his eyes. 'Except myself.'

'In spite of your vows?' His voice had hardened. 'Or do you trust that your Goddess will punish me if I take the virginity of her handmaiden?'

'You are mocking me, lord.'

'You think I'm a barbarian tyrant who takes pleasure in forcing young girls?'

'N–no—'

'Are you much alike, you and Lai?'

'Very much, lord.' Her voice sank to a whisper; was he playing with her, raising her hopes, only to dash them? How could she convince him? 'Twins are revered on Ael Lahi; there is a legend . . .'

'Tell me.'

'The Goddess bore mortal twins. The first man, the first woman. When they grew old and the time came for them to die, She changed them into moonmoths . . . and they flew up into the night sky and became twin stars.'

'Can you see these stars in Perysse?'

Laili went to the arched window and he followed, snuffing out the smirching flame in the silver lamp. As Laili gazed up into the inky skies, she sensed the warmth of his body as he drew closer to her, close . . . yet not touching.

'The skies look so different here . . .'

His hand rose to point; the fingers brushed against her cheek.

'There. Are those your twins?'

She nodded. 'Ainai and Ainaili. But they shine more brightly over Ael Lahi.'

He laughed suddenly and tousled her hair as he might have done with a child.

'Here we know them by another name. The Warriors.'

Night after night the Arkhan returned. And night after night he demanded nothing of Laili but her company. Sometimes he would touch her hair . . . and sometimes he would graze her hand, her arm with his fingers, a fleeting caress, nothing more.

He must have known what he was doing, slowly wearing down her resistance. For she came to crave that touch, she came to long for his fingers to curl about her arm, to pull her close to him . . . She longed to taste the forbidden fruit that she had forsworn in the Grove before the Goddess's shrine.

That night, Sarilla's tower was rimed with the first hard frost of the year.

The Arkhan came late . . . but as Laili rose to greet him, she saw that his eyes gleamed as though he had some secret to impart.

'I have found him.'

'Who, lord?' Laili asked, her heart pounding.

'Your Lai. Your twin.'

'And is he safe? Is he well?'

'He is in my keeping.' Enigmatic words; the lazy green eyes smiled tantalisingly at her.

'But still a prisoner?'

'No. He has been given the chance to earn his freedom.'

'May I see him? Please?'

'Not yet. Maybe in a little while . . .'

'Thank you, thank you, lord.' Laili dropped to her knees and, lifting the hem of Melmeth's ivory robes, pressed them to her lips. She did not want him to see the tears that suddenly burned her eyes. And then she felt his hands on her shoulders, raising her to her feet. She shivered although the fire of pine-cones burned fiercely in the grate.

'Are you cold, child?' he asked.

She nodded.

'Come here, then. I will keep you warm.'

For the first time she let him put his arms around her, for the first time she rested against his breast and felt the strong beat of his heart beneath his ribs.

'There, that's better, isn't it?' His fingers stroked her hair . . . idly, it seemed. 'You're smiling . . . yet your eyes are always so sad, Laili. What troubles you?'

'I . . . I miss Ael Lahi, lord. It is so cold here. I miss the warmth of the sun.'

'If it would make you happy, I would bring back the sun. But I am only Arkhan, dear Laili . . . and there are some things even the Arkhan of the Seven Cantons cannot accomplish.'

He placed one hand beneath her chin, tipping her face up to his, bending to kiss her. For one moment, terror gripped her, she felt she was suffocating beneath the pressure of his lips – and then the pleasure of his kiss trickled through her body, warm as molten honey, and she did not want him to stop.

From the pine-cone fire it was but a few steps to the silk-hung bed.

It was not as she had imagined. There was no tearing, rending pain . . . for he was as skilful as she was inexperienced. Yet at the moment when the need for release overcame him, he shuddered and cried out in her arms and she felt an extraordinary feeling of power . . . mingled with an inexplicable tenderness. The Arkhan of the Seven Cantons was a man like any other, a man with needs, weaknesses, frailties . . .

And he needed her.

Laili awoke at dawn to find herself alone in the silk-hung bed. But on the pillow beside her lay a long, slender parcel wrapped in a tissue as soft as gossamer. Within she found a rosewood flute, intricately carved and inlaid with ivory.

On dry days, the brandslaves trained in the sheer-sided pit Lai had first seen when he entered the compound. The only access was from a damp and rank-smelling tunnel but, high above, a spiked perimeter grille round the rim permitted spectators to observe – and comment on – the exertions of the slaves. Sometimes Lai heard jeering laughter and, glancing up, saw tarkhastars lounging over the grille. Once or twice he had caught a glimpse of floating silks and a faint waft of perfume; shielding his eyes against the pale sun, he had seen women, richly dressed, avidly watching the sweat-streaked bodies as they strained and wrestled in the dirt.

Today, the sun was a thin disc of pale gold, sheened in clouds; Lai shivered as he stripped down to the leathern kilt and padded cuirass worn for blade practice. As he emerged from the dank tunnel, shielding his eyes against the sun's pale sheen, he thought he glimpsed a single figure high above, observing the slaves at their practice.

'You're late, Aelahim!' Orthandor cracked his flail impatiently.

Lai finished fastening the straps on the vambraces worn to strengthen the wrists and forearms, pulling the last one tight with his teeth. They afforded little protection against the bruising impact of the wooden blade: Orthandor believed his slaves should learn how to dodge and parry the hard way and Lai's honeyed skin was already mottled with livid bruises.

'Go find a partner!' Orthandor tossed Lai one of the heavy blades.

The cool air rang to the clatter of wooden blade-staves as Orthandor strode amongst the slaves, bellowing his instructions, seemingly oblivious of the whirling blades.

Lai stared down at the wooden blade in his grip. It was a game now, an elaborate ritual dance of parry and thrust. But one day the wooden blade would be replaced with fine-honed steel. And the ritual would end in blood sacrifice—

Wadhir swung a shattering blow against his blade. Taken off-guard, Lai flinched.

'Scared?' jeered Wadhir. He followed through with another heavy thrust. Lai jumped back out of the way.

'Keep the rhythm, Wadhir!' Orthandor growled. 'How can you develop a technique if you wave that blade about like a windsail in a gale? Watch Dhar. He has control. Self-discipline.'

'Control? Self-discipline?' echoed Wadhir between strokes. He stuck out his foot suddenly and Lai went sprawling in the dirt.

'Clumsy footwork!' Orthandor's flail cracked about Lai's ears as, winded, Lai stumbled to his feet only to fall again as Wadhir slyly tripped him up just behind Orthandor's back. Lai's blade went rolling away and as he made a grab for it, Wadhir neatly scuffed dirt in his face. Lai tried to rear up, only to find Wadhir's foot on his neck, pushing him down—

'Fight! Fight!' The brandslaves began to chant. Yodelling jeers and catcalls egged Wadhir on.

Anger rose in Lai's throat, almost choking him. Blindly he reached for Wadhir's ankle and tugged hard. Wadhir, caught off-balance, crashed down with a yell. Next moment, he was pummelling Lai with blows—

'Break it up!' Lai heard Orthandor's flail whistle down across Wadhir's shoulders.

The chanting died to silence.

'You have broken the first rule of the Tarkhas Memizhon – no brawling.'

Orthandor stood glowering at them. A thin trail of blood trickled down Wadhir's shoulder; the Tarrakh's flail had drawn blood.

Lai scrambled to his feet, brushing the clinging dirt from his body.

'As punishment you will both clean out the bath house – latrines and all. I want every tile spotless. Not one speck of dirt on the floor or the walls. Get in there – and start swabbing!'

As Lai followed Orthandor into the tunnel, he thought he saw the Tarrakh glance upwards and exchange a brief nod with the silent watcher. Dazzled by the pale sun, Lai caught a glimpse of white hair . . . as the watcher turned and walked away.

The bath house floors were awash with dirty footprints; the night watch had just come off duty at Myn-Dhiel and had tramped down along paths muddy with fallen leaves.

Lai got down on hands and knees to wipe the cubicle floors clean, wringing out the muddy water into a bucket.

'Woman's work,' came Wadhir's sour voice. Lai looked up to see him lounging complacently in the doorway. 'Must be why you're so good at it, pretty boy.'

Lai took no notice and turned away to finish the last corner.

'You've done a nice job there,' Wadhir said. His foot kicked out casually, overturning the bucket and sending dirty water swilling all over the clean floor. 'Oh. How careless of me. Now you'll have to do the job again.'

Lai stared at the running rivulets of dirty water. His first instinct was to shove the bucket over Wadhir's head. Clenching his fists, he slowly stood up and walked over to the doorway where he had left his mop. Wadhir, smiling, placed himself deliberately in front of it.

'Looking for something?'

'My mop,' Lai said sullenly.

'He's looking for his mop.' Wadhir mimicked Lai's Aelahim accent with cruel accuracy.

'Then I'll find another.' Lai went to pass Wadhir but Wadhir pushed him back against the wall.

He was trapped. And alone. It was quiet, so quiet, save for the hiss of the steam on the bubbling spring-water beyond the archway.

'What will Maistre Orthandor say when he sees this?' Wadhir began to slop the contents of his bucket around the cubicle; ripe horse manure, fresh from the stables.

'Stop!' cried Lai.

Wadhir slammed him back against the tiled wall. Before Lai could push free, Wadhir had him pinned to the wall, the mop handle against his throat, pressing it into his windpipe.

'Do I have to rub your face in this horseshit to make you understand?' Wadhir hissed. 'No one crosses me and gets away with it. No one does that to Wadhir. Now get down on your knees and say you're sorry.'

'No!' whispered Lai. The mop handle pressed harder into his windpipe, forcing his head back until he felt his eyes begin to bulge from his skull.

'On your knees!'

The steam-sheened tiles swam before Lai's eyes, dwindling to a red-jagged blur . . .

Survival was all – he must break Wadhir's throttlehold – or die.

One knee smashed upwards in Wadhir's groin; one hand, index finger and thumb flexed, jabbed with painful accuracy into Wadhir's sour green eyes.

The mop dropped to the slippery, shit-smeared floor as Wadhir doubled up.

'Damn you!' screamed Wadhir, blundering about, hands clutched to his streaming eyes.

Lai was onto him, knocking him asprawl. The two brandslaves went rolling over and over across the bath house floor, Lai clinging grimly on.

'Enough, Dhar.' Orthandor's great voice roared across the hiss of the waters. 'That's enough!'

Lai felt the weight of a strong hand clamp onto his shoulder, tugging him up and off his tormentor. Two azure-clad tarkhastars had hold of Wadhir, restraining him.

'This place stinks of horseshit.' Orthandor sniffed the air, gazing around him at the fouled cubicle. 'Dhar – you will make this cubicle so clean I could eat my evenmeal off the tiles. And as for you, Wadhir – as you're so fond of manure, you can muck out the Tarkhas stables tonight. And every night for the next seven. If there's the slightest hint of trouble – from either one of you – you'll be stripped and lashed in front of the whole of the Tarkhas Memizhon.'

As Lai limped away to fetch clean water, he noticed a figure uncurl itself from the shadows, caught the glint of sleek white hair and silver-grey eyes.

And he saw a look pass between the stranger and the Tarrakh, an indecipherable look. He did not know what it meant. But he knew it concerned him.

Lai sat in the hall trying to choke down firstmeal, dunking morsels of bread in warm malt ale to soften them.

The anger had drained out of him overnight, leaving nothing but the bitter realisation that he had proved himself to be no different from the rest. The other brandslaves were avoiding him – whether out of respect or fear, he was not certain. Now he knew; he was as violent, as brutal as they – no, he was more violent, for they had not made a life's vow to the Goddess to follow the ways of peace, they knew no better. When put to the test, he had fought as viciously as a crazed beast.

'Dhar!' a sonorous voice called across the din of the hall.

'Maistre?' Lai stood to attention. Wadhir looked up and Lai saw a slow smile spread across his face.

'Outside! On the double!'

Abandoning his meal, Lai followed Orthandor across the compound towards the Tarkhas Gate.

This must be it. The moment they told him he was to be sent to the dye works.

But Orthandor stopped outside a long, barrel-roofed hall beside the parade ground.

'This is the armoury,' Orthandor said brusquely. 'Go in; Maistre Ymarys is waiting for you.'

'For me?'

'To start your training. And he doesn't like to be kept waiting. So, run!'

CHAPTER 4

A gallant, peacock-fine in watered azure silk, stood at the far end of the long armoury chamber. He appeared to be admiring his reflection in a small pocket-mirror. His long hair, silver-sheened in the mote-speckled sunlight, had been braided with strands of gold and blue glass beads.

Lai hesitated.

'I – I was looking for Maistre Ymarys—'

'My name is Ymarys,' the gallant said carelessly, slipping the mirror into his sleeve. 'I am the Arkhan's blademaster. The Razhirrakh.'

'Y–you?' Lai stared in disbelief into the blademaster's face, seeing the kohl-rimmed eyes, the black-crescent beauty-spot, the rouged lips of a court exquisite.

'And you are Lai Dhar.' Ymarys walked around Lai, looking him up and down. 'My new pupil.'

With a languid flourish, Ymarys picked up a curve-bladed razhir where it stood propped against the wall and presented it to Lai, hilt first.

'Let me see what you can do.'

Lai slowly curled his fingers around the silk-bound hilt. It was still warm from the Razhirrakh's hand.

'No, no, you must balance the weight of the blade more evenly or your wrist will lose flexibility.'

Ymarys slipped one hand beneath Lai's wrist to support it as the other hand altered the position of Lai's fingers, each one in turn.

'Now try again. And remove your jacket. It's hot work—'

Lai stripped off his jacket and was rolling up his shirt sleeves when he sensed Ymarys move. He parried instinctively, feeling the shock of steel against tempered steel violently jar his arm from wrist to shoulder. He looked up astonished into the Razhirrakh's painted face.

'Good,' said Ymarys, stepping back. 'Your reactions are abnormally acute. But – as you said – you know nothing. You must perfect the basic blade-strokes and positions before you can progress.'

There was something in the dismissive tone of his voice that stung Lai's pride.

'I can learn. Fast.'

'Very well. You will continue basic training with Orthandor for seven days.'

He sheathed his razhir and turned away; Lai hesitated a moment and then, realising that the lesson was at an end, began to back towards the door.

'Here. After firstmeal. Eight days hence.'

'After firstmeal.'

Lai awoke before dawn from a dark dream-labyrinth, his mind and stomach churning with the old bitter, black anger.

Why me, Goddess? Why?

He had been in training with the Arkhan's blademaster for weeks now; the hardest weeks of his life. Ymarys might look and behave like a court exquisite but beneath the silk Lai had discovered a core of steel. The sleek indolence of a pampered silvercat masked the ferocity of a vicious killer. The Razhirrakh demanded nothing less than perfection from his pupil.

Now murky riverfogs clogged the dawn with dampness, filtering all brightness from the cold air. The last golden days of leaf-fall were past. Lai's body ached for the balmy warmth of Ael Lahi, his soul ached to be free.

As Lai entered the armoury, Ymarys acknowledged him with the usual languid nod of the head and resumed his limbering exercises; lean, supple body of a well-trained athlete, ripple of shoulder muscles beneath the loose linen . . .

Lai peeled off his jacket and threw it down.

'Attack me,' said Ymarys. He was standing, drawn razhir in hand, waiting.

'Wh–what?'

'Attack me.'

Lai suddenly came at Ymarys from the side. Ymarys's blade flicked out, repelled the blow effortlessly; Lai's wrist was wrenched back with the force of the stroke.

'Again.'

Lai hung back. His wrist throbbed. He should have known this would not be so easy.

'Again!'

Lai edged from foot to foot, hoping to trick Ymarys into anticipating a sideways attack. When he moved, he moved forwards, darting in under Ymarys's guard.

Shockwaves resonated up his arm as Ymarys's blade struck his blade aside.

'Come on, come on,' said Ymarys, smiling, beckoning him towards him. 'I'm unguarded. Strike now.'

'Uh-uh. It's a trick.' Lai circled him warily. Wherever he moved he could sense Ymarys's eyes tracking him. Damn the man! Was he a sentient? Though even sentients could be misled . . .

Slide the blade in. Then retract, thrust to the left—

The force of the parry caught Lai off-balance; he toppled down onto one knee. Ymarys's blade-tip nicked his throat; a tiny bubble of bright blood burst on the pierced skin's surface.

'I – I slipped.'

'No excuses. Slip in the arena – and you die. On your feet! Come at me again.'

Lai lunged. Ymarys's blade caught his at the hilt, locked tight. Lai strained to break the lock, leaning towards Ymarys until they were close, so close Lai could feel the warmth of Ymarys's clove-scented breath on his face.

Ymarys broke the lock with a sudden, violent twist of the wrist, sending Lai hurtling down onto his back. Before Lai could struggle up again, the blade-point was at his throat.

'Up. Again. Come on!'

'That wasn't fair—' Lai could have bitten his tongue. Those foolish, childish words.

Ymarys put out his left hand to pull Lai to his feet. Lai stared at the outstretched hand and shook his head.

'Another trick.'

'Trust me.'

'Trust you?' Lai hesitated. Tentatively he took the extended hand and felt himself pulled effortlessly upwards—

And was sent spinning, powerfully propelled across the floor, tumbling asprawl. Instantly he whipped around in the dust, razhir raised to defend himself as Ymarys bore down on him.

Glint of grey eyes, merciless now, hard as honed metal.

Trust you, Maistre Ymarys? I'd as soon trust a coral snake!

44

Lai only just parried the thrust before it drove home, battering the blade down with vicious two-handed strokes, each blade-shattering blow a distillation of the bleak, black anger that was gnawing away at his soul.

Beat him to his knees. Batter the blade from his hand.

But Ymarys stood firm. Endured the hail of blows, braced, balanced.

And Lai began to tire.

'Had enough?' That infuriating mocking quirk in the silvery voice.

'No!'

The blows became clumsier. The blade had never seemed so heavy. Weighted with lead. Sweat trickled into Lai's eyes.

'Concede, Dhar.'

'Never. *Never!*'

Through the sweat-blur he hazarded a last, desperate thrust.

Ymarys's blade flicked deftly beneath his own, twisted, lifted. The razhir corkscrewed out of Lai's hand and crashed to the floor.

'Damn you. Damn you. Damn you.' Lai sank to his knees in the dust, nursing his wrist. He was gasping for breath, angry, sobbing breaths that made his whole body shudder.

'You – you – tricked me. Every – time—'

Something soft thudded onto his bowed head. He flinched instinctively. Then realised what it was. A towel. He wiped his hot face, his sticky palms, his neck.

'You're learning.' Ymarys took a stoup-full of water from the drinking-barrel and drank. He dipped it again and offered it to Lai. Lai looked at it suspiciously.

'It's not poisoned.'

As Lai took the stoup from him, he noticed the dark stains soaking the back of Ymarys's loose linen shirt, the damp strands of hair plastered to his forehead. So the Razhirrakh was human, after all. If nothing else – he had made him sweat.

Lai drank a mouthful or two from the stoup, then poured the rest over his head, feeling the cool water trickle down his face, his closed lids, like monsoon rains.

'He has potential, Ymarys,' came a soft voice from the shadows.

Lai choked and swivelled round, wiping the trickling water from his face.

A man was walking towards them from the gloom veiling the far steps where observers sometimes sat to watch the practice bouts. Lai caught a glint of green eyes before Ymarys's hand settled on his shoulder, pushing him down to his knees.

'The Arkhan!' whispered Ymarys.

'This one interests me,' Melmeth said as he walked past, his heavy robes of scented jade brocade whispering over the boards. 'Tell Orthandor to bring him to my chambers tonight.'

Lai tremblingly raised his head. Chill light flooded the armoury from the open doors. They were alone.

'That was the Arkhan?'

'Melmeth himself.' Ymarys bent to pick up a towel, slinging it around his neck, concealing his face from Lai as he began to wipe his forehead. 'Myn-Dhiel is honeycombed with subterranean passages; he makes use of them to observe his courtiers. He takes particular interest in the training of his bladesmen for the arena. Last year Memizhon lost to the Tarkhas Zhudiciar. The Arkhan doesn't like to lose.'

Ymarys's voice was level but Lai could sense resentment simmering beneath the casual words, acrid as smoke.

Last year Memizhon lost. The implication was clear. Ymarys, the Arkhan's champion, had been beaten – and been lucky to come away from the arena with his life. And now the Arkhan was nurturing new talent, unwilling to risk another defeat. And that new talent . . . was his.

'You're late for Jhered-nai. Hurry!'

They were potential rivals now. No one had spoken the words aloud but the Arkhan's command had made it clear.

Lai grabbed his jacket; in the open doorway white petals began to drift silently down from the leaden skies.

'Maistre Ymarys – is that what you call . . . "snow"?'

Ymarys turned to look.

'Have you never seen snow before?'

'It's . . . beautiful . . .'

Lai went out into the courtyard and, raising his face to the sky, let the first icy caress of the snowflakes cool the heat in his burning cheeks. Glancing back, he caught sight of Ymarys standing watching him through the open doorway, the towel still slung carelessly over one shoulder.

Lai was glad of the warmth of his thick cloak as he followed Orthandor across the snow-slippery courtyard.

'This path leads directly from the barracks into the Palace of Myn-Dhiel. If the Arkhan decides you are suitable to become one of the clan, you will come to know this way so well you could walk it blindfold,' Orthandor said, leading Lai up a steep winding path dimly lit by flickering lanterns. 'I've been coming this way since Sardion – may his name never be forgotten – chose me to instruct young Melmeth in Jhered-nai. Always had a liking for the lad – he had me promoted to Tarrakh – but I can't understand what's happened to him of late . . . Idling his days away . . .'

They emerged under the sheer walls of the citadel and a howling wind slapped them full in the face, wet with stinging sleet.

'*Djhë*! What a foul night!' cursed Orthandor.

They entered beneath a torch-lit archway; two of the Tarkhas Memizhon raised their curve-bladed halberds to let them through.

'Myn-Dhiel,' Lai whispered as they stamped the snow from their boots. *Laili, are you here? Laili?*

There was not even the faintest trace of a response. Mists swirled in his mind, veiling her from his reach.

Orthandor briskly marched Lai through a maze of chilly corridors where silver lucernae suspended by chains above their heads swung and creaked eerily in the whispering snowdraught. Occasionally snowlight from a high casement window illumined the dust-grey walls, occasionally a dark-garbed servitor padded silently past, eyes cast respectfully down.

Lai heard the distant lilt of music, plangent reeds and plucked strings . . . so faint, so wantonly sweet it could have been an echo from another age . . . and came at last to a chamber lit by a fire of sweet-smoked apple logs.

'Wait here,' said Orthandor.

Lai waited, fidgeting with his belt buckle. In spite of the night's winter chill, his shirt and jacket seemed suddenly stiflingly hot, he could feel the sticky dampness seeping out, staining his shirt. From somewhere nearby he became aware of a buzz of voices, voices slowly coming nearer—

'This is the lad, zhan,' came Orthandor's voice unexpectedly close.

And as Lai turned, he saw a tapestried curtain drawn aside and Melmeth appeared.

Lai dropped to his knees.

'Rise,' said a voice, that same soft, persuasive voice he had first heard in the armoury and Lai, stumbling to his feet, saw in the applefire-glow that Melmeth was smiling at him. Behind him lingered in the shadows a dark-skinned, dark-eyed boy; he was carrying an aludh. Had he been one of the unseen musicians?

The Arkhan was austerely dressed, his long russet hair tied back; the only ostentation was a solitary ruby glowing on his ring finger.

'So you are Lai Dhar.'

Such disconcerting eyes, Lai thought, green and yet gold, sunlight behind shifting leaves, not quite human . . .

'Leave us, Orthandor. Yes, Khaldar, you too.'

Lai followed Orthandor plaintively with his eyes but the Tarrakh did not once look back. The boy made a deep obeisance as he withdrew; the panelled door clicked discreetly as it closed behind them.

Melmeth came close, very close to Lai and put his hands on his shoulders. Lai stiffened.

'You must be hot in this cloak,' Melmeth said, unfastening the clasp and letting it drop to the floor. He slowly walked around Lai, eyeing him up and down. Lai could feel the sweat break out again on his forehead. Where was all this leading?

'Hmm. Good stature, excellent bones . . . Any potential champion must look a hero to please the crowds. I think you'll please them well enough.' He touched Lai's arm, his thigh, his fingers pressing deep into the flesh, testing the firmness of the muscles. Lai gritted his teeth.

I belong to this man. I am his brandslave. His property. He could crush me with a word. But I mustn't let him see I care.

Melmeth smiled in Lai's face. Lai noted how white and regular his teeth were, how apple-sweet his breath.

'Extraordinary how alike you both are. You – and Laili.'

Lai's head jerked up as if Melmeth had slapped him.

'She means a lot to you, your sister?'

'Where is she!' Chaotic images tumbled through Lai's mind; Laili in chains, Laili weeping. Laili alone, bruised and dishevelled—

'You would do anything to free her?'

'If she has been harmed—' Lai cried.

'Listen to me.' Melmeth put one hand under Lai's chin, tipping his face upwards until Lai could not avoid the rapacious glitter of his green-gold eyes. 'I could destroy you as easily as a child crushes an ant. You are of no importance. No importance whatsoever. And yet now that I have seen you fight, I want you. I want you to fight for the Tarkhas Memizhon on Mithiel's Day.'

'Tell me what I must do.'

'It's so simple. Win in the arena and you and Laili will be given your freedom.'

'And if I don't win—'

'My dear Lai, you still don't seem to understand. You have been singled out, set apart from the other brandslaves. The training will be punishing – but think of the reward at the end. You could be free. Free to return to Ael Lahi. Of course – if you refuse to continue with the training, you will spend the remaining weeks of winter back in the compound and on Mithiel's Day, you can hazard your chance with the hack-and-thrust rabble – Laili will stay a slave at Myn-Dhiel—'

'No.' Lai knew he was out-manoeuvred. He must fight – and kill – to win Laili's freedom. He must forget that he was ever an adept, that he had once sworn in the Sacred Grove to protect the sanctity of life.

He dropped to his knees before the Arkhan and in a voice trembling with impotent rage, began to repeat the words that Melmeth dictated.

'I, Lai Dhar, pledge my life to your service, Melmeth of Ar-Khendye, Haute Torellan of Myn-Dhiel, Arkhan of the Seven Cantons.'

And a smile of ineffable satisfaction spread across Melmeth's face as he enclosed Lai's hands, raised up in the gesture of fealty, within his own.

'Now, Lai, you are bound to me and to the House of Memizhon. And as token of my faith in you, you will be lodged in the Tarkhas House with my tarkhastars. But, abuse this privilege – or try to run away – and it will go ill with Laili. Do you understand me?'

Lai nodded, too terrified to speak.

'I have ears and eyes everywhere. You will be watched. You will be followed. Never forget.'

As they entered the vaulted hallway which was hung with rich tapestries of faded gold-spun silk, Orthandor put out his hand to hold Lai back.

The sound of laughter drifted through the hall and from a hidden doorway came a chattering group of young women. The air breathed unexpectedly sweet as a spring meadow with their perfumes.

'Lerillys! Kamilla! Sarina!' the tallest of the women called sharply. At once the others obediently abandoned their teasing chatter and demurely lowered their eyes, drifting back to her side.

Orthandor touched his clanmark in salute and nudged Lai to do the same.

'A bitter-cold evening, Orthandor,' said the lady as she passed. 'And who is your companion? I do not think I have seen him before.'

'Lai Dhar of Ael Lahi, lady,' Orthandor said. 'He is Maistre Ymarys's new protégé.'

Lai could not resist risking one glance at the lady's face. Brown eyes, tawny as amber, gold-flecked, golden-lashed, stared back at him in cool appraisement. Her red-stained lips, over-sensuous, curved in a grave yet knowing smile.

'We do not see many with your unique colour of hair,' said the lady. 'And you are from Ael Lahi, Lai Dhar? How . . . intriguing.'

And she walked on, her companions hastening after her.

'Who – who was that?' Lai asked. 'The golden one. The one you called "lady"?'

'You must surely have heard of her! They call her the Duskstar of Myn-Dhiel. She is the Arkhan's consort. The Arkhys. Her name is Clodolë.'

Instead of taking Lai back to the cramped sleeping hall, Orthandor led him to a darkened cell in the Tarkhas House.

'You will sleep here tonight.' He placed a single candle in the wall-recess. 'Till the morrow . . .' And he closed the door; Lai heard the scrape of the key turning in the lock.

Lai sank down upon the narrow bed.

Tired . . .

No way out, now. He had pledged his word. If he was to see Laili alive again, he would have to fight for her, fight in the name of the House of Memizhon whose cursed clanmark he bore and would bear to his dying day . . .

So tired . . .

The snow-speckled draught from the shutterless window made his bones ache with the chill. Child of Ael Lahi, reared in the sun . . .

So very tired . . .

He stretched out on the bed. For a while he tried to keep awake by watching the slow silent fall of snow past the arrow-slit window but his eyelids drooped lower and lower until . . .

Lai, Lai . . .

The low sweetness of her voice charmed his heavy lids open. She was standing at the foot of his bed, her face half in shadow as she drew close to the dying candle-flame.

How – how did you get in here?

I was drawn to your flame, Lai. The flame burns strongly in you.

The winter's night did not tarnish the richness of her tawny hair nor the lazy voluptuousness of her bee-brown eyes. She took a step nearer to him and he watched her warily, wondering what her purpose could possibly be.

I am supposed to pass the night alone . . .

She laughed quietly and came nearer still until he could breathe the heady spiced-musk of her perfume.

You're over-virtuous, aren't you, for your nineteen years? Or perhaps merely inexperienced?

Are you here to test me, lady?

She laughed again and sat on the bed next to him.

You bound yourself to the House of Memizhon. Which means you are bound as much to me as to my consort.

I must be dreaming, Lai said. *You are only a part of my dream.*

Tonight, perhaps, but after tomorrow, Lai . . .

What do you want of me?

I want you, Lai. And she leant towards him, one hand on his shoulder, pushing him backwards, her face coming closer, closer to his, her full lips red as crushed mulberries, her soft tongue touching his, touching and teasing until he could resist no longer and kissed her—

And there came a slight sound, dry, like the incessant rustle of silk. He let her go.

What's wrong, Lai?

His eyes strayed to the dark window-slit behind where the flakes of snow were falling; thicker, whiter, they blew into the cell, eddying around in the whirling wind, flapping horribly towards the candle like moths drawn to a solitary flame—

'Moths . . . ?'

Totems of the Goddess, their wings glittering with stardust . . . How had they found their way here from distant Ael Lahi? And why were they silent, making no music but the rustle of their wings, why were they massing above his head—

'NO!'

He leapt from the bed in terror and found himself suffocating, smothered in a cloud of pallid furry wings. 'Ugh! Get away – get away—'

He tried to beat them off with his hands but dazzled by the bright flame, they blundered into his face, his eyes, his hair, smearing him with their dust, the deathdry powder clogging his nostrils, his mouth, his throat, choking him, *achhh*, choking him—

Lai woke with a shout of fear, sitting up in the darkness, hands flailing wildly about him. He was alone. The candleflame was extinguished, the snow still fell silently beyond the cold cell but the winterblack of the sky was slowly lightening.

It must be near to dawn, Lai told himself, huddling under the thin blanket. His teeth were chattering with the cold.

Only a dream, it was only a foolish dream . . . Moonmoths were too frail to cross the sea to snow-chilled Ar-Khendye; at this time in their brief life-cycle, their progeny were cocooned safe in silken chrysalises, waiting for the first moon of spring.

But why had *she* been a part of it? She had seemed so real.

'Clodolë, Duskstar . . .'

He whispered her name aloud. He could still smell the musk of her perfume, still feel the soft silk-skein of her amber hair.

She was the Arkhan's consort, so far above him that he burned with shame to think of what he had imagined in his dream.

Put her out of your mind. Forget her.

Banging his arms about his body to keep warm, Lai began to pace the cell again, watching the murky sky gradually grow light until the distant blare of the tarkenhorns announced the end of wakenight watch above the snow-crusted roofs of Perysse.

As the light grew stronger he noticed that a folded paper had been pushed under the door.

Puzzled, he knelt to pick it up and broke the scarlet seal:

I am well cared-for, I have had a little fire to warm me in the snows, and enough food. Perhaps they will let us meet, I don't know. I miss you so very much. Your loving sister, L . . .

The signature had been erased but Lai knew Laili's hand as well as his own. He read and re-read it, searching in vain for clues. No hint of where it had been written or when.

He sat heavily down on the bed, the letter clutched in his hand. The fragments of scarlet seal dropped to the floor. After scrabbling around in the dust a while, he retrieved them and fitted them together: the emblem was a flame. The Undying Flame of Memizhon.

It was proof of a kind, proof that she still lived.

CHAPTER 5

The bleak hours of daylight waned and blizzards howled about the gilded domes and spires of Myn-Dhiel as year's end drew near . . . and passed.

The Arkhan had ordered that warm clothes be provided for Lai as well as gloves of supple leather to protect his hands. But in spite of these privileges, Lai was still locked into his cell after evenmeal every night and only released at dawn when the tarkenhorns blew for roll-call. And every day was spent in training: alone with Ymarys or in the company of experienced tarkhastars.

Alone in his cell at night, Lai made himself repeat the invocation to the Goddess. Whispering the familiar words evoked the scent of the Sacred Grove at night, the intricate chatter of the nocturnal insects, the lapping of the moonlit tide. But he found little comfort in remembering . . .

Better to forget.

Laili sat waiting alone, her heart skipping a beat at every slightest sound, her hands tightly folded in her lap.

Where was he?

Past wakenight when the wicks of the scented candles were guttering in puddles of molten oil, she still sat, agitatedly twisting knots with her fingers.

She rose and went to the window, flinging it open, gasping at the sting of the frosty night air. Far below, Perysse lay shrouded in a mist of black-ice.

Why did he send no word? Am I so insignificant that I do not merit one word of explanation?

And then a kind of frenzy welled up within her and she beat with her bare fists at the rough stone framing the casement window until the knuckles were torn and lacerated. She wanted to open her mouth and howl her rage out across the frosted stillness. But instead she put her forehead down upon the cold stone sill and whispered his name into the vastness of the night.

She must have fallen asleep, her head on the sill in the numbing cold, for suddenly Sarilla was shaking her awake, chiding her for leaving the window open.

'Look at you, blue with the cold! Are you trying to make yourself sick? What *is* the matter with you, child?'

Laili stared at her through a veil of mussed hair, hardly understanding.

'He – he did not come last night.'

'Of course he did not come! Do you not know what time of year it is? He has to prepare himself for the Day of the Flame.'

'I know nothing of your customs.'

'My poor little heathen.' Sarilla set about Laili's tangled hair with a brush. 'You must learn our ways if you are to understand him better.'

Laili winced as the brush caught in a snarl of hair.

'This Day of Flame. What is it?'

'It is a ceremony venerating the sacred fire of Mithiel. The Arkhan must perform this in the shrine; in the days beforehand, he spends his time with the priests of Mithiel in prayer and fasting. We recognise it as the first sign of spring.'

'Spring!' Laili said. 'With all this snow?'

'The snow will melt soon. And then comes the day all Perysse has been waiting for – the day of the arena. Those delicious young brandslaves – fighting to the death for their freedom—'

'To the death?' Laili's head jerked up, knocking the brush out of the Torella's hand.

'Now look what you have made me do!' The Torella's hands flew into the air in a gesture of furious exasperation. 'If *he* had not ordered me to take care of you myself, I—'

A timid scratching at the door interrupted what promised to be a stinging tirade. The Torella marched across and unlocked the door.

'Well?' she demanded, tapping her foot impatiently.

'She said I was to bring the gown here.'

Laili caught a glimpse of a waif of a girl in the doorway, staggering under the weight of a rich brocade gown.

'Who said?'

'The dhamzel Lerillys. It's the one you ordered.'

'Fool of a girl! I said I would call for it myself. She's sent you here to snoop, hasn't she?'

'No! I never—'

'Wait outside until you are called for.' The Torella snatched the gown and slammed the door in the girl's face.

'It's beautiful,' Laili said, taking the gown and running her fingers over the delicate stitchery.

'Try it on. There'll be alterations to be made.'

'But I thought it was for you—'

'Ivory! With my complexion!'

Sarilla helped Laili into the gown; the cold brocade slithered against her skin, the seed pearls prickled her neck and shoulders. She had never worn anything so rich – or so stiffly formal.

'But when should I wear such a gown as this?'

'When? At the arena, where else?'

'*I* must attend this – this blood rite?'

'He wishes it so. You'll be masked, of course. No one will recognise you.'

Suddenly Laili felt trapped, confined within the tight-boned bodice.

Alien people. Alien customs. Alien rites.

'Turn around. The hem needs taking up. And the neckline embroidery is unfinished. Look at these loose threads! Take it off.'

Laili obediently stepped out of the gown and Sarilla took it back into the outer chamber, taking care to lock the door behind her.

Laili knelt and peered through the keyhole.

'It won't do. The hem needs raising by a thumb's breadth and this neckline is a disgrace!'

The girl seemed terrified; Laili saw she was shivering, her thin arms wrapped about her as though clutching in what little warmth she could generate.

'What are you waiting for, chit? Get to work!'

'I was up all night to finish it,' wailed the girl. 'It's cost a fortune in candles—'

'No more excuses! I want it by sundown. Now be off with you.'

Laili heard the Torella's voice rising from the courtyard garden, sharp as the cry of a crane. She drew close to her window and, gazing down on the twilit garden, saw that the little seamstress had returned with the ivory gown.

'What's this?' The Torella held it up critically to the fading light. 'It looks like blood!'

She jabbed a finger at the intricate embroidery around the hem.

'It's only a pinprick, it won't show—'

'It won't *show*?'

Laili saw the Torella's jewelled hand flash through the light, heard the smack as she hit the girl across the face, saw the girl stumble and fall to her knees.

'Shoddy workmanship! If you think I'm going to pay you for this, you're much mistaken, my girl.'

'Not going to pay?' The girl was struggling to her feet, one shaking hand clutching at the dress. 'What about my fee?'

'Such insolence!' Sarilla snatched the dress away. 'Be gone with you! Or I'll call the tarkhastars!'

Laili turned away.

There, but for your grace, Goddess . . .

'What kind of a place is this where children work their fingers to the bone?' she whispered.

Lai stood silently in the open doorway of the armoury, observing Ymarys coaching a trio of tarkhastars. A few bleak weeks ago, he would have observed them uncritically, dazzled by their élan and vivacity. Now he found himself assessing their weaknesses: one was unevenly balanced, another ill-guarded on the right flank, so easy to slip the blade through and—

Goddess! He checked himself. *What has become of me? I've begun to think like a killer – a ruthless, calculating killer—*

The battered leathern quintains were brought out, each torso marked in scarlet with the artery points where a sharp slash or thrust would bring certain death. Lai watched Ymarys demonstrate a lunge to the carotid artery. The Razhirrakh moved with the elegance of a dancer, carelessly graceful, more an artist than a lethal blademaster.

As Ymarys stepped back from the quintain, he caught sight of Lai in the doorway.

'Gentlemen.' Ymarys saluted the tarkhastars with his blade. 'Today's session is at an end.'

The tarkhastars saluted in return and filed out past Lai, wiping the sweat from their faces.

Lai began to unfasten his jacket when Ymarys checked him.

'They've cleared the snow from the arena. Bring your blade with you.'

At the back of the armoury a cobalt-stained door led down a deep, winding stair to a sombre, cobwebbed archway; beyond lay a subterranean passage. Ymarys struck a tinderstone to light his lantern and led the way into the darkness. Unlike the noisome passage to the slave-pit, this tunnel was wide enough for four men to walk abreast. After Lai's eyes had become accustomed to the gloom, he began to notice that an intricate pattern had been worked into the ancient stones in a dull glimmer of silver; his fingers traced it, feeling the smooth, cold texture.

'Thylz,' Ymarys said. 'A rare metal, much prized by the ancient Memizhon smiths. It glints faintly in the dark. Even without a lantern you could find your way.'

'These sigils—'

'An ancient tongue that few can decipher now. The Blood Rites trophy – the famed Razhir of Mithiel that Melmeth is so anxious to win back – is forged from thylz.'

A chill draught seeped into the passageway; soon the passageway came to an end in a rising stair. Lai shivered, sensing a sudden echo of terror and dull despair that emanated from the ancient stones. Only one way out – and that led to the arena.

The air grew sharper, cleaner, as they climbed.

'Sarafin's Gate.' Ymarys led Lai through an archway toothed with spikes. 'Your doorway to freedom – or oblivion.'

Lai found himself blinking in daylight on the inner rim of a vast empty circle of carven stone.

'Close your eyes,' Ymarys said softly. 'Imagine. Every seat filled, the stones shuddering to the din of the crowd, all shouting, baying like beasts for blood.'

Lai walked slowly towards the centre. It seemed so far to walk.

'It's vast.'

The frozen sand crunched under his feet. In the distance there were men at work; laboriously raking and sifting.

'Still a trifle hard underfoot.' Ymarys bent and sifted the grains through his gloved fingers. 'But with the thaw so late . . .'

'You mean – we work here today?' Lai blew on his numb hands; his breath sizzled like smoke in the frosty air.

'See the Arkhan's dais?' Ymarys said, pointing. 'That is where you go to receive your token of freedom – if you win. That is where the Arkhan casts the deathstones—'

'What are deathstones?' Lai said, frowning.

'When one combatant draws blood, the Arkhan throws down the

seven deathstones into the arena. If the stones fall in favour of the victor – then he must kill his opponent.'

'Kill?' Lai said. The echo went whispering around the arena. 'You mean execute.'

Ymarys shrugged.

'That is the tradition. If both contestants have fought with skill, the Arkhan may choose to spare the loser. But the crowd comes to see blood spilt. And the Arkhan likes to please the crowd.'

'This – blood rite. It is in honour of your god, Mithiel. Why is this god so hungry for blood?'

'Enough talk!' cried Ymarys in sudden irritation, flinging off his cloak, a fireswirl of brimstone yellow against the white sand. 'To work!'

Each bladestroke was rehearsed and re-rehearsed in slow motion until their movements acquired the grace and pattern of an antique dance.

Zigzag, interlace, then cross, dragonfly, reverse dragonfly, blade-whirring waterwheel . . .

'Bravo, Maistre Razhirrakh!' A burst of applause shattered the stillness.

Ymarys stepped back, his blade lowered. Lai turned around – and saw that there were people watching from the Arkhan's dais.

Melmeth and his entourage were wrapped in costly furs against the chill. Spiced smoke from brewing hippocras drifted across as a servitor poured the hot wine into goblets for the Arkhan and his guests.

'A stirring display, wouldn't you agree, my lord Zhudiciar?'

'It was elegantly executed, zhan.' The man beside Melmeth was robed in crimson velvet. 'But I'll wager neither of these bravos is a match for my champion.'

'That's Jhafir, the Haute Zhudiciar,' Ymarys said in Lai's ear. 'Head of the rival Tarkhas, the Tarkhas Zhudiciar.'

'A wager!' Melmeth cried. 'Do you hear that, Maistre Ymarys?'

Ymarys replied with a bow, hand on heart.

'And what does my lord Zhudiciar bet on his champion's success?'

'A pack of sable-spotted deer hounds. And a pair of grey stallions, bred on the plains of Djihan-Djihar.'

'Hmm. Handsome beasts. An attractive proposition. Come closer!'

Ymarys, still breathing hard on the frosted air, took Lai by the arm and drew him towards the dais.

'You heard my lord Zhudiciar? This leaves me with a delicate decision to make. Which of you two shall I match against his champion? How did *you* decide, Jhafir?'

Lai saw the Haute Zhudiciar smile.

'I made an occasion of it. The men like a clan match – it whets their appetites for the rites to come. I set my two fighting cocks together to spar it out in front of the Tarkhas Zhudiciar.'

'Not to the death, surely!'

'To the first blood. And a most stimulating contest it proved to be. Young Dhussyk against Rho Jhan.'

'And who won?'

'Rho Jhan.'

'Rho Jhan,' repeated Ymarys under his breath.

'Though Dhussyk made him sweat. Learned to fight on a corsair galley, apparently. Only twenty – but a veritable whirlwind of a bladesman.'

'Well, Maistre Ymarys.' Melmeth's words seemed bright and brittle on the cold air; Lai detected a shimmer of anger beneath the brightness. 'A contest it will be. In front of the Tarkhas Memizhon. Unbuttoned blades. Tomorrow at ten.'

'The Arkhan is right,' Ymarys said carelessly. 'Rho Jhan is a formidable opponent. But what he significantly failed to mention is that Rho Jhan is Clodolë's current favourite. What a scandal! To take the rival champion to her bed! Now do you understand why Melmeth would like nothing better than to see his consort's lover publicly humiliated? He'll go to any lengths to ensure that happens. Oh, there's more at stake here than a few lives, Lai. There's the honour of the ruler of the House of Memizhon to be protected. At all costs.'

'So we must fight each other?'

'Yes, we fight each other,' Ymarys said, his voice suddenly chill, winter black-ice, 'for the privilege of besting Clodolë's lover.'

A note had been pushed under Lai's door. He opened it with trembling fingers; it was sealed with the scarlet flame of Memizhon but the writing was unfamiliar.

Be in the Sassistri Gardens by the Windflower Pavilion on the stroke of wakenight tonight. Come alone, unarmed.

No signature.

Lai sprawled on the bed, kicking off his boots, to read and re-read the terse message. He had just come from the bath house; even after a soak and a vigorous pummelling from one of the masseurs, he was ready to drop, every muscle aching with fatigue.

How can I leave this room? I'm locked in for the night . . . and so tired I can not keep my eyelids . . . from closing . . .

The creak of a key turning in the lock . . .

Lai sat up with a start. The lucerna had burnt down and the charred wick was smouldering, a smoking emberlight in the dregs of the oil.

How long had he been asleep? He could only have dozed for a few minutes . . . and yet the lucerna was all but out.

He tested the door handle; the door swung open.

He grabbed his cloak and ran. The thaw had melted the snow and the courtyards were wet with slush. There were lights in the gatehouse and the sounds of singing. Orthandor's rich bass dominating all other voices in a bawdy drinking catch.

I could slip away now – and no one would notice. But then – what would become of Laili? How could I go and leave her here?

Lai sighed and took the shadowed path that led into the gardens.

A slight, wet wind rustled the branches. The unlit path was treacherously slippery with mud.

Lai reached the pavilion as the wakenight bell tolled out, dull bronze reverberations on the moist air and from faraway, the tarkenhorns of the Tarkhas Zhudiciar answered.

There was no one there.

'If this is a trick—' Or worse, a trap. He had not considered that possibility. A clever forgery to draw him here alone, unarmed—

'Lai.'

A girl stood in the open doorway, red hair drifting loose about her shoulders, her face hidden behind a fantastic winged moth-mask, white feathers and silvered sequins.

'Are you – is it really—' He couldn't speak more. He wanted to run to her, to hug her to make sure she was real.

'Oh, Lai—' Laili reached out her hands towards him and the mask dropped to the ground. He flung his arms around her, feeling her clinging to him as if she would never let go.

'Dhamzel.' A voice from the shadows, low yet vibrant with menace. Laili froze, her arms locked tight about Lai's neck.

'Oh no, give us a little longer, it is so long since we . . .' Tears on her voice, like rain on the damp breeze.

'Are you all right?' Lai asked urgently.

'Oh yes, I'm all right. I am well fed, well treated . . . but . . .'

'But?'

'I miss Ael Lahi so much. This terrible aching cold, these sunless days . . . I don't want to end my days in a jewelled cage, my wings clipped, unable to fly.'

'I'll set you free!' Lai said fiercely.

'To be free again – if only I—' She shook her head. 'But it's impossible.'

'Don't cry, Laili, I can't bear to see you cry. Listen to me. You must hold on a little longer. Trust me. There *is* a way.' He tried to wipe the tears from her face with shaking fingers. There was no choice now.

'Be careful, Lai. Myn-Dhiel is full of schemes, intrigues; don't trust anyone—'

'Dhamzel!' There was no mistaking the urgency in the low voice. A woman stood in the doorway, half-shrouded in shadow, her features hidden behind a tufted mask of sable owl feathers. Behind her, Lai could just make out two others, mute harem eunuchs, their drawn blades glimmering in the darkness.

'Lai . . .' Laili raised her fingers to his cheeks, cupping his face in her hands, as though trying to imprint the shape, the memory of it on her fingers.

'You must come now.' The woman placed her hands on Laili's shoulders, slowly drawing her away from Lai.

'No!' cried Lai. 'Why now? We have hardly been together two minutes—'

The two eunuchs in the shadow barred his way, jagged blades thrust towards his throat. Beyond them, he could just see Laili's gown, pale as drifting mothwings. One moment she was there, the next she had vanished from his sight, lost in the tangled wilderness.

'And don't try to follow us.'

Lai craned his head forwards, trying to penetrate the dark hood covering her hair, the sinister owl-mask. Who was she? The voice was muffled by the folds of the hood, yet Lai thought he caught the world-weary inflections of an older woman.

'Follow us – and she will be lost to you forever.'

CHAPTER 6

Melmeth stood motionless as the priests of the flame robed him in scarlet and ochre. The cavernous shrine of Memizhon was bright with the dragon-breath of torches, their fire sparking glints of molten gold in the metallic veins that threaded through the iron-brown rock.

So many times Melmeth had watched his father Sardion prepare to renew the Undying Flame, had stood dazzled by the lights, deafened by the clamour of gongs, watching the stern-faced stranger, clad in robes of flame, slowly ascend the steps and plunge his hand into the flickering tongue of fire – then withdraw his hand whole, unharmed, and show it to the assembled court.

'One day,' the stranger had whispered to him, 'you will take my place . . .' And the child Melmeth had shrunk away from him, fearing his harsh, unfamiliar voice . . . and fearing the searing heat of the flames most of all.

Slowly Melmeth climbed the carven steps. The air vibrated to the booming of tarkenhorns, the metallic shimmer of gongs, the deep chanting of the priests.

He raised his hand – and thrust it into the flame.

Silence fell, soft as winter snow.

He withdrew his hand and held it aloft for the assembled court to see. The flesh was whole, unblistered; the sacred fire had not harmed him. Then the priests burst into a frenetic paean of praise and Melmeth walked amongst his people, touching their heads with the fire-seared hand. All around him, his courtiers fell to their knees to kiss the hem of his trailing robes.

The yearly spring ritual had begun, the ritual that would culminate in the blood rites in the arena on Mithiel's Day, a sennight away.

Over the heads of his court, Melmeth's eyes met those of his consort, Clodolë. Knowing, bitter, ironic, her golden gaze openly challenged him to pass her by at his peril. The carven chair beside hers, the chair where the Arkhmyn, heir to the Seven Cantons, should sit, was conspicuously empty.

'Aren't you going to touch me, my lord?' she asked, her glance sliding to the empty chair. 'Miracles might yet be accomplished.'

Even here she chose to humiliate him, in front of the whole court.

'A show of unity between Arkhan and Arkhys would be auspicious for the coming rites,' Ophar's voice whispered in his ear.

Melmeth hesitated a moment then, seeing the implacable glint in the High Priest's eyes, offered Clodolë his hand to lead her from the shrine.

'So how fares your young protégé?' Her fingertips rested so lightly on his, they hardly touched.

'Nothing seems to escape your attention, lady. I would have thought such matters were of little interest.'

'Oh, everything interests me, Melmeth. I'm told he has red hair. Strange . . . this sudden obsession of yours with red hair.'

Melmeth did not respond. He knew she was trying to bait him; they had pursued this conversation on too many previous occasions.

'Who have you chosen as champion? Not Ymarys, surely.'

'Why not Ymarys?'

'Once they lose their nerve in the arena, they never regain it. Rho Jhan's unbeaten – and he's at the peak of his skills. If they're matched at the rites, Ymarys will be lucky to crawl away with his life.'

'Yes, I heard that you had taken an interest in Rho Jhan's training.'

She snatched her hand away.

'If you're going to lavish money and favours on your protégé, I shall do the same.'

'Even when he fights for the rival Tarkhas? The Tarkhas Zhudiciar?'

'Memizhon is *your* ancestral House, lord, not mine.'

'If your alliance to my House is so displeasing to you, lady, I could so easily find ways of terminating the association.'

She stared at him; suddenly he was aware that the bustle of movement about them was stilled and everyone was watching, straining to catch their every word.

'Are you threatening me, Melmeth? *Me*?'

Then she wheeled sharply away, her dhamzels fluttering after her like windblown butterflies. Melmeth rubbed his hand; the Undying Flame of Mithiel could not harm his unguent-smeared skin, but her nails had left a jagged scratch.

He felt suddenly unendurably weary of his court and the empty splendours of the rites of Mithiel. The sacred robes weighed too heavily on his shoulders; he felt like a puppet, buckling under the weight of pomp and authority.

'Hollow . . .' he whispered. 'Meaningless. A sham.'

He lifted the heavy gilded godmask from his head and handed it to Khaldar who stood silently, faithfully by. His head ached where the cold metal had pressed into his skull.

She would know how to soothe him, only she could smooth the ache from his head and the terrible gnawing emptiness from his soul.

If only he could just slip away unnoticed and—

'A word with you, Lord Arkhan.' Ophar was at his side. 'It has been brought to my attention that Arlan Azhrel has been at his infernal works again. Unnatural explosions. Sulphurous smoke. Heresy, my lord, heresy!'

'There's little danger, surely, in a few firecrackers to amuse the people?' Melmeth said, trying to laugh aside the High Priest's accusation.

Ophar's eyes narrowed.

'Dr Azhrel is a dangerous man. A few firecrackers today . . . but where will it lead tomorrow? What abominations is he devising in his laboratory? The gift of fire was a sacred trust, it is not to be abused or exploited.'

'I fail to see how Azhrel's hobby can be called heresy.'

'Is it not written in the Book of Mithiel, "I charge you, firstborn of Memizhon, to keep my flame burning in the hearts of your people"?'

'Yes . . .' The ache in Melmeth's skull had become more intense. He wished Ophar would leave him alone.

'And is it not also written, "Seek not to exploit the mysteries of my Divine Flame. For the Firebringer will destroy those who wield the fire for their own gain"?'

'Yes, yes—'

'Don't you understand, Lord Arkhan? The man is meddling in the sacred and the forbidden. He must be stopped.'

'I find him to be a good man. A philanthropist. A man of science.'

'Good? I believe our definitions of goodness must differ greatly, zhan.'

'What,' Melmeth said wearily, 'are you asking me to do, Ophar?'

'Close down his laboratory. For if he persists in his experiments, I will be forced to bring him before the Inquisition to be tried. And if his arguments do not stand up before the law of Mithiel then nothing you do, or say, my lord, will protect him.'

*

65

'Maistre Ymarys?'

Marys – rys – ys . . . The echoes whispered to silence.

The armoury was empty.

And then Lai noticed that the little door at the far end of the armoury was wide open. He had never seen it open before and had supposed that it was of little or no significance: a storeroom or disused garderobe . . .

A foul odour came wafting out, sulphurous as the hot springs yet tainted with a more familiar metallic tang.

'Maistre!'

And from deep below he heard Ymarys's voice faintly answering.

'Down here!'

At the foot of the stair lay another chamber, its door half-ajar.

'Come in . . .'

The smell of sulphur grew stronger as Lai pushed open the door.

The air was yellowed with smoke like clinging winterfog; an open grating high in the wall was the only ventilation and source of daylight.

Ymarys beckoned him into the smoke-choked chamber.

A long table was crowded with glass jars, funnels, pipes and alembics. A tall man in shirt sleeves, his face shielded by a leathern mask, was holding a glass flask over a flame. His long black hair was loosely tied back at the nape of the neck with a crimson ribbon. The powdered contents of the flask were slowly changing colour as the flame's heat warmed them to life.

As Lai drew closer, he was overwhelmed by a sudden certainty that he had encountered the stranger before.

'Watch, Lai.'

The powder suddenly glowed jewel-bright, sultry blue as the plumage of an exotic grove bird. The man carefully lifted the flask with metal tongs and placed it to cool on a tripod. Then he raised the mask to wipe the sweat from his eyes.

That face – that hideously scarred face—

'You. It was you,' Lai whispered. 'In the donjon. Afterwards I thought it was just a dream, a feverdream—'

'You two have already met?' Ymarys said. Lai hardly heard him.

'I was delirious. You saved my life. And I never knew your name—'

'Azhrel,' the stranger said abstractedly. 'Arlan Azhrel. I'm glad to see you're fully recovered.'

'Doctor Azhrel,' corrected Ymarys. 'Physician – and Artificiar to the

66

Arkhan.'

'It's a closely guarded secret, the making of firedust, passed down from father to son. The hierophants call it the work of Ar-Zhoth. If they had their way . . .' Arlan Azhrel began to wipe his hands and face clean on a linen cloth.

'Firedust?' Lai was still staring at the doctor, only half-hearing what he was saying.

'For Mithiel's Day. Bright coloured flares, loud bangs, all to excite the crowd.' Dr Azhrel pointed to the dusty row of earthenware jars ranged along the shelf above the table labelled in faded lettering: 'Orpiment', 'Iron Sand', 'Lazuli', 'Antimony', 'Calomel' . . .

'Metallic salts especially refined by Dr Azhrel himself – in his other guise as alchymyst. Whites, yellows, reds . . . even blues and greens . . . He's an artist in fire.'

Azhrel bowed, touched his forehead to acknowledge the compliment, leaving, Lai could not help but notice, a smear of soot.

'And now to work!' Ymarys clapped his hands together.

Dispersing fumes from the firedust began to taint the armoury, drifting up from the cellar; Lai's nose wrinkled at the foul smell, his stomach queased.

'We practise in this smoke?' Lai said.

'Ha! Get used to it now. You heard what Azhrel said – the arena will be wreathed in firedust smoke on Mithiel's Day. On a windless day you can find yourself searching for your opponent through thick fog.'

Throughout the winter the barrel-vaulted roof of the armoury had echoed to the clash of blades as Lai and Ymarys worked alone. Now everywhere Lai looked there were tarkhastars ranged along the whitewashed walls of the armoury; even the Arkhan was there, attended by his silent bodyslave, dark Khaldar, to see Ymarys defend his title.

'Put this on.' Ymarys threw Lai a padded corslet. 'Blood rites rules.' There was a wild, wanton glint in his grey eyes that Lai had never seen before. 'The first to draw blood is the winner.'

Lai tried to concentrate his mind on tugging the corslet straps tight but his heart was pounding. To fight Ymarys was like fighting himself; every move he made would be anticipated.

Orthandor called for quiet and, at a nod from the Arkhan, the contest began.

They circled each other a while, Ymarys languid in his gait, a silvercat stalking his prey.

Lai's nerve broke the first. Blade whirling, he came at Ymarys, intending to tire him with a dazzling fanfaronade of strokes—

Goddess, where was he? Lai blinked, bewildered.

Ymarys's blade came thrusting towards him; he just managed to deflect it, a finger's breadth from his cheek.

'A close call!' Orthandor shouted.

Lai retreated; all the while Ymarys was moving steadily, stealthily closer.

Think of something. Think of something. Think—

Ymarys's wrist twitched, so fast Lai never noticed the moment his bright blade came rearing up, a flicking cobra-tongue stabbing straight for his eyes.

And in that moment, Lai thrust. Felt the jolt of his blade grazing Ymarys's flesh, Ymarys's eyes staring accusingly into his own, cold as razhir steel.

'Damn you to hell, Lai Dhar!'

The razhir dropped to the floor as Ymarys's hand flew to clutch at his face.

'Well, Ymarys?' Melmeth said in the silence.

It was only then that Lai noticed the thin line of crimson trickling between the delicate white fingers, only then that he realised with a shock that he had drawn blood.

A murmur of astonishment went rippling around the armoury as the tarkhastars realised that Ymarys, the champion, had been defeated.

Ymarys gripped Lai's hand and raised it high in the air.

'My lord Arkhan – you have a new champion.' His drawling voice hid the naked anger Lai had glimpsed a few moments before. 'This is your Razhirrakh – Lai Dhar!'

Next morning Ymarys failed to arrive for blade practice.

Ymarys had never been late before.

Lai performed a few solitary exercises, swinging his blade until the air sang.

Where was Ymarys? Sulking, perhaps, resentful that his own pupil should have defeated him in front of the Tarkhas Memizhon clan? Or perhaps the blade-wound had run more deep than Lai had intended. Ymarys took such pride in his appearance; maybe he was refusing to emerge from his rooms until the unsightly scar had healed . . .

'Lai Dhar?'

A servitor clad in the azure livery of the Tarkhas Memizhon stood in the open doorway.

'Follow me.'

He led Lai across the courtyard and in at the great door of the Tarkhas House; a broad staircase of polished oak wound upwards from the panelled hall adorned with the tasselled standards and gilded trophies of past victories. Lai had never been permitted to penetrate so deep into the heart of the clan before.

'Where are we going?' Lai asked as they climbed the stair.

'Maistre Ymarys has risen late this morning. He asks you to join him for a morning tisane.'

'Asks you.' The change of emphasis did not escape Lai's notice. One well-timed blade-scratch – and his position had subtly altered.

Ymarys's rooms were on the first floor; the servitor opened the door and ushered Lai in.

'Good morning to you, Lai,' Ymarys, draped in a morning robe, was reclining on the couch, his hair loose about his shoulders.

'Maistre Ymarys. I – I must apologise. I – I never intended—'

'D'you mean this?' Ymarys lifted the long locks of hair that curtained his face, revealing the cut, a thin crescent of angry red.

Lai flinched.

'A mere scratch. It's healing already.'

Prayer flags of saffron, cinnamon and scarlet hung on the limewashed walls next to a knotted flail of black rope, scourge of the soul as well as the body. Yet the couch on which Ymarys lay was a riot of striped, sequinned silk cushions: mulberried pink, violet, vanilla. The air was perfumed not with bitter incense but with the exotic scents of expensive body-oils. A crisis of identity: Ymarys the hedonist in conflict with Ymarys the ascetic. Lai caught Ymarys unconsciously stealing a critical glance at himself in the round bronze-framed mirror that hung above the bed.

'The preparation of morning tisane is a ceremony of some ritual in my home canton, Langoel.'

The servitor lit the oil to heat water and brought out a flask of exquisitely enamelled beaten metal in the shape of a curled firedrake which he placed on the ebony table at Ymarys's bedside and then withdrew. The water began to bubble; Ymarys deftly poured it over the crushed herbs and spices in the flask and left it to steep. A thin curl of aromatic steam rose from the curved spout, the firedrake's open maw.

A flute, carved from polished ebon wood, lay on a cedar chest. Lai's eyes kept straying towards it. His fingers itched to touch it, to stroke the smooth wood. They began to press a pattern of notes on the palms of his hands.

'Fine, isn't it?'

Ymarys had noticed.

'Take it. Try it.'

Lai shook his head. Lai the flute-player was dead. He had died in the donjon the instant the tattooist's needle seared into his skin.

'You don't play?'

'I used to.'

Ymarys picked the flute up and handed it to him.

'Damned if I could ever get the hang of it. This belonged to my mother. You look as if you know what to do with it.'

Lai found himself lifting the flute to his lips, moistening his lips, drawing a breath. His fingers moved . . . and a whisper of notes brushed the still air. It was instinctive. He could not help himself.

Notes drift upwards into the dark leaves of the Grove, drowsy as wreathing incense smoke . . .

'Ahh,' said Ymarys softly. 'So I was right.'

Lai set the flute down; his hands were shaking.

'I can't.' The whispering notes had awakened feelings, memories he had tried to forget.

Ymarys poured the clear infusion into the enamelled cups and handed one to Lai.

'Tell me about yourself.'

Why should Ymarys want to know now what he had ignored for so many months?

'Nothing to tell.' He replaced the flute on its velvet cloth.

'Where did you learn to play so exquisitely?'

'On Ael Lahi. In the Sacred Grove.'

'The Sacred Grove,' echoed Ymarys, savouring the words on his tongue. 'And what were you doing there?'

'What was I doing there?' Lai slowly sipped the hot tisane. 'It all seems like a dream . . . so remote now . . .'

'Don't you find it's so much more congenial to talk here . . . in comfort . . . away from prying eyes . . . ?'

As Lai inhaled the fragrance of the rising steam, a memory suddenly gripped him, painfully vivid, of the green scent of the island drenched in warm summer rains . . .

'Do you understand me, Lai?'

Lai started, involuntarily spilling the tisane onto his knee, rapidly pinching it out.

'My dear Lai, you are an innocent in a court where intrigue is commonplace and no one can be trusted.'

'Even you?'

'I could so easily have drugged your tea,' Ymarys said, smiling as he raised the enamel bowl to his lips.

Lai looked warily at the smudge of green lees staining the base of the bowl.

Ymarys leaned across and lightly brushed his cheek with his fingertips.

'Be on your guard.'

The words were spoken casually but as Lai looked up into Ymarys's malachite-painted eyes, he caught a glimmer of grim warning.

'You mean—'

'You fight Rho Jhan. *Her* favourite. This isn't just a contest between Tarkhas clan champions. This is the rift that is cracking the House of Memizhon apart. The enmity, the bitter enmity between Arkhan and Arkhys. Believe me, Lai, she is capable of anything – *anything* – to ensure that her champion wins.'

All these long months Lai had sweated in the armoury, preparing for this day. Mithiel's Day. Now it had come.

The hours passed slowly, so interminably slowly . . .

Lai flung open the shutters and gazed up at the high, blank walls of Myn-Dhiel. Somewhere behind those windowless walls Laili was still confined, somewhere within the labyrinthine passages of the ancient citadel.

And yet by wakenight, we both could be free—

Tonight he would face the Zhudiciar's champion, Rho Jhan – and the reality of his own fragile mortality. One error tonight, just one – and he would die.

There came a discreet scratching at his door, so faint he wondered for a moment if he had imagined it.

He tried the door-handle – and found it unlocked.

The landing was empty. But a breath of perfume, faint as the evanescent odour of a crushed petal, lingered in the air. And a little package, wrapped in the finest paper, had been placed outside his door.

He lifted it, sniffing it suspiciously. The faint perfume seemed to emanate from its delicate paper. A note was attached:

Dearest Lai,

They tell me you fight today to secure my freedom. Wear this favour for me, beloved brother. May it bring you good fortune in the arena.

Your loving sister, Laili.

Lai began to unwrap the paper, its frail leaves as transparent as dried rose petals. Inside lay a ribbon of azure silk: Memizhon blue. Attached to the ribbon was a glittering blue jewelstone, carved in the shape of a flame. Lai was about to lift it out when he heard footsteps hurrying along the corridor.

'Lai!' Ymarys's voice outside.

Lai hastily scrunched the note into a ball behind his back.

'What is that?'

'A – a gift. A favour to wear in the arena. It was left outside my door.'

'From Myn-Dhiel? Let me see.' Ymarys took the petal-paper from Lai and sniffed it suspiciously.

'What's wrong? It's only a ribbon—'

'Did you touch it? Did you pick it up?'

'You're talking in riddles. What harm could there be in a length of blue ribbon?'

'No harm in the ribbon. But the jewelled pin,' Ymarys laid the ribbon down with infinite care. 'Come over to the light. Look at the tip.'

Now that they were close to the window, Lai could see that the point of the pin was darker than the silver shaft, as though it had been dipped in some glutinous unguent.

'Poison. Subtle and slow. You would not have felt the first effects until you entered the arena. By then, who would have been able to detect it?'

'Poison . . .' So the note was a forgery. As for the sweet-spiced perfume . . . 'But who would want—'

Ymarys's lips twisted in a sour caricature of a smile.

'Oh, come now, Lai. Who do *you* think?'

CHAPTER 7

All night gangs had roamed the streets of the city, chanting in praise of the Reds or the Blues, Zhudiciar or Memizhon. Fortunes could be made – and lost – on the skills of the bladesmen. Queues had formed outside the arena long before dawn. Scuffles broke out amongst groups of rival enthusiasts and the Tarkhas Zhudiciar had to be called to keep order. Today the markets were shut, the busy quays were silent; everyone was on their way to the arena to see the brandslaves fight to the death for a chance of freedom.

Street-sellers of khassafri were brewing the potent nutmeg punch over charcoal braziers. Marchpanes dyed cochineal red or violet blue were outselling the more traditional treats of halva and spiced nuts. Favours were selling well too, silk ribbons, scarves and flowers in scarlet or azure.

The palanquins of the wealthy began to arrive at a separate entrance; the women, exotically masked with sequinned feathers, could be glimpsed as they flitted into the arena, some with pet marmosets tricked out in red or blue riding on their mistresses' arms. The men followed at a more sedate pace, sniffing at lemon pomanders, attended by dwarfs and dark-skinned bodyslaves.

Amidst the rowdy throng stalked the silent hierophants of the Undying Flame in their sombre robes. They alone remembered that this was a day of sacrifice, a day sacred to their god.

Deep in the labyrinth beneath the arena, the bladesmen made their final preparations for the rite to come. A trail of chanting hierophants passed along the tunnel, thurifers swinging, leaving a cloud of bitter incense smoke in their wake.

'Hmm. You'll do,' Ymarys said as he secured the blue-silk loincloth about Lai's waist. 'We'll have to keep the women from clawing each other's eyes out over you.'

Lai gazed down at his oiled body; his tawny skin glittered as if he had been powdered with gold-dust. He felt naked without the padded practice corslets – vulnerable.

Dark-cowled figures loomed out of the shadows as they left the tiring room. A torch flared into light, dazzle-bright.

'Be one with the Flame,' reverent voices murmured as Lai passed between the priests of Mithiel towards Sarafin's Gate.

The chants, the incense fumes, the ritual costumes . . . if it had not been for the grim presence of the hierophants, Lai could almost have imagined he was preparing for a ceremony within the Sacred Grove . . .

Blue-clad brandslaves came filing past Lai. One turned and gave him a long, resentful stare. Those sour, accusing eyes; suddenly he recognised Wadhir. Growling at their heels came Orthandor's hounds, straining on a double leash.

'On the double there, lads!' roared Orthandor, hauling the hounds to heel. The flail cracked, sizzling the air.

Row upon row of tiered stone seats rose up to the black night sky from the white sand of the arena. The babble of voices from the crowd was like the roar of stormbreakers crashing on the shore.

'So many people!' Lai whispered as they emerged from the subterranean tunnel and stood waiting in the fanged shadow of Sarafin's Gate.

'All Perysse must be here,' said Ymarys. He tossed back his smooth hair which glinted with the dull sheen of antique silver in the dark.

One by one the brandslaves were handed their curved blades by the armourer at the gate and pushed through into the arena, their way back barred by the tarkhastars.

The last of the brandslaves lingered longer than the others.

'Memizhon pigs.' Suddenly he spat in the armourer's face and swung around, blade glinting in his hand.

'Look out!' Ymarys cried.

The tarkhastar at the gate was caught off-guard; he staggered and fell as the brandslave's bladestroke sliced across his belly.

The brandslave went stumbling away down the tunnel.

'Go!' Orthandor unleashed the hounds.

The priests of Mithiel scattered as the slavering animals tore after their quarry. Orthandor seized a torch and strode off after them.

From the tunnel came the noise of snarling – and then silence.

Orthandor returned, with the hounds struggling on the leash, their bloodied jaws muzzled.

'Throat torn out,' he said laconically. 'Damn fool.'

The tarkenhorns brayed out across the arena. The crowd suddenly stilled, the ominous stillness before a storm . . .

'We're one bladesman short. We start at a disadvantage.' Orthandor turned to Lai. 'You'll have to replace him.'

'Me?' Lai appealed to Ymarys but the Razhirrakh looked on him coldly, distantly, almost as if he were a stranger.

'You're still a brandslave. You have no choice.'

'Remember, Lai,' Ymarys whispered in his ear. 'Kill – or be killed.'

Lai shivered. The razhir suddenly felt a lead weight in his hand, so heavy he could hardly lift it.

'Get in there, Lai – and don't let me down.' Orthandor took Lai by the shoulders and pushed him out into the arena.

The sand grains grated cold against the soles of Lai's bare feet.

'We're honoured.'

Wadhir was regarding him. His lips curled back from his teeth in a leering grin.

'Hey, lads, remember the pretty boy?'

Lai tightened his grip on his razhir. Concentrate. Don't listen to him.

'Let's see what fancy tricks you've learned, pretty boy. Let's see this famous technique of yours.'

A gate on the opposite side of the arena opened and a number of brandslaves wearing crimson breechcloths appeared.

The crowd burst into raucous chanting.

'Reds! Come on Reds!'

'Blues! Blues! Blues!'

There was no time to prepare; the Reds came charging across the sand towards the Blues.

'Goddess,' Lai murmured, 'forgive me.'

All the grace and cunning he had learned from Ymarys seemed irrelevant. The Zhudiciar brandslave who confronted him wielded his blade like a scythe; such heavy strokes could shatter his delicate razhir.

The crowd's chanting grew more hypnotic. Lai's heart pounded with every shout, every blade-clash.

Kill or be killed.

One Memizhon slave was down already, rolling in the sand, his face working, contorted in the death agony.

'One to the Reds!' bellowed Orthandor. 'What are you made of,

Blues?'

Another savage cheer bruised Lai's ear. The crowd were hungry for blood.

'Two to the Reds!'

Wadhir's foot shot out suddenly, tripping Lai. He fell heavily; from somewhere in the swirling darkness, he could hear Wadhir laughing. In the same moment, his opponent stabbed downwards – but Lai rolled aside and thrust, a subtle, fluid move only perfected after long hours' practice. Down the man went, the weight of his falling body wrenching the razhir from Lai's hand. As Lai came to tug it out, the man convulsed, blood spurting and Lai flinched away to avoid the scarlet spray. The body twitched once more, then lay still. And in the stillness, Lai realised that he could no longer hear Wadhir's jeering laughter.

'Behind you!'

Ymarys's shout made Lai wheel round, blade raised. He just parried the blow. Dark eyes gleamed in the darkness behind the curved blade. Young eyes; bright with fear and exhilaration.

The white sand was dark with pools of slow-seeping crimson; a hot, sweet stench of blood tainted the air.

Lai alone fought on. He heard the roistering shouts of the crowd, urging him to win. His opponent seemed tired now; Lai could hear him grunt with the effort of each swinging bladestroke. He knew only too well what such slow, wild strokes would lead to. So easy to slip under his guard and—

'Blues! Blues! Blues!'

Lai still stood upright although now he was swaying with weariness; at his feet his opponent lay writhing in the sand, clutching at a gaping slash in his belly, entrails spilling out from between his blood-sticky fingers.

Lai drew in a breath between clenched teeth – and swung the blade again. The dark eyes glazed, rolled upwards, the clutching fingers went limp.

It was over.

'You've done it!' cried Orthandor, caught up in the crowd's frenzy.

Lai hardly heard him. He could scent death on the night wind. They were dragging the dead and wounded from the arena. As the tarkhastars pulled a body out by the ankles, hair trailing through the bloodied sand, he recognised Wadhir; the lips still curled back from the teeth, the leering grin frozen into a chilling rictus.

Even as the evidence of carnage was hastily removed, the winners were being paraded around the arena before going one by one to receive their metal token of pardon from the Arkhan. All except Lai. Who must fight again. Fresh sand was scattered and raked to cover the soaking bloodstains.

High in one of the Mhaell enclosures, a young girl covered her masked face with her fan and turned her head away.

'You're not going to faint, are you?'

'I've seen quite enough.'

'But now it's time for the contest of the champions!'

Her companion thrust a box of cinnamon sweetmeats towards her but she waved it away.

'How can *he* sit there, watching so avidly?'

'I remember Ymarys's first contest as if it were yesterday.' Her companion selected a sweetmeat and popped it into her mouth. 'You should have seen him – he was outrageous! Such a crowd-teaser.'

Orthandor threw a coarse towel around Lai's shoulders and sat him down within the shadow of the Sarafin Gate. A cup was thrust between Lai's lips; he gulped the liquid down, grimacing at the taste: water soured with wine. The armourer passed him a rag to clean his blade. Lai wiped the blood from the steel, not thinking, his mind a blank.

The sudden dazzle of ice-white light that illumined the arena made him fling up his hands to cover his eyes.

For one mazed moment, he believed that She had intervened as flowers of light exploded into the dark night sky, moon flowers, muraq flowers, garlands of golden leaves that wept pale fire into the sand.

Firedust. The silverlight was illusion: magically, ephemerally beautiful . . . but merely illusion, created by Arlan Azhrel in his underground laboratory.

'Look at you!' Ymarys clicked his tongue in disgust. 'You're not ready – and the contest of the champions will begin in a moment.'

Ymarys unbraided Lai's copper-stranded hair and began to comb it until it crackled with electricity.

'Don't relax your concentration for a second. Rho Jhan's subtle as a snake. Remember – you're not the only one playing for high stakes tonight.'

He bound Lai's forehead with a thin band studded with sapphires.

Pungent chymical smoke drifted like fog across the arena, verdigris-green, indigo blue. Lai was grateful now for Ymarys's preparation in the armoury.

An eruption of fire-crackers ripped the black air apart with ear-bruising retorts.

'Now,' said Ymarys in his ear.

Lai walked out into the billowing torch smoke.

A cheer, loud as a rolling clap of thunder, arose from the tiered seats to greet him. Lai faltered.

'Keep walking,' Ymarys said behind him.

The thunder rolled on and on around the arena as, barefoot, he crossed the gritty white sand to stand below the Arkhan's azure-decked dais.

Unable to resist glancing upwards, Lai noticed the Arkhys Clodolë beside her consort, hair rich as ambered honey in the torchlight, fixing him – only him – with her gold-flecked eyes. And he saw the tip of her pink tongue lick along the soft line of her lips; slowly, deliberately, lasciviously . . .

The horns brayed again from the opposite side of the arena and another great shout went up.

Lai could sense the growing impatience of the crowd; it would be so easy to break concentration with so many distractions: raucous shouts, cat-calls, whistles . . .

He turned to see Rho Jhan approaching through the swirls of rising smoke. The torchlight glittered in the fire opals and rubies adorning his crimson headband.

The crowd fell silent as the two men stalked around the arena awhile with measured tread, each warily eyeing each other.

Lai took note of Rho Jhan's air of self-assurance, the calculating glint in his hawk-grey eyes. His ears and nostrils had been pierced with thin golden rings, Enhirran-fashion; his straight black hair had been shaved from the sides of his skull, the aggressively spiked top-knot had been dyed crimson and the rest fell in stiff black braids to his blue-tattooed shoulders. An ivory ribbon, oddly incongruous, fluttered from his crimson headband; Clodolë's favour . . . ?

What is he up to, this Enhirran, biding his time – or waiting for me to make the first mistake?

Lai glimpsed a twitch of shadow out of the corner of his eye.

He whipped about, his razhir wheeling, whirling, to defend

himself. Metal bit deep into thrusting metal, firesparks fizzed into the air and with all his strength, Lai forced Rho Jhan's blade aside.

Instantly Rho Jhan came back at Lai, driving him almost to his knees with his vicious blade-strokes, battering him down, down, down—

Lai lost his footing and thudded headlong onto the arena floor.

Rho Jhan's blade plunged deep into the sand a nail's breadth from Lai's face even as he rolled away, scrambling to his feet, spitting out a mouthful of dust and grit.

Dust in my eye – ahh, curse it – watering – I can't see, can't see—

The blade plunged again, almost spitting him. Lai's eyes wept gritwater as he slid clear.

No time to think. No time to react. No time even to—

Rho Jhan was ready for him and the glint of his white teeth, bared in a grin, taunted Lai as he backed away through the gusting sulphur smoke.

He's going to win. He's going to break my guard. And he knows it.

Lai stepped back, stumbled and fell to one knee.

He would die here on the white sand, twitch out the last of his life in the knowledge that Laili would never be free, that she would end her days a slave in Myn-Dhiel, trapped in the golden cage—

'No!' he shouted. 'NO!'

He beat off the incoming thrust, curling his knees tight to his chest as he tumbled away across the sand, making the older man run to keep up with him.

Rho Jhan's breath was coming faster now. Lai drew him on, ever on, keeping him moving, sensing that he was beginning to tire.

'Rho Jhan!' Lai bellowed across the arena.

Lai lunged. Rho Jhan parried but Lai could see his lips were drawn back in an exhausted snarl.

The frenzied shouting of the crowd had cohered into a regular rhythmic chant as they urged their champions to victory. Stamping feet dinned into Lai's ears; voices calling a name – his name – throbbed like a fever pulse in his head.

'Dhar! Dhar! Dhar! Dhar!'

He must not lose the duel now; even though the sweat was dripping into his eyes, half-blinding him, he struck again and again at Rho Jhan in wild battle-frenzy, whipping the crowd into such an ecstasy of excitement that at the moment he beat through Rho Jhan's guard, cutting open a jagged slash above his right breast, the whole arena seemed to erupt into hysterical cheering.

'*Y'll-th'ai!*' Lai cried, his razhir tip at Rho Jhan's throat. '*Y'll-th'ai!*'

For a moment Lai wondered if Rho Jhan would speak the traditional words of surrender or spit in his face.

But the words came, slowly, pronounced with lingering disgust, as if they had a foul taste.

'*Y'll-m'ai*, Aelahim. I yield.'

Lai let the razhir tip drop. He hardly heard the crowd's exultation as he bent his head, exhaustedly wiping the saltsweat from his eyes with his forearm.

Melmeth rose to his feet, hand poised to cast the deathstones. But Clodolë was beside him, speaking urgent words, touching his arm, his face. Melmeth frowned. Then he raised one hand for silence.

'There has been blood spilt enough tonight. The Arkhys begs clemency for her champion. And I grant it. Rho Jhan – your life is spared.'

The chanting had begun again and it was still Lai's name they were chanting, raising a rowdy paean in the honour of Memizhon and Lai Dhar of Ael Lahi.

'You are their champion now,' Ymarys said. 'Go and receive your prize from the Arkhan – God knows, you've earned it.'

Head ringing from the chanting, Lai began to walk towards the Arkhan's dais; at one moment he hesitated, looking back towards Ymarys, exhaustion glistening in his tear-blurred eyes.

'Go on,' Ymarys said.

The women of Perysse came scrambling, shrieking, shrilling like starlings to lean over the barriers, fighting to touch Lai's hair, his body, his clothes.

'We love you, Lai Dhar!'

'Kiss me!'

'Touch me! Touch me!'

Lai slowly climbed the dais steps until he stood before the Arkhan.

'Listen to the crowd!' Melmeth said. He was evidently delighted. Clodolë said nothing, chewing at a fingernail. 'Perysse has a new idol tonight. The winner's sash, Khaldar.'

The boy came forwards bearing the golden sash over his smooth, dark-skinned arms. As he presented it to the Arkhan, Melmeth let his hand drift over the glossy head, a gesture at once casual yet proprietary. Lai, who had knelt at the Arkhan's feet, looked up to see Clodolë's amber-tawny eyes staring provocatively into his.

Hastily he bowed his head and the Arkhan draped the winner's gold-embroidered sash about his body. Melmeth then raised him to his feet and presented him to the crowd.

'I declare the new champion of the rites to be Lai Dhar.' Khaldar brought Melmeth an enamelled dye-pot and, dipping in an ebony stick, the Arkhan made the ritual mark of freedom on Lai's forehead, a spot of indelible scarlet in the heart of the blue slave brand. 'Lai Dhar – you leave this dais a free man!'

'Well done, lad, well done!' Orthandor slapped him on the back as the cheering began again. 'Wave to them, acknowledge them! Tonight they adore you! Tomorrow they'll be too hungover to remember who won.'

But Lai had turned back to the Arkhan, his eyes searching the dais and tiered seats behind.

'Where is she?'

'She?' Melmeth's face clouded over.

'I thought she would be here. You – you said—'

Clodolë was watching them both intently.

'Later,' Melmeth said brusquely.

'But – I thought—'

'You win this year, Lord Arkhan!' Jhafir bowed to the Arkhan, one hand on his heart. 'Such handsome horses. It breaks my heart to part with them. But a wager's a wager.' He and Melmeth began to walk towards the archway together. Lai, snubbed, stood helplessly watching them. 'I'll have my grooms bring them to Myn-Dhiel at dawn . . .'

Later. When was later?

Clodolë rose and followed the Arkhan. But at the edge of the dais, she glanced back at Lai and beckoned languidly.

'Come, zhan Razhirrakh.'

'Me?'

'You are expected at Myn-Dhiel. Didn't Ymarys warn you? The champion of the rites is always guest of honour at the Arkhan's feast.'

'Shouldn't I bathe first? And change?'

'Certainly not. My dhamzels like the champion to attend reeking of combat,' she said with a lubricious little smile. 'It sharpens their appetites.'

CHAPTER 8

Laili stood alone at her open window, listening to the distant babble of voices drifting up from the hall below. The feast of Mithiel. To which, it seemed, the whole palace – except Laili – had been invited. It was not seemly, Sarilla told her, for a concubine to appear at an official function. Court protocol did not permit it.

The new moon rode high in the sky, a silvered chariot.

Laili touched her forehead, her breast in reverence, whispering the words of salutation.

'Welcome, Goddess, I greet you . . .'

Suddenly she ran back into the room and seized the rosewood flute Melmeth had given her.

They were all feasting, no one would hear her.

She took a breath, then raised the flute to her lips.

Her first hesitant notes were dry as windblown cinders.

Ashes drift like snow across the charred stumps of the burned Grove.

And then, unbidden, the melody of the invocation returned to her. The silver thread spun outwards, filaments of sound, tendrilling down over the citadel, enwebbing the night city in a translucent cocoon.

Flutter of snow-wings . . . the dry ashes stir to life . . .

Laili opened her eyes wide.

Moonmoths?

The music faltered as her fingers ceased to move. She gazed up at the moon's pale face.

Sobs, painful and choking, tore at her throat.

Never to see the moonmoths again, never to hear their song, never again—

The trance was broken, the soundweb torn to tatters.

The flute dropped to the floor.

The palace of Myn-Dhiel was alight with sweet-burning lucernae to

82

celebrate the victory; fragrant smoke drifted through the corridors and pearlescent flames flickered in the high-vaulted hall where the feast was to take place.

A succession of laden platters passed before Lai's dazzled eyes, piled with enough food to feed his village in Ael Lahi for a year: stuffed carp and pike; spit-roast wild duck and pheasant; mountains of spiced rice liberally sprinkled with pine kernels and apricots; tender steamed dumplings with plum sauce . . .

Toasts were drunk to the Arkhan, to the House of Memizhon and then to Lai, the Razhirrakh. Lai hardly heard the cheers, the compliments, the praises. His eyes misted with tears as he stood at Melmeth's side; he could hardly believe that he was free. Free to go home. He longed for the ceremony to end so that he could be reunited with Laili. He scanned the crowded hall, hoping to catch a glimpse of her fire-bright hair . . . but there was no sign of her amongst the painted exquisites and perfumed dhamzels.

'Zhan,' he began when Melmeth turned to him. 'You have been most generous to me. But there is still one thing else—'

Melmeth's russet brows contracted in a slight frown.

'I trust, Lai, that you are not going to raise matters more suited to an official audience than a feast.'

'But we had a bargain, zhan. I have kept my part.'

'Of course we have a bargain! Are you suggesting the Arkhan does not keep his word? You are a free man. You are pardoned of your crime.'

'N–no, zhan, I merely—'

'Good.' Melmeth smiled at Lai, a smile utterly without warmth. 'You must be patient a little longer.' He pressed a money ring heavy with golden eniths into Lai's hand.

Orthandor cried out, 'Look how generously the Arkhan rewards his new champion! A fortune in gold!'

Everyone in the hall, from servitors to Mhaell lords, turned to look at Lai, applauding. The coveted moment of privacy was gone; Lai bowed his head, seemingly to acknowledge the applause, but also to conceal the working fury in his face. He began to suspect a trick. He had been gulled. Laili was not to be set free.

A servitor silently refilled his goblet with wine; Lai swallowed it down as if it had been water, staring resentfully over the rim at the perfumed exquisites of Myn-Dhiel. And one face suddenly caught his attention; a Mhaell lady, plying her way through the throng like a barque in full sail, making straight for Ymarys.

The Torella Sarilla.

As he watched, he saw her kiss Ymarys on both cheeks. So they knew each other! If he could just reach her, he could confront her, demand, 'Where is my sister? Why won't you let her go free?'

But as he moved away from the Arkhan's table, a hand touched his shoulder, a hand with soft fingertips that sent a tingling shiver through his flesh.

He turned to see the Arkhys Clodolë at his side.

'Where are you going, Lai? Not leaving already? You are the guest of honour tonight.'

'You're very kind—' He tried to back away but she took hold of him by the arm.

'Now don't be so self-effacing. The women in this hall are eyeing us jealously; they are all longing for a chance to speak to you.'

It would have been more than discourteous to try to escape; Lai cast one last lingering look over his shoulder towards Arazhel.

'Perhaps I shall keep you to myself. Mmm, yes,' and she ran a hand along his arm, gently pulling him to sit next to her, 'I think I shall for a little. I want to know more about you, Lai Dhar.'

'There's little to tell.' Lai's skin still prickled at her touch, hot then cold, fever-chills.

She laughed. 'Oh, but there is. You're an Aelahim. I find that fascinating.'

He was out of his depths. One moment she was scheming against him with poisoned favours so that her lover, Rho Jhan, could win the rites. The next, she was telling him he was fascinating, the words forming so seductively on her moist, mulberried lips.

'You and I could find much to say to each other, Lai.'

Lai glanced unhappily towards Melmeth. Why did the Arkhan tolerate his consort's flagrant infidelities? But Melmeth was talking to Orthandor, his arm around Khaldar's waist, hand straying idly downwards to rest on the boy's smooth-skinned thigh.

'You have not kissed my hand, zhan Razhirrakh.' Clodolë, brown eyes narrowed, had missed nothing.

'I – I did not dare—'

The slender fingers brushed across his cheek, his lips.

'Dare,' she whispered. Her breath was spice-sweet, more intoxicating than wine . . .

Perhaps if he came to know her better, he could gain information from her, information about Laili. She seemed willing enough at this very moment.

He took her hand and pressed his lips to her fingers, and then her palm, her wrist . . .

'My warrior!' Sarilla came up to Ymarys in a cloud of scented silks and kissed him with exaggerated affection on both cheeks. 'My poor wounded hero.' She stroked the crescent scar.

'Sarilla, *please*.' Ymarys gently but firmly removed her hands from his face, kissing the tips of her fingers.

'But isn't this what you wanted? A new Razhirrakh to take your place? There's nothing binding you to the House of Memizhon now, you're free.'

'Free!' Ymarys let out a disdainful laugh. 'Free to do precisely what, Torella?'

She hesitated.

'Surely you can't have forgotten our little . . . understanding.'

'We have an understanding?'

'But you promised.' Her exclamation was so piercing that several guests nearby turned around to stare. Instantly she raised her fan and continued in a whisper. 'We can retire to my demesne in Mynezhil. It's true that the kastel is in need of some considerable refurbishment . . . but with your winnings—'

'Retire! At your stage of life, Torella, retirement may be all there is left to contemplate. But I—'

'Cruel! That was needlessly cruel!' she whispered. She seized a goblet of wine from the table and took several shuddering gulps. Ymarys noticed that her hand shook.

'Torella—' His fingers closed around hers, trying to prise the goblet from her hand.

'To mock my age. After all we have shared, all I have lavished upon you— There was a time you were not too proud to be seen with this raddled old harridan.'

'I never said you were—'

'What need of words? Your eyes say it all.' She drained the goblet down and beckoned a servitor over to refill it.

'Enough, Sarilla.' Ymarys took the goblet from her hand and waved the servitor away. 'I think you've had enough.'

'Yes, I've had enough. Enough of men's empty promises! Enough of being Melmeth's bawd. Enough of Myn-Dhiel—' She broke off.

'Well now, will you look at that?'

Ymarys turned in time to see Lai slip out of the hall after Clodolë.

'Did you see?'

'I saw well enough,' he said crisply.

'Ohh! So that's the way the wind blows, is it?'

'Sarilla, that's absurd.'

'I should have guessed. He's pretty enough, I grant you. But what did you expect?'

Ymarys winced.

'I don't mind. You know I don't mind.' Her tone had become plaintive, tears brimming over, staining her rouged cheeks. 'I've never minded, have I? Those gorgeous dark-eyed boys . . . We've always understood each other so well, Ymarys. That's why we need each other.'

'Where are we?' Lai whispered.

'Hush.' Clodolë had brought him along one of the hidden passages within Myn-Dhiel, a claustrophobic, winding tunnel, sticky with spiderwebs.

Beyond lay a dimly lit bedchamber; its viridian ceiling was spangled with gilded stars.

'We will not be disturbed here,' she said, pulling him into the room by the hand.

'B–but the Arkhan—'

'Relax, Lai. Sit down.' She pressed him gently down onto the couch. Her fingers kneaded his neck, his shoulders. 'All knotted up! You're so tense!'

Lai glanced uneasily about him, still fearing some trap, some deceit.

'Wine?'

He shook his head.

'What is troubling you?' She stroked his shoulder. 'Do you think I devour young tarkhastars for firstmeal?'

Devour. He wished she had used some other word.

'Then what about Rho Jhan?'

The tawny eyes narrowed again, cat-slits in the dusky light.

'I have no interest in losers, Lai.' That spice-scent again, wafting from her ambergold hair, so sweet, so tantalisingly evocative of . . . of . . .

She was unpinning her hair from its jewelled fillet, letting it tumble from the confining pins about her shoulders, rivulet after rivulet of molten gold. His hand lifted against his will, reaching out, wanting to touch—

'Don't deny you find me tempting,' she said, laughing quietly, almost under her breath. 'Come now, Lai, surely you will not refuse me? How many men can say they have pleasured the Arkhys of Ar-Khendye?'

Dumbly he shook his head. Her spicescent was irresistible, each breath that he took of it seemed only to sharpen his desire for her, to dull all earlier misgivings.

'You're bound to the House of Memizhon? Well then, you are bound to me as much as to my consort . . .' She wound her arms around his neck.

Those words. He had heard her say them before. That night of snow and shadows he had pledged his allegiance to Melmeth. But that had only been a dream – hadn't it? Dull stirring of fear, even as she pressed her body against his, even as her slender fingers slid beneath the waist of his loincloth, questing downwards, sending shivers of arousal through his whole body.

'No,' he said faintly. He wanted her. And yet he didn't want her. There was something at once alluring and repellant about the way she was offering herself to him.

'You say no,' she said. Her fingers gave a mischievous little tug and the folds of the loincloth slipped to the floor. He was naked – naked and helplessly aroused. 'But look at you. Your body says yes.' He could see her ivory teeth when she smiled, small and sharp like those of a predatory animal.

'Clodolë—'

'Why so shy? You're no virgin, surely!'

And then she was kissing him and the dizzy spicescent flooded his senses. They were falling back onto the bed, caught up in the silken draperies, his hands were moving over her body and yes, her soft breasts were white, the whitebloom of apple blossom as he freed them from her tight-clinging dress, and yes, her pink nipples tasted blossomsweet to the tongue and yes, oh yes below that white, soft belly, tangled goldenhairs, thighs parting, inviting, drawing, sucking him into her throbbing darkcentre.

In the Grove white petals are falling about his head, he is smothering in their sweet snowfall, jasmine blossom, datura blossom, suffocating surfeit of sweetness—

'No!' Don't let me suffocate, breathe, must breathe—

'Yes,' Clodolë had bound her long hair about him, entangling him in its wild golden tendrils as she writhed her body against his, 'yes, Lai, yes yes *yes*—'

Whirl of whitewings, clustering above him, ahh, all over him with their softfurred bodies

He could not control himself. He came, whole body pulsing with the release, slumping back shuddering against her. Sated. Spent.

Like the feast . . . Gorged on over-rich, over-spiced delicacies, he rolled over onto his back amidst the tangled sheets, staring up at the dizzying swirl of gilded stars whilst she traced patterns on his chest with one long diamond-studded fingernail.

'You are very alike. You and your sister.'

'What?' He struggled to sit up.

'Did you think to use me tonight, Lai? Did you?' The sharp-honed nail dug into his tender flesh until he yelped. 'To get to your beloved Laili?'

'I thought—'

'I should punish you for that, Lai Dhar. But – you please me.' She withdrew her nail from his chest and slowly licked the drop of bright blood from its tip. 'There is a resistance in you which I find quite irresistible. If you continue to please me . . . then I will plead your case with Melmeth.'

Lai looked up into her tawny eyes. She was smiling at him. How could he trust her? Twice she had played him false tonight.

'You know where she is kept? You have seen her?'

'Oh, Lai.' She pushed him back onto the silken sheets. 'You're going to have to be nice to me, oh so very nice, if you want to learn such secrets.'

CHAPTER 9

The sun's light kissed the gilded rooftops of the city of Perysse, shimmered on the rippling Yssil waters, warmed the earth. Deep in the corruption of the quay middens, something deep-buried sensed the warmth, awoke and stirred to life . . .

Tarkenhorns brass-blaring noonwatch.

Lai groaned, raising his face from the mattress, hastily burying it again to muffle the sound. Bright daylight streaked the shutters. He reached blindly out for the jug of clear well-water he had left on the floor last night, lifting it, spilling it, swilling the water around his drink-fouled mouth, pouring it down his throat.

Clodolë. Voracious, insatiable Clodolë. He lay back, remembering. The Arkhys of Ar-Khendye, flaunting her white body, shameless as a whore; already he hated her for the hold she had over him. Yet a glow of lust flickered through his body as he remembered what they had done together last night. Playing with fire. Memizhon fire. He was playing with the fire that could destroy him.

The bath house was empty as he had hoped; at this hour most were at noonmeal or on duty. He wanted no questions – just solitude. Time to think.

Tearing off his clothes, he dived straight into the cold bath, immersing himself in the freezing water, trying to rid his body of her cloying perfume. Not until he was shivering with cold did he haul himself out and towel his body vigorously until his skin glowed.

Clodolë. Even now her scent seemed to cling to his skin, his hair—

'Oh there you are, Lai. I've been scouring Myn-Dhiel for you. No one knew where you were. Although I could guess . . .'

That nudging, knowing smile in Ymarys's silky voice; Lai felt the blood burning his cheeks at the unspoken insinuation.

'Don't say a word, Ymarys. Promise me. Please promise me.'

'Your secret is safe with me. But a word of caution . . .'

'Caution?'

'You made an enemy last night. A dangerous enemy.'

'You mean Rho Jhan?'

'You should have run him through whilst you had the chance,' Ymarys said, silver eyes glinting maliciously through the steam drifting off the hot bath. 'Do you think he'll let this slur on his honour pass unavenged?'

Lai slipped his arms into his blue jacket.

'Tsk!' Ymarys's fingers briefly touched the worn linen, then withdrew in disgust. 'This will never do.'

'Whyever not?'

'My dear Lai, you are the Arkhan's Razhirrakh now. You must dress like a champion!'

'But surely you are still—'

'Unless you have other plans?'

'What do you mean, Ymarys?'

'It is customary for the victor of the rites to serve the Arkhan as Razhirrakh.'

'But that is *your* position. I never intended—'

'What precisely did you intend?' Ymarys said softly.

'To leave Perysse. To go home.' Lai leaned his head against a marble pillar, gazing into the mists of steam, seeing the verdant shadow of a distant island far beyond.

'And what is to stop you?' Ymarys's voice was so quiet now. Lai barely heard it.

'One – who is still enslaved.'

Ymarys glanced around and then slipped his arm through Lai's.

'My dear young friend. You are in need of distraction. And a good tailor. Come – let me show you the delights of Perysse.'

'So . . . how does it feel to be free?' Ymarys asked slyly as they walked unchallenged through the gates of the Tarkhas Memizhon.

Lai took in a deep breath; the light spring air was tartly sweet with wafts of medlar blossom from a terraced garden nearby. It tasted like new wine, fresh and sharp in the mouth.

'Heady. I can't describe it.'

At first Lai was overwhelmed by the noise, the turmoil of the city. He saw nothing but the magnificence of the public buildings, the marbled fountains, the tree-shaded squares.

After a while he began to notice the street-children. Hiding behind stalls, in cobwebbed alleyways, they stared out at him, their eyes dark and wary.

The day was passing. Ymarys made Lai sample clove sweetmeats from one stall, sizzling caraway pastries from another.

Little hands reached up to him, begging, clawing, broken finger-nails dark-encrusted with dirt.

'Food, zhan. We're hungry. Please.'

'Take no notice.' Ymarys walked on, brushing the clinging fingers from his clothes.

'But they're only children—'

'If you feed one, a hundred more will pop up to take its place. Yes, there's people starving in Perysse. What did you expect?'

Lai looked at the pastry in his hand; he looked at the hollow-eyed face staring hungrily up at him.

'Here,' he said in a whisper. The child snatched the food and went scampering away.

A few paces on, Lai glanced behind him and saw a little trail of ragged children following in his wake.

'What did I tell you?' Ymarys said wearily.

Lai detached a handful of coins from his money-ring and flung them spinning into the air.

'Must you be so profligate with your winnings? You'll have nothing left for your new clothes.'

'I don't need new clothes.'

'Nonsense! We're only a few steps from the silk bazaar . . .'

The silk bazaar was held every day near the river; here the traders from the cantons, from the red deserts of Enhirrë, even from distant Djihan-Djihar, came to barter with the silk merchants of Perysse for their wares. It was the fast-beating heart of Ar-Khendye's trade; fortunes changed hands for the exquisite Ar-Khendye silk was prized above all other fabrics. The dyers and weavers had passed down the jealously guarded secrets of their trade from generation to generation, perfecting their techniques until no other country could match their invention or their artistry.

Ymarys stopped at the entrance to the covered bazaar beneath the brilliantly coloured swathes of silk that formed a billowing canopy above their heads, ivory marbled with cornelian, jacinth and jet.

'Zhan Ymarys. Illustre. Welcome.' A merchant greeted Ymarys, beckoning him into his alcove. 'See what treasures I have on show this week . . . this pale citrine is a perfect match for—'

Ymarys waved one hand languidly.

'Not for me. For my young friend here. Let's see what exorbitantly over-priced stuffs you have to show us.'

The merchant insisted on holding swathe after swathe of silk up against Lai.

'The sapphire. It matches your eyes, zhan. Definitely the sapphire.'

Lai shook his head impatiently. The silks were too gaudy, too bright. In his heart he felt nothing but emptiness. He was free . . . and she was not.

He pointed towards a bale of sombre grey, so dark it was almost black.

'That,' he said.

'Anyone would think you were in mourning!' Ymarys said disapprovingly.

'That's the one I want.'

Mourning. For Lai the adept. Lai the man of peace. Now he would wear the colour of winter, no-colour.

'Maybe your esteemed friend would consider slashed sleeves, knots, ribbons in a contrasting shade, zhan Ymarys? Lavender, silver or scarlet . . . ?'

The merchant was ready to haggle over the price; but after two token disagreements, Lai agreed his third offer.

The merchant's slaveboy poured spiced qaffë for Ymarys and Lai whilst the merchant cut and wrapped the silk.

'Perhaps this shade would suit you better, zhan. Lily-white for a lily-livered slave.'

Lai choked on the qaffë and turned to see Rho Jhan mockingly holding out a length of ivory silk.

'Though from what I hear, my lady Arkhys prefers to see you divested of all clothing.'

Lai's hand shot instinctively to his razhir hilt.

'Say that again.'

Lai felt Ymarys's hand on his arm, checking him.

'Easy, Lai.'

'Come on, boy, that contest was only half-finished.' Rho Jhan tweaked the golden sash about Lai's waist. 'Victor of the arena? You won on a technicality. That little scratch – that was nothing.'

'Nothing?' The red rage of the arena suddenly blazed in Lai's brain; the razhir hissed from its sheath. 'You call it nothing?'

The merchant's slaveboy let out a shrill scream of excitement at the sight of the drawn blade.

'Fight! A fight!'

'A year's too long to wait till next Mithiel's Day.' Rho Jhan was smiling at him as he drew his razhir, that insolent, contemptuous smile. 'Let's finish it here.'

'Sheath your swords!' Ymarys flung himself between them, suddenly lithe, charged, all languor dissipated.

Lai glanced around, aware that the bustle of the bazaar had hushed and everyone was staring at him.

'Lai!' Ymarys hissed.

Ymarys was still his maistre; Lai slowly lowered his blade.

'Fighting in a public place?' Ymarys glared at Rho Jhan. 'You know the penalty.'

Rho Jhan still held his razhir at Ymarys's breast; Ymarys stared coolly back at him.

'Yes. Run me through here – unarmed – in front of witnesses. There's no second reprieve from the donjon.'

Rho Jhan gave a little shrug and with a flourish, sheathed his razhir. But the while he kept his eyes fixed on Lai's over Ymarys's shoulder.

'Maybe not today. Maybe not tomorrow. But I'll be looking out for you, Aelahim. So be on your guard. I'll be there when you least expect me. You can depend on that.' He turned on his heel and walked out.

Seeing the entertainment was at an end, the merchants and customers turned back to their business and the haggling began again. Lai sank down on a bale of material.

'What's happened to me?' He looked at his hands; they were sweaty and trembling. 'I would have spitted him. Without a thought. What have I become?'

'A razhirrakh.'

'But I thought now that it was all over—'

'You can never lose that instinct now. You can't shrug it off.'

'Once a killer, always a killer,' Lai whispered. He let his head sink into his hands, trying to block out the babble of the bazaar. He had become the very thing he abhorred.

Dark eyes stared wildly into his above the slashing blades, seeing nothing there but oblivion . . .

How could he ever hope to be received back into the Grove? He had blood on his hands.

As if from far, very far away he heard Ymarys's voice.

'This dragging tristesse. It always follows Mithiel's Day. First the elation – your blood burns, your head dins with the shouts of the crowd. Then comes the fall. The despair. There's no cure – only diversion.'

Lai pushed past Ymarys and went running out of the bazaar, hurtling headlong down the cobbled lanes, not caring where he went, just running, running until he could run no more and collapsed, gulping for breath, in a dark cul-de-sac deep in the worm-eaten core of the street marshes.

He stumbled aimlessly on until he heard the lapping ripple of the river Yssil, smelt the unmistakable odour of the dye works.

Drawn against his will, he found himself outside the works, staring through the bars of the high perimeter fence.

The smell from the dye vats almost choked him; foul, leaving an acrid burn at the back of the throat. Clouds of smoke boiled over the top of the nearest vat; the rags of the slaves toiling to stir the noisome brew were plastered to their bodies with the steam.

Lai watched, his eyes stinging, though whether with the fumes from the vats or with tears of rage, he neither knew nor cared.

This was the blood that fuelled the fast-beating heart of Perysse; the human misery on which the city had grown rich and renowned. Those gorgeous bazaar silks might as well have been dyed in the blood of the dye works slaves.

'Water, zhan, for the love of Mithiel—' A slave, voice cracked with the heat, stumbled to his knees, hands outstretched to Lai. Lai could see the festering sores the shackles had rubbed on his emaciated legs; he could remember only too well the grinding pain of the shackles he had borne in the donjon before—

Water. Helplessly, he looked around, seeing no sign of a water butt or fountain.

'Get back to work!' An overseer appeared, whip in hand. The slave cringed away, a cowed dog, retreating on hands and knees.

'That man is thirsty!' Lai cried.

The overseer came sauntering up to the grille.

'So, what's it to you?'

Lai drew out his money ring and pulled off a handful of eniths.

'Give him water.'

'Very generous,' said the overseer, taking the coins and pocketing them. He then turned and went sauntering away, ignoring the slave.

'Hey!' Lai cried, rattling the bars. 'Give that man a drink!'

'What business is it of yours? These slaves are convicted criminals.

Little better than animals. They'll get fed and watered. When I say.'
He raised the whip and brought it stinging down over the slave's
back; Lai heard the man gasp with the pain. 'That's for stepping out of
line.' The overseer looked back at Lai. 'I don't like interfering do-
gooders. Be off – or he'll get another dose.'

Lai stared back, speechless. Then he struck the bars with his hands
and turned, stalking away, his brain singing with anger. Corrupt,
cruel city – the sooner he and Laili were away from it, the better.

The twilit quay was empty; somewhere in a warehouse behind him
rats piped a thin, high nocturne. And . . . in the distance a burst of
rowdy music: drunken voices raised, droning over a wheezing
hurdy-gurdy and jangling fiddle.

Laili.

No one turned a head as he entered the wineshop. No one
recognised him. The taproom was crowded: tattooed sailors off the
silk barges; whores tantalisingly clad in rainbow gauzes of scarlet,
violet and viridian . . . The wine was cheap, sharp and strong, tart as
unripe berries on the tongue. It was a penance to drink it.

Laili walked the twilit confines of Sarilla's courtyard garden, up and
down, up and down, a caged bird, constantly prowling the limits of its
enclosure.

She had rehearsed and re-rehearsed her speech to Melmeth; now
she murmured it through once more under her breath.

'My lord. You must forgive me – but I cannot keep silent any longer.
You believe yourself to be a devout man. And yet you allow these
atrocities to continue—' Atrocities. She bit her lip. The word was
strong. Yet there was nothing else to describe what she had witnessed
in the arena.

Did she dare to confront him? Her position was still so precarious.
Lai was free, she had seen him receive his token of freedom. But an
all-powerful Arkhan, if angered, might revoke that gift. Melmeth was
so unpredictable, sometimes a vulnerable, weary man whom she
loved – and at other times so cold and unapproachable, she wondered
if she truly knew him at all.

'You look so sad.'

She started. He was watching her from the archway. And she had
not even heard him approach. He came towards her across the
courtyard, his robes brushing against the sweet herbs, enfolding her
in his arms. She let him embrace her, steeling herself.

'What's worng, Laili? I could not come before now. You know I would have come sooner had not court affairs detained me.'

'I know,' she said, detaching herself from his embrace, wandering over to the edge of the pool.

'Are you angry with me?'

She shook her head but did not look round. The pool waters were glassy, a mirror of polished amethyst in which their reflections seemed as insubstantial as shadows.

'So what is troubling you?' He drew closer until his hands rested on her shoulders.

'That – that shameful business in the arena. That butchery. What kind of a god demands the sacrifice of innocents?' She turned around and stared up into his face. 'Is this the supreme being who guides your life?'

His hands dropped away from her shoulders.

'Innocents, lady? Condemned criminals, every man. Each one given the chance to begin a new life – or die a hero's death in the arena.'

'You made Lai fight. You made him kill. He is a gentle man, a good man. Why did you do this to him?'

'Your brother was already a criminal. He almost killed one of the Zhudiciar's men, remember.'

'He did it to save me,' Laili said stubbornly.

'So you would rather he had been executed? Or left to die in the donjon? An interminable, cruel death.'

'There has to be some other way.'

'There is no other way. It is the law. It has always been this way.'

Laili thought she detected a tone of hopelessness in Melmeth's words.

'Maybe it is time to change.'

'But the god must be requited.'

'The god, the god, always the god. My lord, are you Arkhan – or do the priests of Mithiel rule?'

He stared at her, his green eyes hooded.

Now I have gone too far. Now he will punish me.

'Forgive me. I should not have spoken against your god.'

'No. No.' He seemed to be struggling with some inner dilemma. 'Maybe it is time someone spoke out. Maybe—' His words trailed away into silence. It was so dark in the courtyard now that she could see nothing but the glimmer of his eyes. 'Lai wants to see you, Laili.

He wants to take you home.'

'Home.' A faint sigh escaped her lips.

'I gave him my word. But now . . . I do not think I can bear to let you go.'

Laili turned to him in the darkness; her heart singing. He loved her.

'Then tell Lai I cannot go home. Not while my lord still needs me.'

It was late when Lai returned to the Tarkhas Memizhon; the moon was already high in the sky and the panelled corridors of the Tarkhas House were dusted with moonshadows. Maybe Ymarys was asleep . . . or out at one of the pleasure houses of the city.

Lai knocked softly at Ymarys's door.

'Come . . .'

The room beyond was lit only by the moon. Ymarys was sitting cross-legged on his couch, cloaked in his unbraided hair. A thin wisp of dreamweed smoke rose from the bowl of the glass pipe, pearl-escently blue in the moonlight.

'Lai.' A lazy, drawling laugh, soft as the purr of a wildcat came from the back of Ymarys's throat. 'Well, well, well . . .'

The wafting fumes were like dark, sweet vanilla, yet with a lingeringly bitter undertone that made Lai's eyes sting. He hesitated.

'Come in.' Ymarys gestured with the pipe, a long, languid gesture, drawing Lai closer. 'Sit. So to what do I owe the pleasure of your company?'

He seemed half-drowsed on the opiate; Lai was already regretting his decision to come, seeing that Ymarys was unlikely to give him any kind of lucid answer.

'The Torella Sarilla. I saw her greet you last night.' Lai lowered himself onto the tasselled cushions. 'Have you ever seen a bodyslave, a girl with hair my colour in her household?'

Ymarys slowly blew a thin breath of blue smoke from between his lips.

'I might have done.'

'Come now, Ymarys! Are there that many redheads in the court?'

Elegant fingers reached out and gently brushed Lai's hair.

'Moonlight on flames. Frost-dusted autumn leaves.'

'Ymarys—'

'Hair your colour? She is related to you?'

'My sister Laili. Sarilla bought us as a pair. If there were any way you could introduce me to the Torella so that I might—'

97

Ymarys let out a disdainful snort. '*Tcha*! Still so naïve, Lai Dhar. You've much to learn of the ways of Myn-Dhiel.'

'Is the Torella too exalted then to receive me?'

'Heavens, no! She adopted me as her protégé some years ago. She adores the attentions of comely, well-made young men.'

'Then what's the problem?'

Ymarys drew in on the pipe; the burning weed glowed in the bowl of the pipe, a firefly in the darkened room.

'There's nothing you can do tonight. Here, have some dreamweed . . .' He took the pipe from his mouth and placed it to Lai's lips; Lai pushed it away.

'Go on. You look so driven, so haunted, Lai. Take the smoke in, let the fumes release you . . .'

'I don't want dreamweed. I want answers!' Lai rose to his feet and went towards the door.

'Stay a while,' Ymarys said, pleadingly. He placed the pipe down on a metal tray tarnished with a thin layer of weed ash. 'Don't go. I could help you. It's just that . . .' He paused delicately. 'Do you remember I once hinted to you that Melmeth has a secret mistress, one he keeps hidden away?'

'No. Oh no.'

'Hush. I've said more than I should have said.'

'Laili.' The realisation pierced like a violent stab in the stomach. Lai doubled up, clutching the pain in.

'It's an honour. To be the chosen mistress of the Arkhan. If you can survive long enough, that is, to enjoy the privilege.'

'But why this secrecy? Why can't I see her?'

'Bide your time. Be patient. He's bound to tire of her, he usually does if Clodolë doesn't get to her first—'

'If she's in danger—'

'She's safe in Sarilla's keeping. The Torella is experienced in these matters. She was Sardion's mistress and heaven knows, enough rivals tried to poison her in her time.'

Suddenly the sickly sweet fumes of the dreamweed seemed to be stifling; desperate for clean air, Lai went to the window and pushed the shutters open, leaning out into the night.

'Laili. Melmeth's mistress.'

The moon suddenly shone full over the rooftops.

And from the darkness of the moonhaunted night came a distant silvershimmer of sound.

Lai raised his head, listening.

'What's that?' Ymarys whispered.

'*Ymarys!*' Yet as Lai leaned forwards, straining to catch the echo of the elusive sound-source – it began again. Thin silver music wreathing dreamily over the sleeping city, distant, high, fluting . . .

'I don't believe it. It's not possible.'

'What is it?' Ymarys came to stand close behind him.

Thread after silver thread of intricate moonspun sound unravelled. A sound to ravish the heart. To make the heart ache almost to breaking.

'*Hai* . . . so beautiful . . . Where is that music coming from, Lai?'

Lai could not answer. The words had choked in his throat; if he spoke, he would weep aloud.

Down they came, drifting from the moonblue sky like flakes of snow.

'What *are* they?' Ymarys said. His drug-haunted eyes seemed transfigured in the moonlight.

Lai struggled to find the words to tell him.

'Moonmoths. Sacred to our Goddess.'

'Moonmoths?' Ymarys repeated. They both gazed out into the night, mesmerised by the swooping, glittering flight of the frail-winged insects. The dark air sparkled with the iridescent dust from their bodies.

'Moonmoths,' Lai said again mechanically. 'They sing . . . just one night, the night of the spring moon . . . then they mate, lay their eggs and die.'

'I've never seen these moonmoths of yours before.'

He hardly heard Ymarys, he was listening to that insistent, persistent music so pure, so liquid it had flowed through his consciousness like a crystal stream of clearwater. It was a struggle to wrench his mind to focus on what Ymarys was saying. Far below he could hear delighted cries from the courtyard; other casements were opening, tarkhastars and servitors were leaning out to stare, to gaze at the wonder.

Is this a sign to your servants, Goddess? A sign of forgiveness? Or a call, summoning us home to the Grove?

'How can I bring her home now?' he cried aloud to the bland face of the moon.

He stopped, realising that Ymarys was staring at him in utter incomprehension.

CHAPTER 10

'It's such a beautiful night.' Melmeth took Laili's hand between his own. 'Come, walk with me in the gardens.'

Laili's heart quickened; it was such an ordinary thing to do, to walk hand-in-hand with a lover in the moonlight – and yet he had never before asked her to accompany him beyond the confines of her tower room.

'But if someone should see us?'

'What will they see? Two moon phantoms haunting the Grove of Blue Terebinth.'

Outside the dark air was deliciously fresh, the grass still wet underfoot. The last high tatters of cloud drifted away and the moon suddenly shone full over the gardens.

And from the moonshadowed Grove of Blue Terebinth a distant shimmer of sound rose to greet the moon.

'What is that?' Melmeth stopped, his hand clutching hers.

'I – I don't know,' Laili said in a whisper, head raised, listening.

Down they came, drifting from the moonblue sky like flakes of snow. And the summer night was filled with the beat of their soft wings, their febrile silvered song.

'Look, Laili!' Melmeth, delight trembling in his voice, showed her his cupped hands; as he slowly opened them she saw the delicate creature trapped inside, its velvet wings dusted with scented spangles, its dark eyes huge beneath white wisps of antennae.

'Moths. Moonmoths,' she said wonderingly.

'Have you ever seen the like before?'

She nodded.

'What can have brought them to our shores? Where have they come from?'

'Ael Lahi . . .' The name was just a whisper. A whisper of longing. A sudden aching homesickness.

'Ael Lahi! They are far from home. Just like you, my Laili—' He suddenly shook the moth away; it fluttered weakly to the ground as he clapped his hand to his mouth.

'What is it? Let me see!'

'It stung me.'

'Surely not!' Laughing, she prised his hand from his lips to examine what damage had been done. 'I can't even see the—'

'So sweet on the tongue,' he said, puzzled, his goldgreen eyes softening.

There was a tiny mark, a puncture-mark, no bigger than the end of a pin below his thumb; even as she looked at it, it closed over, leaving the skin smooth. 'There's – nothing here.'

'The taste. Taste, Laili. Sweeter than dreamweed . . .'

She drew away from his outstretched hand, from the dust still glimmering on his palm.

'You must not taste it. Not unless you seek to invoke the Goddess—'

'You are not in Ael Lahi now, Laili.'

No. And these were not, perhaps, the same moonmoths that had haunted the Sacred Grove, though the adepts had always believed them to be unique. There was something indefinably different about them, something that made her feel uneasy . . .

Laili gazed out of her window. The moths were everywhere now, in the moonlit gardens, swirling like snow about the tower. Melmeth had not come. Perhaps something she had said last night had displeased him . . . he had seemed abstracted.

'Laili!'

The Torella stood in the doorway. Her eyes were huge and dark, swimming with secrets.

'Sweet child! You're unhappy. You must have some dust!' Her steps wavered drunkenly as she crossed the room. A strange scent clung to her hair, her warm breath as she embraced Laili. Laili drew back, shaking her head.

'But it's wonderful! I knew you'd be alone tonight. I said to myself, poor little neglected Laili, I must go and cheer her up.'

'You know where he is?' Laili seized hold of her hand. 'Why hasn't he come?'

'Ssh,' she said, pressing one wavering finger to Laili's lips. 'He's the Arkhan. He can do as he pleases.'

'Who is he with, Sarilla? Is it Clodolë?'

'Clodolë!' She began to giggle. 'He hasn't bedded her in a year.'

'Another mistress?'

'O, is my little protégée jealous? And only a few months ago you wouldn't let my lord even touch your little finger. Listen, sweeting, my lord has always been . . . how shall I say . . . ? catholic in his tastes. Sometimes he tires of female company . . .'

Laili stared at her blankly.

'Forget him! Take some boskh.' She opened the stone on her ring, pushing it under Laili's nose. 'I almost killed to get this. It cost me a pair of ruby earrings. One taste of this and you'll forget your heartache.'

The spiced sweetness wreathed upwards from the glittering cavity beneath the ringstone. Just the scent of it evoked the moonblue sands, the silvered sea of Ael Lahi. But Laili could see only Sarilla's drug-hazed eyes staring enticingly back.

'No. No thank you.'

'You're turning down a glimpse of heaven . . . Yskhysse. Ecstasy that goes on and on . . .'

'People are using the dust? Eating it?'

'But yes, my dear.' She fluttered her eyelashes mockingly. 'What *did* you imagine they were doing? It really is the most exquisite experience . . .' She began to giggle again. 'Don't conceive for a moment that my lord hasn't tried it too. It won't be long before he invites you to share in his glimpse of heaven . . . They say it increases a man's virility sevenfold! My dear – just think!'

It was a warm summer's night and yet Laili suddenly felt chilled to the bone. The moon's cold light illuminated the madly skittering mothflight, specks of darkness flitting across her silver face.

And in the stillness came a curious, dry rustling, sere as the fall of withered magnolia petals.

A single moonmoth had strayed into the room, drawn to the pale flame of the lucerna. Laili reached up her hands and caught it as, singed, it dropped towards the heart of the flame.

'So far from home,' she murmured, feeling its last shudders beating against her enfolding hands.

Laili tried to settle to sleep . . . but the silken sheets seemed to stick to her skin in the sultry heat. She kept imagining Melmeth embraced in another's arms, naked, whispering those endearments she had thought were hers alone . . .

And her lord's absence was not the only worry preventing her from sleep.

She lay counting days on her fingers in the darkness. At length she could bear it no longer.

She rose, wrapping a thin gown, purple and gold, embroidered with heartsease petals, about her naked body. Her thick hair was sticky with sweat, she tied it back with an opalescent gauze scarf, one of his first gifts to her. She lit the lucerna, sat at her desk and scribbled down a record of the days that had passed since . . . since she had last bled.

The waning moonlight faded from the chamber wall. She should have started to bleed two mooncycles ago. But when they first captured her, she had ceased bleeding for several cycles; then, a gap had meant nothing.

Her loose gown gaped open as she wrote. Her breasts were swollen, the translucent veins blue as iris petals. They burned. If her fears were correct she must be at least twelve weeks with child . . .

And no concubine of Melmeth's had ever produced a living child, Sarilla had told her so. Clodolë had seen to it. Most miscarried. One died. Clodolë was Arkhys of Ar-Khendye. She would not tolerate any rival.

How long could she keep it a secret?

'The Arkhan will see no one else today.'

'Fhedryn . . . *please—*'

'I can't make any exceptions – not even for you, Lai Dhar.' Fhedryn, the Arkhan's chamberlain, barred Lai's way with his ebony staff. 'He's not to be disturbed. You'll have to come back tomorrow and wait your turn like the rest of the petitioners.'

Lai went striding angrily away from the audience chamber.

'Psst! Zhan Razhirrakh!'

A dhamzel was beckoning him to follow her. Plump Lerillys, Clodolë's favourite and confidante.

Lai glanced about him uneasily, wondering if she truly meant him. There was no one else in sight.

'Come,' she called softly. 'My mistress is awaiting you.'

Clodolë was sitting, one leg curled beneath her, on a cushion-strewn couch, feeding sweetmeats to a snuffling lapdog.

'Have you missed me, Lai? I've missed you,' she said, smiling up at him.

'You promised me,' he said, determined not to be diverted this time. 'You promised me for news of my sister. You promised me you would speak with the Arkhan. Every time I try to see him, I am sent away.'

She shrugged.

'You're so impatient . . .'

'He said she would be freed if I won in the arena!'

'To hear you rant one would suspect something more than a fraternal relationship between you and your beloved Laili . . . Do I detect a whiff of incest, dearest Lai?'

'Incest!' Lai cried. 'You twist everything around, don't you, you see the whole world through your own warped vision. I don't have to stay here listening to your insinuations!'

'Stop!' She rose to her feet, the dish of sweetmeats sliding to the floor; the little dog greedily pursued the remaining sweets as they rolled under the couch. 'How dare you go before I have dismissed you?'

'I am not your pet lapdog,' said Lai coldly and made for the door.

She reached the door before him, blocking the way out, arms spread wide.

'Oh, no! To leave you must first remove me. And if you lay a finger on me, one finger, I shall scream for the tarkhastars on duty. What will Melmeth say when I tell him you tried to force me?' She tore open the front of her goldgauze gown, the filmy fabric ripping, baring her breasts. Her voice rose hysterically. 'There. Explain your way out of that!'

Lai stared, open-mouthed.

Her white breasts were painted with whorls, stars and flowers: indigo, henna and gold.

'Oh, Melmeth, Lai Dhar was like a madman, he tore off my gown and threw me to the ground in spite of my protests, my tears—' She flung herself to her knees before him, still strategically blocking his way to the door. Dishevelled hair, tear-flooded eyes, she looked the very picture of ravished virtue.

'What do you want of me?' he asked defeatedly.

She smiled.

'What do you think?' She swiftly turned the ornate key in the lock. 'There. Now no one can disturb us.'

She took Lai's hand and drew him towards the couch. The little dog came cringing out from underneath and slunk off towards its silk-lined basket.

'You must learn to be more subtle, Lai. You must play the courtier's part with a better grace.'

He said nothing, crossing his arms on his chest, still angry with her for her deceits, her play-acting.

'Be patient. I am sure Melmeth will keep his word . . .'

'And meanwhile you twist me around your little finger like a silken thread.'

'You really are angry with me, aren't you! How can I sweeten your mood? Wine?'

He shook his head. He wanted to keep a clear mind this time.

'Why don't you try one of these.' She held out an open silver box; a delicious honeyed fragrance wafted out.

'What are they?' he asked suspiciously.

'Little sweetmeats. Let's indulge ourselves.' She popped one into her mouth. 'Mmm . . . they are so *good*. Try.' She selected another and held it up to his lips. 'What's the matter now? Afraid I'll poison you?'

Reluctantly he opened his mouth like a child forced to take bitter medicine and let her place the sweetmeat on his tongue.

As he began to chew, the sweetmeat released a luscious sweetness, the almondine savour of wild apricots. He could even see the colour of the apricots as the taste melted in his mouth: soft, fragrant ochre, stained with darker flesh at the heart of the stone . . .

'Another?' She slid another one into his mouth before he could refuse, darker than the dark heart of the rose, scented with subtle driftspice . . . an all-pervading spice, a stimulating, sensuous spice that set the blood burning . . .

She slid onto the couch beside him, pressing close to his body. Her perfume was so strong, a shaded spicemarket in the sultry summer's heat. When she spoke, she seemed to breathe spices over him.

'Don't you like what I have done?'

'The – the flowers?'

'There are more.' A low, shuddering laugh, daring him to find them.

Head reeling, he set the glass down. There was something he must remember. A reason he had come. But . . . what was it? She was undoing the fastenings on his shirt, deft fingers pulling at the lacing of his breeches. Mustn't forget—

'Did you see them last night? Did you hear them?'

The room wavered drunkenly before his eyes; dazzle of light, dazzle of ambergold hair.

'The moths, Lai. Weren't they magical? That music . . .'

'W–wait.' His tongue would not work its way around the words. 'You – saw the moths too?'

'Better than saw.' That low laugh again. 'I was walking in the gardens with Lerillys. And I had such a terrible headache . . . nothing would relieve it. Then *they* came fluttering down, settling a while on the tamarisks above our heads. The air was full of the dust from their wings. It was – sweet on the tongue. And when they flew away, the tamarisk leaves were powdered with the dust, sparkling like stardust. Can you imagine it, Lai? So sweet to the taste. And my head had stopped aching, it felt so clear, so clean—'

'You tasted the dust?' Lai said thickly.

'It cured my headache.'

Crimson mouth pouting now, a sulky moue. Indulged, spoilt childwoman; he didn't know whether to despise or pity her.

'What was wrong with that? What do you know of these things anyway?'

'It . . . could have poisoned you.' Panic rising inside him. She was disappearing in a dazzle of moonlight, silver aura gilding the gold.

Her voice came to him remotely from within the dazzle.

'Then by that token you are poisoned too, Lai Dhar. I had my kitchenboy sprinkle some of the dust on the sweets. Good, isn't it, so very, very good?'

Constellation upon constellation above her head, the painted stars collided, burst, spun about the vaulted ceiling.

'Do you know . . . the exquisites are devising names for the drug even now? Moongrains, starsparkle, boskhdust and other such pretty titles . . . They say it can reveal your most secret desires.'

'N–no—'

'Who am I, Lai?' She was caressing him, kissing him. She tasted of allspice.

He blinked. There was something wrong with his sight. Her face wavered, precious oil spilt in water, rainbow iridescence.

Her hair – soft russet, bright with threads of copper. Thin dusting of freckles on her little nose. Eyes of that same dream-hazed, sentient blue as his own. Laili's mouth on his own, inflamed, incestuous kisses, Laili's arms around his body—

'Clodolë – stop this!' He forced her hands away.

106

'Don't you like it? But perhaps none of these are anywhere near your most secret desires.'

'Be yourself! Be you!'

Glimmer of moonsilver . . . Laili's likeness dispersed in swirls of night-mist . . . yet behind her another woman stood in shadow . . . Slowly She raised Her head until, with sudden recognition, he knew Her. Light streamed from Her in cold rivulets. Her face in its archaic pallor was unendurably beautiful; Her eyes, darker than a moonless night, lit upon him, their expression remote yet tender. Slowly, Her arms opened to him . . .

And a voice whispered in his head. 'Isn't this what you have always desired, Lai, the ultimate union, to be One with the Goddess?'

The moon went out. She had gone.

'Why did you do that?' he cried to Clodolë. 'Why?'

And then the boskh blurred all senses and he no longer knew where he was or greatly cared.

They lay naked on the edge of a great cliff. Below, far below, breakers pounded against the rocks, spray rising in salty clouds.

'*I don't want this, Clodolë—*'

'*You don't know what you want, do you?' She shouted back at him over the roar of the waves. 'But I know what I want!' She was weeping. 'I want a child!'*

She writhed up to meet him – and in that moment their minds touched, opened, and he saw horrors, oh Goddess, appalling horrors within the secret sealed chambers of her mind, horrors that made him scream for release—

An attic corridor along which he runs, opening door after door only to see in each bare room a bier and on each bier the waxen corpse of a malformed foetus, lying puddled in a mess of blood and afterbirth.

'*Let me out! Let me out of here!*'

The walls crumble away.

No release. Still locked within each other, they are falling, falling over the cliff-edge to oblivion—

'*Goddess – help me—*'

Mist of saltspray, crash of heaving breakers,

'*We'll be smashed on the rocks, smashed and broken open—*'

They cleave the waves. Down. Powerful sea currents rack his body, the pulse of the deep waters, the enclosing, suffocating darkness—

'*Goddess . . .*'

Beached, he rolls gasping onto his back on the sand . . .

Clodolë was staring down at him through the golden mermaid-strands of her hair. Her eyes seemed larger than ever, the cloudy dark of deep sea waters.

'I thought I was drowning.' He tried to sit up, only to collapse again – not on damp sand but on the hard boards of the floor. Dull light sullied the walls. The night was ebbing fast.

'I had no idea the boskh would affect you so . . . so drastically . . .' She was naked. Had he torn her clothes off? Had his fingers left those marks on her soft flesh? The sweet scent from the moist tangle of golden hair between her bruised thighs nauseated him now. He wished she would leave him alone.

'What – hour is it?'

'Near dawn.'

He struggled up onto one elbow.

'You mean we've – we've been—'

'Fucking all that time?' she said crudely. 'Yes. A whole night. Impressive?' She seemed upset. 'Who else could give you that, Lai?'

'Listen.' He caught her by the wrist, pulling her close. 'Don't ever do that to me again. No more boskh.'

'I lavish my most precious possession upon you and you complain!'

He began to search around for his clothes.

'Are you leaving me?'

'It's day.' He went to the window, pulling open the painted shutters.

'Close them!' She hissed with pain, pressing her knuckles to her eyes to protect them from the sunlight. 'Close them, close them!'

Her agony was so palpable, so intense that, shocked, he banged them shut again. In the halflight, she knelt, shuddering in the aftershock.

'Are you all right? Clodolë!'

'White needles – in my head—' She rocked to and fro. 'A little more . . . will stop the pain . . .' She fumbled blindly with one hand for the silver box.

'A little more will only make it worse!'

'P–please—' She raised her head; her dazzled eyes streamed with tears, a cloudburst.

Pity overcame him. She was not play-acting now. He found the box and took it to her; she stuffed two, three, four sweetmeats into her mouth, chewing till the saliva dribbled out of one corner of her mouth.

'You're addicted.'

Brittle-bright notes shimmered in the dawn air. The tarkenhorns were blowing for dawnwatch, rousing the city from sleep.

108

He heard her sigh.

'Mmm . . . s'better now . . . so much better . . .'

She lay back on the silken cushions, her eyes vague, wandering, fixing on some distant point.

'Come, Lai . . . join me . . .' One white finger beckoned lazily.

He shook his head. He had to get out, had to get air, fresh air—

The dawnlight pierced his brain like sheet lightning. He grasped at the wall of the tower, teetering on the vertiginous rim, as the morning spun dizzily in front of him.

'Your most secret desires . . .'

He had glimpsed Her, in that one fleeting moment of transcendence, as he had once seen Her within the secret silence of the Grove.

And now he had abused the sacred substance, he had used it for his own sensual gratification . . . and She had withdrawn, leaving him but a drear aftertaste . . .

A void had opened up within him, a great and desolate emptiness . . .

CHAPTER 11

The light of the Undying Flame flickered palely in the Shrine of Memizhon; Ophar narrowed his eyes, wondering if the veiled woman who knelt before the flame was more shadow than substance, the revenant of some long-dead Arkhys . . .

As he approached, she looked around, startled.

'My lady Arkhys,' he said, surprised. Her face was pale, her eyes blurred with tears, her hair usually so immaculately dressed, escaping in wisps from under the loose hood. 'What is wrong?'

She shook her head and turned her face away from him, as though ashamed.

'My lady,' he said as kindly as he could. Kindness was not an emotion he permitted himself to indulge in, yet her distress moved him. He had always felt a certain tenderness for Clodolë since the day he had first seen her, a girl whose hair seemed kissed with the tawny warmth of the sun. 'Tell me what is troubling you.'

'If only I could, Ophar.' Her voice, stifled with tears, was a whisper of its usual self, a shadow-whisper. And then she turned from him as another bout of weeping overcame her and she covered her face in her hands. 'Ohh . . . she must have cast a spell over him . . .'

'She?'

'Why else would he have rejected me, Ophar?'

'Are we discussing your royal consort?' Ophar said carefully.

'She is from Ael Lahi. Have you seen her, Ophar? They say she bears a crescent mark on her brow that marks her as a servant of their goddess. She's a moon-worshipper. What kind of moonmagic has she worked on Melmeth to drive him from me?'

'The Arkhan has had these little infatuations before, lady . . . They last a short while and then he tires of his latest conquest and returns to you, his one, true love.'

She gave a bitter little laugh.

'Maybe in the past. But this time . . . no. He is under a spell. An

Aelahim enchantment. I truly believe he intends to put me aside in favour of this pagan slavewoman.'

'But what makes you so sure?'

'The night of Mithiel's Day, she was seen at her open window. Playing a flute and singing, chanting strange hymns to the moon. Worshipping her pagan goddess on the day sacred to the god! And – is this not more than a coincidence, Ophar? – the very next night, these moonmoths appeared in the city. Suppose,' and Clodolë knelt up, clutching at his hands, 'suppose this is all part of her subtle witchcraft, designed to bend Melmeth to her own desires and turn him away from the ways of his forefathers, the Way of the Flame?'

Ophar stared above her dishevelled head into the heart of the flame. Was it his imagining – or did it seem to burn less brightly?

'But the moonmoths. Are you suggesting she summoned them? And for what purpose?'

'The dust on their wings, Ophar.' Clodolë's eyes had darkened as she spoke, her voice low, breathing secrets. 'It is a powerful aphrodisiac.'

'So you believe this Aelahim woman is practising black arts – to seduce the Arkhan?'

'It must be so.' Clodolë raised her tear-streaked face to his. 'Oh, Ophar I am so afraid – so very afraid—'

He patted her hand in a tentative attempt at consolation.

'Take heart, daughter. You were right to come to me. There is more to this than I had realised. Aelahim witchcraft . . . and here in our midst, a canker eating away at the heart of Myn-Dhiel . . . it must be stopped.'

'Qaffë for my lord's favourite. Spiced with cinnamon and dark honey. Why – what's up, sweeting? Not feeling well?'

The aromatic smell of the qaffë in the little porcelain bowl made Laili's over-sensitive stomach churn. She lay back on the silken pillows, turning away her face, waving one hand.

'So pale, little one.' Sarilla's fingers stroked her brow. 'I hope you are not sickening. They say the marsh fever's rife in the city again. There's even talk of plague. *Ouf . . .*' she fanned herself languidly with her silk fan. 'This heat . . .'

'I'm just a little tired. I'll be all right, Sarilla . . .'

'Perhaps you should sit here by the open window. Let me help you . . .'

111

'I'm not an invalid. I can manage quite well myself!'

Laili leaned on the sill, taking in breaths of fresh air; already the roof tiles and spires were shimmering in the first golden heat of the day.

'Laili,' Sarilla said slyly. 'How long is it now?'

Laili started. 'How long?'

'Since you conceived? Oh, come now, you can confide in me. Did you think I hadn't noticed? Green-faced in the morning, turning away your favourite sweetmeats . . . I've already had to get the seamstress to let out the bodice on your white silk gown.'

The turret room was spinning round, Laili felt herself falling, falling . . .

Sarilla caught her and helped her into a chair, forcing her head onto her knees, stroking the back of her neck.

'You are in danger, sweeting. You know that, don't you? I won't tell a living soul. You can trust me, Laili. But – how long will it be before others notice?'

Laili spent the day in an agitation of indecision; unable to concentrate on her usual tasks. Her fingers slipped as she twisted Sarilla's hair into the elaborate jewelled and feathered construction the Torella favoured. Even the aromatic flower oils she had been mixing to perfume Sarilla's rooms made her feel queasy.

When should she tell Melmeth? He had been so preoccupied of late . . .

But when he came to her chamber, he smiled on her, stroked her hair and when he kissed her, his breath tasted strangely sweet.

'I've missed you so, chaeryn.'

Chaeryn. Beloved. Laili's heart sang in silence to hear him call her that name again; in the last days, he had not once called her his beloved and she had begun to fear that his affections were straying elsewhere. Sarilla had warned her enough times.

'Laili,' he said, staring intently into her face, 'I think your Goddess has spoken to me.'

Laili gazed back into his eyes. The delicate rivergreen of the iris was dominated by wildly dilated, swollen pupils . . . the eyes of the initiate who has ingested drugs to seek the trance-state in which the voice of the Goddess may be heard.

'What did She say?'

He let go of her and went to the open casement to gaze out at the stars, each movement erratic, restless.

'It was more vision than speech . . .' His voice drifted back to her, dream-laden. 'And a songthread weaving through it, so ravishing it tore the heart to hear it – I tried to remember the notes when the dream faded but they were beyond my skills to recapture . . .'

'And the vision, my lord?'

'A dreaming place where I felt at peace. Even as I wandered there amongst the whispering trees, the path led me away and when I tried to find my way back, I couldn't, every turning led me into twisted brambles and foul mires.' He seized her hands, crushing them between his own. 'Help me find that place again, Laili. And that music. It wreathes around my head, it won't let me rest, it won't let me sleep . . .'

She raised one hand to stroke his forehead; it was hot, hot as firestones.

'If we were on Ael Lahi, I would say that the Goddess had called you to the Grove, my lord. But here in Perysse I would be accused of talking heresy. Heresy against your god.'

'My head is burning and your hands are so cool. You are like a still forest pool, Laili, deep, unfathomable . . . I want to drown myself in your dark waters . . .'

He was babbling, as though delirious. But he was her lord and she loved him, so she surrendered to his desires, letting him drown again and again until, exhausted, he gave a sigh and slept in her arms.

Lai opened his door. A folded paper had been pushed underneath. Heart beating faster, he unfolded it, clumsy in his haste. There was no scarlet seal this time. Just a few untidily scribbled words:

Be at Sulirrian's gazebo tonight. Unarmed. Wakenight. *Please*. L.

So it had come to this. Melmeth had tired of her, had cast her aside. Why else would her note have been so urgent – yet so oblique?

Lai went to the carved chest of cherrywood in which he kept what little money he possessed; he counted it out, coin by coin. Would it be enough to buy them both passage home?

Arkhan Sulirrian the Visionary had built his gazebo in the highest part of the Sassistri Gardens where the ground dropped steeply away, overlooking the winding river and the weather-vaned turrets of the barracks beneath. High on the brow of the hill stood the gazebo's slender structure: twisted columns of serpentine white marble supporting a fragile dome whose ceiling was inlaid with a golden-glass mosaic.

Occasional wafts of faint music and laughter drifted upwards from roof gardens and open casements, embellishing the mellow silence of the warm summer's night.

But all Lai could think of was Laili – alone, abandoned. Stale, used goods that had lost their novelty . . .

The milkwhite columns of the gazebo shimmered faintly in the moon's chaste light. A glimpse of movement caught his eye, a swirl of shadowed draperies.

'Laili?' he called uncertainly.

'In here.' Her voice was muffled.

He hurried up the steps and entered the gazebo.

She was waiting in the furthest corner, her veiled face averted, as though ashamed to look at him.

'Laili,' he said gently. She did not move, she just stood there. 'It's all right. Don't be afraid.' He reached her, put his hands on her shoulders, turned her to face him, raising her veil—

'Clodolë!' He drew back, stumbling in his confusion.

She was smiling, evidently well pleased with her little deception.

'You really thought I was Laili, didn't you?'

Now that he had recovered from the initial shock, he was angry. So angry he could not speak.

She stroked one finger down his cheek.

'You've been neglecting me, Lai.' Her crimson-stained lips pouted. 'I don't like to be neglected.'

'And I don't like this play-acting,' Lai burst out. 'This pretence. What do you want of me?'

She gave a little laugh.

'What do I want? Now who's play-acting? Playing the fool?' She slid her hands onto his shoulders, fingering the sombre cloth of his jacket.

'I don't think we have anything more to say to each other.'

'There are ways of communication other than conversation . . .' Her fingertips worked their way down to unbutton his shirt.

He caught her hands in his.

'Who *are* you, Clodolë? And do you know who I am? Or doesn't it matter as long as my prick is in good working order?'

She snatched her hands away.

'You just don't begin to understand, do you?' he said in a whisper. 'There's more to life than Myn-Dhiel. You're sated. Sated with

114

meaningless, mindless pleasures. Look. Down there.' He pointed to the rooftops of Perysse far below. 'Your city. Teeming with life. Teeming with hunger and misery. When have you ever troubled yourself to find out how your people live?'

'You call it my city. It is Melmeth's city.'

'But there's so much good you could do, Clodolë. There are children, starving homeless children in those tortuous streets who desperately need your help.'

For a moment, he saw her hesitate and a fleeting look of longing softened her bee-brown eyes. And then the look vanished and her gaze hardened again.

'An Arkhys does not concern herself with the common people.'

'These common people – have you ever troubled yourself to go and see how they live? How they scrape some kind of existence together from one long day to the next? Babies abandoned on rubbish tips, left to the rats, emaciated children thieving scraps, selling their bodies for—'

She hit him across the face; hard.

'How dare you preach at me!'

'You don't want to know, do you?' He could taste blood; her rings had grazed his lip.

'They live their lives as they please. If you're so concerned about them, little priest, little lapsed priest, why aren't you down there distributing soup?'

Her words stung. Little priest. How had she found out? Or had the Torella put it about the palace that her Aelahim slaves had been members of a barbaric religious order, sworn to chastity . . . and therefore all the more delightful a conquest?

'Escort me back to Myn-Dhiel.'

He hesitated.

'What point is there in staying here? You were right; we have nothing to say to each other.'

They descended the winding path without speaking.

'Where are they tonight?' she said after a while. 'The moonmoths?'

'They have a brief lifespan. And the moon is waning . . .'

He heard her give a little sigh. In her moonpale silks she seemed to have become a creature of the night, her eyes dark and huge, her drifting hair more white than gold. A trick of the fading moonlight? He didn't know, he only knew that she looked eerily, ethereally beautiful, a woman of moonshine and shadows.

'Lai,' she said in a whisper. 'You're so passionate about the issues you care about. I love that passion in you. Can we not forget our differences – for one more night?'

She drew closer to him, one fingertip touching his swollen lip where her ring had drawn blood.

'I hurt you. Let me kiss it better.'

She drew closer still, lifting her pale face to his.

'No,' he said although he longed to let her kiss him. 'I won't play your games any more, Clodolë.'

She stared up at him.

'Games. You think this is a game?' Her voice hardened. 'Then let me remind you that the welfare of one who is dear to you depends largely on whether I still find you pleasing company or no . . .'

'You're threatening me!' he said, astonished.

'I've put up with Melmeth's infatuations in the past. But I am losing my patience with this one. Oh, you know who I'm talking about, don't you? Disappoint me once more – and she will suffer.' She gathered up her skirts and went running down the path in between the trees.

'Clodolë – wait!'

She turned and faced him, her eyes blazing like a cat's in a last gleam of moonlight.

'Wait? For what? If I want a sermon, I can go to the priests of Mithiel.'

He watched as she crossed the velvet-grassed bank and disappeared into Myn-Dhiel by one of the secret Memizhon doors.

'I could have loved you, Clodolë,' he whispered. 'Perhaps that was what you really wanted of me . . . love? And there was a time when I thought . . . before . . .'

Before she had threatened Laili.

Starflecks, now green, now blue, now pure white ice glittered in the cloudless dark above his head.

There were stars on the vaulted roof of her bedchamber, gilded stars, a feeble imitation of these brilliant pulsations of light.

A sham. Like your protestations to me, Clodolë. Like all the promises of the House of Memizhon – empty.

Little street sparrows, their dark eyes dulled with hunger, the ragged children crept out from noisome alleys and doorways, their hands upraised to Lai, silently begging.

If you're so concerned about them, little priest . . .

They must have smelt the delicious odour emanating from the basket of fresh-baked bread he had bought.

He began to tear the loaves up into chunks – and suddenly he was almost knocked off his feet as the children surged around him, clawing for the bread.

'There's plenty—' he cried. A tiny boy was knocked face-down into the mud; Lai scooped him up and thrust a piece of bread into his hand. When he turned back to the basket, it was empty and the children had fled.

He picked up the basket and shook the last crumbs out onto the cobbles, smiling wryly. What had he hoped to achieve with one basket of bread? He would have to return tomorrow . . . and the next day and the next . . . Then, maybe, they might come to trust him . . .

A plumed palanquin came swaying towards Lai across the crowded square, its bare-chested bearers grunting in the heat.

As it passed Lai, the curtains parted and a ringed hand let drop a scarlet muskrose at his feet. A waft of an opulent perfume stirred a memory of another hot day a year ago at the slave market by the Ylliri Fountain, a painful memory he had tried to forget . . .

The palanquin passed on without slowing its pace towards the palace. Could the unseen passenger be the Torella Sarilla?

Puzzled, Lai knelt to retrieve the rose. As he lifted it, he saw that a wafer-thin paper had been inserted amongst its ruched petals. He stepped back into a shadowed doorway to read the message:

Be in the Sassistri Gardens near the grove of silver myrrh at wakenight.

Just those laconic words. No signature. Lai's heart beat faster, a soaring wingbeat in his chest. Was all the waiting over – were they to be reunited at last?

The shrine of Ala Sassistri, mistress of the Arkhan Sulaimon, was still a favoured place for lovers' trysts. Here, where the grieving Arkhan had scattered the ashes of his dead beloved, a grove of rustling myrrh-trees and sombre incense cedars had been planted. And on the shrine of pale marble, the bleak, bleached taint of mourning, hung wind-harps, their unearthly, thready timbres troubling the grove's quiet when the sky darkened with storm clouds.

No breeze stirred the plangent strings of the wind-harps as Lai entered the odiferous grove; the summered nightscent of the whispering leaves, some crushed underfoot in the dank soil, was rich and bitter as pyre-spices.

She was by the shrine. A still figure, her loose robe pale as the funerary marble, her bright hair veiled in gossamer.

Lai hesitated. This revenant, frail moon-phantasm of Ala Sassistri . . . this could not be Laili.

Staying within the cover of the grove, he edged forwards. His foot pressed on a concealed twig, the tiny crack tweaking the warm air.

'Who's – who's there?'

The voice. He knew it. Still he dared not go any further, fearing some obscure Memizhonian subterfuge.

'Lai?'

'I'm here. Are you alone?'

She nodded her head. Still she did not move. He ventured out from the myrrh-trees, crossing the moonsilvered grass towards her.

'Why?' asked Lai. 'Why tonight? Why here?'

'I don't know.'

'Are *they* watching us? There must be a catch.'

She put out one hand towards him, fingers feverishly feeling for his face, touching, informing.

'What have they done to you, Laili?'

'Listen.' She pulled his head close to hers. 'You must believe me. I am well. I am cared-for. I want for nothing . . . You must be content with that.'

'Content! When I cannot see you, cannot even speak your name aloud for fear that—'

'Hush.' She sealed his lips with her fingertips. 'I know. You risked your life for me in the arena, for my freedom. You cannot yet understand what I am saying to you. That – in a way – I am happy.'

For a moment Lai could not believe what he was hearing.

'They've made you say this. They've threatened you as they threatened me.'

Gently she shook her head.

'I want you to be happy too. If only you would stay at court. Then you would still be near at hand—'

'Stay! In this dissolute travesty Melmeth calls a court! And what would I do to maintain my position? Kill a few more slaves in the arena?' He saw her shake her head. 'Have you ever left Myn-Dhiel, Laili? Up here, surrounded by pleasure gardens and fountains, it's so easy to forget the city beneath, the starving children, the shaven-headed slaves toiling in the dye works—'

'You judge Melmeth too harshly . . . he is a good man at heart.'

'A good man who enjoys watching his slaves fight to the death for sport?'

'Lai.' She took his hand in hers. 'You are so . . . so changed. So bitter.'

'I can't live with what I have done. Every night I . . . I find myself back in the arena, my feet slipping on the bloodied sand. Every night I wake shouting out aloud in terror. I can't stay here, Laili. I have to go back to the Grove. Only there will I find some kind of peace of mind—'

'Then this is where our ways part, Lai. Because I can never go with you now.' There was a sudden shiver in her voice.

'Why? Because you're Melmeth's concubine?' He tipped her face up, each word a sharp sliver of bamboo slid under fingernails. 'Violating one of the adept – that must have appealed to him.'

'No! It was not like that!'

'Just like them to choose this grove for our meeting-place . . . dedicated to fragrant Sassistri, Sulaimon's whore. And how did she die? She was poisoned by his jealous Arkhys.' He snatched away his hand. 'He'll keep you locked away in some secret chamber until he tires of you, until this game goes stale . . . then you'll receive a pretty gift from Clodolë: gloves or a scented pomander. Laced with her most virulent poison.'

'No, Lai!'

'Come with me. No one will notice if we slip away. And there's bound to be a spice barque in port that's heading back to the isles—'

'You still don't understand, you're not listening to me! I don't want to go.'

'You – don't want to?'

'What would be the point of returning to Ael Lahi? To hear the singing, to ache to be part of it . . . yet to be barred from the Grove, always on the outside.'

'They would understand. You were taken by force—'

'Force . . .' An enigmatic little smile flitted across her lips, brief as a moonshadow. 'I have come to love him. And he loves me.'

'And when it is no longer politic for him to love you?'

'I bear his child, Lai.'

'His – his child.'

Stunned, Lai could only stare at her.

119

'Now do you understand?'

Melmeth's seed, Melmeth's heir. Oh yes, he understood only too well. She could never go with him now to Ael Lahi. He would return alone.

'It was selfish of me to want you to stay here. Of course you must go. Remember – a part of me will be always with you.'

'And a part of me here with you,' he said, his voice breaking.

'Lai, oh Lai.' She wound her arms around him and pressed her cheek to his. For a moment he hid his face in her hair, letting himself drown in the memory of that lost closeness, that time when they thought as one, acted as one. She kissed his forehead, brief brush of rose-velvet lips.

'If ever you need me, Laili—'

It sounded so foolish, so empty. When you are the beloved of the Arkhan of Ar-Khendye you need no one. And yet . . .

Danger . . .

The chill of presentiment drenched him as it had done once before, that distant twilit evening when the gilded slave-galley rounded the headland.

He looked back. She was still standing there. When he looked again, there was nothing but moonlight.

CHAPTER 12

Moonlight filtered into the first chamber of the mausoleum of the House of Memizhon. A faint red eye of flame glimmered from an alcove where the wakelight burned incessantly. Like a film of greying powdersnow, dust lay on the crumbling sarcophagi, drifted across the flagged floor. Melmeth stood still, still as the painted stone statues that stared at him from every niche in the vaulted chamber. Behind each effigy were neatly piled mouldering skulls and bones; wherever he looked, hollowed sockets of darkness stared at him, yellowed teeth-stubs grinned.

And all around stood the ancient ancestral effigies, lifesize, some still draped in rotting fragments of ceremonial garments; their staring eyes glinted in the moonlight.

Melmeth ventured a step towards the nearest statue.

For one sickening moment he was convinced the stiff figure was mummified human flesh. The hair appeared to be real hair, matted and spider-webbed with age. But on closer inspection, the hideous sunken face was sculpted yellowing wax; the glazed eyes were precious stones. Emeralds, perhaps . . . their chill, dead glint terrified Melmeth as the moonlight animated them, until they appeared to stare directly, accusingly at him.

'Lord Melmeth.'

'Who's there?' Melmeth whispered. His throat was suddenly dry, choked with dust. Had someone followed him? Or was the sepulchral voice issuing from one of the antique sarcophagi?

'Did I startle you?' A man moved into the silvered path of moonlight, a gaunt old man, his priest's vestments darker than shadow. In his hands he held a glass cruse of sacred oil, red as blood. Ophar. 'I've come to perform my nightly duties. But what has drawn *you* to the mausoleum at so late an hour?'

Melmeth took in a slow, steadying breath, a breath that tasted of mould and decay.

'Here,' he said, 'here lies the greatness of the House of Memizhon, crumbling quietly and inexorably to dust. Each Arkhan, each tyrant of Ar-Khendye, reduced to a neat stack of bones.'

Ophar nodded his head. Moving to the wakelight, he carefully replenished the sacred oil and replaced the guttering wick. A breath of cinnamon and bitter myrrh wafted through the chamber.

'And what will they say of me when I am dust?' Melmeth swept one finger along the dust clogging the carven legend below the figure, peering at the ancient letters. 'What will I have left behind me? What will they call me? Melmeth the Weak? No. I've decided that things must change – and I must change them.'

'Ah.' Ophar did not turn around yet from his stillness, Melmeth was aware that he was listening to him with utter attention.

'The rites of Mithiel. They are barbaric.'

'Hardly barbaric when condemned criminals are granted the chance to gain their freedom in hand-to-hand combat.'

Melmeth faltered a moment; he was still in awe of Ophar. But even as he faltered, he heard Laili's clear voice, saw her eyes, blazingly blue with anger, accusing him . . .

'Is there no other way to let them earn their pardon? No other way to requite the god?'

There was a pause. Then Ophar asked acidly, 'What precisely are you suggesting, lord?'

'A contest of skill. But the killing must stop. No more deaths.'

To his surprise Ophar began to chuckle, a dry, mirthless sound, as if he had almost forgotten how to laugh.

'My lord, this is absurd. The people expect a fight to the death. It is a necessary part of our judicial system. It is also a deterrent. If they want to amuse themselves with a harmless contest of skill, they can watch a bout of Jhered-nai any time they wish—'

'You are not hearing what I'm saying, Ophar. I want it to stop. I'm putting an end to it.'

'And the god?' Ophar said in the softest of voices.

'Surely the god can still be honoured with incense and prayers. Is that not more fitting than the shedding of blood?'

'And what has brought on this sudden crisis of conscience?' Ophar asked still softly, oh so softly. 'You cheered on your Memizhon champion to victory as loudly as any of the rabble.'

'I see matters differently now.' Melmeth tried not to sound defensive.

'You have invested so much in the training of your champions. You've always taken such an interest in their selection,' persisted Ophar. 'Are you going to deny them their chance of glory?'

Melmeth found himself seized with a violent desire to strike the old man.

'Are we always to be at cross-purposes?'

'Whilst you neglect your duty to the god of your House, yes.'

'So you're going to oppose me.'

'It is my duty as High Priest to oppose you. What you are proposing is an insult to the god. And Mithiel is a warrior's god. It pleases him that the blood of warriors shoud be shed in his honour. The spilling of warrior's blood onto the earth in spring ensures a good harvest—'

'I will not be opposed this time!'

'Melmeth, my son.' Ophar had not called him by his first name since he was a child; this sudden benevolent tone was unsettling. 'I understand your desire to make changes. Changes which you consider to be for the better. Only consider the consequences of your actions. Don't do anything rash, anything you might later regret.'

Melmeth said nothing.

'Tomorrow, I am confident you will see the whole matter in a different light.' Ophar bowed to the Arkhan and withdrew, his robes dragging a trail through the drifting charnel dust.

'By tomorrow,' Melmeth said in a whisper, 'all Perysse will know what I have done. And there is nothing you can do to change it, old man.'

Ymarys made his entrance into the Arkhan's audience chamber. He had dressed with exaggerated ostentation for the occasion and heard, to his satisfaction, little gasps of envy and admiration from the assembled exquisites and courtiers. His tailor had excelled himself. Metallic-sheened silks embroidered with threads of gold and bronze were set off by tassels of a shockingly vivid mulberry-pink adorning his razhir-sash and tight-fitting breeches. He looked dazzling. Dazzling – and dangerous.

If this was to be his last official appearance at court, he wanted it recorded in the annals, right down to the last detail of his tasselled shoes.

He approached Melmeth's throne and bowed with a lazy grace, flicking his silky hair back from his face.

'Is it true what they are saying in the barracks, zhan? Have you banned the rites?'

'Not banned. Altered. Now I realise that your role in this will be significantly diminished . . . But I want you to remain at Myn-Dhiel and retain the title of Memizhon Razhirrakh – as my official blademaster.'

'You are very generous, zhan,' Ymarys said, one elegant brow lifting slightly. 'But what about Lai Dhar? Surely he has first claim to that title.'

'Lai? I thought you knew. He asked to be released from his court duties – and I released him. He has gone to seek a passage home.'

If his years at Myn-Dhiel had taught Ymarys anything, it was how to conceal his feelings. And he was a consummate courtier, well-skilled at concealment. He contrived another graceful bow, hiding the sudden gleam of pain that flashed through his kohl-lined eyes. Lai – leaving Perysse. Without even telling him.

'And what will my official duties entail, zhan?' Ymarys heard himself asking in a tone of supreme self-control whilst his mind tried to make sense of the hurt.

Lai. Gone forever.

'We will still require your skills as bladetutor to the Tarkhas Memizhon. But you are no longer required to risk your life in the arena. There will be no more bloodletting on Mithiel's Day.'

The courtiers broke into a chorus of shocked whispers.

'He's banning the rites . . .'

'And what about the brandslaves?'

'Orthandor will take charge of the contest. The slaves will compete for their freedom in Jhered-nai.'

Did I mean so little to him? So little I didn't even merit a word of farewell?

'Well?' Melmeth said. 'Do you accept?'

Ymarys started. He became aware that all eyes in the chamber were fixed on him, awaiting his response; Sarilla, in particular, was staring at him with fixed attention above her fan.

'We should miss you, Ymarys, if you were to retire. You, our arbiter of court fashion.'

Ymarys acknowledged the Arkhan's compliment with an elegant obeisance.

'When you put it so graciously, zhan, what can I do but accept?'

A soft sigh of approval greeted his words. But as he bowed his way from the Arkhan's presence, he caught Sarilla's eye once more. Her elegant painted mouth, bright as japonica petals, framed one word.

'Traitor.'

The sky was sheened with faint, high cloud, sheer as finest silk as Lai went towards the river. To the west, the dipping sun glimmered, pale and pure, a glaze of liquid gold, promising fair weather on the morrow.

All day he had aimlessly wandered the streets of the city, trying to make sense of it all.

How could Laili do this to him? How could she stand in the moonlit gardens and tell him, 'Forget me'?

How could she have changed so in the passing of a single year?

Night after night he had crawled exhaustedly back from the armoury to his bare cell and sworn that he would give up, he could take no more . . . and then her wan face had haunted his dreams, her eyes swollen with weeping. Next morning at dawn, that vision had driven him, bruised and stiff, back to the armoury.

He had killed to set her free.

Swallows dipped and skimmed over his head: he looked up, a smile of regret twisting his lips. So many things he had not noticed for so long, so many simple things that would have once delighted him: the fluting dusksong of a merle perched high on a carven weathervane; the first bright flowering of the quinces festooning the crumbling walls of Sulirrian's ancient summer palace near the quay . . .

Yet what was there left for him here? Laili was far beyond his reach, the favoured darling of her royal master. And Clodolë, opulent Clodolë . . . she had merely used him for her own purposes.

He was not to be used.

All that remained was the promise of Ael Lahi . . . and the tenuous hope that, in the service of the Goddess, he might find some way to atone for the blood he had shed.

He stood a moment on the river-bank, watching the anchored ships dipping gently on the river-tide. Even the dilapidated, tar-caulked hulks of the shabbier vessels seemed transformed by the golden light of the setting sun.

A shack at the end of the quay served as a recruitment office for the river barques; as Lai approached, a light flowered at the window as someone inside lit a lantern.

Lai pushed the leathern curtain aside and went in. A grizzle-bearded sailor was lighting his clay pipe from a tinder, hands cupped to shield the flame.

'Closed for the night.'

'I want a passage to Ael Lahi.'

The sailor removed the pipe from his mouth and gave a short grunt of laughter.

'No one goes that far. No one but madmen – or castaways.'

'The Spice Isles, then. I'll do anything. Scrub decks, mend sails, push a galley-oar—'

'You seem very keen to get away from Perysse. In trouble with the law?'

Lai did not answer.

The sailor bent over a stained parchment chart on the table, squinting at the writing in the fading light.

'You'll have to wait for the El'Thera; she won't be back till the new moon rises. There've been storms out in the straits. I could put a word in with her maistre, if you made it . . . worth my while.' He stared at Lai suggestively in the fading light.

But Lai had begun to learn the ways of Perysse . . .

'I'll make it worth your while when the El'Thera's back in port.'

'Can't guarantee anything . . .' the sailor called after him.

So even in this he was frustrated. Now that he was free to return home, the only ship going anywhere near Ael Lahi was caught in storms . . .

Am I never to get out of this place?

As Lai walked slowly back along the quay, a faint, delicious spicescent drifted towards him. And with it came a memory, achingly vivid, of bee-tawny eyes, soft skin, luscious-fleshed as apricots . . .

Boskh . . .

Above his head a trail of moonmoths came darting towards the rising moon, leaving a cloud of dust shimmering in the warm air.

'Quick! There they go!' Children ran out from an alleyway, laughing and waving nets, making vain leaps as the moths fluttered high into the air.

Lai stopped one of the children, a boy in a tattered jacket several sizes too big.

'Lemme go! They're getting away!'

Lai held an enith in front of the boy's eyes.

'Tell me – why are you trying to catch the moths?'

'Because you can sell 'em for a hundred of these!' The boy snatched the coin and scampered off across the cobbles in pursuit of the fleeting moths.

'It's true.'

Lai looked around and saw Arlan Azhrel, the scars on his ruined face weirdly lit by the flame of his lantern.

Daemon-mask. Lai was sucked back into the pit of his donjon nightmares, into that dark delirium of fever dreams from which Azhrel's physic had rescued him.

'They're fetching exorbitant prices. Especially at Myn-Dhiel, I hear. D'you want to accompany me on a moth-hunt?'

'I—'

'Good. Hold the lantern. I'm onto something, I think.' Azhrel strode off across the quay. 'I heard reports that they were seen clustering over here . . .'

A foetid stench drowned out the faint sweetness of boskh.

'The middens!' Lai said, drawing back.

'Indeed so. The smell is less pungent by night. Also there are fewer curious onlookers . . .' Azhrel began to poke around with his stick in the rotting rubbish heap.

'But why are you searching for moonmoths?'

'This is the most fascinating natural phenomenon to occur in Perysse in my lifetime. Besides, there's something I don't quite understand— Ah. Bring the lantern closer, Lai.'

In the circle of lantern light, Azhrel pointed with the stick tip.

'What do you make of those?'

'Dead leaves.'

'Maybe . . . but have you never seen chrysalises before?' Azhrel knelt down and carefully extracted some of the dry fragments, holding them up to the light, sniffing them.

'Chrysalises? You're saying that the moonmoths hatched in a midden!'

'Maybe . . .' Azhrel slipped the fragments into a glass jar and stoppered it. 'It may be the clues are right beneath my eyes and I cannot see them.'

'A midden,' Lai repeated. Was this the mystery of mysteries that the Eldest One had kept from the youngest adepts? That the sparkling-winged messengers of the Goddess hatched in dung and detritus? 'No,' he whispered, revolted at the thought. 'It must be a coincidence.'

'What must be?' Azhrel said.

Lai found Azhrel staring intently at him, his dark eyes lit by the lantern flame.

'You know something of these moonmoths?'

'I come from the island of Ael Lahi. We believe the moonmoths to be sacred, the gift of the Goddess.'

'And Ael Lahi lies far from here?'

'East of the sun and west of the moon,' Lai said wryly.

'If you could just spare me an hour or so of your time, I'd like to ask you a few questions. I live in the Old Quarter, not five minutes' walk away.'

Lai shrugged. There was no ship leaving for the islands . . . and time seemed to stretch ahead, empty and purposeless. What had he to lose?

Galingal Lane led away from the river, its houses hidden by a high, crumbling stone wall overgrown with vines and jasmine; the poignantly sweet scent from the creamy flowers enriched the drowsily warm night. Azhrel stopped at a little door set in the wall, half-hidden by creepers, its warped timbers silvered with age and, unlocking it with an iron key, ushered Lai inside. Within the tangled garden, the winding path fragrant with herbs, nestled Azhrel's house.

'So . . . what brought you down to the quay tonight?'

'I came to book a passage home.' Lai tweaked a leaf-tip from a coriander plant and sniffed at the sharp green scent it left on his fingertips.

'Home! But of course – you must have family in Ael Lahi.'

'Family?' The word pricked at his heart. His only surviving relative was Laili. And now she would never return to the island. He would be the last of their bloodline on Ael Lahi. 'Not still living—'

'Dr Azhrel! Dr Azhrel!'

Someone banged on the garden door.

Azhrel went hurrying back down the path. Lai followed, curious. A ragged boy stood in the lane outside.

'Can you come to the dye works? There's been an accident.'

'How bad an accident?'

'A vat-spill. There's boiling dye everywhere. Please come quick.'

'Run back and tell the foreman I'm on my way.' Azhrel turned to Lai. 'Forgive me—'

'I'll come with you,' Lai said on impulse.

'Wait here.' Azhrel disappeared into the house. A few moments later, he appeared at an open window holding a leathern bag.

'Catch!' He threw the bag down to Lai.

A moment later he had slammed the house door shut and was hurrying down the path towards the lane.

'Why were they working at this hour?' Lai asked, hastening to keep up with Azhrel's swift stride.

'Slave labour. They work shifts throughout the night. The silk trade is the beating heart of Perysse, hm? It never stills.'

A sudden waft of dye fumes blew down the dark street, rank as rotting vegetation. They turned a corner and Lai saw the high spiked railings black against the dull glare of fires beyond. Shadowy figures hurried to and fro in confusion; greasy smoke belched out, fouling the sweet evening air.

Azhrel went up to the gates and called, 'Who sent for a doctor?'

Lai peered into the billowing smoke. From somewhere within he thought he could hear a faint, insistent moaning.

'Come in, Dr Azhrel.' A man appeared through the smoke and with a clanking of keys, unlocked the gates to admit them. His face was shiny with sweat.

'How many injured this time?' Azhrel asked.

'One's dead. Fell asleep whilst he was supposed to be watching the vat.'

'If you fed and rested your workers properly, these accidents wouldn't happen,' Azhrel said quietly.

The foreman spat.

'Workers! Condemned criminals, every one, Dr Azhrel. Scum of Perysse. Look at this mess. We'll be days clearing it up.'

The hard-trodden dirt underfoot was pooled with leaks of congealing, cooling dye. Steam hissed and wisped from puddles and still-running rivulets.

'And not just any dye, oh no. Only the most expensive, the Llyrian purple.'

A miasmic cloud hung over the works like fog; condensation ran in rivulets down the sides of the walls, the dye-encrusted metal vats. In the warm damp air Lai felt his clothes begin to stick to his skin.

Torches lit the shed where the injured had been laid on sacking. Lai faltered on the threshold, overwhelmed by the sight that confronted them. Some of the casualties were groaning, others lay still. There was an all-pervasive smell of burned flesh and vomit.

'And you remembered what I told you last time this happened?' Azhrel stripped off his coat, rolled up his sleeves.

'Yes, yes, sponge them in cold water. Mithiel knows, we've little

129

enough fresh water to spare in this heat . . .'

Brandslaves, ankles still shackled together were dipping rags in buckets of well-water, ringing them out and laying them over their injured companions.

'Scalds, steam burns,' Azhrel muttered, moving down the shed, glancing from left to right, assessing the situation. He stopped by one brandslave who lay motionless; only the thin hiss of pain that issued from between his clenched teeth gave any clue that he was still conscious.

The foreman caught hold of Azhrel's arm, steering him towards a pallet set apart from the others.

'Pheryn, my nightshift overseer.'

Lai saw Azhrel stiffen, the muscles tightening in his neck. He pulled his arm free and turned back.

'This man first. Pheryn can wait. And get some strips of clean linen. These filthy rags will only cause infection!'

The foreman hesitated a moment, then left the shed.

Azhrel bent over the brandslave, lifting up the sodden rags. Ribs and hip bones protruded through the emaciated flesh. Boiling dye had stained the skin lurid patches of purple. Beneath the slave's filthy loincloth Lai glimpsed a tracery of ill-healed scars of the gelding knife.

'Help me raise his head,' Azhrel said, opening his leathern bag.

Lai slipped his hand under the thin shoulders; the slave began to moan in pain as he touched him.

'I'm sorry—' Lai whispered.

'Open his mouth. That's right.' Azhrel took out a glass phial and tipped a little of its contents onto the injured slave's parched tongue.

Lai saw the glistening dust, caught a breath of its fragrance, sweet and pure amidst the stench of dye and sweat. The terrible, mindless moaning gradually died into a soft exhalation of relief.

'Boskh?' Lai said, his eyes meeting Azhrel's over the slave's lolling head.

'You disapprove?' Azhrel shook a little of the dust over the scalded, weeping blisters. Even as Lai watched, a pearlescent film seemed to form over the skin.

'Miraculous . . .' Lai shook his head in disbelief.

'Did you know it could heal so efficiently?'

'I had no idea . . .'

'Here.' Azhrel passed the phial to Lai. 'I have another. You take that side of the shed, I'll take this.'

130

'Zhan.' A pale-skinned slave tugged at Lai's sleeve. 'She's going fast. Help her.'

'Her?' Lai knelt beside the prone form and saw as the companion drew aside the dye-stained shift that this shaven-headed brandslave was a woman. 'But I thought—'

'The Arkhan's justice makes no distinction between men and women when the dye works is the sentence,' her companion said expressionlessly. 'Has she a chance?'

Lai let his hand rest on the woman's brand-stained forehead; the skin felt clammy and chill. Beneath the bruised lids, he caught a glimpse of white.

'She's almost gone . . .' he said, swallowing down his anger. How could Melmeth permit this cruelty – had he even any idea of the conditions?

The phial of boskh glimmered in the torchlight as he unstoppered it and poured a little into the woman's slack mouth. A sigh, almost imperceptible, escaped her lips. His hand reached for her slender wrist, feeling for a pulse.

Live, he willed her, feeling the bones protruding beneath the paperthin skin, the pulse so faint it was hardly there. *Live.*

Live for what purpose? a faint mindvoice whispered. *Day after day of endless toil and heat. No hope of reprieve. No hope. Rather let me die . . .*

'No!' Lai cried aloud, pressing the woman's hand between his own. 'It doesn't have to be that way. There is always hope.'

The bruised lids flickered, opened. The woman stared curiously up into his face, her dry lips moved.

'Eryl?' said her companion in painful eagerness.

'Why?' Eryl whispered. 'Why did you bring me back?'

'Because you mustn't give up,' Lai said with quiet fervour. 'Don't let *them* defeat you. You have friends outside. Friends who will not forget you.'

Eryl's hand lifted a little, pointing towards Lai's forehead and the tattooed mark of Memizhon.

'You . . . you are one of us . . . and yet you are free . . .'

'I had to fight for my freedom. And I will fight for yours.'

'Be careful,' her companion said. 'They are watching us.'

Lai nodded, understanding.

'I won't forget,' he said again and, drawing away, moved on to the next pallet.

*

Distant tarkenhorns blew from the ramparts of the Tarkhas Zhudiciar, announcing wakenight.

Lai felt a hand on his shoulder. Wearily, he looked around and saw Azhrel.

'Wakenight. Time to go.'

'I had no idea it was so late.' Lai rubbed his eyes, blinking away the blur of tiredness.

'I'll return in the morning. But we've done all we can for now.'

Lai stood up, stretching his cramped muscles. As he followed Azhrel, he glanced back over his shoulder into the torchlit shed; Eryl was lying with her head on her companion's lap. Her thin chest gently rose and fell in the natural rhythm of sleep.

The iron gates clanged shut behind them; the key creaked in the lock.

'It works!' Azhrel said under his breath. 'Sweet Mithiel, it really works!' His dark eyes caught the glitter of the starlit sky; he seemed charged, transfigured with excitement. His glossy hair, usually so neatly tied back, had come loose about his shoulders. Lai glanced at him and their eyes met, conspirators sharing the same secret.

'Have you any idea what this means? All those cases of gangrene I try to treat at the weavers, the loom injuries . . . now they can all be cured. No young mother need die of puerperal fever again, no child succumb to the smallpox—'

Lai stumbled on a loose cobblestone, Azhrel steadied hm.

'You're exhausted. What am I thinking of, rambling on in this way? I never meant to keep you out so late.'

'You didn't keep me. I chose to stay,' Lai said.

'The gates of the Tarkhas Memizhon will be locked by now. But you can sleep at my house in Galingal Lane – if you like.'

Bunches of dried herbs and flowers hung low from the ceiling of Azhrel's study, brittle seed pods and fronded leaves brushed their heads. The room was filled from floor to ceiling with books: old books, their spines cracked open, spilling yellowed pages. Even the desk was littered with tumbled papers and stained alembics.

Azhrel delved beneath a pile of papers and brought out a glass bottle half-full of a translucent liquor, pale as snow-melt.

'Alquer?' As Azhrel poured out a generous measure each, Lai thought he detected a faint odour of bitter jhynzar berries. 'Try it – it's excellent.'

Lai took a sip; it was clean and pleasantly sharp in the mouth but when it reached the back of the throat it turned to liquid fire.

'Powerful?' Azhrel said, a smile twitching at the corner of his mouth.

Lai let his breath out slowly, convinced that he would breathe flames like a firedrake.

'Powerful,' he wheezed, nodding.

'It's something of an acquired taste.' Azhrel raised his glass and clinked it against Lai's. 'A good night's work.'

'A good night's work.'

'I watched you tonight. You have the makings of a healer in you.'

'No,' Lai said curtly. 'I'm no healer. I did what anyone would have done.'

'Anyone? Is that what you think? You saw those terrible injuries – and yet you didn't flinch.'

Lai shrugged. 'I've seen as bad in the arena. I've inflicted worse.'

'Just because you were compelled to take part in that barbaric blood rite, doesn't mean you have become as brutalised as those who compelled you.'

'Doesn't it?' Lai said bitterly. He swallowed down the alquer; it seemed to have lost its bite.

'Lai.' Azhrel reached out across the desk and seized hold of his hands, turning them palm upwards in the puddle of light from the lucerna. 'Look. What do you see?'

'Blood,' Lai said in a whisper, staring down at his hands. 'The hands of a killer. A trained killer.'

'Is that what you see? I see the hands of a healer.'

Lai got up, knocking over his chair and walked away to the unshuttered window, staring out into the night.

'You must put the arena behind you,' Azhrel said fiercely. 'Yes, it has changed you. But it has not destroyed you. It will only destroy you if you let it.'

'Don't preach at me, Azhrel. How can you know? How can you possibly know what it's like?'

'Me?' Azhrel said, pouring himself another measure of alquer. 'Oh, I know. Believe me – I know.'

Lai glanced at him, seeing the harsh lines of his ruined face cruelly highlit by the lucerna light. But at that moment he was too wrapped up in his own anger to greatly care about Azhrel . . .

'It'd be better if I left.'

'To wander the streets all night?' Azhrel's mouth quirked into a mocking smile. 'To sleep rough?'

'I need to think.'

Azhrel shrugged.

'Go, then. Go think.'

Lai opened the door; a waft of creamy jasmine scent floated in – but all he could smell was the indigo stink of the dye works.

'You know where to find me,' Azhrel called after him, 'if you need me.'

CHAPTER 13

'Dhamzel, Dhamzel!' The urgent whisper penetrated Laili's dreams; Laili woke to see a pale, pinched face hovering above hers. It was Miu, the little slavegirl who brought their food from the kitchens.

'What's wrong?'

'The Torella. I think you'd better come see.'

Wands of gilded sunlight lit the bed, the polished floor; it must be mid-morning and yet the apartments were eerily hushed, with no usual bustle of activity . . .

Laili reached for her overgown and drew the woven cord tightly around the waist, hoping the curve of her swelling belly was not too obvious.

Miu beckoned her across the antechamber towards the closed doors of Sarilla's rooms; Laili thought she could hear someone muttering on and on distractedly inside.

'She won't let me near her,' said Miu. 'Says her head hurts. Threw the qaffë pot at me and smashed all the cups.'

'Maybe an infusion of feverfew would help her . . . or willowbark. Can you run back down to the kitchens and see if they have any?'

Miu shrugged.

'Cook beat me for breaking the cups.'

'Please, Miu.'

As soon as the girl had gone, Laili tapped on Sarilla's door.

'Go away.'

'It's Laili.' Laili opened the door a crack and slipped inside. The room was smothered in darkness and for a moment, she could see nothing. Then as her eyes became accustomed, she made out a pale figure, insubstantial as a ghost, felt a breath of movement as Sarilla wandered past her.

'I've sent for some feverfew for your head. Why not lie down and rest?'

'No, no, no . . .'

Laili caught hold of her and began to guide her towards the bed.

'Let me just open the shutters a crack—'

Sarilla clutched her head, turning away from the sudden brightness.

'*Ai*—' Her fingers wove convulsively through her unbound hair, twisting, tearing.

'It's all right,' Laili soothed, trying to prise away the clawing fingers. 'Let me bathe your forehead . . .'

'Close the shutters. Close them!'

Sarilla's unpainted face had become a shrivelled mask: an old woman's face. Laili, shocked at the alteration, turned to close the shutter again. Sarilla was instantly at her side, clutching at her hands.

'Get me some, Laili. Here.' She tugged at the heavy emerald ring on her finger, pressing the cold stone into Laili's palm. 'Sell this.'

'But I can't leave the palace,' Laili said, 'you know that.' Especially now that my condition is becoming so obvious, she thought.

'Then get Miu to go buy some.'

'Buy what, Sarilla?'

'Boskh!' cried Sarilla shrilly. 'It cures headaches, megrims . . . I must have some more! How can you stand there and watch me suffer?' She began to moan, clutching at her temples, swaying her body from side to side.

Boskh. Laili took in a breath to steady herself; the stale darkness of the shuttered room was oppressive and now Sarilla's cries grated like the scratch of sharpened talons.

'I'm sending for a physician.'

'What use are physicians?' Sarilla wailed.

'Who else should I send for? I don't know who to ask for help. Zhan Ymarys?'

'No!' Sarilla sank to the floor, rocking her body as though consumed with grief. 'Don't let him see me like this. Don't tell him.'

'But what can I do? I can't leave you in this state.'

'Just get me some more boskh. Please, Laili.' She stroked Laili's hand with hers, held it up to her withered cheek. 'Be kind to your poor Sarilla—'

'I've brought the infusion.'

The slavegirl stood in the open doorway, holding a fragrantly steaming bowl.

'Infusion? I ordered no infusion!' Sarilla suddenly strode forwards and struck the bowl from the girl's hands, sending scalding liquid splashing across the room.

'*Hai!*' The girl fled.

Laili hurried after her, catching her as, sobbing, she fumbled for the doorhandle.

'I'm so sorry. Are you hurt?'

'I'm not coming back. Don't ask me,. She's gone mad. I'm not coming near that madwoman again.'

'Please do just one thing. Call the physician. Just that. You don't have to come back. But tell him it's urgent.'

Still sobbing, Miu pulled open the door and went running out down the stairs.

Laili went back into Sarilla's room to find her seated before her shadowed mirror, applying paint to her face in the semi-darkness.

'I must look my best for Ymarys,' she was muttering. 'For my dearest friend. My hero. There!' She turned to face Laili. 'Will I do?'

Rouge smeared her mouth into a lopsided gash; kohl and malachite blurred the dark circles around her eyes. The effect was both garish and grotesque; a mask to frighten children.

Laili swallowed.

'Maybe you would let me finish your toilette for you?'

'It doesn't matter . . .' Sarilla rose, her trailing sleeves knocking pots onto the floor and went wandering away into the antechamber. 'He doesn't love me any more. He doesn't even call.'

'Do lie down, Sarilla. Please.'

Laili went after her and put her arms about her shoulders, easing her onto the couch.

'There. Let me wipe your face.' Laili began to remove what she could of the smudged paint whilst Sarilla twitched and mumbled on the couch.

'Look Ymarys, the damask hangings are not too badly worn. But so much dust! I know it's quiet here in Mynezhil . . . but it's so peaceful . . . you'll come to like it, I'm sure . . .'

'Sarilla,' Laili said. 'I'm Laili. Don't you recognise me?'

'Laili?' Sarilla peered at her as if from a great distance away. 'What are you doing in Mynezhil? It's such a long journey to make . . . and you in your condition . . .' Laili glanced around, hoping no one had heard, wondering what other secrets Sarilla might babble in her confused state.

'Just a little more dust . . .' Sarilla whispered. 'Just a few grains more . . .'

*

137

Lai sat huddled on a coil of thick rope, watching the sun come up over the Yssil. He had walked the streets of the city till dawn, until, numb with tiredness, he had ended up here on the quay, watching the brown rats scavenging in a rubbish heap.

The anger still gnawed though it had dwindled to a dull ache in the pit of his stomach.

Damn Arlan Azhrel. What business was it of his, what he did with his life?

It sounded so logical – to expiate the guilt by devoting himself to a selfless life caring for the sick.

And somewhere inside the pain and confusion he knew a part of him desperately wanted to accept that role. The pull was so strong. He had felt that pull last night as he knelt beside Eryl, wanting to help her, to cure her.

But for the wrong reasons.

Maybe he should have let her drift away into the darkness . . . away from that living hell of heat and foul fumes. But the only true cure would be to end the inhuman conditions the brandslaves were forced to endure. And how, where would he begin?

Memories of fire and terror danced across his sleep-starved brain. Shackles burned into his wrists and ankles . . . He cowered in fear before his tormentors again. Enslaved. They could do anything with him, to him. His abused body protested, his mind screamed for release.

He found he was shivering, shivering in the chill of dawn.

No. He could not challenge the might of the Tarkhas Zhudiciar alone.

'Goddess,' he whispered, 'tell me what I should do.'

Silence. Baby rats chased after their mother, shrilling piercingly.

If he had learnt anything during his long apprenticeship in the Grove, it was that there were no easy answers.

And all he had wanted was to go home. A wave of black, bleak homesickness washed over him, engulfing him.

Nothing had gone right since the night he left the arena a free man. All his plans had been frustrated, all his dreams shattered.

The quayside blurred; he knuckled his eyes, wiping away the salty wetness. He was not crying. He would not cry. To cry was a sign of weakness – and he could not afford to be weak. His eyes were watering with weariness, that was all.

Now he regretted rejecting Azhrel's offer of a bed, now the thought of crisp, clean sheets seemed like a promise of heaven.

On the quay an old woman was brewing up khassafri; its sweet nutmeg aroma drifted enticingly towards Lai. He got to his feet and walked stiffly, slowly across to her stall. Sipping the hot liquid from a mug, he felt its warmth seep through his body.

A sudden echo of hunger, aching hunger, seared his belly.

How many times in the donjon had he lain, half-starved, unable to move from weakness, longing for food, any food . . . ?

And he still had the money he had saved for his passage home to Ael Lahi.

A short while later, he rattled the gates of the dye works.

'Go away!' growled a hostile voice. The foreman came out, eyes bleared from lack of sleep.

From somewhere beyond the sheds Lai heard the creak of the treadmills; the morning shift was already at work.

'I've brought food and drink for the injured.'

'The slaves are not allowed to accept gifts. Understand?'

'Don't you recognise me? I was here with Dr Azhrel last night.'

The foreman peered at him.

'Dr Azhrel came back before dawn. He mentioned no food or drink.'

'It's only fresh bread – and khassafri. It'll nourish them – and they'll recover the sooner.'

'Well . . .' The foreman opened the gate a crack.

Lai made to go in – but the man's arm shot out, barring the entrance with his coiled whip.

'I'll see they get it.'

'Can't I just—'

'Not unless you're with the doctor. Zhudiciar's orders. A special dispensation for Dr Azhrel – no one else. Give the doctor my thanks.'

He took the steaming jug from Lai and the fresh bread. Lai watched him lumber away towards the sheds . . . and wondered whether the slaves would ever receive his gift.

Scents of herbs sweetened the sun-baked air, feathery tamarisk and golden fennel. Half-hidden in creeper was a rusted bell-chain; Lai tugged it and heard the distant clamour of a silver-tongued bell.

He waited in the dusty lane, sun hot on his head. Birds rustled in the creeper, drabbet wrens and squabbling sparrows.

He was just going to leave when he heard footsteps approaching;

the door opened, affording a glimpse of the verdant haven beyond. An elderly woman stood staring suspiciously up at him.

'Is the doctor in?'

'He's been called up to the palace. Torella someone-or-other's been taken ill. Touch of the sun, shouldn't wonder. Is it urgent?'

'I'll call back . . . later.'

The Arkhan stood on his balcony, watching the sun setting behind the distant hills. The breeze that stirred his hair, his clothes, was welcome after the heat of the day. Below, Perysse still shimmered in a haze of heat, a mirage-city, insubstantial as a dream.

Melmeth passed a hand over his eyes. Maybe it was only a trick of the failing light—

He adjusted the folds of his silken robes, squaring his shoulders, bracing himself to face the coming encounter. He had rehearsed in his mind many times what had to be said . . . and yet this dull feeling of dread would not leave the pit of his stomach. He was sure that what he was doing was right, was inevitable, could even be justified as for the good of his people – and yet . . .

'Ophar is here, Lord Arkhan.' Fhedryn's voice was low, discreet; Melmeth was so preoccupied he had not even heard the steward enter the cabinet.

'Show him in. And see we are not disturbed. By anyone.'

Melmeth turned to greet the High Priest of Mithiel. A servitor, busy lighting the lucerna over the Arkhan's desk, hastily extinguished the taper and withdrew, bowing.

'Sit, Ophar. Wine?'

'I do not partake in this sultry weather, zhan.' The High Priest sat down stiffly opposite Melmeth at the desk. In spite of the heat he was wearing his full priestly regalia as though to emphasise the formality of the occasion.

'The reason I called you – to consult you, that is—' Melmeth was already stumbling over his well-prepared words, daunted by the old man's austere manner. 'I – I intend to divorce Clodolë.'

Ophar said nothing.

'You disapprove.'

Ophar considered for a moment or two longer, prolonging Melmeth's torment.

'There are few precedents. One or two of your illustrious ancestors felt obliged – when they tired of their consorts – to accuse them of heinous crimes. The resulting sentence of death enabled them to take a new consort of their choice. But these are legal matters more pertaining to the Haute Zhudiciar than to me—'

'I don't want her to die!' Melmeth cried. 'It's just that I have come to realise that we have nothing in common. We are utterly unsuited.'

'And she is barren.'

'I need an heir, Ophar. I want an heir.'

'But a legitimate heir.'

'Five times Clodolë has conceived, five times she has miscarried. The physicians say she can bear no more children.'

'Mithiel could still bless you both with a child. I hear you have not been near my lady's bedchamber in over a year.'

'Oh. So you are suggesting it's my fault?'

'The lady Clodolë is of one of the oldest Mhaell families in Ar-Khendye. I prepared the astrological charts myself; there was no one more suited to you out of all the eligible brides. Your stars were well-matched.'

'But we are not.'

'You risk angering the other members of her clan if you put her aside. Her dowry brought you the lands to the—'

'Yes, yes, I have thought of all this too.'

'Then why did my lord call me here to ask my opinion – when his mind is already made up?' Ophar asked drily.

'I—' Melmeth raked his fingers back through his hair which felt hot and lank with sweat. 'I wanted your blessing.'

Ophar pursed his lips together.

'As High Priest of Mithiel, I could only bless a second union once your consort elect had made a public profession of her faith in the Temple of the Flame.'

'And if she were not of our faith—'

'Out of the question. She would have to be converted to the Way of the Flame. I would, of course, undertake her instruction myself.'

The High Priest must have heard the rumours, must have guessed his intentions. How could he ask such a sacrifice of Laili? How could he ask her to give up the beliefs which had shaped her, made her the woman he had fallen in love with? For a brief second he was gripped by the desire to take the tyrant's way out, to call his tarkhastars and have the crafty old man put to death. But he was no tyrant – and Ophar knew it. He would have to find another way.

'Very well.' He waved a weary hand in dismissal. Ophar took his hand, kissed the ring of the flame and withdrew a few steps.

'One thing else, lord—'

Melmeth looked up.

'A signature. That is all I need. It will take but a moment of your time.'

'What's this?' Melmeth scanned the document, trying to focus on the looping script, bringing it close to the lucerna. His eyes ached; the letters seemed to blur together in the dim light.

A moonmoth drifted in, drawn to the lucerna, and blundered into the flame.

Melmeth gazed down at the dying creature; its wings were brown and sear as a fallen leaf.

'They were so beautiful. And now they are dying.'

'Dying by the hundred. Your signature, zhan.' Ophar dipped the quill in the ink, placed the pen in Melmeth's fingers.

'But this is a warrant for Dr Azhrel's arrest!' Melmeth threw the pen down, ink spattering the marble desk.

'He is at his arcane practices again. He must be stopped.'

'Your proof, Ophar?'

'I have witnesses. Azhrel has been seen collecting the dead husks of these creatures, brushing the powder from their wings into a jar. He alleges he is making a study of its effects on the human body; he says it cures wounds and infections. But I have proof that here in Myn-Dhiel they are putting the dust to other uses.' Ophar's eyes narrowed accusingly. 'I hear it is much in demand as an aphrodisiac, a narcotic.'

'I will not sign this warrant.' Melmeth pushed the parchment aside.

'The city is half-drowsed on this invidious stuff.'

'If the moths are dying, then why worry? It's over.'

'Is there something the matter with your eyes, my lord?'

'Just weary . . . weary of reading too many documents.'

'Maybe I should call your physicians—'

'Azhrel is my personal physician,' Melmeth said pointedly, 'and my friend. Understand me, Ophar?'

Ophar hesitated a moment – then snatched up the warrant and with the most perfunctory of bows, turned on his heel and left.

Alone. The silence of the empty audience chamber lapped about Melmeth like a cool tide. He rested his head on his hands.

He loved Laili and he knew that she loved him. They deserved to be together. Why was Ophar putting so many obstacles in his way?

For a moment he wondered that if he had signed the warrant,

Ophar might have been prepared to be more flexible.

But how could he sacrifice Azhrel to placate the hierophants? Some compromise would have to be found . . . but what? The needling ache at the back of his eyes was becoming difficult to ignore. Like the insidious whine of an insect it pervaded his consciousness until he could no longer think coherently.

Boskh. Boskh would dull the pain.

His fingers moved across the marble to the dead moth.

What am I doing!

He watched himself, as if from a distance, disgusted at his craving yet unable to stop. A little more, just a little more to deaden the ache . . . The fingers lifted the dry body, tapped the dust onto one palm. The palm was rising, his parched mouth opening to welcome the dust—

Ahh. The dust-grains seemed to melt to snow on his tongue, spreading a cold, white luminescence through his brain. Pain receded into a distant frost haze. His thoughts were clear, lucid as glassy ice.

A white calm enveloped him, a calm of drifting petals on a dark, deep pool . . . Nothing mattered any more . . . All he had to do was lie back in the dark waters and . . . float . . . float away . . .

'Torella? Torella?' The little slavegirl rapped at the door to Sarilla's bedchamber. 'The physician's here to see you.' She rattled the handle vigorously. 'She's locked it, Dr Azhrel.'

'Is there another key?' Azhrel said, frowning.

'I don't know.'

'I was told the Torella was not in her right mind. Why did no one stay with her?'

'The dhamzel Laili stayed until she was called to attend on the Arkhan.'

'Torella!' Azhrel cried, knocking loudly on the door.

There was no reply.

Azhrel took a blade from his leather bag and, after some intricate fiddling, managed to release the door catch and the door swung slowly inwards.

Sarilla, her hair in wild disarray, was standing at the moonlit window, surrounded by a cloud of whitewings. She wore only a thin silk shift.

A starspun shiver of sound tingled through the dark room; Azhrel felt the hairs at the back of his neck lift.

'Torella,' Azhrel said.

She turned to him, smiling serenely. The moths clustered to her breast and shoulders, a heaving cape of white down.

'Do you like my new gown? Do you think Sardion will like it?' She pirouetted unsteadily around, moonmoths crawling from her arms and breast, their wings ragged, all glitter dulled. Some dropped sluggishly to the floor.

'It is charming,' Azhrel said, moving towards her, 'and I would like so much to see you more clearly. Shall I light the lucerna?'

'No! No!' She seized hold of his hands, clutching them, nails digging in. 'No light! It hurts so . . .'

On her bare arms and breast there seemed to be a fine tracery of purpled lines, punctuated by tiny puncture marks freshly dark-stained with blood.

'Then let us move closer to the window . . . turn around for me again. Torella. That's right.'

Humming to herself, she twirled about whilst he strained to see the lines staining her skin more clearly. At length, he caught her by the hand and gently drew one finger up her arm, following the track of the line. She was burning with fever and she winced as he touched her.

'Since when did these appear?'

She did not appear to hear his question. At her feet the dead moths lay, a carpet of pale husks.

'Oh dear,' she cried, sagging suddenly to the floor, sifting the disintegrating moths through her fingers. 'Now what shall I do? There's none left . . . and they're all dead . . .'

Azhrel shut and barred the windows and then lifted Sarilla into a cushioned fauteuil; she weighed hardly more than a child and her translucent skin felt oddly dry, brittle as petalpaper.

'You are not well, Torella. You must rest.'

'All dead . . .' she repeated desolately. He was not certain she knew he was there or had heard a word he had said.

A light tap at the door startled him. A young woman stood in the doorway, shielding a lantern flame with her hand.

'I was told the Torella was sick,' she said. 'I will sit with her.'

'She has a fever. Make sure she drinks this powder with plenty of water.' He snapped the catch on his bag shut. 'Fan her, sponge her with cool water – but above all keep the windows shut. Don't hesitate to send for me if there's anything you're at all concerned—'

'Don't worry, Dr Azhrel. I'll take good care of her.'

As soon as Azhrel had closed the door, Lerillys took her hand from the lantern and the golden light splashed out into the darkened room.

Sarilla hissed with pain.

'No light!'

'I said I would stay with you,' Lerillys said petulantly, 'but in the dark? Am I supposed to do nothing all night?'

'It hurts *so*.'

'And what would make it hurt less?' Lerillys asked.

'You're cruel. You know very well.'

'Ah, but it will cost you, Sarilla dear. What pretty gift will you give me this time?'

'My casket. In – in the red lacquered chest. My black pearls.'

Lerillys found the casket and began to sift the jewels through her fingers.

'I remember seeing an emerald set in gold . . .'

'It was Sardion's last gift to me,' Sarilla said distantly. 'I – I couldn't give it away.'

Lerillys snapped the casket shut; Sarilla flinched at the sound.

'I can get a better price in the city.'

'Not my emerald, Lerillys. Take the amethyst earrings . . .'

'Amethyst doesn't suit me.'

'Take anything you like . . . but leave me Sardion's emerald.'

'Anything?' Lerillys said greedily.

'Just give me the dust.'

Lerillys took a little twist of petal paper from between her breasts.

'Here you are, then.'

Sarilla's fingers jittered as she tried to unwrap the twist.

'Don't spill any, sweet Sarilla.'

Sarilla put one fingertip into the white dust and licked it.

'Are you sure it is pure? It has a strange aftertaste.'

'It is from the Arkhys's own supply.'

Sarilla tipped the contents into her mouth all at once.

'That's better, isn't it?' Lerillys said, softly. She took another slip of petalpaper from her sleeve and left it on the open jewel casket.

'Better,' echoed Sarilla, her eyes closing.

Lai, lost in a haven of dreams, heard a distant blur of voices.

'He said he'd wait for you, doctor. I told him you might be some time.'

'Thank you, Mirali.'

'I wasn't sure what the young gentleman wanted . . .'

'He's a friend.'

'I left your supper in the watercrock to keep it cool—'

'Yes, yes, Mirali . . . now go to bed.'

Click of a doorlatch. Lai opened his eyes, still half-asleep, wondering for a moment where he was.

Azhrel was standing in the doorway, watching him.

'I must have dozed off . . .' Lai pushed the tangle of hair from his eyes, blinking in the dying lucerna light.

'So how can I help you?' Azhrel went over to the lucerna, trimming the charred wick, replenishing the oil until the dying flame suddenly flowered, illumining his face. He seemed preoccupied, remote.

'I wanted to know how they were. Eryl and the others at the dye works. The foreman wouldn't let me in without you.'

'No.' Azhrel sat down and pulled the alquer bottle towards him.

'What's wrong? Has one of them deteriorated? They were all doing so well—'

Azhrel poured himself a glass and offered the bottle to Lai; Lai shook his head.

'Nothing like that.' Azhrel took a long, contemplative mouthful and picked up a sheaf of papers from the desk, flicking through them.

'What, then?'

'Ach, I don't know.' Azhrel took another mouthful. 'Things I've seen tonight. Things I don't begin to understand. Maybe I made a mistake. A grave mistake.'

'What do you mean?' Lai was fully awake by now. 'What kind of mistake?'

'Playing god.'

'You mean using boskh?'

'You'd think I'd have learned by now. There are no miracle cures.'

'But you saw what happened – I saw it too. It works.'

'Yes, it works. But I was wrong. To use my patients to prove a point when I knew so little about it myself.'

'You saved their lives.'

'Does that make me any less contemptible than the overseers who wield the whips? I used them – I experimented upon them.'

'They would have died if you hadn't experimented—'

'Have you read my notes?'

Azhrel pushed the papers across the desk-top to Lai. Lai scanned the lines penned in Azhrel's clear, strong hand.

'"Observations on the use and abuse of the substance known as boskh . . ." You tried the dust on yourself!'

'I'm not entirely unscrupulous. Yes, I experimented on myself first. See?' Azhrel showed Lai his left hand. 'A careless slip of the knife in my laboratory.'

A thin, deep scarline was gouged across the palm below the thumb; the scar tissue bore the same, pearlescent film that Lai had seen form on the injuries in the dye works.

Lai ran his finger along the iridescent scar.

'Healed to perfection. Not a trace of swelling or infection.'

'So why this crisis of conscience?'

'I like to call myself a man of science – but I can't find any explanation for this – premonition.' Azhrel pointed to a glass display case. Looking over his shoulder, Lai saw a series of moonmoth specimens pinned out. 'This sense that something's gone awry . . .'

'Awry?'

'Chrysalis; male, female. See the spiked tip to the ovipositor, curved like a wasp's sting?' He tapped the case with his nail. 'That intrigues me. But no mothgrubs, no caterpillars. It just doesn't add up.'

Where was their mystery now? Dry, decaying shells, pinned to a sheet of card, they seemed no more magical than dead flies found on the sill of a locked room.

'Miracle cures . . . and pernicious addiction. I know there's a connection – but I can't prove it. If only there were time to conduct proper tests. Investigations.'

'I'll help you,' Lai heard himself saying.

'I thought you were waiting for a ship to Ael Lahi.'

'I am. But until it arrives, my time's my own. Tell me what to do.'

'You watch . . . and listen. Any report of moonmoths, go straight to the source and collect any trace of their presence you can find. I'll give you phials, tweezers, all you need. Write down all details in this notebook, no matter how trivial they may seem.'

'And you?'

'Me?' Azhrel yawned. 'I'm going to bed. I've been out since dawn.'

CHAPTER 14

Laili woke in the night, certain she had heard screaming, a woman's screaming, high-pitched, crazed, terrified. She turned to Melmeth – only to find he had left her bed; the place next to her was cold, in spite of the night's warmth. And she had not even noticed him go.

She tried to sleep again but she kept seeing Sarilla's face, her wandering eyes glazed with fever . . .

'I've brought you your morning qaffë, lady.'

'Don't you remember, Sarilla, no more qaffë . . .' Laili turned over sleepily, nose wrinkling in disgust at that distinctive aroma – and then she realised it was not Sarilla standing at her bedside.

'Who are you?' She sat up. 'And where is Sarilla?'

'My name is Lerillys. Sarilla is dead.'

Laili felt the room spinning, twisting about her; she clutched at the bed post, determined she should not faint. If she fainted, Lerillys might guess her secret.

'Dead? But – how? And why was I not called earlier?'

'The physician said it was some kind of pestilence, there have been similar cases in Perysse . . . They've sealed off her chamber.' Lerillys seemed impassive, limpidly untroubled by Sarilla's death. Laili wanted to grab her by her plump white shoulders and shake her.

'Pestilence?' Laili tried to work out how many hours it had been since she saw the Torella, had she touched her, might she have caught the infection from her?

'They're burning the body tonight.'

Poor vain, silly Sarilla. Tears started to Laili's eyes. To die so swiftly, so horribly from this virulent disease.

'Do drink this qaffë, lady, I prepared it myself especially.' Lerillys had such a soft voice, the cooing of a plump white-feathered pigeon.

'I do not take qaffë in this heat,' Laili said carefully, blinking back her tears. 'I brew my own infusions. Perhaps you would like to drink it yourself?'

Lerillys smiled, shaking her head. 'I have already broken my fast. Let me help you dress.'

'I thank you,' Laili said hastily, 'but I need no assistance. You may leave.'

Lerillys did not move. Whoever had sent Lerillys had told her not to take no for an answer. Anyone who helped her dress would see the evidence her clothes so cunningly concealed.

'I have no desire to dress yet,' Laili said, taking up a book, opening it, pretending to lose herself in reading one of the verses. Still she stood there. But now Laili could sense her will had begun to waver.

'I told you,' Laili said, suddenly looking her directly in the eyes. 'You may go.'

One last hesitation; Laili caught the involuntary flicker of fear in her limpid grey eyes. Suddenly she snatched the enamelled bowl, qaffë spilling onto the embroidered sheets and left the bedchamber.

Laili stood taut, unmoving until she heard the outer doors slam shut. Then she sank back on the bed, trembling.

Sarilla was dead. Now there was no one left whom she could trust.

The shutters in the Arkhys's bedchamber were closed to protect the room from the day's sultry heat. A faint breeze stirred the feathers in the fans that two bodyslaves wafted to and fro above the Arkhys's head as she lay listlessly on a couch, eyes half-closed.

Lerillys entered the room.

Clodolë clapped her hands. 'Go!' she said sharply to the body-slaves.

Lerillys waited until they had left the bedchamber.

'Well?' Clodolë demanded.

'Sarilla's servants were right. Four, maybe five months, I would guess,' Lerillys said in a soft, sweet voice.

Clodolë drew in a thin, gasping breath.

'How can you be sure?'

'I can't be sure. But she has the look . . .'

'Lack of exercise.'

'The seamstress's evidence? The dresses altered, the loose robes fitted?'

'Too many cakes and sweetmeats.'

'And she would not drink the qaffë I brought her. It is well known that pregnant women cannot abide the taste of qaffë.'

'Four, five months,' Clodolë repeated tonelessly.

'The child will be born before leaf-fall is over.'

'I can work that out for myself!' Clodolë rose from the couch and went over to the table to pour herself a glass of sherbet. With trembling fingers she prised open the stone on her ring and tipped a white sparkling powder into the glass, then drank the sherbet down in one draught.

'I want to see Ophar,' she said, without turning around.

'The foreign woman was seen at her window, worshipping the moon. Invoking a pagan goddess.' Ophar's bony finger jabbed at Melmeth, sharp as a sacrificial blade. 'Now is it not a strange coincidence, my lord, that these moths arrived the very next night?'

'You're surely not implying that *she*—'

'Sorcery, my lord. Witchcraft. Moonmagic.'

'She's no witch! I know her and I love her. This talk of witchcraft is superstitious nonsense.'

'And they're saying that she has used her powers to beguile you, to ensorcel you, my lord.'

'Who has been spinning you this moonshine?'

'They are serious allegations. Allegations of heresy. As scion of the Undying Flame, it ill behoves you to be seen consorting with unbelievers. With pagans.'

'This is Clodolë, all Clodolë,' Melmeth whispered.

'Consider, my lord. The very fact that you defend her so stubbornly proves how strong her enchantments are.'

'But of course. I must be enchanted!' Melmeth said, his voice harsh with irony. 'Why else would I prefer an Aelahim woman to my own faithful wife?'

'I urge you – make an example of her. Give her to us to be tried.'

Melmeth felt a sudden shimmer of fear for Laili; Ophar was utterly serious in his accusations.

'But what proof have these rumour-mongers furnished against her? Is it a crime to sing at an open window? To play the flute?'

'If my lord is so certain of the woman's innocence . . . then he can hardly object to a routine interrogation.'

'It is out of the question.'

'Her refusal to be examined could be seen as an admission of guilt.'

'I will not permit it!' Melmeth cried, rising to his feet, overturning the chair.

Ophar remained seated, staring obdurately into space.

'So be it.'

Azhrel arrived at the Torella's apartments to find the doors guarded by two of the Tarkhas Zhudiciar.

'No one's allowed in.'

'But I've come to check on the progress of my patient, the Torella.'

'Haven't you heard? She's dead. Died in the night.'

'Dead!' Azhrel said, puzzled. 'Why did no one call for me?'

'They say she caught the pestilence – and took poison to end her agony.'

'Poison? What poison?'

'The death of white crystal. That's what the note said. The note she left.'

'I'd like to see the body.' Azhrel made to enter, one hand reaching for the door-handle.

'Sorry, doctor.' The halberds clicked together, blocking his way. 'Our orders are – no one's allowed in.'

'But I'm her physician, damn it.'

'They're fumigating the apartments now. The body's been taken away. It has to be burned. To stop the spread of infection.'

'So where are her servitors? Who found the body?'

'Some little slavegirl from the kitchens. No one knows where she's gone. Took fright and ran off.'

Azhrel went down to the kitchens; but no, no one had seen the slavegirl since the morning's grim discovery.

'That lazy little runt, Miu? She's no great loss,' said the cook, sniffing scornfully. 'Probably caught with her fingers in my lady's jewel casket.'

Fuming with frustration, Azhrel went hurrying up the kitchen stairs. Miu was the only witness, the only one who could answer his questions.

Someone tugged at the sleeve of his gown. He looked around and saw a little eunuch boy was beckoning him to follow. They climbed up and up, a spiral servants' stair that led to the top of the tower, to the poky garret rooms. In the last and meanest of them all, she lay on a mattress, curled up like a sleeping kitten.

'Miu.' Azhrel knelt beside her, gently touching her arm.

'Mmm . . .' She did not wake. Beside her lay an empty screw of petalpaper. Azhrel picked it up, sniffing it. A faint trace of boskhscent still lingered, though all last traces had been licked from the paper. A little pile of discarded papers lay in the corner of the room.

'How long has she been taking boskh?' demanded Azhrel.

The eunuch boy shook his head, pointing to his mouth. He was mute.

'And how long has she been like this? One hour? Two, three?'

'Mmm . . .' sighed Miu.

'Keep a watch over her. And fetch me if she wakes. You'll find me in Galingal Lane.'

At the dye works the huge slave-manned treadmills were rumbling round, the vats were bubbling, steam billowed across the yard. Lai stood, face pressed to the high iron railing, watching the human machinery in motion.

The Arkendym treated their animals with more care than their slaves. Even Orthandor's watch-hounds were better fed and groomed than the unfortunates condemned to toil in the steamheat and stink of the dye vats until they dropped from exhaustion.

To his dismay he realised that he knew one of the toiling workers. That thin frame shuffling across the courtyard, weighed down by a bundle of indigo leaves, was Eryl.

Lai whistled softly to attract her attention; slowly she raised her drooping head. Sunken eyes stared dully at him – through him, as if he were a phantasm of her imagining. And then he saw a glimmer of recognition light her lustreless eyes. She remembered him.

'Why are you back at work?'

'Your miracle dust healed me. They say I am fit.' He could scarcely hear her voice above the rattle of the treadmills.

'But you need to rest!'

She shrugged and, hefting the basket up onto her hip, continued her slow trudge towards the vats.

A clear, cold rage washed through him, cleansing all other thoughts from his mind. Days had passed since he had made her that promise. He had seen the gleam of hope flicker in her eyes as she recognised him . . . and die away again. And as he knew from his own enslavement, once hope died . . .

He walked around the spiked perimeter walls, looking for a hole in the defences. Armed overseers prowled the perimeters; chained guard dogs protected the boundaries. But skeins of raw silk had to be brought in to be dyed and dyed silk came out again to be taken to the weavers. If he watched and noted the times of the deliveries . . .

A slave dropped a laden basket of skeins; he knelt in the dust to pick them up, knocking them against his thigh to remove the dirt. Some went rolling across the yard close to the iron grille and the slave crept closer to retrieve them.

'Remember me?'

Lai started.

'I am Mirghar, Eryl's brother. You said you would help us.'

'My name's Lai. Lai Dhar.'

'Pretend to shake a stone from your shoe. Even now they are watching.'

'If I brought you weapons . . .' Lai shook his shoe vigorously.

'Food, first. We are too weak to fight. And these shackles . . .' He pointed to his ankles and wrists. 'You can't get far with these.'

'Food. Then knives. You can pick the locks with knives—'

'Hey there!' A whip cracked across the dust, sending up a little puff of dirt. Lai looked up and saw one of the overseers hurrying towards him. 'No talking to the slaves.'

Mirghar snatched up his basket but not before the overseer had caught him a crack across his raw-scarred shoulders with the lash.

'And that's for clumsiness.'

'There was no need!' Lai cried, facing the overseer through the bars.

'Relative of yours, is he?'

'The man's exhausted – no wonder he's clumsy.'

'Are you trying to tell me my job?' The overseer came towards Lai, tapping the whip-handle menacingly against his palm. 'Why . . . wait a moment. That ginger hair. I know you. You've been here before.'

'And what of it?' Lai spat back.

'Looks suspicious to me.' The overseer jabbed his whip at Lai through the bars. 'You hanging around here, talking to the brand-slaves . . .'

'Ah, Lai, there you are.'

The strong dark voice startled Lai. Azhrel came striding along towards him, his leathern bag in one hand.

'Anything the matter?' he asked the overseer briskly.

'You know this young man, doctor?'

'Know him? He's my new assistant. I'd arranged to meet him after I'd seen my morning patients . . . but I was late. Come, Lai, have you bought that red ginseng from the herbalists that I asked for?'

153

Lai stared at Azhrel in amazement.

'Why didn't you say you were Dr Azhrel's assistant?' growled the overseer.

'He's foreign . . . still has a few difficulties with the language.' Azhrel took Lai by the arm and started to lead him away. 'Must hurry – patients to be seen, physic to be prepared—'

Once they were out of sight of the dye works, Lai pulled his arm free from Azhrel's grip.

'I spoke with Mirghar, Eryl's brother. If I can smuggle weapons into the works—'

Azhrel stopped dead.

'Weapons!' He whirled around to face Lai. 'What the hell d'you think you're playing at?'

'Playing! Is this a game? They're suffering. Their lives are a living hell.'

'And you think nothing's being done?'

'Nothing's changed. Nothing's been achieved.'

'Oh, and you are going to change things? All by yourself?'

'Someone has to,' Lai said defiantly.

'Fine! Very heroic!' Azhrel walked off down the street. Lai went after him.

'Better to try than let things continue as they are.'

'You'll be crushed underfoot, destroyed. Who are you, one man, to stand alone against the might of the Arkendym empire? This city was built on slave labour, made rich by slave labour.'

'I can't just stand by and watch. I have to do something—'

'And who will you have helped? You'll find yourself back in the donjon – and there's no second reprieve from the Zhudiciar's justice. You've seen the bodies hanging from the spikes. Carrion-fodder.'

A flock of pigeons drinking and bathing at a water-trough took to the air, startled by the raised voices.

'I never thought to hear *you* saying that. To hear you sound so defeated.'

'You would have released a horde of convicted criminals into the streets?'

'Most of them are political prisoners, people who dared to speak out against the Arkhan, and you know that full well, Arlan. The violent criminals are trained for the arena.'

'You know that, I know that, but the people of Perysse believe otherwise. And if you set the brandslaves free, the people will raise the cry of slave-riots! They'll send out the Tarkhas Zhudiciar and, "to keep the city safe", there'll be a massacre.'

They had come to a halt in the middle of a lane.

'You believe that, don't you? That's what they want you to believe. And that way, nothing ever changes. You're condoning the system. You're just as bad as they are!'

'Maybe I am. But I won't see you throwing your life away needlessly – and scores of other innocent lives in the process. How can you help Eryl and her fellow slaves when you're put to the question by the Zhudiciar's Torquistar in the donjon? How can you help them when you're left to die on the spikes? Believe me, it's a slow death, Lai. It was devised to be slow. Excruciatingly slow.'

'And your way is better? Do nothing – or little better than nothing? Prolong their lives, prolong the living hell with a little food here, a little medicine there . . .'

'Is that all you think I do?' Azhrel's eyes blazed, dark fire in his ruined face. Lai saw he had gone too far this time – but he didn't care, he was in a mad, fighting frenzy of anger. '*Djhë*, Lai, if you knew how close you'd come to spoiling it all, spoiling everything I've been working for all these years—'

'You never told me,' Lai said defensively.

'I couldn't risk telling you. Not yet. You were too close to the court. And I had to know I could trust you. Besides, to know too much would have endangered you.'

'And you couldn't trust me?' Lai cried.

'The time wasn't right. It's not right even now. But he's beginning to listen.'

'He?'

'Melmeth. It's the only way things will ever change . . . when the Arkhan tells his people he wants it so. He's had to live in the shadow of his father for too long. And only now is he beginning to emerge into the light, to question the old ways.'

'Can't you trust me now?'

'Maybe.'

'There are others?'

Azhrel nodded. 'No names,' he said, glancing over his shoulder as if fearing he might be overheard.

'Can't you let me in on this?'

'It's risky. You're so easily recognised.' Azhrel gently tugged a lock of Lai's bright hair. 'And they're already suspicious.'

'I'll cut my hair, dye it if need be—'

'That,' Azhrel said with the trace of a smile, 'would be a pity.'

Lerillys came running in to Melmeth's study, her plump bosom heaving in distress.

'Don't you ever knock, dhamzel?'

'Lord Arkhan, my mistress is asking to see you.'

'Asking?' This was unlike Clodolë; she usually expressed her wishes in a more forthright way.

'She is sick, very sick. Didn't you know, lord? I am so worried about her.'

'And what form does this sickness take?' Melmeth had heard stories like these before; Clodolë's 'sicknesses' were often a cry for attention, a way to attract his notice.

'She is listless, weak, she just lies in the darkness.'

'You have, of course, brought the physician to her—'

'She will see no one, lord, she will let no one near her, not even me. And she cannot bear bright light – either of sun or lucerna. It is just as it was with the Torella Sarilla – before she lost her reason. I fear – I fear—' Lerillys dabbed at her brimming eyes with a lacy kerchief.

'What do you fear?' Melmeth demanded.

'That she is dying, lord. Please go to her. Don't turn your back on her now.'

Clodolë dying? Another exaggeration, no doubt. But Melmeth felt a slight pang of conscience. He had treated her badly . . . but hadn't she provoked him, taunting him with stories of her lovers?

Melmeth slipped unannounced into the Arkhys's apartment. Several of Clodolë's dhamzels were lolling around on cushions in an outer chamber, dipping berries into spiced sugar and gossiping as they ate the ripe fruit. They seemed little troubled by their mistress's sickness. He glimpsed their juice-stained mouths, glimpsed them licking the tips of their fingers and laughing. Or was it merely sugar? The white powder gave off an unnatural sparkle and the chamber smelt deliciously sweet, sweet as boskh . . .

Once he would have lingered to watch, tantalised by their laughter, their languorous gestures . . . Now he moved on unseen, a ghost haunting his own palace, silently entering Clodolë's bedchamber.

The balcony doors were open to the warm night; a light breeze stirred the swathes of summer muslin that were draped around the Arkhys's bed.

156

She lay unmoving, beneath the drifting gauzes, her tawny hair tumbled about her bare shoulders. As he drew closer he saw how pale she looked, pale as the ivory petals of funerary lilies.

Once on a distant moonlit night he had approached this bed, a bridegroom of eighteen summers treading a carpet of rose petals, parting the gauzes to greet his bride. He could still remember how he had felt, that trembling sensation of exhilaration and apprehension, how his hand had risen to draw back the curtain—

'Clodolë,' he said.

She seemed not to hear him. Suppose what Lerillys had said was true—

He took her slender wrist, feeling for a pulse.

'You came,' she said, her eyes opening. 'So maybe you do still care for me . . . just a little . . .'

He tried to step back but her arms were around him, clinging to him.

'You tricked me! They told me you were sick.'

'Don't be angry with me. Please.'

'What do you want, Clodolë?'

'You. You, Melmeth.'

Dizzying spicescent of her hair, her breath. Boskh. The very scent of it made him hungry for more.

'Irresistible,' she whispered. 'It's irresistible.. Can't you taste it in the air?'

White snowpetals drifting on the night breeze, falling incense flowers, paler than moonlight . . .

Moonmoths came floating in through the open windows and encircled her in a halo of white wingbeats.

Clodolë shook out her hair and the moths fluttered to settle amongst the loose tumble of dark gold, exotic, furred whiteflowers adorning her head like a bridal wreath.

'Twelve years ago . . .' Her dark-filmed eyes were radiant, her full red mouth smiling, ecstatic. 'Remember?'

His lips opened, hoarse sounds struggled to become words. He stood mesmerised, as though his feet had merged with the marble floor, unable to move away.

The moths rose from her hair in a puff of sparkling dust, the spiced fragrance bewitching his senses as they fluttered overhead, emitting their eerie twittering calls.

The dust was clogging his eyes, his nostrils, his mouth, he could not help but breathe it in and the sparkling dust-granules fizzed acid-sweet. The air burned dazzling white, searing his skull; he gasped, staggering, finding Clodolë's arms wound about him.

'Say you still want me, Melmeth. Say it. Say it.' Her voice, rich as the purpled evening sky, trickled like dark wine into his senses as her full grapesoft lips nuzzled his cheek.

Knees buckling, he was borne back down onto the bed, ensnared in her arms, her cloudy gauzes, her writhing hair.

Boskh-tranced, his senses slid drunkenly askew.

White, all white, white of rushing clouds . . .

'We can start again. Maybe the boskh has cured me . . . maybe I can carry a child . . . at least we can try again, Melmeth, we should try again, Ophar says so—'

'Wait.' His hands caught hold of hers, gripped, pushed her away from him. He had not noticed till then how huge and dark her eyes had become; they dominated her pale face. 'Can't you understand, Clodolë? It's not just the question of a child. It's us. It was never right. We were ill-matched from the start.'

'How can you say that when you know I love you?'

'You don't love me,' he said bitterly. 'You don't even know me.'

Child-bride, consort, Arkhys – but not lover. Never lover. She had touched the animal lurking within him – but not the soul. There was so much of him that she did not know, had never even troubled herself to know. There was so much he could have given her in return. And would have given, willingly . . .

Now he saw the futility of trying to change the way it was between them.

In the darkness she began to speak in a dull monotone.

'The boskh is the only thing that makes me feel alive, truly alive. Everything else is grey without you. Colourless. Pointless.' Her hands dropped into her lap; moths scattered wildly into the air. 'Empty.'

He tried not to look at her, hearing the utter despair in her voice, the despair that he knew he could never comfort nor assuage. He began to edge away, one step at a time.

'Come back, Melmeth.' She reached out her arms, imploring. But the panic was rising, a choking floodtide that would drown him and all his hopes.

He ran to the door, stumbling, holding himself up by a chill twist of marble column, running on and on past her astonished dhamzels, making for the gardens.

There he was violently sick. Even when he had stopped retching, grinding stomach cramps doubled him up again, moaning. He rolled in the dew-damp grass until the pain in his belly slowly quietened.

Whisperings in the gloom of the grove, sere voices whispering his name . . . Eyes were watching him from the dank foliage . . .

The night garden was devouring him, clinging webs brushing his cheeks with spiderslime, whirred winged shadows flying into his face—

A warning bell was tolling a dull tocsin somewhere in the ruins of his mind.

She would never be satisfied. And one pathetic little bier after another would fill the locked attic of her mind. Dreams of dead children. Dreams of a dying dynasty.

The fall of the House of Memizhon . . .

CHAPTER 15

At the foot of Laili's bed lay a little carved box of sandalwood; the pungent scent of the rosy wood perfumed the morning air.

Kneeling on the bed, she picked up the box to find a note attached.

'Laili, flame of my heart, wear this for me. Melmeth.'

Had he guessed, then? She had meant to tell him last night but he had been in no mood for talking, he had only wanted to hear her play. And as music always seemed to soothe him, she had played her flute for him, as he desired.

She opened the box. There, nestling against a lining of silk, lay a bracelet of gold, set with a ruby carved in the form of a flame whose blood-dark heart glowed crimson in the morning light.

What did it mean, so rich a gift? He knew she cared little for jewels . . . and yet there was something formal, almost contractual, in the sending of this flame-fashioned stone, the emblem of his House.

Fragments of Sarilla's malicious gossip whispered in her mind, a chill draught, wreathed with bitter pyre-smoke.

She took the bracelet between finger and thumb, easing it from its casing, turning it round to find the catch—

The door opened and Melmeth came in.

'This gift,' Laili stammered, 'it is too precious for me, my lord—'

'Gift?' he said, frowning. 'What gift—'

And then with a cry, he struck it from her hand.

Laili just stood there, amazed, tears starting to her eyes, watching the golden bracelet roll away across the floor. Her wrist throbbed with the force of the blow. He had never struck her before.

'Let it be – don't touch it—' He was breathing hard, moving warily to where the bracelet lay, as if it were some poison-fanged snake about to rear up and strike.

'M–my lord?'

He looked at her, the green of his eyes piercing her like splinters of jade.

'I sent you no gift.'

'But – the note said—'

'What note?'

Trembling, she picked up the card and handed it to him. He glanced at it and then threw it down on the floor.

'A poor imitation of my hand.'

'My lord?'

He took up the fire-tongs from the fireplace and gingerly turned the bracelet over. Then he beckoned her closer.

'But not too close, Laili. Look. On the inside of the bracelet; here.'

A thin barb of gold, darkly discoloured, was concealed beneath the clasp. She would never have noticed it as she pulled the bracelet on her wrist, not until the barb had pierced her skin.

'Poison?'

'Deadly poison. You would have been dead within a few minutes. If I had not come when I came—' He turned from her, his voice choking.

'Who – who wished me dead?' she asked dazedly, although she knew the answer.

'She has overreached herself this time.' He replaced the bracelet in its box and closed the lid.

Laili was still gazing fixedly out onto the distant city hazed in summer heat when he put his arms around her, his hands sliding down to cover her belly.

'Laili, Laili, why didn't you tell me?'

'I was going to, my lord. I wanted to be sure. And then you were so preoccupied with . . . other matters . . .' She was still in a state of shock, uncertain of what she was saying.

'When will the babe be born?'

'I cannot be sure . . . but most likely after the summer's heat has died. When the leaves are falling.'

'A child,' he whispered, resting his head against hers. Suddenly he tensed. 'She will stop at nothing now to try to kill you . . . and our child. Touching in a way, her devotion to me.'

'She is still your consort, my lord,' Laili said stiltedly.

'You cannot stay here. Too many of the servitors are in her pay. I must hide you in a safer place until I have dealt with her.'

'Nowhere is safe now.'

'Don't be afraid. I will protect you. I know of just the place. She will not be able to touch you there.'

161

'Away from you?'

'Only for a little while. I will look after you, Laili.' He kissed the top of her head. 'You . . . and my heir.'

'Make way for the Arkhan, make way, make way—'

Melmeth paused a moment in the hallway, steeling himself for what was to come. The little box was concealed in the folds of his sleeve.

If only there were some other way . . . but the only other way was the one she favoured. And he would not demean himself, he would not stoop to murder. If he was to be remembered, he would be remembered as Melmeth the Just, not Melmeth the wife-murderer.

Now it was too late to turn back. The arrangements were made; the documents had been drawn up. All that remained . . .

The gallery filled with whispering courtiers, many fanning themselves in the oppressive heat with citrus-scented fans of painted silk and feathers. They parted, bowing, as Melmeth appeared, his ceremonial robes of ivory brocade brushing the floor with a sleek silken hiss as he walked to the porphyry throne and sat down. Jhafir came to stand at his right hand, carrying a roll of parchment.

'What does this mean, my lord?' Clodolë came stalking into the chamber, followed by an armed escort. 'I am ordered to appear before you? Not requested, but ordered? Marched here by your tarkhastars, like some common criminal?

'I have a gift for you,' Melmeth said in a quiet voice.

'A – a gift?'

He beckoned her closer.

'Hold out your hand.'

Slowly, questioningly, she extended her graceful white fingers, fingers a court poet had once likened to magnolia petals, Melmeth remembered bitterly. If only things between them could have gone otherwise, if only . . .

He slid the sandalwood box from his sleeve and placed it on her palm, closing the slender fingers around it, feeling them begin to tremble against his own.

'Open it.'

'Here?' Her eyes still defied him. 'In front of the court?'

'I wish it so.'

The audience chamber was silent now, not even a whisper from the upper gallery stirring the air.

Her fingers fumbled with the clasp until the lid sprang open.

'Now try the bracelet on.'

He saw her bite her lip.

'No.'

'The gift does not please you?' he said, frowning.

'I didn't say that . . .'

He rose from the throne and approached her.

'Then try it on.'

'No. I will not.'

'Must I put it on you myself, then?' He reached towards the glint of gold, wondering as he did so whether she would dare him to go so far.

Suddenly she gave a rasping cry and dashed the box to the floor. The bracelet rolled out of its silken nest. As one of the tarkhastars bent to retrieve it, Melmeth shouted, 'No! It's poisoned! Don't touch it!' Turning back to Clodolë, he gripped hold of her by the arm.

'And you knew it was poisoned, didn't you, Clodolë? For this was not my gift to you. This was your gift to the Lady Laili, intended to kill. I even have the accompanying letter you sent, mimicking my hand. Only by the grace of Mithiel did I arrive in time to save her. And this is not the first time, my lady Arkhys, is it? There have been other deaths, other wasting illnesses in my court that the physicians have been unable to explain.'

She stared coldly back at him.

'You have no proof.'

'Jhafir has the letter. He has had the court scribes compare the hand with mine – and yours. There is no doubt that you wrote it. You have become careless of late, Clodolë.'

She still stared at him, silently reproving. After a while she drew in a slow, shuddering breath. 'Oh, you are more cruel than I imagined, Melmeth. Trying me in front of the court – with no means to defend myself. So.' She drew herself up to her full height, chin held high. 'What is my sentence, lord? Death?'

Melmeth glanced at Jhafir. The light in the audience chamber seemed bright, too bright. His eyes stung. No one moved, not even a fan lifted to waft a breath of air through the stifling heat.

'The Lady Clodolë is henceforth banished from the court of Myn-Dhiel to the summer palace at Shandaïra.' Jhafir unfurled the parchment and began to read aloud. '"All contracts between the Lady Clodolë and the Arkhan Melmeth are, of this day, annulled. The Arkhan has made a very generous settlement on the Lady Clodolë on condition that she never returns to the city of Perysse."'

'Banished!' Clodolë hissed.

'The Arkhan gives you the summer palace and all the estates that surround it.' Jhafir rolled up the parchment and handed it to her. 'Exceptionally generous, in the circumstances.'

'You call this generous! Consigned to a living death! Why didn't you have me executed?' Clodolë cried to Melmeth. The parchment fell to the marbled floor. 'Did you think you were being kind, Melmeth? Or were you just too weak-willed to sign the death-warrant?'

Melmeth just looked at her, saying nothing. Her pale features, distorted with contempt, seemed to blur in the painful sunlight. He remembered another day, bright with sunlight, when he had first seen her, a slender girl with eyes as brown as striped bees . . .

'I demand a fair hearing. I demand the right to appeal. I demand—'

'Lady.' Jhafir moved forwards and took hold of her arm. 'Accept what you are offered. The Arkhan is merciful.'

She pulled away from him.

'He is bewitched. By his Aelahim concubine. Look at his eyes – glazed, dull – she is poisoning his mind with love-philtres, binding her to him with witchcraft!'

Melmeth shook his head. At a click of Jhafir's fingers, the tarkhastars moved forwards and surrounded her.

'Take the Lady Clodolë away.'

A curious straggle of onlookers followed the Arkhys's jade-striped palanquin as its bearers made their way down to the river-quay. Street children ran alongside, hopeful maybe that the Arkhys's entourage would fling a few eniths in their direction. The armed escort seemed somewhat excessive for what was said to be a pleasure-trip.

A sultry breeze stirred the half-furled sails of the royal barque and the dusklit riverbank was alive with gnats.

Sombre-robed figures moved amongst the gathering crowd on the quay. Whispered rumours spread. The Arkhys was in disgrace. She no longer pleased the Arkhan. He had divorced her.

'Clodolë!' clamoured the onlookers. 'Clodolë!'

But the blinds of the Arkhys's palanquin remained closed. Clodolë would not show herself to her people.

'If the patient's been dead some while, there's little I can do!' Azhrel said in irritation.

The tarkhastars of the watch looked uneasily at each other; the youngest wiped his mouth as though he had just been sick.

'We think you'd better take a look, doctor. Before we remove the body. In case we need to close off the building.'

They led him to a dilapidated tenement on the edge of the Street Marches.

'If it's plague, we've orders to put the sign on the door and inform the Haute Zhudiciar.'

'And you think it's plague?'

'You're the doctor – you tell us.'

Azhrel began to climb the rickety stairs; as he neared the top, a sickeningly familiar smell surrounded him. He drew a balsam-impregnated handkerchief from his sleeve and clapped it over nose and mouth.

'Right at the top – it's not locked!'

Azhrel pushed the door open.

A boy's body lay in a desolate room, jagged broken panes, a buzz of blowflies over the filthy bed. Swollen tracks under the greying skin, broken pustules of corruption, jagged fleshholes as though the swarming flies had not just laid eggs in the putrefying flesh . . . But something else had already eaten its way through . . .

All that long, gilded day, Laili had waited for Melmeth, starting at the slightest sound, not daring to eat or drink the food that was brought for fear they had been tampered with.

At first she thought the faint fluttering inside her to be no more than the rumblings of her empty stomach . . . Then as they grew more insistent, she laid her hand tentatively on her belly – and felt something stir beneath her fingers.

At what age did a babe quicken in the womb? Was that what she could feel, lithe and vital, kicking inside her? Her child? Melmeth's child?

She longed to take his hand and place it over the taut skin and see as he felt his child move the same, amazed glow warm his eyes she had glimpsed that morning.

The heat of the day grew stifling and she drew the shutters across, their carved slats casting an intricate trellis of shadows and sun on her floor. She began to feel weak for lack of food. She loved the warmth of the sun balming her bare skin, her closed lids . . . If she lay still, she could let her mind drift back to the sun-drowsed sands of Ael Lahi, the cool shadows of the Grove . . .

A hand touched her shoulder.

Laili sat up, blinking dazedly, to see Melmeth standing over her. The room was dim with twilit shadows.

'Come with me.'

'Where are we going?'

'Just come, Laili. Please.'

Sleepily she reached for her silken overgown, felt with her toes for her slippers.

'*Hurry.*'

'What's wrong?'

He took her hand and hurried her out into the antechamber.

'You have heard me speak of Khaldar, my bodyslave, my musician?'

Laili had heard of dark-eyed Khaldar, the eunuch boy with the golden voice. She had also heard Sarilla's sly insinuations.

Sometimes he tires of female company . . .

The apartment doors were open; taking up a lantern, he led her across the threshold and out into the darkened palace.

'There is something wrong with his eyes. If anyone comes near with a light, he screams with pain. I've sent for Dr Azhrel.'

Melmeth stopped before a little door of silvered greywood.

'Then why me?'

'Because you're the only one in Perysse who knows anything about moonmoths.'

He lifted the latch and slowly let the door swing inwards.

'Look,' he whispered, his fingers tightening around hers.

A youth lay motionless on the bed. The window was wide open and a flock of the moonmoths fluttered about the room, crawling all over the boy, a heaving coverlet of white down.

'Khal?' Melmeth said softly, stroking the boy's cheek.

Khal's lids flickered open, his lips moved.

'My lord is . . . too good to me . . .' he murmured.

'Look, Laili,' Melmeth said tremulously, 'they have calmed him. Perhaps it is true, what they are saying, that the dust heals . . . ?'

Laili moved closer to Khal. The creatures were slowly crawling off him, their wings ragged, all glitter dulled. She brushed some away and they dropped sluggishly to the floor, unable to fly. Her fingers were smeared with dust from their decaying, disintegrating wings. Khal groaned, muttered incoherently.

'Can you bring the lantern closer?'

'He cannot bear the light, I told you—'

'Melmeth!' There was something in the urgency of her voice that made him comply. As he held the flame over the boy's slim body, she could see clearly what she had glimpsed in the gloom. Puncture marks. Bruised puncture marks, freshly dark-stained with blood, marring the perfection of Khal's dark skin, on chest, smooth belly and groin – as if he had been stung by a swarm of envenomed bees.

'Sweet Mithiel.' The light flickered as the lantern rattled in Melmeth's shaking hand and he caught hold of her, pulling her back. 'I should never have brought you here. I didn't realise—'

A discreet tap at the door interrupted him. Laili looked up to see a tall man, sombrely dressed in grey physician's robes, in the doorway. For a moment she noticed only the terrible scars pitting his face. And then, hoping he had not seen her staring, she realised he was not the old man she had anticipated; with his broad shoulders and glossy dark hair, she judged him to be close in age to Melmeth.

'Arlan,' Melmeth said. 'What's happening? Look at him. Those marks. What do they mean?'

Azhrel lifted the boy's slender wrist, searching for a pulse.

'He's still breathing. But the pulse is sluggish.'

'He was covered in moonmoths, they were swarming over his body. I've never seen the like before. Have they drained his blood, are they leechmoths, are they—'

'No.' Azhrel picked up one of the dying moths with a pair of tweezers and, screwing up one eye, examined it through his eyeglass. 'Not leeches . . .'

'Then is it a kind of pestilence?'

Azhrel popped the moth into a glass phial and stoppered the lid.

'You attended Sarilla. She could not bear the light near her – did she show any sign of these marks?'

Azhrel bent over Khaldar and with gentle fingers, tried to raise the boy's eyelid. Khaldar screamed.

'I don't understand,' Azhrel murmured, shaking his head. 'Swollen lids, dilated pupils . . . Has he been taking the dust? Ingesting it?'

'Maybe a little,' Melmeth said vaguely. 'He said it gave his voice extra resonance, his songs extra poignancy.'

'Maybe it started with a little.' Azhrel turned the boy's wrist over, pointing out a tracery of incisions, barely noticeable in the dim light. 'And then he found he needed more – and more – to feed the habit.'

'But what does this prove?' Melmeth said with a little laugh. 'There must be hundreds within Myn-Dhiel who have been taking the stuff.'

'Maybe it proves nothing,' Azhrel said, frowning. 'I'll give him a sedative; tincture of black poppy.'

Laili watched the physician measure out a few drops of dark liquid onto a glass medicine pipe and drip them between the boy's parched lips.

'Is there anywhere we can talk undisturbed?'

Melmeth drew aside a tapestry curtain and ushered Laili and Dr Azhrel into the painted chamber beyond. Laili saw the boy's aludh lying where he had left it on the table, one of the strings snapped, awaiting repair.

'This is the Lady Laili, Arlan.'

The courtesy title took her by surprise.

'She – like these moonmoths – comes from Ael Lahi.'

Laili found herself looking into Azhrel's eyes; shrewd, honey-dark and surprisingly warm, they made her forget the harshness of his scarred face.

'You're very like your brother.'

He was smiling at her.

'You've met Lai!'

'He's been assisting me.'

'Lai? Still here in Perysse?' The news confused her; she was sure he had returned to Ael Lahi. What had made him stay?

'Let me get out my journal. You won't mind if I jot down a few facts? Now tell me – do moonmoths usually behave in this way? Do they sting? Or draw blood?'

She shook her head. 'I have never seen anything like this before.'

'What do they feed on?'

'I don't know. The Elders teach the secrets to the newest adepts at the moon ceremony – I and my brother would have been initiated into these secrets had – had—' She faltered, glancing at Melmeth.

'Go on,' he said.

'Had the slavers not destroyed the Grove with fire and captured us.'

'So those who understood the nature of these creatures were killed in this raid?'

'Yes,' Laili said unhappily.

In the adjoining bedchamber Khaldar stirred, moaning under his breath.

'If you want my honest opinion, lord,' Azhrel said, 'I would ban the

168

use of boskh.'

'But only last week you were telling me that it's caused miraculous cures!'

'I was wrong to leap to conclusions. I don't know enough about it. I need to find out more.'

'Ban it! How can I ban it?'

'Send out your tarkhastars to confiscate all supplies and impose severe fines on anyone who does not comply.'

'That could be difficult to enforce.' Laili saw that Melmeth's fingers had begun to twitch. She wondered if he was aware he was doing it.

'I do advise it. It seems a highly volatile substance. Khaldar is not the only case I have seen in the city.'

'How can you be sure there is a link?'

'I can't be sure. But if many more are reported, we'll have an epidemic on our hands—'

Khaldar began to call in a faint, dry voice, 'Water . . . water . . .'

'Someone must stay at his bedside,' Azhrel said. 'I'll leave instructions and physic.'

Melmeth's hand strayed out, began to finger the snapped aludh string, winding it one way, then the other.

'That golden voice. That glorious, golden voice,' he said after a while. He passed a hand over his eyes.

'I'll stay with Khal,' she said.

'You?' He looked at her, blinking away tears. 'No, no. I can't risk it, chaeryn. I shouldn't have brought you here tonight. We know far too little about this affliction . . . and I can't put you – and our child – at risk.'

'I don't understand—'

'I'm going to make arrangements. Trust me, Laili.'

'You're sending me away?'

'A plague-infested city is not the place for a pregnant woman.'

'I want to stay with you. Please don't send me away.'

'And I want you to be safe. When did you say the babe is due?'

'Leaf-fall.'

'Listen.' He took her hand, stroking it with his fingers. 'Clodolë left Myn-Dhiel today. I have divorced her. She has gone to Shandaïra.'

'She's gone?' Everything was moving so fast – too fast for her to assimilate.

'And the only thing that prevents our union is Ophar's insistence that you convert to the way of Mithiel. Now—' He stopped her cry of protest with one finger, gently placed on her lips. 'This is something which will require delicate negotiation. But believe me, Laili, I'm not going to let him come between us.'

She leaned across and kissed him gently. This much she understood. He wanted her. He wanted her enough to have divorced Clodolë. She could only begin to imagine what that decision must have cost him, what risks he had taken to make this commitment to her.

CHAPTER 16

The tarkhastars of the Arkhan's guard threw open the doors of the audience chamber. Lai looked questioningly at his escort.

'You're to go in.'

The audience chamber at Myn-Dhiel was deserted; Lai walked slowly forwards over the marbled tiles, gazing up at the carven columns, jewelled snakes twisting and writhing through the trunks of trees whose gilded branches upheld the painted ceiling.

The porphyry throne was empty.

Painted birds and apes peeped through the branches, bright-eyed and predatory. Lai sensed he was not alone. Gauzes billowed at an open window.

'Out here.'

Melmeth stood on the balcony high above the gardens; from this height the formal knots and groves became intricate patterns on an unfolding carpet of basil and cedar green.

'I hear you have been making plans to leave Ar-Khendye.'

'I won my freedom,' Lai said defensively. 'There was nothing to keep me here in Perysse.'

'Not even your vow of fealty to me?' Melmeth said softly. 'Or was that broken the night you entered Clodolë's bedchamber?'

Lai felt the blood rushing to his cheeks. He bowed his head.

'I wronged you, lord. I – I am sorry for it.'

'You committed an offence against my honour. Against the honour of the House of Memizhon.'

Lai stared at Melmeth. The greenjade eyes looked back, betraying no hint of emotion. It occurred to him that at one snap of Melmeth's fingers, he could be hurled from the balcony to die on the stone terrace far below.

'But I haven't summoned you here to punish you for her indiscretions. No, this concerns you – and your sister.'

'Laili?' Lai's head was reeling.

'A strange sickness has broken out here at Myn-Dhiel. And because your sister is very dear to me I am concerned for her health. I think you know why. So I have been making plans to send her from Perysse. Will you go with her and protect her until it is safe for her to return to court?'

'Where are you sending her?'

'I have written the instructions in this letter.' Melmeth handed Lai a folded paper, his fingers closing around Lai's for a moment as though sealing a bond. 'Even here we may be overheard,' he said quietly. 'There are orders here for Ymarys to accompany you.'

'Ymarys! But I have not seen him for days—'

'My sources inform me that you will most likely find him at the Pleasure House of Ysmodai. That's where he goes when the melancholy fit is upon him.'

Perysse at sunset. One bright star hung low in the twilit sky, a teardrop of crystal. Duskstar.

Lai stopped outside a mansion set apart from the others; a hideous gilded daemon's head leered down at him from the doorway.

Could this be the place? The Pleasure House of Ysmodai, Melmeth had said. Knock three times on the door, the letter instructed, then wait.

The door opened a crack; eyes stared at him from the smoky gloom.

'I am looking for Ymarys,' Lai said. 'Is he here?'

'Zhan Ymarys?' The soft voice betrayed the speaker: a eunuch. 'Please follow me.'

The walls were hung with silks, hot, lascivious colours: burnt ochre, sensuous pomegranate red, lascivious purple, dark as the split flesh of ripe figs.

Smokescent wafted around Lai in the dim, hyacinthine light, lilac and spikenard mixed. Dancers wreathed in and out of the lilac shadows moving slowly, seductively to the beat of a velvet-skinned drum. There were boys in the shadows, beautiful almond-eyed boys watching the customers through the smoke. Lai could detect another scent, more subtle yet strong in spite of the masking incense fumes. His eyes pricked.

'Boskh?' A boy smiled at him with dark-rouged lips, offering an open enamelled box filled with dust.

Boskh. Lai shook his head and turned away although he felt a sudden, desperate craving at the sight of the sparkling powder; the air seemed thick with the opulent perfume of the drug.

He scanned the smoke-clouded room, wondering where Ymarys was amidst the crowd of painted, masked exquisites.

The drum beat more slowly, more seductively as a single dancer wound sinuously in and out of the onlookers, scattering trails of filmy gauze, a moth emerging from its cocoon. His eyes, darker than moonlit pools, seemed mazed with drugs.

It seemed that he had arrived as some arcane erotic masque was being enacted. Was this what he would have been made to do if they had sold him to the brothel? To be made to dance, drugged, naked, before rich Mhaell customers until the highest bidder took him? Lai watched, fascinated yet repelled, as the strong, slender body beneath the scattering gauzes was slowly revealed, the dark skin painted with trails and whorls of sparkling silver, the dancer's pubic hair dyed to match his waist-length serpentine locks in wild streaks of moonwhite. Weirdflutes skirled and as the drumbeats quickened, a beating of wings disturbed the air.

Moonmoths came spiralling lazily down from a high, open casement as the dancer came to rest, a sacrifice sprawled in sensual abandon, head thrown back, star-streaked hair spread about him like flung streamers. Moonmoths settled on his body, his hair, clustering over the silently heaving ribs. A murmur of amazement rippled around the watchers.

And suddenly Lai realised that he was witness to some obscene parody of the moon rituals of the Sacred Grove, designed to stimulate the jaded palates of the Mhaell audience.

He turned away, disgusted.

What could possibly amuse Ymarys in this tasteless pantomime? And where was Ymarys?

He began to move through the slowly swaying revellers. The smell, the taste of the boskh was maddening him, his mouth watered at the memory, his stomach contracted in a pang of longing.

Damn Ymarys! Where was he?

Grotesquely painted faces leered at him through the boskh clouds; someone stroked his hair, his cheek . . . A hand slid up the inside of his thigh . . .

He twisted aside with a curse.

Get out. Must get out of here.

He stumbled away from the dancers . . . And then, only then, did he catch sight in the smoky shadowlight, of a shimmer of pale hair. Ymarys sat slumped in an alcove, a stained dreamweed pipe on the table in front of him and an empty alquer bottle.

'Ymarys. I've been searching everywhere for you!'

Ymarys slowly lifted his head; his hair, usually fresh-washed and scented, fell in lank, greasy strands about his shoulders.

'Lai?' he said muzzily.

'What's the matter with you?'

The silver eyes gazed, glazed and dull, into nothing.

'She's dead.'

'Dead? Who's dead?'

'Sarilla.'

A cry arose from the revellers; glancing back, Lai saw that two of the watchers had joined the dancer and were licking the boskh from his belly and breast, urged on by the other watchers and the orgiastic drumbeats.

'Sarilla!' Fear for Laili knifed through him. 'How – dead?'

'They say she caught the pestilence . . . and took poison. Why didn't she send for me, Lai?'

Pestilence. No wonder Melmeth wanted Laili away from the heat of the city. Suppose it was too late, suppose she had already caught the sickness—

'And now I'm Torellan of her estates in Mynezhil.' Silent laughter shook his body. 'Torellan of some crumbling, deserted kastel and acres upon acres of moorland.' The laughter ceased. 'Yes. She left it all to me. And I said some cruel things to her. Needlessly cruel. Now I shall never have the chance to tell her – to tell her I didn't mean them.'

Lai heard the bitter self-recrimination in Ymarys's whispered words. His hand slid across the table, closing around Ymarys's.

'Burned on the pyre. Ashes and a few charred scraps of bone. Is that all there is, Lai? All that awaits us?'

A shadow appeared behind Ymarys, materialising out of the smoke. Lai blinked, wondering if the insubstantial form were merely drug-induced hallucination.

'Who is your friend, Ymarys? I don't think we've been introduced.'

The shadow took substance, flesh and bone. Dark hair, striped moonwhite, floated about his shoulders. Lai felt fingers, light as gossamer, touching his cheek.

'Lai – meet Jhofiel.'

'The dancer,' Lai said. Jhofiel's floating hair seemed to exude a cloud of boskh; the scent stirred a host of erotic sensations.

'And you are Lai Dhar. Champion of the arena.' Jhofiel smiled at him; with dark, enigmatic eyes, hazed with secrets. 'You saw me dance? I'm flattered.'

Such smokegrey eyes . . . Lai found himself staring into them, mesmerised.

'I – we – have to go—' He heard his voice as if from far away.

'What's the hurry? Stay a little longer.'

Soft fingers touched his hair, his face, his throat. His eyes were closing, he was drifting into a drugdaze . . .

'N–no.' He struggled to his feet. 'Mustn't stay. Come. Ymarys.'

'Come where?' Ymarys said vaguely.

'Arkhan's orders.' Lai caught hold of his arm.

'Can't go. Too . . . too . . .' Ymarys sank back.

'You're coming with me.' Lai grabbed him, pulling him to his feet. 'Fresh air. That's what we need.'

Jhofiel shrugged and drifted away from the alcove. In the boskh-haze no one seemed to care whether they stayed or left.

Out in the street, Ymarys slid down onto a doorstep, a huddle of arms and legs. Lai sat down beside him, his head still swimming.

'Arkhan's orders?' Ymarys said; he began to smoothe out his creased jacket and to fasten his collar in a vain attempt to smarten his appearance. 'I – can't appear before Melmeth looking like this.'

'There's still time,' Lai said. 'We're to report at wakenight.'

Ymarys staggered to his feet, clutching at the doorpost to steady himself.

'I – thought you'd left Perysse. Disappeared. Back to Ael Lahi.'

'Would I have gone without telling you?'

'Yes. It was in your eyes. I don't know what's made you change your mind . . . but it isn't anything I said to you, is it?'

Although it was almost wakenight, a single light was still burning in Azhrel's study. Lai, not daring to disturb the formidable Mirali, went round to the creeper-framed window and tapped on the pane.

Arlan looked up from his papers; his face looked grey and haggard in the lamplight.

'What are you doing trampling on my herb garden at this time of night?' he asked brusquely, opening the window.

'I had to see you. Can I come in a moment?'

Azhrel shrugged. Lai clambered up and over the sill. The desk was strewn with papers, drawings, moonmoth specimens.

'Look – I'm sorry. I won't be able to help you as we'd planned. I have to leave Perysse. For a while. Melmeth's orders.'

'Maybe that's all for the best,' Azhrel said obscurely.

'And what is that supposed to mean?'

'Nothing, nothing . . .' Azhrel dragged his hands over his face, as if trying to wipe away the fatigue.

'You look exhausted. You're doing too much. You really do need an assistant. If only I—'

'You're under Melmeth's orders. And as for exhaustion – it's something one learns to live with in this profession.'

'I won't keep you from your work any longer.'

'Decent of you,' Azhrel murmured, picking up his pen, dipping it into the ink, starting to write again.

Lai swung his leg over the sill.

'Wait. The moonmoths on Ael Lahi,' Azhrel said suddenly. 'You said they came every spring. They mated, laid their eggs, died. *Where* did they lay their eggs?'

Lai turned around, puzzled.

'I don't know. I never really thought about it. Till now. I suppose there was some tree they favoured in the Grove . . .'

'And no one ever picked some little crawling thing off a leaf and said, "Oh look, here's a moonmoth caterpillar"?'

'No.'

'Doesn't that strike you as odd? And yet I'll bet that as a child you collected beetles, you chased butterflies and maybe dropped a caterpillar or two down someone's back . . .'

'The moonmoths were sacred to the Goddess. And as for crawling things . . . we treat them with respect. Some – like the scarlet sandspider – can kill with a single bite. What exactly are you getting at, Arlan?'

'Take no notice. Talking in my sleep, that's all . . .'

'Sleep well,' Lai said softly.

When he reached the little door in the garden wall, Lai looked back. He could still see Azhrel, outlined in shadow against the lamplight, hunched in concentration over his papers.

A sharp, insistent jab startled Laili; the baby was restless tonight, kicking and squirming. Could it sense her anxiety, her fears for the future?

'Hush now,' she whispered, placing one hand over the distended wall of her belly.

A painted panel slid open in the wall; Melmeth came into the bedchamber.

'I have made the arrangements.'

'You're sending me away.'

'Have you ever heard me speak of Langoel?' She heard him give a fleeting sigh as he pronounced the name. 'I spent the happiest years of my childhood there. At a place of study and contemplation. Azhrel was my companion there, my fellow student.'

'Dr Azhrel?'

'The very same. That was before my father had me brought back to Myn-Dhiel, saying that it was no fit education for his only son to be cloistered with mystics and scholars.'

'You didn't want to leave?'

He did not answer her question.

'The house overlooks the sea. I know you'll feel at home there. I have sent word of your coming to my mentor Pherindyn who is Venerable Hearkenor there. They will take good care of you until the plague has run its course and it is safe to return to Perysse.'

'But you—'

He took her hands in his own.

'I will come to join you. I promise, Laili. I would go with you now – only—' She saw him blink tears away; his lids seemed swollen, the intense green beneath filmy, clouded.

'Is there something the matter with your eyes?' she said, concerned.

'Just lack of sleep . . .'

'You must take care of yourself.' She pressed his hands, raising them to her cheek, not wanting to let go.

'I will sleep more easily once I know you and the babe are safe.'

'Is it far to Langoel?'

'Several days' journey by boat and by land.'

'And I must go alone?'

'I have asked your brother to go with you to protect you on the journey. Oh, don't cry, chaeryn, please don't cry.'

'I'm not crying,' she said even though she could feel the tears trickling down her cheeks.

'It will only be for a little while, a very little while. Maybe only a few days. I shall come to you as soon as I can. Trust me, Laili.'

*

The royal barque rocked gently on the broad river in the early morning breeze. Lai and Ymarys, dressed for travel, stood waiting on the landing stage. Melmeth's orders had stipulated they should be here, beyond the Ahrimel Gate, at dawn.

The river marshes stretched away into the distance, a yellow sea of velvet butter-rushes and goldeneye, already resonant with the hum of bees.

'Here they come,' Ymarys said, nudging Lai.

One of the ancient Memizhon tunnels, legacy of more unsettled times, opened out on the river bank beyond the city walls. Now Lai saw the rusty grille opening. The Arkhan came out of the gloom of the tunnel entrance with Laili beside him. Tarkhastars of the Tarkhas Memizhon followed discreetly several paces behind.

The pale morning sky seemed to have leeched all colour from Laili's wan face; she walked slowly, reluctantly, as though unwilling to leave Melmeth's side.

Now Lai saw what he had refused to acknowledge before. It was true; she loved Melmeth.

'Lai.' She acknowledged him with a glance, a brave attempt at a smile.

He found his hands moving out to touch her face in greeting, her wind-tousled hair. Her cheeks were cold, chilled by the breeze off the Yssil.

'Take good care of her, Lai.'

Lai nodded.

'Come soon,' Laili whispered.

Melmeth took her hands in his and, raising them to his lips, kissed them. Choked for words, he turned away to where his tarkhastars stood waiting. Overhead gulls wheeled and soared.

Lai and Ymarys helped Laili up the gangplank onto the deck of the barque.

The sailors began to untie the mooring ropes, the heavy coils slapped onto the deck. The barque shuddered, oars dipped, the drum began to pound a brisk rhythm as she headed out into midstream.

Laili stood at the rail of the barque, looking back as Melmeth and the blue blur of the tarkhastars' uniforms dwindled to a dot . . . and disappeared from sight.

The barque reached the estuary port of Phaeros two days later. The canton of Langoel was another day's sailing – given fair winds and auspicious tides – southwards along the coast. At sundip the following day the barque-maistre set them down on the shore of a little inlet.

Wading birds, their plumage pink in the setting sun, rose off the salt flats in a great flock, wheeling and wheeling again over their heads, giving eerie, plangent cries as they flew across the sands.

Where the birds had risen up in a cloud of wings, Lai saw a long white wall enclosing the silvered domes and towers of the House of Hearkening of Langoel, built on the seashore itself, within perpetual sight and sound of the sea.

'It's miles from anywhere!' Ymarys said in tones of disbelief.

Laili squeezed Lai's hand in hers.

'Doesn't it remind you – just a little – of home?'

Pherindyn, the Venerable Hearkenor, received them in his room, a white-washed cell decorated with patterns of seashells set into the plaster; coral-tinged cockleshells and the whorls of whelks and periwinkles.

'Ah! The Lady Laili.' Pherindyn laid down his gull-quill pen and rose to greet them, looking intently at them over the top of his rimless spectacles. 'You are most welcome. We have been expecting you and your escorts since we received the Arkhan's letter.'

'You are most kind,' Laili said softly.

'As the Arkhan explained to you, this is a house of contemplation and study. Please feel at liberty to go where you will, to read in the library if you wish, or to walk in the gardens. But I must warn you – some of our elder appellants here are devoted to their studies and hate to be disturbed!' Pale blue eyes, light as a summer sky, twinkled benevolently at them from a wrinkled, sun-browned face.

'We make music too, so it may please you to listen to our playing . . . or even join us, if it pleases you.'

'I've brought my flute,' Laili said, looking up at Lai as she spoke, 'though I am sorely out of practice.'

'This news of pestilence in Perysse is most unfortunate. Sultry summers seem to breed disease in the stews of the city. But I'm sure it will die with the summer's heat. Some of our most dedicated students work in the city as physicians and apothecaries. I know they will devote themselves to finding a cure.'

The tide was far out, a glisten of silver on the hazy horizon, when Lai

179

went to walk along the sands next morning. The wet sand oozed beneath his feet, the salty wind tousled his hair.

He closed his eyes, letting the bleached calm of early morning cradle him. Beyond the hazed horizon lay Ael Lahi . . . the white island, the safe haven . . .

'You were going home.' Laili was standing on the edge of the dunes, watching him. 'And now you've had to stay in Ar-Khendye – because of me.'

'There wasn't a ship bound for the Spice Islands for weeks,' he said, shrugging it aside.

She came down the sands and slipped her arm through his, resting her head against his shoulder.

'I'm so glad you're here. I'm so glad we're here together.'

He nodded . . . but his eyes strayed over the top of her head, gazing longingly out towards the distant horizon and beyond . . .

CHAPTER 17

Melmeth stood with Azhrel at Khaldar's bedside. Azhrel drew back the thin sheet covering the boy. The plague marks, the swollen red tracery that covered him from neck to groin, had not faded; if anything they seemed more angry, more inflamed than before.

'Any change, Arlan?' Melmeth asked anxiously.

The doctor shook his head.

'Periods of lucidity . . . then the fever returns and with it, this utter prostration. I begin to fear he may be losing the fight.'

'Mel–meth! Mel–meth!'

Melmeth looked up, puzzled. 'What's that?'

He went to the window, pushing open the rain-speckled glass. Sun suddenly flooded Khaldar's bedchamber, piercingly, wetly bright. Melmeth shut his eyes, turning away from the light, gasping with pain.

'My lord?' Azhrel was at his side, supporting him. 'What's wrong?'

'My – eyes.' He fumbled his way into a chair, averting his face from the light.

'Let me look,' Azhrel tipped Melmeth's head upwards, gazing searchingly into his eyes.

So gentle, Azhrel's supporting hands, they were like a caress. So close, he could feel Azhrel's breath, warm, yet fresh and sweet, on his light-seared eyes . . .

'Well?' Melmeth demanded. Whenever he tried to focus on Azhrel's face, the image slipped and slurred out of focus. It was like peering in through a steamy window on a wet winter's day.

Azhrel slowly took his hands away.

'Have you been taking boskh?'

'Maybe a little . . .'

'How little is "a little"?'

'How can you tell I've been taking it?'

'Sarilla, Khaldar, others in Myn-Dhiel, all presenting with the same

181

symptoms: abnormally enlarged pupils, swelling, sensitivity to light. And all had been ingesting the drug; not a grain or two but considerable amounts.'

'And is there no remedy?'

'I'll put some eyedrops in for you. A tincture I have concocted myself from a prescription in one of old Galendryn's *Journals*; it seems quite efficacious.'

Azhrel took out a dropper and a little phial of translucent liquid from his physic bag.

'These drops sting like nettles – but the pain soon passes.'

The tincture splashed into Melmeth's right eye, then the left and all was fire, bright fire, tears of fire were running down his cheek, he could not blink them away . . .

He gripped the arms of the chair until he felt his knuckle bones would burst through his skin.

'Melmeth! Melmeth!' The chanting grew louder.

Melmeth came through the fire, blinking away the last molten tears.

'It's worse. Everything's blurred again.'

'Patience, zhan, patience. Give it time to work.'

'You must tell me the truth.' There was an acrid taste in his mouth. 'Am I losing my sight?'

'It's hard to tell.' Azhrel stoppered the little phial tightly. 'I haven't seen enough cases yet to prove any pattern . . .'

'The *truth*, Arlan.'

'The truth,' Azhrel said heavily, 'is that you could lose your sight at any time. The deterioration is irreversible. And exposure to intense light – even strong sunlight – and the damage will be permanent.'

Melmeth, numbed, sat staring blankly into emptiness. Blind. Condemned to walk out of the sun for the rest of his life – or to walk forever in perpetual dark.

'And you must not neglect to apply this tincture. I'll make you up a bottle, drops to be administered four times a—'

'*Mel-meth!*'

'What is that noise?'

'My lord!' Jhafir came hurrying into the chamber. 'Are the rumours true? Are you planning to leave the city?'

Melmeth swallowed. Had he been naïve enough to think he could slip away to Langoel without anyone commenting?

'Only for a little while.'

'But your people need you. Listen to them calling for you. For

Mithiel's sake, do not leave Perysse until this crisis is past. Have you heard what they are saying in the city? They are saying that this plague is the god's punishment on you. That you should never have sent Clodolë away.'

'And is that what you believe, Jhafir?'

'I believe there is a real risk of riots unless we can prove to the people that we are doing all we can to halt the spread of the sickness.'

'But there is always plague in the city in summer.'

'This plague is unlike any other. They are afraid.'

'Then let me speak to them. Let me reassure them.'

'We can't just "speak" to them, my lord Arkhan. We have to do something.'

'What are the opinions of the physicians? Azhrel?'

'You know my opinion already. Ban the use of boskh. And enforce the ban rigorously.'

Melmeth looked back at Jhafir.

'Edicts, then,' he heard himself saying. 'See to it, Jhafir.'

Without moonlight Melmeth might have lost his way in the dark groves of the gardens, but the moon hung over the night-tranced city, a pale globe, mothwhite in the starry sky.

At the top of the hill, Melmeth paused. Perysse lay far below him, a maze of winding alleys, tottering chimneys and ramshackle roofs. He was so high, he felt he could run to the edge and take wing, soaring like a hawk above the dreaming city.

Laili. If only you were still here. If only we could face this together, if only . . .

He made his way to Sulirrian's gazebo. Here he would not be disturbed.

With shaking fingers he removed the nacred pill-box from his sleeve. Azhrel had warned him of the risks. But what else could he do? He was so sure that the answer lay within this pearl-inlaid box.

It had to be done.

'In the dust-trance,' Laili had said, 'the Goddess speaks to the Elders.'

He prised open the lid and saw the grains of precious boskh shimmering in the moonlight.

'Goddess of the Grove. Speak to me.' If Ophar heard him commit this sacrilege . . . 'Tell me what I must do. Guide me.'

Sparkling granules fizzed acid-sweet on his tongue. The air burned dazzling white, searing his skull; he gasped aloud.

Power went coursing through his veins; he shuddered, then stood tall, feeling the healing fire scorching his fingertips. Looking at his hands he saw – he was *sure* he saw – a whiteglow radiating from his fingers.

'Sweet Goddess,' he whispered, dropping to his knees. 'Is this your doing?' He waited for her answer. But the night was silent . . . and in the silence he heard only the rushing pulse of his own blood.

He tipped the last grains of boskh into his mouth. *Ahh . . .* that pure, white burn . . . A serene, dreaming calm lapped over him, lulled him like a pale drifttide . . . It was true, it must be so. She had given this gift to him, this gift of healing. She had shown him his purpose in life, his true path. At last his life had meaning. Relevance.

'Yes,' he said, quietly exultant. 'I will do it. I will heal them all, the sick, the plague-ridden. Let them come to me. To Melmeth the Healer.'

No one seemed to be about in the Torella's apartments – no one challenged Azhrel as he slipped in and began to climb the attic stair. Where had they all gone?

Miu lay without moving, beneath fine drifts of long hair, so fair it seemed almost white. He was sure – certain sure – that the last time he had seen her, her hair had still been plain mouse-brown. He reached for her wrist – and saw that her eyes were open.

'Miu – can you hear me?' he asked.

There was not even a tremor of response. Her pulse, her breathing, everything had slowed – she slept the deep sleep of the narcoleptic, of the comatose.

He sat down beside her and took out his notebook, scribbling in his observations with a stump of pencil, noting the day, the time.

What exactly am I witnessing here? When she wakes – if she wakes – what will emerge from this soft-spun chrysalis of hair? And has this bizarre transformation been precipitated by ingestion of the dust?

Fhedryn draped the heavy ceremonial robes over Melmeth's shoulders and secured them with chains of antique gold. Bodyslaves combed his hair about his shoulders and sprinkled it with cool rose-scented water. He let them minister to him, scarcely noticing what they did.

'Ophar is here, my lord Arkhan, and—' Fhedryn began to announce but the High Priest swept past him, sending the bodyslaves scurrying out of the chamber.

'What is this I hear, my lord? A healing?'

'You said I should not neglect my people.' Melmeth smiled at Ophar.

'But you have never conducted a healing in your life! Is it wise that you should start now – and at such a volatile time?'

'I can think of no better time,' Melmeth said serenely.

'But you have not fasted, you have not been ritually cleansed in the hot springs, you have not spent the night-shrine vigil customary in these matters.'

'These are not necessary, Ophar.'

'Are you feverish, my lord?' Ophar drew nearer and stared up into his face. 'Your eyes . . . seem to glitter. Let me postpone this ceremony until you are more . . . yourself.'

'It must be now!' Melmeth said with sudden fury.

'Now? Why is now such an auspicious moment?'

Silvervoice . . .

Melmeth put one hand to his brow; for a moment the room seemed to sway giddily about him.

'The power still burns in my blood. I can feel it, tingling at the tips of my fingers. You said that you could see the glitter in my eyes.'

'And if the healing should fail?' Ophar said gratingly.

The silvery boskh-voice sang on in Melmeth's ears, lulling away all worries, all doubts.

'I will not fail,' he said dreamily.

They must have forgotten her. From the thick dust still drifting across the stairs and the floor of the garret, it was obvious to Azhrel that he was the only person who had been here. All for the best, maybe . . .

'Miu,' he said softly.

This time he was certain he saw her stir. He drew closer, his heart pounding with sudden excitement. If she reacted to the sound of his voice, she must be close to waking. And when she awoke, he would be the first to witness, the first to record this extraordinary metamorphosis.

Moonlight powdered the dusty threads of her transparent shroud. She seemed so weirdly beautiful, lying there swathed in the white filaments of her hair. From the skinny body of a drab little kitchen slave, a new creature was emerging, white, virginal – Changed.

*

185

The arena was full. But no raucous shouts bruised the mild summer night; no rowdy apprentices of rival clans hurled cheerful abuse at each other. Instead a silent, subdued crowd had filed in to fill the tiered seats. Some had carried their sick on improvised stretchers or in palanquins. The Zhudiciar had insisted that medicinal herbs be burnt to cleanse the air from the taint of infection; blue drifts of aromatic smoke wafted across the sand.

The moon rose high in the sky. Melmeth watched from the dais as his tarkhastars carefully carried Khaldar to a shaded plinth.

'You're certain you wish to continue with this?' Jhafir murmured.

'Yes,' said Melmeth. 'Oh yes.' He clicked open the stone of his ruby ring and tipped the last of the boskh into his palm. Ahh . . . the silversweet scent of it, clear as moonwater . . .

Swiftly he tipped it onto his tongue and closed his eyes, shuddering as the drug melted into starcrystals of sensation in his mouth. Flares of whitelight burst against his closed lids.

'My lord,' came Jhafir's voice as if from far away, 'they are ready for you.'

'Lord Melmeth . . . help us, Lord Melmeth, help us . . .'

They were calling his name. They needed him. And he would go to them and he would heal them.

Melmeth felt himself moving forwards across the sand, cloaked in a pale aura of moonshine. He passed by the sick where they lay at the rim of the arena, gliding his hand across their pallid brows, touching their trembling fingers as they tugged avidly at his sleeves, his hem. And it seemed as if Her phosphorescent light glimmered on his fingertips, passing through him into their fevered bodies. Such a transcendent sense of peace enwreathed him, such a pale, drifting calm . . . he was the vessel of the Goddess, he was Her representative, through him Her healing light radiated.

Everywhere he noticed the same, strange tracery on the plague victims' skins that Khaldar bore, the same raised, discoloured lines and ridges . . .

Beside him, Jhafir drew his scarf up over his mouth and nostrils, muttering irritably about danger of infection.

But it didn't matter. He was safe. The boskh sparkled in his bloodstream, protecting him. Couldn't they see how it glowed on the tips of his fingers? Didn't they know he was Her Chosen One?

He reached the central plinth where Khaldar lay and, placing his hands gently on the boy's forehead, gazed up into the heavens, full into the bright face of the full moon.

So bright the Goddess's face that he could not look at Her; Her silver stare burned through his clutched hands, silverfire penetrating his clenched lids, searing away his sight—

Melmeth gave a cry, throwing up his arms to protect his eyes. He dropped to his knees in the sand.

'Is this part of the performance?' Jhafir asked wryly. And then when the Arkhan did not get up, he started forwards to help him.

'Dark,' Melmeth whispered. 'All dark.'

'My lord?'

'Jhafir—' Melmeth's hands scrabbled at his arm, clutching at him as he tried to struggle to his feet. 'Jhafir – I can't see—'

Jhafir swore under his breath.

'Azhrel! Call for Dr Azhrel!'

A murmur of concern began amongst the nearest bystanders.

'My lord, please take my arm,' Jhafir said softly. 'Please try to act as if nothing were wrong.'

'What's the matter with his eyes?' demanded a woman.

Jhafir attempted to lead Melmeth away but after a faltering step or two, Melmeth sagged to his knees again.

'Please, zhan,' Jhafir begged, between gritted teeth. Two of the Tarkhas Memizhon came running up to help him. They dragged Melmeth to his feet, supporting him between them.

'He's blind!' someone screamed. 'Look at his eyes!'

'Blind,' Melmeth repeated in a mazed voice. 'Blind.'

The word went rippling around the hitherto silent crowd. Some began to heckle; cries of 'Fake!' rang out above the rising din.

'Get him out of here!' said Jhafir, backing towards Sarafin's Gate. 'Into the tunnels. Rho Jhan!'

Rho Jhan came hurrying across the sand, crimson-clad tarkhastars following close on his heels.

'Calm them down, for Mithiel's sake!' Jhafir said. 'Or we'll have a full-scale riot on our hands! And where's Dr Azhrel when he's needed?'

'Follow me,' Ophar said briskly to the tarkhastars supporting the Arkhan.

'People of Perysse!' Jhafir raised his arms to the crowd. 'Your Arkhan has been overcome by the emotion of the situation—'

A loud jeer of derision drowned his words and a bottle crashed into the sand a handspan from where he was standing, staining his crimson robes with splatters of liquid. Other missiles followed, a hail of stones and medicine bottles.

'Go with the Arkhan!' Rho Jhan hurried the Zhudiciar towards Sarafin's Gate, shielding him with his drawn blade.

The tarkhastars heaved shut the fang-toothed gate; the clang of iron resonated like thunder behind them. At a wave of Rho Jhan's hand more tarkhastars came running in, wielding pikes and halberds. A bottle hurled into the arena hit one tarkhastar; he staggered and went down with a bloodied head.

The shouting could still be heard within the musty damp of the Memizhon tunnels. Ophar and Jhafir stopped for breath; Melmeth slid slowly downwards until his forehead rested against his buckled knees.

'Rho Jhan and his men will contain them,' Jhafir said, distractedly dabbing at the stains on his robes. He did not sound over-confident.

'And if they decide to go howling up the hill to Myn-Dhiel?'

Jhafir bent down beside Melmeth.

'My lord, you've heard what Ophar says. You must give the word to defend the citadel. Call out the Tarkhas Memizhon.'

Melmeth let out a whimper.

'A show of strength will soon cool these hot tempers.'

Melmeth reluctantly nodded his head.

'Go on ahead.' Jhafir signalled with one hand to the tarkhastars; they sped away into the darkness of the tunnel.

'And now you, my lord. Can you walk?'

'I – c – can't see, Ophar.'

'Rest a while longer. But you cannot stay here, my lord.'

Jhafir drew Ophar away from the Arkhan and whispered in his ear.

'Is he acting rationally – or under the influence of that pernicious drug? Next thing he'll be trying to fly from the top of the Tower of Perpetuity.'

'We must hide him somewhere safe until the situation in the city is less volatile. Not Myn-Dhiel – that's the first place they'll go to look for him.'

'And where else do you suggest? With a riot raging in the streets?'

'We can reach the mausoleum by these tunnels. I know the way. Who would think to look for him there?'

'The mausoleum? The charnel house?' Jhafir said coldly.

'Your concern is to subdue the riot. My concern is the Arkhan's safety – both physical and spiritual.' Ophar's eyes glittered, polished jet in the gloom. 'Leave him with me.'

Ophar stood on the battlements of the citadel, Rho Jhan at his side. Small fires still smouldered in the city, twists of thick smoke blackening the clear sky like windblown streamers. Beneath them, the tarkhastars of both clans were clearing away bodies, flinging them onto carts.

'Everything is under control,' Rho Jhan said, saluting the High Priest.

'We rely on you and your men to keep everything under control,' Ophar said smoothly.

'The Zhudiciar has ordered the imposition of a strict curfew. All exemptions must carry a signed permit.'

'Good, good. Things must not be allowed to get out of hand again.'

'The Haute Zhudiciar asked me to deliver this document to you. He asks you to do with it whatever you will.'

Ophar opened the parchment and scanned it.

I, Melmeth, renounce all the dissolute and corrupt practices of my forefathers. I authorise Jhafir, Haute Zhudiciar, to free all brand-slaves and end the inhuman practice of gelding malefactors. Slave-owners to be compensated for their losses from the royal coffers. The slave-market on the quay is to be closed down and all traffic in human flesh is to cease.

'Mad,' he muttered under his breath. 'Utterly mad.'

A charcoal brazier smouldered close by; he thrust the parchment into the glowing embers and watched it slowly curl up and char to ashes.

'And the Arkhan?' Rho Jhan asked.

'Is resting. I and my priests will be caring for him until his health is restored. But I want you to bear a message for me. A message of vital importance. The Haute Zhudiciar will release you from your duties.'

'And where am I to take this message?'

'To the summer palace at Shandaïra. To the Lady Clodolë.'

Clodolë paused on the upper terrace of the summer palace, her hands resting on the stone balustrade, to gaze out over twilit water gardens. Night-flowering waterlilies, pale ninufars, opened their scented petals to the stars. White peacocks wandered like ghosts amongst the dark foliage, their sharp cries echoing forlornly through the empty

189

groves. Beyond the distant hills lay the steep gorge of Shandaïra . . . and beyond that the river plain crowned by the steep hills and escarpments where the Arkhans of the House of Memizhon had built their citadel.

Shandaïra had been built centuries ago as a pleasure palace, a retreat from the dusty summer's heat of the plains. Shaded by groves of oranges, bays and cypresses, lulled by the sound of running waters, the empty terraces of Shandaïra had once echoed to the brilliant laughter of courtiers. Now Clodolë, a ghost of the Arkhys of Ar-Khendye, haunted the terraces by night, shunning the heat of the day, remembering other starlit nights when she had been the centre of an attentive circle of admirers . . .

All day she lay listlessly in her gauze-draped bed, neither reading nor sleeping, drinking little, eating less, taking a few grains of her dwindling supply of boskh to dull the needling ache behind her eyes. At sunset she rose, dressed and went out to tread the empty garden paths alone whilst her little entourage watched from the palace, whispering and worrying.

But that misty evening a sound disturbed the soft burblings of the frogs and krikris in the reeds.

Horses' hoofs. A distant commotion of voices within the palace – then footsteps clattering over marble steps. She looked around.

'My lady Arkhys!' A man was hurrying towards her, a man covered with the dust and dirt of travel. She recognised him.

'Rho? Rho, is it really you?'

Bowing his shaven head, Rho Jhan handed her a paper weighted with the seal of the Haute Zhudiciar. She began to open it – then looked at him, her eyes wide and dark with sudden apprehension.

'Rho – what is this?'

'Open it!'

She tore the paper open and, in the dying light, read what Jhafir had written.

A little huddle of her retainers had gathered anxiously on the steps, watching for her reaction.

She clutched the paper to her breast. Her eyes closed a moment. Then, in a strong, triumphant voice, she cried out, 'At last!'

'My lady?' Lerillys ventured down the steps towards her.

'Pack at once! We are returning to Myn-Dhiel.'

CHAPTER 18

Petalfall from the white-bloomed oleanders, soft as snow, on her uptilted face, everywhere falling petals . . .

And through the softswirl of white, Laili sees a figure coming slowly, stumblingly towards her, glint of redgold hair in the sweet snowfall.

'Melmeth?'

'Laili! Where are you? I – I can't see you—'

His arms are outstretched, blindly feeling his way through the white petalfall. She and Lai played this game as children.

'Here. I'm here.' Laughing, she reaches out to him through the wind-swirled blossom.

Petals brush against her face, vibrate against her cheek. She brushes them away but they settle again.

Not petals. Mothwings. Fluttering mothwings, drifting to settle on his face like a mask of pale feathers.

'My eyes, Laili—'

He tears at the crawling moths with his hands.

'My eyes!'

This is no game.

She plucks at the powdery, clinging creatures, trying to pick them from his face, pulling off dusty wings, furred antennae—

Beneath the living mothwing mask, the jade of his half-eaten eyes is filmed with dust.

'Blind. I am blind, Laili . . .'

Dawnlight woke her. She lay still, trying to calm the dreamfear beating like a trapped bird in her breast.

Ill omen to dream such terrors.

Every morning Laili went to the highest point of the house, laboriously climbing the stair that wound to the ironwork balcony encircling the silvered dome. There she would stand gazing out across the empty sea-road, her hair streaming about her face like rusted ribbons, shading her eyes against the dazzle of the sun, patiently searching the horizon . . .

Lai watched her from a distance.

Only thirteen days had passed since they arrived. But it seemed, in the absence of news from Myn-Dhiel, as if they had been at the house for an eternity, each day passing more slowly than the one before.

What could they do but wait? 'Soon,' Melmeth had said.

Ymarys drew close to Lai, gazing up at Laili as she scanned the empty sands.

'Quite frankly, Lai, I'd assumed we'd be on our way back to the city by now.'

Lai sighed.

'Surely your sister has begun to wonder? It's already two weeks. Doesn't it seem a little strange to you?'

'I'm sure there's a good reason for the delay,' Lai said staunchly.

'Are you?' That now-familiar malicious gleam illumined Ymarys's eyes, lightning over grey water.

Melmeth opened his eyes. Fingers fumbled for the bandages that covered his face, peeling them away—

Still dark.

Greydark against which vague shadows were etched, no more.

He felt the tears well against his swollen lids, felt the wetness spill helplessly down his unshaven cheeks.

In his dreams his sight had been restored. He had been so certain that when he tore away the bandages—

'Is anyone there? Can anyone hear me?'

His voice echoed in the sealed chamber. It sounded hollow; cold with the resonance of stone, cold as a tomb.

'Where am I?'

A confusion of voices whispered in his memory . . .

For your own safety . . . Riots . . . Mausoleum . . .

They had entombed him with his ancestors. They had locked him in a chamber of the mausoleum. For all he knew, they might never return and he would die here, a slow, lingering death in the dark, deprived of food and water . . .

'Let me out!'

A pang convulsed him; he recognised the symptoms now. The griping emptiness, then the terrible craving that drove all other thoughts from his brain.

Boskh.

He dropped to the floor, knees drawn up to his chest, clutching the gnawing pain in.

'Boskh . . . I must have boskh . . .'

Pains griped his belly, blueblack as thunder.

'Please . . . someone . . . anyone . . . help me . . .'

The Razhirrakh lay on his bed in the seastained twilight, his head pillowed on his hands, staring into nothing.

'What's wrong, Ymarys? Are you ill?' Lai, his sleeves rolled up, stood in the doorway. 'You haven't left this room for two days.'

Ymarys managed a slight shrug of the shoulder.

'What, then?'

Ymarys slowly stretched out one arm, then the other, yawning.

'It's so tediously dull here. What is there to do?'

'Plenty!' Lai said. 'Why not come and help in the gardens?'

Ymarys's lip curled slightly in disdain.

'Me work in the gardens? Have you any idea what gardening does to the hands? All that engrained dirt under the nails—'

'It's good exercise. The soil's poor, too sandy. They use a mixture of dried seaweed and seagull droppings to enrich it.'

'So that's the distinctive odour . . .' Ymarys delicately wafted one hand in front of his face, as though fanning away the offending smell. 'No. I miss the delights of Perysse, plague or no plague.'

'But Sarilla's left you her estates – you could begin a new life for yourself as a country torellan . . .'

One eye opened, fixing Lai with a look of scorn.

'You know my opinions on gardening. Can you imagine me running a country estate? I would wither and die from boredom. I need gaiety, scandal, stimulation!'

He rose from the bed and went to stare at his reflection in the mirror he had fixed to the lime-washed wall. Through the casement beyond Lai saw that the moon was rising over the sea, silvering a path across the waters . . . A path that led to Spice Islands and beyond . . .

Soft fingers closed about his shoulders, kneading, massaging. And he had not even heard Ymarys move from the mirror.

'Tsk! All tense, knotted up. The curse of too much gardening. You need to relax . . .'

Ymarys's breath, sweet with fennel, warmed his cheek. Lai felt his eyes closing, felt Ymarys's lips brush the back of his neck, his caress lulling him into a sensual daze . . .

'Ymarys.' He stilled the roving hands and turned around to face him. 'Ymarys. Stop. This won't work.'

'Why not?' Ymarys's voice, no more than a grating whisper.

'My vows.'

'You broke them with my lady Arkhys enough times. What's one time more?'

Lai shook his head.

'After Clodolë I made a vow not to let myself get involved again. With anyone.'

'You don't find me attractive.'

Lai shivered. On the contrary – he found himself drawn to Ymarys in a way he had never imagined possible. That veiled, catlike sensuality excited him, that sense of sheathed claws in velvet pads, claws that could rend him to his very soul—

'I do find you attractive. Disturbingly attractive,' he heard himself saying. 'But you're also my friend. My closest friend. I don't want to spoil that friendship.'

'Why do you get such satisfaction in denying yourself? We're talking an hour or two's pleasure here, Lai sweeting, not a lifetime's commitment.'

'Look – you're bored, you've admitted as much. You relish a challenge. Why not seduce the Aelahim, it'll make the hours pass more swiftly . . .'

'A game? Is that how you think I meant it, Lai?' Ymarys's eyes held Lai's a moment, grey and unfathomable as mistwater in the twilight. Then the wild glint of malice returned and he laughed. 'Yes, of course it was a game.' But the laughter sounded false, forced, to Lai's ears.

'I'd better go.'

'Yes, go.'

Ymarys was not looking at him, he was staring at his reflection in the mirror. He tugged back his long hair from off his face and twisted it into a severe knot, stabbing it secure with one black thorn-pin.

Lai paused in the doorway.

'I'm sorry.'

'Just go.' ·

Suddenly Ymarys savagely tore out the pin, letting his hair tumble back about his shoulders, a silkfall of moonstained ashsilver.

'Forget it ever happened.'

*

194

The royal barque moored at the quay in the heart of Perysse. Crowds had gathered to see the Arkhys make her triumphal re-entry into the city. Tarkhastars of both Tarkhas Houses lined the quay, a chequered pattern of crimson and blue.

Jhafir and Ophar waited at the quayside to greet the Arkhys.

Clodolë appeared on the deck of the barque, Rho Jhan at her side. Instantly a deafening cheer arose from the crowd. As she made her way towards the waiting palanquin, she was showered with rose petals. Smiling, she turned to wave to the cheering crowd, before stepping into the palanquin.

Jhafir, somewhat piqued at being granted little less than a nod of the head, leaned towards the High Priest as the palanquin was lifted high onto the shoulders of the bearers.

'I shouldn't say this . . . but don't you think her exile has put years on her? Her hair . . . faded almost white. And her eyes—'

'It seems quite understandable in the circumstances,' Ophar said. 'The Arkhan treated her most cruelly. She was driven to distraction by Melmeth's endless affairs. I'm surprised she didn't retaliate sooner.'

'Isn't this a little unconventional, Ophar? The House of Memizhon ruled by a consort?'

'If we regard the Arkhan and Arkhys as one flesh joined in the sight of the god . . . then it is the logical way to proceed in the Arkhan's absence. In my opinion, the Arkhys will prove an excellent substitute for her consort. We need a strong leader to see us through this time of troubles.'

'My first allegiance is to Melmeth,' Jhafir said. 'You speak as if he had already abdicated. As if he were dead.'

Melmeth shuffled his way around the narrow chamber in which they had confined him. He had learned its dimensions by counting paces, so many to the right, so many to the left . . .

How long had he been in hiding? He had lost days in fever and delirium; he was not even sure when day gave way to night.

They had told him he must remain here until the mobs in the city were subdued; it was for his own safety. But now he began to suspect he was being kept prisoner; the door was always locked.

Servitors brought food and drink twice a day; he guessed they were hierophants by their soft, deferential voices.

'What's happening? I demand to know what's happening.'

'You have been very ill, my lord, you must not excite yourself.'

'I want to see Jhafir! Send him to me at once!'

Hands gently took hold of him, restraining hands, coaxing him back onto the bed.

'You must rest, zhan.'

'Where is Khaldar? What has become of Khaldar?'

'He is being cared for.'

'And my personal physician? Dr Azhrel? Bring Azhrel to me.'

But no one obeyed his commands, no one listened.

Dream memories . . . A woman bent over him, her hair brushing his forehead . . . He raised one hand to caress her cheek and saw the intense seablue of her eyes awash with tears.

Why have you betrayed me, Melmeth? Why have you left me here to give birth to our child in shame and silence?

He woke whispering her name.

'Laili . . .'

And with his memory came the realisation that she must believe that he had abandoned her. What could he do? If he sent word to her, he would betray her whereabouts. Yet if he sent no word, she would believe herself forgotten. There must be something—

He lurched to his feet and stumbled towards the door, feeling his way, hand over hand along the rough, cold stone of the wall.

When his hands touched wood, he began to pound with his fists, shouting.

No one came. No one even answered. He hammered until his hands were bruised and sore.

He might as well be dead.

The Razhirrakh sat hunched on the sand, disconsolately skimming pebbles across the grey waves.

'Ymarys!' Lai hailed him, slithering down over the dunes towards him. He had put on the loose bleached robes worn by the community; his feet were bare.

Ymarys turned and, when he saw what Lai was wearing, his plucked eyebrows arched in amazement.

'This is just for convenience's sake. It doesn't mean anything.'

'You look,' Ymarys said pointedly, 'as though you belong here.'

'And you look as if you wish you were anywhere else but.'

'I'm bored, Lai. So desperately, utterly bored. What is there to do here but stare at the sea? Besides – doesn't it give you the slightest twinge of concern?'

196

'What?'

'The lack of "news" from Perysse.'

Lai glanced over his shoulder, almost as if he feared Laili might be listening.

'Maybe the plague's out of control.'

'Or maybe our fickle Arkhan has found another interest. Women do lose their charms when they're so grossly pregnant . . .'

'What are you suggesting?'

'You want news. Laili wants news. And I'm bored. Why don't I return to the city and find out what's going on?'

Lai considered for a moment or two.

'Very well. What have we got to lose? But if you're questioned, where will you say you've been all this time?'

'Sarilla's estates. I left the royal barque at the estuary, having satisfactorily discharged my escort duty. As far as I knew, you both were planning to go back to Ael Lahi.'

'It sounds credible.'

'My dear, Sarilla's estates are so far to the west, no one would even consider going to check if my story was true!' Ymarys's eyes, seasilvered in the morning light, seemed to glitter again at the prospect of returning to Perysse.

'So your mind is made up?'

'If I stay here amongst these good scholars a moment longer, I swear I'll die from tedium. To have to listen to another absorbing discourse on the forty different types of sea holly – or the migration habits of the terns—'

'I'll miss you,' Lai said.

'Will you?' Ymarys said. He reached out and brushed Lai's cheek with his fingertips.

Clodolë pensively fingered the gilded arms of the porphyry throne of Memizhon, savouring how it felt to be sitting in Melmeth's place.

'Are we alone, Ophar?'

'For a few moments.' The High Priest glanced warily about him. 'But even here one can never be too discreet.'

'Then tell me what you can. Where is he, how is he?'

'He is blind. And with the blindness a kind of madness has afflicted him. It appears he had become dependent upon the dust and, in some drugged fit, believed he had gained godlike powers.'

'And is he still in the grip of this . . . madness?' Clodolë asked carefully.

'We have confined him. For his own safety, of course, you understand, Arkhys.'

'Oh, yes. I understand,' she said. 'And were many killed in the riots?'

'It was difficult to obtain precise figures of casualties amongst the populace. Jhafir lost ten men, the Tarkhas Memizhon eight. There are still mutterings, of course, but we are putting those down with all severity.'

'And these rumours of plague?'

'Not rumours. Whether the infection is carried by the moonmoths or is mere coincidence, no one can be certain. But it is rife amongst all circles of the city from the street marshes to the palace itself. Jhafir's edicts have had very little effect. Quite frankly, we are at a loss as to how to control it.'

Clodolë walked slowly towards the balcony.

'You remember what I told you about the Aelahim woman summoning the moonmoths?'

'What are you implying, Arkhys?'

'If she summoned them . . . then she must know how to lift the curse.'

'But no one knows what has become of her – or her brother. They disappeared some while ago. Melmeth had that preening popinjay Ymarys escort them to the coast. The word was they had returned to Ael Lahi.'

'And you believe that?'

'In the absence of other information—'

'She is carrying Melmeth's child!' Clodolë said in a cracked whisper. 'Do you really believe he would have sent her back home? No. He's hidden her somewhere. And someone must know where she is. Find out who was on that barque – and interrogate them. Even if it was only a single word overheard it might give us the clue we need.'

The barque-maistre was blunt with Ymarys when he took the Razhirrakh on board at Phaeros.

'Can't think why you should want to go to Perysse. Haven't you heard? There's plague there. I'm only going to deliver these casks of berindë – I'm not setting foot on shore. Trade's trade – but I'm taking no risks.'

There were tarkhastars of the Tarkhas Zhudiciar on the quays of the city. They were checking papers. It seemed to Ymarys as he watched from the deck of the barque, that no one was being allowed beyond the quay without a permit.

He would have to wait for nightfall.

At sunset the tarkenhorns blew and the tarkhastars departed. Ymarys slipped ashore in the gathering twilight.

The quay was almost dark now. If he shut his eyes, he could see it as it used to be, the waterside taverns gaudy with jewelled paper lanterns, strains of music and rowdy laughter gusting from open doorways.

All the taverns were boarded up, their lights long since extinguished.

He wandered along the empty quay, staring up at the blank shutters in the dwindling light, silently whispering the names of the wine shops, the pleasure houses: 'The Medlar Tree. At the Sign of the Blue Asfodyl. The Pleasure House of Black Khassia . . .'

On each door was pinned the same notice: *Closed by order of the Haute Zhudiciar.*

'. . . The Pleasure House of Ysmodai.'

Ymarys stopped a moment, remembering that last soft-balmed night, the interwreathing dancers, the alluring dark perfume of sweet vanilla on warm, young breath . . .

Where had they gone, the whores and the painted dancers? Had they succumbed to the plague? Had they all faded into the darkness?

Help me . . .

'Who's there?'

A sudden breeze off the Yssil set the tavern signs swinging and creaking above his head. Ymarys's skin had gone chill and cold.

Please help me . . .

The herbs in the Hearkenor's walled garden had been blighted by the first frost. Lai knelt on the rough stone path, cutting away the dead seedpods, his breath clouding the dank, dark air.

'You have been taking such good care of my garden.'

He turned to see Pherindyn behind him, well-muffled against the damp.

'I had to do something useful with my time, mhaestyr.'

'Such a short time you have been here . . . and already you seem like one of us. Why should that be, I wonder?'

Lai saw that Pherindyn was regarding him warmly, his rough,

windburnt face crinkled into a smile.

'Come, walk with me. Tell me about yourself. I'd like to know more about you. You are no stranger to a community such as ours, are you, Lai?'

The kindness in Pherindyn's voice almost melted Lai's reserve.

'I do feel at home here,' he said, the words awkward, half-formed. 'Once – before I was enslaved – I—'

'I had guessed as much.' Pherindyn nodded his head. 'And if you wish to stay with us, we can offer you time to think, time to rediscover your original path . . . But you must put aside the accoutrements of your profession.'

'No weapons?'

'We are opposed to violence – of any kind. I keep an armoire in which new members of the community place all such relics of their life outside the house. A locked armoire. I'll take you there, if you wish.'

The tall armoire was of dark-stained, knotted wood; it smelt of beeswax and dust. Lai hung his razhir on a hook inside and placed his riding clothes and golden victor's sash beneath.

A symbolic gesture. But as Pherindyn locked the door, Lai felt as if he had shrugged off an intolerably heavy burden. He had taken the first step on the long path back to the Grove.

Please help me.

The faint, failing voice still resonated through Ymarys's brain. The night was silent but for the wheezing of the creaking sign.

'I've cracked. Finally gone crazy. I'm hearing voices.'

In here . . . Up the stairs . . .

Each word etched itself upon his mind, the filigree scratchings of a silver nib. He looked up again at the shuttered building. The mask of the lesser daemon of Ar-Zhoth leered down at him: lascivious Ysmodai, Ysmodai the Trickster.

What's happening to me? Where is everyone? Can't anyone hear me?

Curiosity overmastered Ymarys. He slipped down the noisome side-alley, searching for another way in. Perhaps a back door might have been left unlocked, unbarred . . . Or a side window . . . He had to know if the mind-voice were real – or imagined. He had to find out.

On the first floor, a leather-paned window had been left slightly ajar; if he could clamber his way up, using the gutter as a toe-hold . . .

His foot dislodged a tile which fell to smash on the courtyard beneath. He froze, suspended in mid-air, waiting for the sudden clamour of voices, the cries of discovery.

No voices disturbed the dreary silence of curfew. No one appeared. Ymarys's straining arms began to protest; he swung himself lightly up, nudged open the window and squeezed inside, brushing cobwebs from his clothes. Damn! He had snagged a thread of his sleeve.

'Anyone there?'

Upstairs . . . I'm upstairs . . .

There was no doubting the clarity of the voice now.

Ymarys blinked in the shuttered gloom of the landing, then edged his way along until he almost fell up the open stairwell. Warily he climbed the precariously winding stair, back to the wall, one step at a time.

Open the door . . .

The door swung inwards . . . The attic room was dim, clouded with nightshadows.

Someone . . . or something . . . lay in the corner, shrouded in pale gauze, cocooned in cobwebs, white strands straying onto the dusty floor.

A faint, sweet scent . . . drifting moonpetals . . . tainted the air.

Here.

The voice rang clear in Ymarys's mind as the note of a glass bell. Yet the only sound in the bare attic was the gasp of his own ragged breathing.

'Who – who are you?'

My name was . . . was Jhofiel . . .

'Jhofiel?'

Smoke-grey eyes, meeting his through the lilac haze of dreamweed, enticing, daring . . .

How could this shrouded skeletal bundle of arms and legs be Jhofiel the dancer? Jhofiel who, skilled in the erotic arts, had made him forget for a night or two the emptiness in his heart left by dead Sarilla, unattainable Lai.

Ymarys took a tentative step towards the prone figure.

Don't . . . come too close . . .

'Why have they left you here alone?'

They were afraid . . .

'Your hair,' Ymarys whispered, bending down to sift his fingers through the soft, pale strands. They felt as frail as spidersilk, slightly sticky to the touch. 'But Jhofiel's hair was dark.'

Why are you not afraid . . . like the others?

'But what has happened to you?'

They call it the Changing . . .

'Is it a sickness? Are you ill?'

They say it is caused by the boskh . . .

'How long have you lain here?'

Two, three, four days . . . I've lost count . . .

'Since the Zhudiciar's edicts were posted?'

Maybe . . .

'When did you last eat?'

Can't eat . . . can't speak . . . aloud . . . Jhofiel tried to prop himself up on one emaciated elbow, his huge dark eyes staring suspiciously into Ymarys's. *How come you can hear me? No one else could understand me . . . since the Changing . . .*

Ymarys gave a light, insouciant shrug. 'I'm damned if I understand it myself—'

A muffled shout outside on the quay.

They've come for me. You're an informer! You're—

'Ssh.' Ymarys edged across to the dormer window and peered down to the cobbles far below, hoping his moving shadow could not be glimpsed from the quay.

Torchlight lit the sluggish river water with splashes of gleaming gold. A patrol was coming along the quay. Ymarys counted six tarkhastars in all. They were methodically checking each boarded door, each shuttered window, rattling the locks and bolts to ensure they had not been tampered with.

Three dizzy storeys beneath, he saw them approach the door of the empty pleasure house, heard them pound on the door with mailed fists.

He held his breath as the empty building echoed with each blow . . .

The patrol moved on to the next house.

'Now do you trust me?' Ymarys whispered to Jhofiel. He began to move silently towards the door. This was the moment to slip away, when the patrol was just out of sight.

Where . . . are you going?

'You're too weak to move, I have to bring you food, water.'

Why? Why are you doing this for me?

Why?

Ymarys forced himself to look at the Changed features, the thin-sculpted face, white marble mask, out of which stared the slanting dark eyes, no longer weird but weirdly beautiful . . . Jhofiel's sensuality had not been lost in the Changing but heightened, translated into this pale, slender nightwraith.

'I don't know,' Ymarys said.

Fogs had rolled in off the sea, encasing the house in a chill, damp cloud. Lai doggedly worked on in the Hearkenor's garden, trying to dissipate his growing anxiety in hard physical labour.

'Lai.' Pherindyn appeared in the archway of the walled garden, beckoning Lai to him.

Lai went carefully: fallen leaves had made the paths slippery.

'You have news?' Lai said, his voice raw with the morning's cold.

'Only rumours – and disquieting rumours at that. I thought I should tell you first – and then you could decide on a suitable moment to tell your sister.'

'What rumours?' Lai stopped.

'There appears to have been some kind of insurrection. A minor one, swiftly put down.'

Insurrection. Riot. A sudden fear for Ymarys seared through Lai's mind.

'You don't think that the Arkhan—'

'Has been overthrown? It's unlikely. But maybe he has decided to stay in Perysse until the situation has stabilised. Maybe it's nothing to be concerned about.'

And there was no news yet from Ymarys.

'Maybe,' Lai said sombrely. He took out his pruning knife and began to trim the climbing fig on the southern wall.

CHAPTER 19

The High Priest paused on the rickety tower stair to catch his breath.

'Right on up to the attic, your reverence,' called the cook from the bottom of the stairwell.

'It would help if you could show me where you found this – this creature.'

'I'm not going up there again for a thousand eniths. Scared the life out of me. I've never seen the like—'

Ophar reached the attic and sniffed, wrinkling his nose in disgust. That sherbet-sweet smell again: boskh – unmistakably boskh.

The door at the end had been left ajar. He pushed it with his staff and ventured in.

In the far shadows lay what seemed at first to him to be nothing more than a crumpled bundle of cobwebbed rags.

He moved closer, impelled to see what he must see, no matter how horrible.

'Blessed Mithiel, what abomination is this?' he muttered.

A frail figure lay there, clothed only in long drifts of floating hair, white as spun sugar. Was she sleeping? Or in some kind of drugged trance? And what *was* she? Closer still . . . Now he could see that the long fingers of the slender hands were webbed, the tracery of veins in the transparent skin as delicate as a skeletal leaf, hoar-dusted by winter frosts. Soft curves of a translucent body beneath, breasts whose delicate nipples were round and pink as little shells—

'Stay a moment,' he murmured, drawing back. The boskh must have infected his brain, stimulating unnatural lusts with its insidious musksweet fragrance. He was sweating. What had possessed him?

Was this the result of the Aelahim woman's sorceries? Was this what became of those who took the dust? The smell of boskh was everywhere, clinging to the gossamer threads of hair of the thing that had once been human – and now was something else, some succuba summoned from the daemon hordes of Ar-Zhoth, to provoke and enflame obscene desires—

Feelings, long suppressed by years of continence and self-denial, re-awakened, all the more potent for being so long denied.

She stirred.

Could she sense his thoughts, could she feel the heat of his desires?

A rage, mingled of disgust and desire, consumed him. Destroy. Destroy the vile creature so that it should not inspire such carnal lusts in others—

He had no doubt now as to what he must do. As High Priest he must protect the faithful from the influence of such lascivious monstrosities.

'Why was I not told of this before?'

'We had no idea it was hiding up there.' The cook shuddered.

'And no one's been up there in weeks?'

'Only Dr Azhrel.'

'Azhrel!' Ophar echoed, grimly triumphant. 'Oh, I have you now, doctor. I have you.'

A single moonshaft lit Sarilla's tower, the high open casement with its cracked panes. And from the open casement a single thread of ethereal music issued, liquid as moonkissed waters.

Azhrel stopped, mesmerised, and looked up.

At the window of Miu's moonlit garret stood a frail figure, a whitewraith, tall and slender.

'What . . . is that?' Azhrel murmured.

Clothed only in its long drifts of floating hair, white as spun sugar, the figure lifted one skeletal hand towards him.

With a sudden shock of recognition, Azhrel felt himself lifting his hand in salutation, moving slowly, involuntarily across the cobbles—

'Why, Miu – you're *awake*!'

The distant silverthread of melody floated towards him, borne on the nightbreeze, faint as a half-remembered dreamvoice from the far side of sleep.

She was awake. And she was singing.

The nagging ache in his temples and behind his eyes slowly eased. He forgot how tired he was. Tranced by the wreathing melody, he felt the looming towers of Myn-Dhiel melt away and he stood on moonbleached sands, lulled by the whisper of tidefall . . .

The sound of chanting shattered the trance. A splash of fire lit the archway.

Torches.

A group of hooded hierophants came towards Azhrel across the palace courtyard, mumbling chants and burning bitter herbs in their clanking thuribles.

The night grew bright with their spluttering torches, the air harsh with their monotonous chanting.

'You're out late, Doctor Azhrel.'

The last of the hodded torch-bearers stopped in front of the physician, throwing back his hood to reveal his lean face.

Ophar.

'So many patients to attend to,' Azhrel said pointedly.

'I am told there's one of *them* sequestered hereabouts—' and Ophar glanced up at Sarilla's tower, '—and the edict demands that they must be destroyed.'

A terrible apprehension gripped Azhrel.

'Who – or what – must be destroyed?'

'Oh come now, Doctor. Are you telling me you haven't come across one of these poor wretches?'

Miu. Someone had discovered her.

'Fire.' Ophar smiled. 'They cannot resist it. Moths are drawn to the flames—'

'You'll excuse me but I have patients waiting—'

Ophar grabbed him by the arm, fingers digging into his flesh.

'Watch.'

They had gathered at the foot of the tower in a ring of torchflames.

'Is that one of your patients, Dr Azhrel? Hm?'

Azhrel saw Miu's pale figure at the window, more moth than human. All the while the chanting was growing louder, dinning into his ears with its merciless, mindless monotony.

'Miu!' Azhrel cried.

For a moment, she seemed to hang, to float in the very air above the flaming torches. Azhrel could not avert his eyes, hoping for a moment against all hope—

Then the fires caught light. Gossamer whiteness crackled, burned as the creature came thudding to the ground and the hierophants closed in, hacking, stamping, crushing—

Azhrel tried to push his way through to her but the hierophants caught hold of him, held him back.

'It is counted a heinous crime to harbour one of these daemon-spawn, Azhrel.' Ophar's breath stank of smoke and stale incense.

'If you arrest me, who will care for the plague victims?'

'You are not indispensable. There are plenty of other physicians.'

'But none with my specialised knowledge—'

'It is your "specialised knowledge" that gives us grave concerns. We shall be watching you, doctor. Oh yes, we'll be watching. You may not always know we are there . . . but meddle once more in temple matters – and we shall crush you as we crushed that cursed mothspawn. No one – not even the Arkhan – will be able to save you.'

The hierophants flung Azhrel down by the charred remains. She was nothing now but a smouldering, blackened shell, her gossamer hair burnt to a handful of cinders.

'Miu,' Azhrel repeated brokenly. Now he would never learn her secrets. His sight blurred . . . but in his distress he could no longer tell whether his eyes were watering with the acrid smoke . . . or tears.

Ymarys knelt down and – after a moment's hesitation – slipped his arm beneath Jhofiel's shoulders. He was so light it was like lifting a child . . . But no child had such wildspun glimmering hair, there seemed to be skeins and skeins of it, cascading about his shoulders, his waist . . .

'Drink,' Ymarys said. 'It's honey and water.'

Turn away.

'Why?'

Just turn away.

The slender tongue uncurled from Jhofiel's mouth seeking sweetness. Ymarys stared, half-revulsed, half-fascinated, as Jhofiel began to draw up the honey-liquor, sucking as though through a straw. The level in the beaker slowly went down . . . until none was left.

I warned you.

Jhofiel was watching him through his moondark eyes. The feathery fronds of eyebrow-antennae trembled slightly.

You don't find me strange? Monstrous? Deformed?

The direct question confounded Ymarys. He could not begin to define what he felt about Jhofiel, except that it was something quite other than disgust. Jhofiel exuded a subtle, sensuous aura, almost as if his natural sensuality had been enhanced by the Changing.

Ymarys drew away, his senses swimming, aware of the moondark eyes still watching him. How could he feel so strongly attracted to this weirdling?

I remember you now.

Jhofiel's dark eyes stared at Ymarys in the gloom of the shuttered chamber.

The Arkhan's champion. I saw you in the arena once, your body oiled for the fight. Of course I was way up in the cheap seats, not close enough to see your face, only the way you moved, so graceful, so – dangerous . . .

Jhofiel glanced slyly at Ymarys, almost provocatively. Before Ymarys could stop him, Jhofiel had reached out to touch his hands with his own; a brief, seductive gesture that left a tingling trace of desire.

'Jhofiel—'

No. It was obscene to even contemplate it. Obscene to imagine such a thing possible. Man and Changed, bodies intertwined, touching, kissing . . .

He went towards the door, slamming it behind him, running down the stairs, stumbling in his haste. He was stifling in this shuttered, gloomy house. He had to get away.

Autumn rain fell on the city. Summer was over. Ymarys lifted his face to the rain, letting it drench him.

Here on the street, his mind felt cleaner, clearer.

He had wasted so much time.

There were plague warnings, the sightless eye of Ar-Zhoth, black as tar, daubed across doors and shutters in every street he passed through.

There were edicts pinned to every noticeboard.

By order of Jhafir, Haute Zhudiciar for the protection of the citizens of Perysse, it is decreed that:

1) All citizens shall obey the curfew from dusk until dawn. Anyone found abroad during the hours of darkness without a permit will be taken to be a looter or rioter and arrested.

2) All boskh and moth carcases to be destroyed. Anyone found in possession of the drug will be arrested and his possessions confiscated.

3) Anyone known to be harbouring the unfortunates known commonly as the Changed is to be immediately reported to the authorities.

4) Punishment for the crime of looting: loss of right hand.

Punishment for the crime of rioting: loss of both hands.

Punishment for the possession of boskh: blinding and castration.

Punishment for harbouring the Changed: execution.

There also were posters offering ludicrously generous rewards for anyone coming forwards with information as to the whereabouts of one Ymarys, the Arkhan's Razhirrakh:

Tall, slender yet with broad shoulders, the Razhirrakh can be easily identified by the ornate razhir he wears. Physical peculiarities: grey eyes, long straight hair, ash-fair, which he may wear braided after the fashion of the Tarkhas Memizhon.

He threw back his head and laughed aloud. 'So I'm a wanted man. How flattering.'

He tore down one of the posters and, folding it, slipped it inside his jacket as a memento.

The rain had soaked his hair to dark strands. Who would recognise him now? The few who had ventured out onto the rain-churned streets hurried past, their heads down. Nevertheless, for Lai's sake, maybe it was better to be cautious.

Rain drove across the parade ground of the Tarkhas Memizhon in stormbursts. Inside the Tarkhas House, Ymarys climbed the broad stairs, leaving a trail of wet footprints on the polished wood, and reached his rooms unchallenged.

But when he opened the door he saw that the room had been ransacked. All his possessions and papers lay strewn across the floor, all his precious suits of silk and taffeta had been flung on the floor and trampled underfoot.

'Not the paeony sarcenet—'

He sank to his knees, stifling a silent cry of anguish in the crumpled fabric of a much-beloved jacket.

They had slit the seams in their search for clues. Perhaps they had thought to find a concealed paper with a name, a destination on it? Not one garment remained undamaged. They had even ripped the silken rosettes from his shoes.

'Ah well,' he said defiantly. 'They were all outmoded, last season's styles. I would have thrown them out anyway.'

Orthandor was sitting hunched over the dregs of a brew of khassafri: Ymarys could still smell the last lingering fumes of nutmeg scenting the Tarrakh's room.

'What's this, Tarrakh? Drinking on duty?'

'Yma—' Orthandor started up clumsily, upsetting his stool.

'Ssh,' Ymarys said, smiling. 'You haven't seen me. I'm a phantom. A figment of your imagination.'

Orthandor smothered him in a bear hug.

'Ugh. You're soaked. Have some khassafri to warm you.'

'I'd appreciate a dry jacket too.'

Orthandor set a mug of khassafri down in front of Ymarys. Ymarys cradled the mug between his cold fingers to warm them.

'What's going on, Orthandor?'

'I might ask you the same. You're a wanted man. What have you done?'

'Look. Just answer me one question. Where's the Arkhan?'

'Haven't you heard? He's sick. Brain fever. Doesn't even remember his own name.' Orthandor lumbered over to a linen chest and drew out a jacket. 'Will this do?'

'So where is he?' Ymarys peeled off the wet jacket and pulled on Orthandor's, which was several sizes too big.

'He mustn't be disturbed, apparently. "The slightest disturbance could break the slender thread attaching him to life." Or so says Jhafir.'

'Poetic words. But what do they conceal? He's dead already? Murdered? Or just thrown to rot in some oubliette in the donjon?'

Orthandor shook his head slowly.

'When did you last see him, Orthandor?'

'In the arena riot. Two of the Tarkhas Memizhon dragged him into the tunnels. A day or so later they were both dead. The pestilence.'

'How convenient,' Ymarys said acidly. 'And no one's seen Melmeth since then?'

'Myn-Dhiel's crawling with Jhafir's men. There's more crimson than azure nowadays.' Orthandor let out a sigh. 'We're demoted.'

'You said they dragged him into the arena tunnels. Which lead to Myn-Dhiel – or the mausoleum.'

'The charnel house? You think he's been murdered?'

Ymarys gulped back the khassafir and got to his feet.

'There's only one way to find out.'

Ymarys was in a dangerous mood now, spoiling for a fight. They had ruined his wardrobe, raked through all his personal possessions. If anyone challenged him, he would skewer them – Memizhon or Zhudiciar, he didn't care which.

He had only once taken the way of the dead to the mausoleum and that was when, as a young tarkhastar, he had followed Sardion's bier. Then the tunnels had been lit with torchlight; now he had to follow the snail-phosphorescence of the thylz trail in smothering dark.

Maybe the rumours were true and Melmeth was grievously sick. But suppose Clodolë had taken advantage of the rumours – and had Melmeth killed? Ymarys had been a courtier too long at Myn-Dhiel not to be aware of the animosity between Arkhan and Arkhys.

As he drew near to the mausoleum, he sensed a stir of movement ahead. Flattening himself against the grimy walls, he edged forwards and saw a glint of torchlight.

Two of the Tarkhas Zhudiciar stood on guard in front of the arch that led into the mausoleum.

Why would they place a guard over the bones of Melmeth's ancestors? No one ever went to the mausoleum except the hierophants.

Two. Ymarys's fingers closed around the hilt of his razhir. Only two. And he had the element of surprise on his side.

Maybe he could just brazen his way in.

'Good day to you, gentlemen.'

They started, blinking in the murky torchlight at the sudden pale-haired apparition which had appeared, grinning, before them.

'I've come to pay Arkhan a visit.'

To Ymarys's delight, the two tarkhastars seemed utterly confounded. One even began to fumble for the keys at his waist.

'Identify yourself,' the other said uncertainly.

'Surely you know who I am.'

They glanced at each other.

'You need a permit. From the Haute Zhudiciar.'

'Oh, damn the permit.' Ymarys's razhir flashed from its sheath to hover neatly beneath the tarkhastar's chin. 'Just let me in.'

The tarkhastar's eyes slid questioningly to his companion's. The other one gave a terse nod. Ymarys saw his hand twitch; in a second, he had filleted the man's blade right out of his hand.

'*Ai!*' The man dropped to his knees, nursing his wrist. Ymarys made a grab at the keys.

'What in the name of Ar-Zhoth is going on down there?'

Rho Jhan. Ymarys cursed under his breath.

Tarkhastars came running towards him from the darkness; he swiftly assessed the odds. He was outnumbered.

'Intruder in the mausoleum, zhan!'

Ymarys gracefully executed a mocking bow.

'Get him!'

'Come on, then. Come and get me!' He kissed his fingertips to them – and disappeared laughing into the darkness.

He knew the arena tunnels better than anyone. He would lose them – and be back at the Pleasure House of Ysmodai whilst they were still stumbling around in the dark.

Must get out of Perysse. Must get out before they catch me. They know I'm here, even now they'll be searching for me, asking questions . . .

Ymarys sat cross-legged on the floor of Jhofiel's attic, fingertips pressed together in an attitude of meditation.

Jhofiel floated past him. The dancer had been restlessly drifting to and fro across the attic room since Ymarys's return.

I feel so trapped . . . I need fresh air, moonlight . . .

Maybe I should leave tonight, thought Ymarys. The longer I stay, the greater the risk.

The moon is high in the sky . . . just let me out for a few minutes in the gardens. Who's going to see?

The secluded gardens of the Pleasure House of Ysmodai were overgrown, neglected since Jhafir's edicts. Jhofiel flitted through the darkling garden, his bare feet scarcely leaving a print on the dew-wet grass.

Weeds were already choking the paths and borders. But the tangle of climbing roses was starred with late milk-blush blossoms and their creamy scent still perfumed the moist evening air.

Ymarys.

When Ymarys looked around he saw that the moon had silvered Jhofiel's cloudy hair, creating a misty aureole around his pale features. He realised that Jhofiel was holding out his hand to him. He shook his head, unable to find his voice, dazzled by the moon-wrought transformation.

Why do you keep away from me? Are you afraid?

'Afraid! Why should I be afraid?'

I'm infected, tainted. You fear to catch the contagion if you touch me.

'Is that what you think?'

Isn't that why they seek to destroy us? They fear they will become as us? This condition is a divine punishment for the sinful, lascivious lives we led. The All-Seeing could not permit the wickedness to continue . . . so he sent this

212

curse to afflict us. He took away our powers of speech, he rendered us hideous—

'That's what the hierophants preach. Do you believe them?'

Not now that I have met you. You understand.

Ymarys still did not look at Jhofiel; he could sense the dancer's nightmoth eyes staring directly at him, into his mind.

'Only imperfectly.'

The air is so sweet. And the new moon is rising. It's a sign. Jhofiel glided over to stand behind Ymarys.

I'm grateful that you saved me, I want to thank you . . .

Pale lips, soft as jasmine petals, pressed the skin at the back of his neck. Ymarys gasped, taken aback by the potency of this alien kiss.

Yskhysse . . . don't you want to learn the secrets of the forbidden art? Aren't you in the least curious?

'Curious?' Ymarys murmured. Softsilver hair all about him, a mist of floating hair, exuding that tantalisingly evanescent scent he had first noticed in Jhofiel's attic room. Moonlit jasmine with an undernote of something indefinably animal. *Alien.* 'Wait. Not now.'

Jhofiel let out a sigh, faint and light as the brush of a moth's wings; Ymarys felt his soft breath on his face, his neck.

You. Even you reject me . . .

'Did I say that?'

You don't have to make excuses.

'Jhofiel, I—'

I'm unnatural. You can't bear to touch me.

'For Mithiel's sake!' How did Jhofiel know how to play on his emotions so well? The last thing he had felt was repelled – not by Jhofiel's kiss, nor by the touch of his slender androgynous body. 'I came back to Perysse for information. That's all. I'll be leaving – just as soon as I can spirit myself on board a coastbound ship.'

Ymarys . . . come here.

'No,' said Ymarys softly.

Jhofiel's arms encircled Ymarys.

Stay one more night. Just one more.

Ymarys could feel his resolve melting faster than honeyed candlewax.

'One more night, then.'

The coastline was perpetually shrouded in seafogs; drear, damp mists that dripped from every roof of the house, veiling the light of the sun.

213

Laili now walked with the rolling gait of the heavily pregnant. She had found a companion in one of the appellants, an older woman, Cariel, who knew all about birthing. Cariel estimated that if the child arrived to time, it would be born by Sh'amain, the Day of the Dead.

And still no word came from Ymarys – or Melmeth.

That foggy morning Lai was at work in the Hearkenor's garden when he heard a sound that stopped him in the midst of digging up a particularly stubborn rosemary bush.

Low notes wreathed upwards, smoky as autumn leaffires, sad and forlorn.

She was playing her flute. No one could play with such subtlety as Laili . . .

He let his spade fall and followed the sound of the drifting notes, out of the walls and onto the shore.

A little flurry of notes, a darting fall, then a slow, lingering descent into silence.

She was standing on the sands, staring out to sea, the flute still in her hands.

'I love the sound of the sea. It reminds me of Ael Lahi. It's the only place where I feel truly at peace.'

'We can still go home. If that's what you want.'

'How can I go home now?'

She looked at him then and he saw that her eyes were clouded with unshed tears.

They walked in silence for a while along the empty strand. A grey seamist hung low over the waters.

'You're not hiding anything from me, are you, Lai?' she said suddenly.

'Me? What should I be hiding?'

'News. News about Perysse. About – Melmeth.'

'I've told you all I know. I've heard nothing.'

'Not even from Ymarys?'

'No,' he said, brow creasing in a frown.

They sat down together in the shelter of a sand dune tufted with whispering marram grass.

'Why hasn't he come, Lai?' Her hands rested over her swollen belly, as though protecting her unborn child. '"Just a short while and we shall be together." And now all these long weeks have passed and no news has come, not even a simple message. I'm so worried.'

Lai sifted sand through his fingers, such soft grains, so different from the coarse sand of the arena . . .

'Every night I hear him calling me. Just one, insistent message. "Help me, Laili. Help me!" He needs me. I know he needs me. I should go to him.'

'You can't go anywhere in your condition,' he said, trying to make her smile.

'I knew what I was doing was wrong. But it was also so very right. Can you understand that, Lai?' Tears clouded her clear eyes. 'I knew. In here.' She laid her hand on her breast. 'And not a day passes when I don't miss him, when I don't listen for the sound of his voice, his footfall . . .'

He put his arms around her, rocking her gently, wishing he could find words to comfort her.

'Laili, I'm sorry, I'm sorry.'

'If that was the test the Goddess set me, then I failed Her.'

'Don't cry, I can't bear it when you cry.' He took out a kerchief and gently wiped the tears from her eyes.

Stormclouds were massing overhead, lit underneath by the light of the sun, veins of fire streaking the grey.

'Rain's coming. We'd better go back.' He helped her to her feet and they set off slowly towards the white walls of the house.

Was that someone moving across the unlit quay? Ymarys rubbed his aching eyes and looked again. Was the house under surveillance?

You've been watching at that window for hours.

Feathery touch of fingers at the back of Ymarys's neck, teasing undone the knot of stiffened muscles.

I could make you feel so much better, ease this tension a little . . . you're all twisted-up inside, Ymarys . . .

Ymarys removed the massaging hand from his neck.

'Jhofiel, you know I find you attractive. You can read my mind better than I can myself. I just can't—'

Whyever not? Huge eyes widening in surprise, white eyebrow fronds visibly vibrating in amusement. *Regard this as a professional arrangement. Payment for services rendered by a grateful client. I was a professional, myself, remember?*

Ymarys began to smile, in spite of himself. Jhofiel seemed able to assume this chameleon guise, projecting a rainbow array of emotional auras, one moment violently jealous, the next, playfully seductive.

'You owe me nothing, Jhofiel.'

But haven't you ever wondered what it would be like . . . ?

Slowly, hypnotically, Jhofiel began to move as if to an inner rhythm, letting the loose robe he was wearing slide off one shoulder, then the other, slide down to his waist, his hips . . . his feet.

He stood naked before Ymarys, his moonlit body almost translucent, clothed only in the silvered strands of drifting hair. An unblemished body almost too perfect in its silken smoothness, slender yet unmistakably male, penis a pale moon-orchid, a bud ready to burst into full bloom.

Touch me. Hold me. I won't break.

Ymarys gazed at him, his breath caught in his throat, wanting to touch – yet—

You fear you may become like me. You fear that if you kiss me, if you possess me, you will become infected . . .

Jhofiel bent down over him, veiling him in a cloud of soft hair, pushing him backwards, his feathery fingers deft and swift as they undid his shirt, his breeches, peeling away his outer skin of clothes, until he lay naked on the bare boards.

'Jhofiel—' Ymarys gasped.

Now you will find out. Jhofiel's boskh-scented breath warmed his face as he opened his lips with his own . . . and the slender tongue came snaking out, curling itself about Ymarys's tongue.

Ymarys cried out—

And then as he tasted Jhofiel's translucent saliva, colder than the empty waters of the moon, he felt the struggle drain out of him and a white void open within his mind.

He could not even remember who he was.

Torch-flares gashed the darkness.

Dazzled, Ymarys flung up one hand to cover his eyes, groping with the other for his razhir.

A booted foot stamped on his searching hand; he doubled up in silent agony, clutching his crushed fingers.

The attic room was full of moving shadows; rough hands seized him, flung him against the wall.

'Bring him downstairs.'

'Jhofiel!' Ymarys shouted. 'What have you done with Jhofiel!'

They grabbed him by the arms and hustled him, naked, down the stairs and out into the neglected garden.

The hierophants forced him to his knees on the grass and closed in a tight circle around him. Pitch torches wept gouts of flame onto the damp ground.

The one nearest shrugged off his hood; Ymarys looked up and found himself staring into the shrewd, cold eyes of Ophar.

'The Arkhys has missed you at court, zhan Ymarys. Why have you neglected your court duties these long weeks?'

'The Arkhan granted me leave of absence,' Ymarys said. His crushed bladehand throbbed; the pain took on a pulse of its own. 'I've been at Sarilla's estates.'

'And before that?'

'I told you. I visited Sarilla's estates which are now mine.'

'Don't play games with me, Ymarys. You went to Phaeros with the Aelahim woman. We need to know where she is now.'

'I really have no idea what you're talking about,' Ymarys said, trying to affect his habitual nonchalant tone.

'Oh, come now, zhan Razhirrakh. Is your memory so poor? Or perhaps you don't realise how serious your predicament is? Do you know the penalty for harbouring one such as this?'

Ophar raised his hand. At his signal, Rho Jhan appeared, dragging a slender figure whose pale hair streamed behind him like moonspun gossamer.

'Jhofiel,' Ymarys whispered, agonised. 'Oh, Jhofiel.'

Dazzlebright . . . sunbright . . .

'Don't be crazy!' Ymarys hissed. 'It's torchlight, nothing more. Look away!'

Jhofiel's frail body began to shudder beneath Rho Jhan's restraining grip.

'You know how sensitive they are to fire, zhan Ymarys. Perhaps you would prefer to spare the wretched creature any more suffering—'

He made a sudden thrust towards Jhofiel with his torch. Jhofiel let out a shrill, keening cry. Ymarys flinched as the cry pierced him, a jagged silverblade of fear, the unearthly voice strident in its distress.

'Let him go. Put me to the question if you must – but let him go, he is innocent.'

'Where is Laili Dhar, Ymarys? That's all we want to know. Such a simple answer. She need never know who betrayed her. It could have been anyone – even the Arkhan himself.'

The light – the light—

Jhofiel was struggling to escape, struggling as the flames burned brighter. The harsh glare of the torchflares was reflected in his huge, dark eyes.

'I can't hold him back, Ymarys,' Rho Jhan said softly. 'He just can't resist the flames.'

'Don't look, Jhofiel!' Ymarys implored. 'Hide your eyes!'

So bright . . . It calls to me . . .

'Jhofiel,' Ophar echoed, still so softly, so seductively, 'come to the fire, Jhofiel . . .'

'If I tell you,' Ymarys heard himself saying, 'you'll let him go?'

All the while that the torchflames scarred his vision, he was calculating the odds – even if he told them what they wanted to know, he could still get a message through to warn Lai.

'Oh yes,' Ophar said. 'Of course we'll let him go.'

'Then – she is at the house by the sea – in Langoel.' Each word burned Ymarys's mouth like caustic soda. 'Well? You've got what you wanted. Let him go!'

'Rho Jhan.' Ophar nodded to the Enhirran.

Rho Jhan turned to Ymarys, smiling.

'As you wish.'

The hierophants turned their torches towards Jhofiel.

Ymarys scrambled up, frantically tearing at the hierophants' cloaks, their coarse robes, only to be knocked down again, trampled underfoot.

He heard their triumphant shout as the flames caught.

And Jhofiel's cry. He heard his cry. Ecstatic as the bright ring of flames engulfed him – then wordless, mindless agony as his silkspun hair became a tracery of fire, as the fire shot heavenwards in an explosion of starsparks and the frail creature that had been made of moonshine burned like a moth in a candleflame – until something charred, blackened, dropped lifeless to the ground.

CHAPTER 20

Cariel came knocking on the door of Lai's room before dawn.

'Get up, Lai Dhar! Get up at once!'

Lai blearily flung on his clothes and went stumbling across the murky yard after Cariel's bobbing lantern. As he climbed the stair, he heard a mewling cry coming from Laili's room.

Laili still sat in the birth chair, her freckled face white with exhaustion. But as Lai came in, she smiled at him, such a smile of exultation that it made his heart melt. Wrapped in white linen, tucked in to her breast, lay a little, snuffling thing, its head covered with a down of soft copper.

'Is it—' Lai came closer and peered down at Laili's baby. Eyes of a startling blue looked back at him.

'A boy,' she said, holding the babe close in the crook of her arm.

'Born several weeks too soon,' Cariel said. 'Poor little scrap of a mite.'

'He's not a scrap. He's perfect,' Laili crooned.

Lai took Cariel to one side, out of Laili's hearing.

'Is he going to be all right? And Laili? Why didn't you call me?'

'She wouldn't let me call you. Said she had to do it on her own. And it's too early to tell with the little one. He's small, but he's strong. A fighter.'

'Lai?' Laili called. He could hear the weariness in her voice now. He went back to her side. 'Isn't he beautiful?' she said.

Lai nodded.

'What will you call him?' He put out a finger, stroked the baby's soft cheek. The baby pursed up its mouth as the finger touched the side of his lips, ready to suck.

For a moment, Lai felt as if from a great distance, Clodolë's pain. This was what she had been denied. The simple pleasure of holding her own live, undamaged child in her arms.

'An Aelahim name?' She ruffled the coppery down on the baby's shell-pink head. 'Look at him. He's an Arkendym. His name is Dion. Dion-Dhar . . .'

'That's enough talking for now,' said Cariel officiously. 'She needs rest. She's been up all night.'

'When did the labour start?' Lai asked Laili.

'On the way back from the seashore, if you must know. What a narrow escape you had!'

'Look at this gluttonous baby. So full of milk he's fallen asleep.' Laili lifted the heavy drooping head from her breast; the baby gave a little grunting snore but did not wake. 'Bed for you, my lord.' She settled him down in the crib on his side, tucking the soft shawl around him. 'However did mother manage with the feeding of two of us?'

Lai watched her. Echoes of their mother in the way she moved, the way her hair slipped from the loose knot at the nape of her neck as she bent over the crib, the way she brushed it back with one hand. But the sigh she gave as she straightened up again . . . The sigh betrayed her.

'I've decided,' he said. 'I'm going to Phaeros tomorrow.'

'Phaeros!' She gave a little start. 'Suppose you're recognised?'

'We can't stay here for ever. We have to know what has happened.'

She clasped her arms around herself as though she were cold.

'And we have to know when the next ship leaves Ar-Khendye for the islands.'

Her eyes met his, pleading; he saw how wan she had become, how worry and sleepless nights had eroded her stamina.

'Not yet. Just wait a little longer.'

'Winter's coming on. How long can we wait?'

She went to the window, gazing out across the darkening sea.

'What do you think has happened to him, Lai?'

'Pherindyn spoke of riots in the city. If it were safe for you to return, Melmeth would have sent word.'

She swung around.

'But to have sent no word at all!'

He could find no answers to comfort her. Sooner or later he would have to tell her the news even though he did not understand what it meant: Clodolë had returned to Perysse.

'Kneel before the Arkhys!'

Blinds shaded the Memizhon audience chamber so that at first Azhrel could not see clearly in the dim light.

Strong hands pressed on his shoulders. Irritably he shrugged them off and, with as much dignity as he could muster, went down on one knee on the polished marble floor. Looking up, he saw that Clodolë sat in Melmeth's place, a pale shimmer of heavy silks and veils draped across the throne of Memizhon.

She raised one languid hand to dismiss the tarkhastars.

'What are you doing at Myn-Dhiel, Azhrel? No one sent for you. Haven't you patients enough to attend to in the city?'

'I've come to attend on the Arkhan.'

'There's no need.'

'As his personal physician, I beg to disagree. I was treating him for a serious disorder of the eyes.'

'You heard what happened in the arena?'

'I heard all kinds of fantastic stories. A shaft of light from the heavens struck the Arkhan blind.'

'The stories are fanciful.'

Azhrel's knee began to ache. He made to get up.

'Who gave you permission to stand in my presence?' Clodolë cried. 'Stay where you are until I have finished!'

Azhrel shrugged. Better to humour her; only that way might he learn anything about Melmeth.

'So you admit that you were treating the Arkhan for a serious eye disorder.'

Azhrel nodded, wondering where this was leading.

'Could it be that your physic was responsible for his affliction?'

The accusation astonished Azhrel.

'So he *is* blind.'

'You've made mistakes in the past. You said I could never bear Melmeth a healthy child. You will soon be proved wrong again.'

Azhrel was taken aback. Was she pregnant? The silks she was wearing gave no hint of her condition, but they were so loosely cut that her figure was concealed.

Suppose he was wrong and she had conceived? What would become of Laili Dhar and her child?

'If I could just be allowed to examine—'

'We do not require your services any more. You are dismissed.'

'I am the Arkhan's physician,' Azhrel said stubbornly. 'Only he can dismiss me from his service.'

She rose in a dry shiver of silks; dry as the rustle of mothwings.

'If you value your freedom, you will leave Myn-Dhiel now before I

221

order your arrest. On suspicion of causing the Arkhan's blindness.'

'Let me at least see my other patient, the boy Khaldar.'

'Melmeth's catamite?' Her rich voice soured, a sharp, thin whine. And then she smiled. 'I have no idea what has become of him.'

Azhrel had been a servant to the House of Memizhon for too many years not to have leaned some of the concealed ways that honeycombed the ancient rock on which the citadel stood. He allowed himself to be escorted to the outer gate . . . then slipped back into Myn-Dhiel by means of an obscure garden door.

Khaldar's rooms were empty. From the thick film of dust coating every surface, he guessed that no one had entered for some time. The servitors he passed in the marbled corridors shook their heads when he mentioned Khaldar's name.

With every blank look his anxiety increased.

Night was falling. He entered a garden courtyard, wondering whether to abandon his search.

The moon silvered the Harkentower with a shimmering halo. Aware of a sudden tremble of movement, he stopped, gazing up at the moon-crowned tower.

They issued from one of the high barred windows in a starsilvered cloud, like soap bubbles blown from a pipe, their frail wings glistening in the moonlight.

Moonmoths – newly hatched.

Azhrel went clambering up the steep watchtower stairs two at a time. At the top lay a dim chamber, dusty moonlight shafting down from a high slit-window. And a scent wafted towards him, the sweetspice of boskh – yet here its sweetness was overlain with another sicklier stench.

'No.' Azhrel's voice was soft with nausea as he backed away. 'Oh no.'

Moonlight blanched the discoloured skin of the corpse, bleaching the corruption dazzling, purified white. The swollen body lay on a filthy pallet, tight-bursting skin crawling with erupting sletheris. Pupae cases like withered leaves hung from the wasted limbs, from the threadbare blanket. Moonmoths clustered in a patch of moonlight, their fast-drying wings vibrating. Even as Azhrel stood there, some began to drift to the high window, to flutter through the bars, drawn to the moon's pale disc.

'Khaldar,' Azhrel said. 'So they left you here to die. Alone.'

He took off his jacket and gently laid it over the eunuch boy's putrefying body.

'What a fool I've been. What a cursed fool. The answer was here beneath my eyes all the time.'

The clues were all there – the chrysalises found in the middens, the infected ridges and skin eruptions in the plague victims. How could he have missed them? There must be two patterns of addiction. Most addicts ended like this: hosts to the voracious moth larvae. But those who ingested so much boskh that it provoked the Changing he had observed in Miu seemed untouched. 'They do not prey on their own kind,' he murmured.

There was a certain ruthless efficiency about the parasitical process that as a scientist he was forced to admire. If only he had brought his journal—

'In the tower!'

The alarm had been raised. Tarkhastars came running up the stairs; turning, Azhrel saw drawn razhirs glinting in the moonlight. Too late for escape now.

'Trespasser!'

They caught hold of him by the arms and began to drag him down the stairs. When he tried to fight free, one struck him on the side of the head with his razhir hilt. The stairs crashed past in a dazzle of moonlight and nightblack.

At the bottom, he attempted to pull himself to his feet.

'You were ordered to leave, Azhrel.'

'Warn – the Arkhan—' His tongue would not work properly; he could taste blood. 'P–parasites—'

A kick caught him in the stomach; scarlet gashed the black as he went down, gasping. Blood dripped in front of his eyes. Voices swam in his head.

'Throw him out.'

They hauled him, feet dragging over the ground, until he heard a door pulled open and found himself tumbling down a steep bank, over and over until a gravel path stopped his fall.

He thought he could still hear their laughter, callous and mocking, before a black rising tide swept consciousness away.

Ymarys could not remember how long he had lain in Jhofiel's empty room. Sometimes he heard voices in the street far below.

Leave me be.

223

Nothing mattered now. He had lost Jhofiel, beautiful, ethereal Jhofiel, destroyed by the flames. And he had betrayed Lai.

Maybe there was still time to warn Lai – but that would mean admitting his guilt. And how would Lai ever understand that he had betrayed his sister to try to save a freak, a monstrosity?

The attic room was dark. Only the outline of the arched window was limned in glistening silver.

Moonrise.

The coverlet was so soft against his naked skin, soft as the finest velvet . . .

As his eyes became accustomed to the moondusted darkness, he looked down at his body—

He leapt up with a cry, trying to brush the moths off his chest, his belly, where they clustered, clinging on until he struck them to the floor.

Moonmoths flapped dizzily about him, wings ragged from his assault, powdering the air with the sweet spicedust from their wings.

Gradually the frenzied flailing subsided. His spent body slackened, lay still.

They drifted down, settling on his skin, soft as the first fall of snow.

There were no more fluting calls, no cloud of glittering dust; they covered his body from head to naked feet, squirming, scrabbling – *stinging*—

'*Ai!*' Tiny needlepricks of fire, hot as wasp-stings, jabbing into his tender flesh.

Darkwoods . . . Drifting through the black web of thorn branches . . . The hooked thorns tear at his flesh . . .

A gust of breeze trembled through the chamber; moonmoths eddied, swirled, a turbulence of windblown petals. When the breeze died down, only a few still clung tenaciously to his arm. The others began to drop to the floor, blighted orchard blossom, their white wings fading, decaying, disintegrating . . .

Rising slowly on the nightbreeze . . . Floating over dark waters . . . Catching an echo of a voice, a whisper, a memory . . .

'Jhofiel?'

All about him lay drifts of dead moths, their papery wings crumbling in the moonlight.

A terrible, debilitating lassitude was spreading through his body, he could hardly raise his head. Moonlight silvered the floor, silvered the dead moths littering the chamber . . .

'Jhofiel . . .?'

No answer. Only the faint rushing pulse of blood in his own ears.

A crisp breeze arose off the sea, rattling the spiny sea-holly as Lai approached Phaeros along the cliff path.

It was quiet. Too quiet, Lai reckoned. There had been such a bustle of activity in the port when they sailed through weeks ago. Now he could see no movement of masts or sails – nothing stirred on the water.

He caught the sound of voices, raised voices, far below. He edged forwards to the cliff's edge until, lying on his stomach amidst the coarse marram grass, he could see the port walls and the cliff gate.

'What do you mean, the port's closed? For how long? By whose authority?'

'Can't you read, old man? By order of Jhafir, Haute Zhudiciar.'

Lai edged a little closer; there were tarkhastars in the gateway, three or four, their crimson jackets bright blots against the chalkwhite stone like hedgerow poppies.

'But I'm here to pick up my cargo. I'm a merchant, I'm expecting qaffë beans from Tai-Goa, vanilla pods—'

'I told you, the port is closed. No one is allowed in until the Haute Zhudiciar revokes the edict.'

'And when might that be, pray? When my beans have rotted and the pods have been eaten by weevils?' The irate merchant had dismounted from his horse and was waving his fists in impotent rage. Behind him a servitor idled, picking at his thumbnail.

The gate was already shut and barred.

Laili stared out over the green waves lapping at the walls of the house; high falltide, the turn of the year towards the dark side.

'What is the meaning of this intrusion? You have no right—'

Laili heard voices in the courtyard, the protests of the appellants.

'Take me to the girl. She is a runaway slave. You have been harbouring a criminal!'

The fast tread of booted feet was coming closer, closer. She snatched Dion from his cradle and ran towards the door—

The door burst open and Rho Jhan strode in.

'Laili Dhar? You are accused of heinous crimes against the Arkhan and the people of Perysse.'

'Crimes?' She tried to steady her voice. 'I have committed no crimes.'

'I bear a warrant for your arrest.'

Dion began to whimper at her breast.

'You are to be transported back to the city to stand trial.'

Cariel elbowed her way through the tarkhastars clustered outside the door and planted herself in front of Rho Jhan.

'She's just had a baby. Can't you see? She's in no condition to travel.'

He clicked his fingers and two tarkhastars came in, seized Cariel and flung her out of the room.

'No!' cried Laili, starting across the room towards her. 'Cariel! Cariel!'

Rho Jhan gripped hold of her by the arm and held his knife to Dion's throat.

'Come quietly – or I kill the child.'

Lai sat down on a tussock of reeds and tugged off his boots. His feet ached. It had been a fruitless journey to Phaeros; he had learned nothing but that the Haute Zhudiciar had stopped all river traffic in and out of Perysse until the plague was under control. High overhead, curlews wheeled above the salt marshes. So human, their plaintive calls . . .

Gradually, the realisation came to him that, mingled with the birds' keening cries were distant, desperate screams and cries for help.

He went splashing back through the reed clumps towards the sand dunes, splattering his robes with mire-water.

A carriage, escorted by crimson-clad horsemen, was fast vanishing over the dunes.

He ran on, his bare feet thudding on the damp sand. But there was no way he could catch them up; even as he ran, they dwindled into the sea mist glistening on the horizon and disappeared from sight.

A huddle of appellants met him at the open gateway, all talking at once in hushed, frightened voices. Cariel was crying.

'What—' he leaned against the gatepost, panting, '—has happened?'

'They took her! They took Laili!'

'Who? Who were they?'

'They forced their way in. Their leader was tattooed,' Cariel said. Lai saw the raw bruises marring her face, her swollen mouth.

'Rho Jhan,' Lai said, stunned.

'We tried to stop them. They wouldn't listen to us, the leader just arrested her, bundled her and the babe into a carriage and drove away—'

Pherindyn came out into the courtyard.

'Give me the key to the armoire, mhaestyr,' said Lai.

The heavy armoire door swung open and he lifted down his razhir.

'Is there no other way?' Pherindyn pleaded.

'No other way.'

CHAPTER 21

'So . . . this is Melmeth's whore.'

Laili lay sprawled, shivering on the floor where Rho Jhan had flung her. She raised her head, trying to squint through bruised lids and a veil of matted hair to identify the owner of the low, honeyed voice.

Soft footfall of delicate silk-slippered feet, coming nearer, pausing.

'I warned you, Rho, not to play with her too roughly. I want to question her myself. Before I hand her over to Ophar.'

Pain of aching limbs, pain of beaten body, pain like fire in her lungs at every breath.

'I often wondered what he saw in her . . .'

A thin groan of denial escaped Laili's cracked lips.

'Do you know where you are, whore?'

'Baby. What – have you done with – my baby?' Her voice, worn to a whisper, could hardly frame the words.

'Give her some berindë, Rho.'

Rough hands yanked her upwards. That male musk-sweat odour she had come to hate in the last days; seasoned leather and black liquorice. Rho Jhan.

An open flask was thrust between her lips, grating against her teeth. Berindë scorched her mouth, her throat, making her choke.

'Do you know who I am?'

Laili blinked. The room was in twilight but even in the dimness she could make out a slender woman sitting observing her, a blur of white and gold, cream and honey mixed, her luminous skin paler than the creamy silk of her robes.

'You are – the Arkhys.' Laili tried to focus on Clodolë's face in the duskhaze. Her eyes. So large . . . So weirdly dark . . .

'You see, Laili,' the Arkhys rose from her couch and came slowly towards her, 'you will be of use to me in a way that you could never have anticipated.' As she came closer, her perfume seemed to enfold Laili in a summercloud of sweetspice; her very breath seemed laden

with this strange, delicious perfume. 'I know he cares for you still.'
Laili's eyes flicked open suddenly. 'Oh, not as you fondly
imagine . . .' A cool, soft hand drifted across her cheek. 'If he loved
you and you alone, little whore, would he have left you in the house
by the sea?'

'And if he loved you so much – why did he banish you from
Perysse?'

The soft hand drew back sharply; Laili flinched, expecting a blow.
The blow did not fall.

'Ah, there is so much you do not understand . . . You are too naïve
to know these things, to know how to keep a man in thrall even when
he is far away . . .' A hushed whisper of silk as the Arkhys moved
away. 'Is everything prepared for her, Rho?'

'Everything.'

'What are you going to do with my baby?' Laili asked hoarsely.

'Your baby?' Clodolë began to laugh. 'My baby. My beautiful son.'

'Yours?' Laili said in a gasp.

'My long-awaited heir.'

'Where is he?' Laili reared up. 'Where is my son?'

Clodolë rose and drew aside a gold-threaded tapestry; beyond lay a
gilded cradle hung with silken drapes of the palest Memizhon blue.

'Look.'

Laili strained to see, catching the merest glimpse of a soft tuft of
copper hair before Rho Jhan pulled her back.

'Sleeping soundly. But soon he will wake – hungry . . .'

'And how will you be able to feed him?' Laili said, scorn tainting her
voice. She could already feel the milk burning in her swollen breasts.

'An arkhys never feeds her own children! She employs a wet-nurse.
And you will have to do for now . . . until Ophar calls you to answer
the charges against you. By then I shall have found someone more
suitable.'

Lai made the last stage of the long journey back to Perysse on a
farmer's cart laden with baskets of glossy egg-plant and okra.

They were still letting food into the city. And none of the
tarkhastars on the city gate recognised him, as he sat beside the
farmer, his face smeared with earth, his hair tucked into the wide-
brimmed straw hat he had worn to tend Pherindyn's garden, his
razhir concealed beneath a pile of old sacks.

But what a change had befallen the city! The once-busy streets were silent and deserted. The silk bazaar was closed; the clacking looms had stilled. Only the stench of the dye works hung like a cloud over the rooftops . . . mingling with the thickening pall of smoke from funeral pyres.

Dusk found him sitting on the edge of the quay, the turgid waters lapping against the stone wall beneath his dangling feet. Soon night would smother the city, extinguishing all lights as curfew was called. Perysse: city of ghosts and shadows.

Where had they taken her? Was she in the donjon? How could he get news of her?

If only he could find Ymarys.

Think. Think back. Where had he found Ymarys the night they left Perysse? The Mhaell pleasure house. The House of Ysmodai. Close to the quay.

It was dark now; he stood up and made his way from doorway to doorway along the cobbled quay, searching for the gilded daemon's head: Ysmodai the trickster.

'A moment of your time, zhan Razhirrakh.'

Lai whirled around, hand on razhir-hilt, razhir half out of its scabbard – only to see Arlan Azhrel in the doorway.

'Arlan! I could have skewered you.' He thrust the razhir back into its sheath.

'Foolish of me. I was tired, I didn't think.'

'I'm looking for the Pleasure House of Ysmodai.'

'I've just come from there.'

There was something tense, something twisted in Azhrel's face.

'Oh – and it's not what you're thinking. I've been with a patient of mine.'

'I didn't imagine you were visiting the House of Ysmodai on pleasure.' Lai forced a wry smile.

The twisted expression relaxed; suddenly Azhrel's hands were on his shoulders, pulling him into a quick, fierce embrace.

'In all truth I never thought to see you again. What in Mithiel's name persuaded you to come back?'

'I've got to find Ymarys. I thought he might be here – but the place seems deserted.'

'The Haute Zhudiciar had all the brothels closed down when the plague got out of control. But you have come to the right place. He *is* here.'

'In hiding?'

230

'He has fallen sick.'

This was a setback Lai had not anticipated.

'The plague?'

'Maybe.'

'Is he conscious?'

'Intermittently so.' Azhrel put one hand on Lai's shoulder, gazing searchingly into his face by the fading light of the wandering moon. 'I have to warn you. He's not . . . as you remember him . . .'

'Arlan?' Lai tried to scry the physician's scarred face but shreds of ragged cloud hid the moon and a shadowveil fell between them.

'See for yourself, if you must.'

Ymarys lay in an upper room, naked beneath a threadbare linen sheet. He seemed not to hear the door open or the footsteps as they softly crossed the bare boards to his bedside. Beneath the medicinal smirch of burnt fever herbs, lay another, more insidious scent, a sweeter taint that Lai could not yet identify . . .

Azhrel gently drew back the crumpled sheet; Ymarys did not ever stir.

Lai gazed at the emaciated body, once so extravagantly praised by court poets, at the tumbled, lank hair, the dried and peeling lips, the several days' growth of beard stubbling the sunken cheeks.

'Ymarys,' he murmured, shocked at the devastating change the sickness had wrought.

'I have watched by his bedside for three days and nights now. He has not once regained consciousness.'

Pallid grey light had slowly begun to leak into the room. Lai leaned forwards, peering in the half-light at Ymarys's body, noting the irregular rise and fall of the taut ribcage. Ymarys, sensing the shadow, mumbled something in his sleep and shifted.

'What is – *that*?' Lai whispered, pointing. 'There. And there again, another one – above the groin.'

Ymarys made a sudden convulsive movement, clutching at his thigh, slapping at it as though to dislodge some clinging insect.

'You saw?' Azhrel said, grimly triumphant.

'Surely it was just the twitch of a muscle?'

'Keep watching.'

'There – again. Like a rippling, a wriggling beneath the skin. Arlan—' Lai looked up at Azhrel over Ymarys's body.

'Can't you smell it in here? It clings, long after the moths have died, almost as if every pore were still exuding the stuff.'

231

'Boskh?'

'Oh, they're subtle creatures, these moonmoths. They dull the senses of their victims with the dust on their wings. Then when the victim is too drugged with the dust to care, they inject their eggs deep below the skin. So when the grubs hatch, they have a plentiful supply of living food to sustain them.'

'No!' Lai cried. 'It can't be so!'

'Is this the secret that your fellow adepts kept from you? That these transient, ethereal moonmoths are nothing but voracious parasites? Parasites that feed on human tissue?'

'No,' Lai repeated stubbornly.

'I was slow to put the clues together. I couldn't understand where they were breeding, how they were breeding—'

'Isn't there something you can do to save him? Anything?'

'I call myself a physician, Lai, yet he's beyond my skills and it pains me to sit here, just – watching him die.'

Despair and fatigue had dulled Azhrel's eyes; Lai saw in the greylight how worn, how exhausted he was.

'When did you last get any sleep?' he asked gently.

'I forget.'

'You need to rest,' Lai said. 'I'll stay with him.'

'I can snatch a nap in the chair here . . .'

'If he takes a turn for the worse, I'll send someone to fetch you. Go home. Go to bed.'

'I wouldn't say no to a bath, that's true. And a change of linen. But Lai—'

'Go,' Lai said, steering him towards the door.

'I'll come back by noon.'

When the physician's footsteps had died away, Lai unbelted his razhir and, laying it on the floor, settled himself in the chair at Ymarys's bedside. From the open window the first sounds of morning began to disturb the silence: the clatter of cart wheels over cobbles, ordinary sounds on an ordinary day. And if Ymarys heard them, he gave no sign.

'Jho . . . fiel . . .'

Lai woke. The room was bright with daylight; for a moment he had no idea where he was. He tried to straighten up, wincing as his stiff-cricked neck protested – and realised that the voice he had heard was no dreamvoice but Ymarys's.

The still body on the bed had begun slowly to undulate, to writhe, as though griped by some silent internal agony.

'Ymarys?' Lai said, his voice thick with sleep. 'Can you hear me?'

The hands began to flex, to move over the writhing body, the head began to thrash from side to side.

Lai reached out to grasp one of the wayward hands between his own.

'*Ymarys.*'

For a moment the lids flickered apart, revealing the dark-filmed eyes underneath then squeezed shut as the fingers clawed into Lai's hands.

'Close – shutters—' A whispering hiss of pain, piercing in its sibilance.

Lai stumbled across to the window and swiftly pulled the shutters across; as he looked at his hand he saw that the clutching fingernails had drawn blood. A pattern of light spots still speckled the floor by the bed, bright pollen on polished wood.

'Water . . .'

Lai poured water into a glass and knelt to try to raise the limp head and tip the glass to Ymarys's parched lips. Ymarys took a few feeble sips, water dribbling down his stubbled chin – and then turned his face away.

'Ahh – it burns—'

Lai drew hastily back as Ymarys began to flail about, disjointed fragments of words gritted out from between clenched teeth.

'Gnawing – inside—'

He rose up, dark-veiled eyes staring unseeing into the sun-speckled gloom, grabbing blindly at Lai's hand.

'For Mithiel's sake, let me put an end to this! Give me my blade, give me the death crystals, kill me before they – before they—'

'Ymarys. Do you know me?' Lai gripped hold of the wild-flailing arms.

'Know you?' Sweat-sticky fingers moved to touch his face. 'Lai. Oh Lai. It *is* you.'

'What has happened to Melmeth? Where is Laili?'

'My protégé. You know where to cut for a clean, quick kill. Do it now.' Ymarys dropped back onto the mattress, panting for breath.

The door creaked open and Azhrel came padding softly across the polished boards to Ymarys's bedside.

Lai caught hold of his arm, pointing at Ymarys's erratically jerking body.

'Look.'

Pustules were erupting along the ridges on Ymarys's smooth skin. And as Lai watched, something began to emerge from the largest pustule, something yellowish-pale and glutinous, like an oozing jelly.

Ymarys began to whine, a terrible thin, searing sound. The physician bent over him.

'Easy now, Ymarys . . .' With surgical tweezers he began to draw the emerging creature from Ymarys's body until it hung, slowly squirming its translucent coils from the tips of the instrument.

'What is it?' Lai said, his gorge rising.

'A moonmoth grub,' Azhrel muttered. 'Now do you believe me?'

Ymarys's hand reached blindly out, clawing for Lai's.

'Lai – do it – do it now—'

'Can't you do anything to help him, Arlan? Poppy to dull the pain?'

'Nothing works. He can't keep it down. He's eaten away inside.'

'Lai – I beg you—' Scream of pain wrenched out, words barely intelligible.

Lai looked at Azhrel; Azhrel looked hopelessly, defeatedly back.

'How long will he last like this?'

'Another day, two even . . .'

Lai drew in a breath, then let it out in a slow, jagged sigh.

'You go, Arlan. *I'll* stay.'

Azhrel nodded his head. He packed away his instruments and left without another word.

Lai knelt by Ymarys's side and stroked the sweat-soaked hair from his forehead.

'Can you hear me, Ymarys? I'll do as you ask. But you must grant me one last favour in return.'

The phantasm of a wistful smile passed across the sunken features.

'Am I still . . . that attractive, darling? You . . . flatter me . . .' The words ended in a gasp, the emaciated body arched in a sudden spasm of pain.

'Laili's in danger, Ymarys. I have to find Melmeth.'

'Melmeth – in mausoleum—'

'The mausoleum? Is he dead?' Lai clutched Ymarys's hand tightly. 'You must tell me, Ymarys.'

'N–no. Arena tunnel – follow thylz—'

The arched body collapsed, the words degenerated into an inarticulate whine, the whine of a dying animal. A trickle of black blood issued from one side of the cracked lips.

Lai closed his eyes a moment, his lips moving in a silent prayer to the Goddess.

The razhir slid from its sheath with the hiss of sharp-honed steel. It glinted, a pale sickle of moonshine, in the dim room.

Ymarys's teeth were bared in a grimace.

'Do – it—' he whispered.

Lai grasped the hilt two-handed. Braced himself. Swung – arcing flash of moonshine – and struck.

The room was silent now but for the buzz of a trapped insect beating against the shutters. But even as Lai wiped the blood from his blade, he saw a wriggle of movement beneath the skin of the still body, moth-maggots still at work in a corpse not yet cold.

He wrapped his cloak about him and went slowly, numbly down the stairs.

CHAPTER 22

Darkwater. Chill darkwater many fathoms down below a frozen, sunless sea. Nothing stirs, not even a thread of current.

'Laili – help me!'

Only the black engulfing waters, cold as the realms of Ar-Zhoth, cold as death—

Melmeth woke, clawing at the air, reaching out into emptiness. His skin was moist with cold salt-sweat, the crumpled sheets clammy as he clutched the fading darkness to him.

'You were dreaming.'

'Dreaming.' He clutched at his heaving chest, trying to drag air into his lungs. Drowning. He had been drowning, not dreaming, even now the bitter brine taste of the black waters racked his throat.

'And now you are awake.'

'Clodolë. But you should be in Shandaïra.' His thoughts were so muddled – he couldn't remember why she had gone to Shandaïra, only that there had been some reason for it—

'Oh, no. I am here. Touch me.' She bent over him, her hair brushing his chest, her breath warm and boskh-sweet.

His hand rose shakily, seeking hers, imploring.

'Do you have just a little of the dust?' To his shame he heard himself begging.

'That depends.'

'Depends on what?'

She paused.

'Would you like to see our son?'

'*Our* son?' He fought the dizziness to pull himself up. 'What are you talking about?'

'We have a son, Melmeth.' Her voice seemed radiant, golden in the gloom. 'His name is Dion.'

'Impossible! We haven't slept together in over a year. And I'm not acknowledging some ill-gotten lovechild of yours as heir to the House of Memizhon—'

Her finger jabbed him in the chest. 'Who are you to rant about ill-gotten lovechildren, my lord Melmeth?'

Suddenly he knew.

'Where is Laili?' he asked hoarsely. 'What have you done with her?'

'One thing at a time.'

'And the child? My son?' He rose clumsily from the bed; his legs seemed to be made of straw. 'Where is he?' He made a grab for her; his arms clutched empty air.

'I had not realised till now.' Her voice came to him from the far corner of the cell, quietly disdainful. 'You really are blind. Blind – and helpless.'

'He is not your son. He is Laili's. If you've harmed her—'

'I want the child. He is, by rights, mine – you can't deny it.'

Want. Mine. Clodolë had the power to crush all he held dear. The anxiety gnawing at his heart intensified.

'Where is Laili?' he repeated.

'Alive. For as long as it suits my purposes.'

The wanton cruelty in her voice enraged him.

'And you can help to keep her alive if you co-operate with me.'

'And if I choose not to—'

'Rho-Jhan has her in his keeping. She would not die quickly.'

'Laili, Laili . . .' He stood, useless, defeated, disgusted at his own helplessness.

'Here, my lord.' Clodolë came close to him – and suddenly he could smell a delicious perfume. 'Console yourself with this. A little of the dust would ease your mind and body . . .'

So long since he had tasted the dust . . . a terrible hunger invaded his body. He must not give way to it. Not if he was to save Laili.

'Take it away.'

'What harm can it do you now? Mmm . . .' He could hear her sampling the dust, he could almost taste it himself, his mouth had begun to water. 'It's so refreshing . . .'

The scent wafted around him like perfumed smoke; her voice had melted to a murmur of soft, subtle persuasion. He turned away, feeling his hands trembling uncontrollably; he clenched them until the nails bit into his palms. He had a son now, he must be strong.

'No? Then I'll leave some for you. Help yourself whenever you wish.'

He blinked, suddenly seeing a milky aureole in the darkness.

'Clodolë – what is happening to you?'

'To me?' A new, vulnerable note in her voice. 'What do you mean?'

'There is a kind of glimmering about you. An aura.'

'A – a trick of your diseased eyes. There is nothing the matter with me.'

A shadow fell across Laili's bed. A lantern flame, bright as a glowing coal, lit the stern face gazing down at her.

'Who are you?' Laili whispered, drawing the thin blanket up to her chin. 'What do you want?'

'To talk with you.' The stranger set the lantern down on the table.

'I don't know who you are.'

'I am Ophar, servant of Mithiel.' It was difficult to tell his age; his face had the worn, weathered quality of carven stone. She sensed no warmth or compassion in the man – only an immutable sense of duty, achieved by long years of prayer and self-denial.

'Is this some kind of interrogation?'

'Tell me about the Goddess of Ael Lahi.'

Laili, dishevelled, still half-asleep, had begun to piece the clues together. Wasn't it Ophar who had insisted that she convert to the Way of the Flame before she could become Melmeth's consort?

'What do you want to know?'

'I want to know what kind of deity would send a plague of such devastating power as this plague of moonmoths that is ravaging my city.'

Laili gave a little shake of her head.

'You believe the Goddess sent the moonmoths?'

'Arkendym slavers defiled Her Sacred Grove.'

'Yes, but—'

'And now She revenges Herself on us for their crimes.'

'No! That is not Her way! She is above such human emotions as revenge. She does not hunger for blood sacrifice.'

'And how do you know this?' Ophar's voice was low, subtly soft.

'I served Her in the Grove. I was taught Her ways, Her wisdom. She is the rhythm of the tides. She is the pattern that underlies our lives.'

'You talk of pattern.' He snorted. 'But how can you pattern your lives on such vague principles? Where is the discipline of ritual and prayer, of self-denial and abstention?'

From the crib at the foot of the bed came a grumbling cry. Dion was waking for his next feed.

238

How could she explain the ways of the Grove? The celebration – the calm – the sense of purpose? His life had been dedicated to a lonely path, a path that had demanded the ultimate self-sacrifice, the submerging of all personal needs in the service of a savage and merciless god. He had come to question her at her most vulnerable and at the darkest hour of night; she was alone, imprisoned. He was waiting to trip her up, to trap her in her own words. She would not give him that satisfaction.

'To enter the Grove is to give up the life outside the Grove,' she said, choosing her words with care. 'I gave up everything – but in return I gained so much more—'

'This has been most instructive.' He cut her short. 'So you believe your Goddess is incapable of acts of vengeance?'

The grumbling from the crib grew louder. Soon, Laili knew, it would become a roar of hunger.

'I believe the Goddess shapes our lives in other ways,' she said, 'ways we do not always understand.' She could see Dion's fists and feet kicking furiously free from their wrappings. Ways you could never understand, you dessicated old man, she wanted to say. Can't you see my baby's hungry? Can't you leave us together for what little time we have left?

She seized Dion and held him to her.

'My baby needs feeding,' she said, staring challengingly at Ophar, daring him to gainsay her.

But he said nothing and, covering his head with his hood, rapped on the door three times to be let out.

When he had gone and the keys had turned in the lock behind him, she still held Dion tight, rocking him, hushing him.

'We have to get away from here, baby. We have to find your father. But how?'

Lai tugged the battered straw hat over his hair and, face well concealed, followed Ymarys's bier to the Place of the Pyre. There, he watched as the hierophants poured pungent pyre oils over the body.

'The Flame warmed you to life, to the Flame now return . . .'

It seemed a bleak and joyless ceremony, with little consolation in it.

At moonrise Lai and Azhrel went down to the banks of the Yssil to scatter the ashes on the fast-flowing waters.

'It was not how he wished to die,' Lai said. 'He wanted a glorious death, blade in hand . . . He used to jest about it . . .'

'But you were with him at the end. He called your name in his delirium. You must have been . . . close.'

Lai caught the slight hesitation in Azhrel's voice though, wrapped up as he was in his own misery, he did not read any great significance into it.

'He taught me all he knew about bladesmanship. All his tricks, all his secrets. Without his training I would have died in the arena. Yes. I suppose we grew to be close.' He swallowed down the rising tears; he could not afford to weep now, he needed to be strong. 'I would have given anything to spare him such a death.'

'I've just come from the bedside of another victim,' Azhrel said. His eyes were blank, empty of emotion. 'A flute-girl, not fifteen summers old. And I can do nothing for her.'

'The Goddess's sacred creatures turned against us.' Lai shuddered, seeing again Ymarys's pain-drawn face.

'Against us? But maybe this is how they have always been. Maybe your elder adepts knew this all along.'

'No. It's impossible.' But even as Lai said the words, he began to think that Azhrel might be right.

'Suppose the adepts had found a way to control these voracious creatures? Suppose that was what they would have taught you – had you not been snatched away by the slavers?'

'"The secret of the Goddess's wisdom lies in understanding the pattern, the rhythm, the dance . . ."' Lai whispered. He gazed out across the rain-swollen waters. Suddenly he turned to Azhrel. 'But the pattern has been broken. I don't see the Goddess's purpose in this. I see only human greed and corruption. And someone has to stop it.'

The moon's light broke low over the oil-dark waters of the river. Pale as moon sylphs, they came floating from the dilapidated tenements on the quay, to dart and dance over the waters.

'But how?' In the moonlight Lai saw the dark smudges of exhaustion shadowing Azhrel's eyes. 'They are everywhere. Fumigation has failed. Every house burns moth herbs and incense – but still they find their victims and still they breed—'

'Fire.' Lai gripped Azhrel by the arms. 'But not just any fire. Firedust.'

'But firedust burns so fast—'

'And so brightly. Brighter than any bonfire. It would be irresistible.'

'Maybe . . .' Azhrel sounded unconvinced.

240

'Could you make a display that burned bright enough to draw the moonmoths from all over the city?'

'I don't know if I have the skill – or even enough firedust.'

'There must be firedust in the Memizhon armoury.'

'Haven't you heard? The plague has even struck to the heart of the Tarkhas Memizhon. The Zhudiciar's closed the barracks until they can be fully fumigated. No one's allowed out – or in. He's moved the tarkhastars into Myn-Dhiel – a sensible precaution, in the light of the arena riot.'

'But you could try—'

'Of course I'll try – I'll try anything!' Azhrel snapped back. Then he seemed to make an effort to control himself. 'Forgive me. I'm a little short-tempered. Lack of sleep, that's all. There are a few barrels of firedust in the powder room in the tunnels below the armoury. A leftover from Sardion's day. If the dust's not deteriorated I might be able to put it to good use.'

Crick in his neck; Lai groaned as he tried to move his head. One hand rose to rub the spasmed muscles.

Muted daylight lit the untidy piles of papers littering Azhrel's desk; the blinds were still drawn. Shadows of branches flickered across the yellowed linen, stained with age and sun.

Lai slowly raised himself to his feet. His mouth was dry and foul, his eyes sticky with sleep. He must have fallen asleep in the old leathern chair in Azhrel's study. How long had he slept? No one had disturbed him. He had some vague recollection that . . .

He opened the door and looked down the passageway.

'Arlan?' he called.

The wood-panelled passageway was silent, the dusty patina of the old timber mellowed by the sunshine.

Lai opened the garden door and went to the well. The water he drew from the mossy depths was clear and bitter, it tasted of stone rich in metal ores, the ancient bedrock on which Perysse was built.

When he had finished drinking, he dipped his hands into the bucket and splashed the cold, astringent water onto his face, his head, his neck.

He shook water droplets from his dripping hair; they glittered like crystal rain in the autumnal sunlight.

Inside, Mirali was busy kneading dough on the floured kitchen table.

'Qaffë's brewing on the hob,' she said without looking up from her work.

Lai poured the dark liquid into a bowl and stirred in a generous spoonful of spiced honey before wandering back into Azhrel's study.

He flicked through the pages of Azhrel's open journal: the jottings of a physician had become a record of the progress of the plague. One passage in particular caught Lai's eye; he set the bowl of qaffë down and began to read:

> Ophar, in his infinite wisdom, has pronounced these Changed Ones to be abominations of Ar-Zhoth. People fear what they do not understand. But suppose we have misunderstood the nature of these creatures? Suppose they hold the answer to the curing of the plague?

'I trust you slept well.'

Azhrel stood in the doorway watching him.

'Who are the "Changed Ones"?' Lai pointed to the entry he had been reading.

Azhrel let out a halting sigh.

'It seems . . . that the repeated ingestion of boskh affects some individuals more drastically than others. Most – like Ymarys – are used as hosts by the moths. But in others the boskh precipitates a form of metamorphosis into a state of being quite . . . inconceivable. Not human. Yet not inhuman. Something . . . else.'

In the darkest shadows of the Grove the Goddess Changes the Chosen One to her will, bestowing gifts of Healing . . .

'You've witnessed this metamorphosis?' Lai gazed intently at Azhrel.

'Yes. Oh, yes.' Azhrel shuddered. His dark eyes had become shadowed, haunted.

'What happened?'

'The hierophants torched her,' Azhrel said bleakly. 'If only you had seen her, heard her sing . . . Ah, that silver sound. It haunts me still, Lai. Does my hypothesis sound too eccentric to you? We know that boskh heals. Suppose those who are Changed by boskh are healers, healers by touch, by the touch of sound upon the body?'

'Suppose . . .' Lai murmured.

'And, in our fear and ignorance, we have destroyed our only hope of survival?'

'But there must be others—'

'Not one of the Changed has escaped the flames. What hope is there for us while the fanatics control the city?'

'Fanatics?'

'Ophar brought Clodolë back to the city in triumph. Oh, she believes she is sole ruler now – but in everything she does I smell the dubious sanctity of the Way of the Flame. Look at this' He drew a poster from his robes and placed it on the desk in front of Lai:

> The Arkhys is happy to announce her recent delivery of a healthy son and heir to the royal House of Memizhon. Before proceeding to the Shrine of the Flame to give thanks for this auspicious birth, the customary donation of birthgifts will be made from Myn-Dhiel when she will show the Arkhyn to the people . . .'

'Clodolë – delivered of a son?' Lai went through the proclamation again, unable to believe what he had read. 'But – she is barren. You said so yourself. How could she have—'

'Your sister's son? The one who was taken by Rho Jhan?'

'Dion,' Lai said in a whisper. 'Could it be Dion? And if it's so,' he looked up at Azhrel in an agony of anxiety, 'what's become of Laili?'

CHAPTER 23

The Arkhyn's robes were of ivory satin, the tiny cuffs and hem intricately embroidered in gold and scarlet thread. Laili looked at them – and looked at Dion. Such a shame to wake him. He would hate to be undressed – and hate even more being confined in these antique, uncomfortable garments. She knew her reluctance to do as Clodolë had bidden her stemmed from a much deeper fear. Once he was dressed in the official clothes of the heir to the House of Memizhon, he was no longer her child – but Clodolë's.

'Well?' Clodolë said. 'Is he ready?'

'He's asleep.' Laili let her hand rest protectively over the rim of the crib.

'I told you to have him ready!' Clodolë said, fretfully waving her silken fan. 'There are crowds gathering outside. They've come to see him. Can't you hear the noise? Dress him now. Or do I have to do it myself?'

I'd like to see you try, Laili thought. She leaned over and stroked Dion's cheek.

'Wake up, little one.'

He let out a grunt as she burrowed her hands beneath him and lifted him out onto the bed. He was too drowsy at first to notice but as she untied and peeled off his robes, he gave a convulsive shiver of displeasure.

As Laili worked, she glanced up at the open doorway. If she were to seize him and run—

Hawk-grey eyes met hers. Rho Jhan stood outside in the shadows. Of course, Clodolë would not have come alone, unguarded.

'I'm waiting,' said Clodolë, tapping her fan against her fingertips. She seemed unduly agitated.

Laili tried to coax and squeeze Dion's chubby little arms through the ornate cuffs. Dion was not pleased with this new indignity. His face puckered up as her fingers fumbled with the ribbon ties.

244

'You should take a clean cloth to protect your gown,' she said, staring directly at the Arkhys as she lifted Dion off the bed.

'And why?'

'He has a tendency to bring up a little of his feed.' It was a small and bitter triumph to see the unmistakable expression of disgust on Clodolë's face.

They stood a moment, the baby held between them, Laili unable to let go, Clodolë suddenly tentative, almost reluctant. In the silence, Laili became aware of a far-off clamour of voices.

'The crowd's growing restive,' Rho Jhan said from the doorway.

Clodolë snatched the baby out of Laili's arms and swept out of the room.

Laili rushed after her, only to find the door slammed in her face. Rho Jhan had locked it before she could drag it open again. In rage she beat her fists against the gnarled wood until they were bruised and sore.

'Dion!' she cried. '*Dion!*'

Nothing in her training in the Grove had prepared her for this. She had learned the disciplines of endurance and self-denial. But this separation roused a deep animal instinct within her; they had taken her child from her. She could find no inner calm until she had him back with her again.

The shouts of the crowd grew louder as Clodolë climbed the steps of the gatehouse. She climbed slowly, awkwardly, afraid to drop the squirming bundle.

Emerging into the daylight, she was greeted with a tumultuous cheer; servitors and citizens thronged beneath the walls, gazing up at her. Her eyes ached in spite of the gauze veil; the autumn sun seemed overbright even though there were clouds gathering above the heights. She smiled, and lifted the baby to show them.

'Mithiel has blessed me with a son!' she cried, triumphantly. Her dhamzels brought forward baskets and threw down handfuls of sugared almonds and silver eniths into the cheering crowd.

She hugged the baby to her triumphantly.

'Now you're mine, Dion,' she crooned. 'All mine.'

Lai shaded his eyes against the cloudy light and gazed intently upwards.

Clodolë. He felt a strange stir of emotion as he saw her appear on the ramparts, a distant vision of drifting golden veils and pale hair.

He did not join in the scrabbling for almonds and coins, but stayed gazing upwards, jostled to and fro by the crowd.

Dion. She had taken Dion from Laili. From the awkward way she carried the baby, he was sure his suspicions were true.

And if she had taken Dion – then where was Laili now?

Dion began to snuffle in his gilded cradle. The snuffling soon deteriorated to a quiet but insistent grizzling. Clodolë crept closer, wondering what she should do. The baby's face crumpled up, its fists clenched tight as it began to hiccup its rage. Its face had turned bright scarlet.

'There, there, baby,' Clodolë said. She patted its arm ineffectually.

Dion's toothless mouth opened and he let out a yell. A terrible yell, as if all the daemons of Ar-Zhoth were raging in his belly. He drew his knees up, his little body convulsed.

What was she supposed to do? Was he hungry? Cold? Wet?

Uncertainly she reached into the crib and picked him up. Ugh. The linen robe was damp and stained. As she lifted him, his lower lip drooped and he let out another shivering cry.

'Hush now.' She tried to hold him close but it seemed hard to get a safe grip on this quivering, hot, damp little body. She began to rock him in her arms. 'Hush. What's the matter?'

Dion only yelled louder.

'Quiet, baby.' Why was he not responding? This was what mothers did, wasn't it? How could he tell she was so inexpert at it? How could he tell she was not his real mother? She began to pace up and down the little room, patting at the furious baby on her shoulder. 'Quiet, Dion.' His sobs were beginning to affect her; tears stung her eyes. If this were her baby, it would not cry so. If this were flesh of her flesh, it would nestle close to her heart, it would know the sound, the rhythm of her heartbeat. How could it go on crying so? Did it know what she intended? Did it know it was to be taken from its mother?

Panicking, she dropped it clumsily back in the crib. It went on yelling piteously, its knees drawn up to its chest, as though in agonising pain. Perhaps it was in pain. Perhaps even this one would die, as every baby of her own had died—

Tears streaming down her cheeks, she seized the silver bell and rang it hard.

One of her dhamzels came hurrying in.

'Take the baby away.' Clodolë had to shout to make herself heard above Dion's yells.

'I think he's hungry, Arkhys.'

'Then bring the wetnurse. The one with red hair,' snapped Clodolë.

'I thought you said her milk had dried up—'

'Just bring her here! Bring anyone!'

In his mother's arms, Dion's frenzy gradually subsided. Laili drew him into the little room, talking to him, hushing him, rocking him . . . all the things Clodolë had tried to no avail.

Clodolë lingered outside the door, watching them: mother and baby, locked in a charmed circle which she could not penetrate. They seemed so absorbed in each other. So content.

Well, it would not last much longer. Laili was dispensable. Clodolë had sent into Perysse for wetnurses; as soon as a suitable woman with a good supply of milk had been found, Laili would be disposed of.

Someone gave a discreet cough; Fhedryn stepped out of the shadows.

'My lady Arkhys, there are petitioners from the city waiting to see you about the ravages of the plague—'

'I will see no one else today, Fhedryn. I have a headache.'

'But I really think you should—'

'No one!' Clodolë cried.

But when she had closed her chamber door, she crumpled slowly to her knees, burying her face in her silken sheets, weeping and clawing at the soft-sheened fabric with her nails.

Lerillys crept up to the door, listening, terrified to knock to see what her mistress wanted and yet terrified to leave her alone in such a passion of weeping.

'He knows,' wept Clodolë, rocking herself to and fro. 'He knows I'm not really his mother.'

'Lerillys!' Clodolë rang the little bell to summon her attendant. She called again. 'Where are you, girl? Lazy slut. Still asleep?'

She went into the antechamber and flung open Lerillys's door. And stopped, mouth open. The air was filled with moths; they fluttered everywhere, coating the silken draperies with their sweet-scented dust. And on the bed lay Lerillys, naked, head lolling back, eyes unfocussed, moaning with pleasure beneath the vigorous thrusts of the tarkhastar who had mounted her.

'Lerillys!' said Clodolë again, gazing with fascination and loathing at the lovers. They neither heard nor saw her. They were trapped in a trance of sexual ecstasy that would go on and on . . .

Yskhysse . . .

Moths swirled about them, dusting their sweating bodies with stargranules of boskh, brushing one against the other in their own darting, swooping dance of mating.

Clodolë inhaled the boskh-laden air, the sense-stimulating tingle flaring through her brain like a kaleidoscopic orgasm of flame – and dying to ashes.

She shivered, hugging her arms to her body. The room had turned winterdrear and cold, her mind was draped with dull mourning sheets.

Moonmoths began to settle on the lovers, their shimmering wings covering their hair, their naked flesh, like lacy wedding gauzes.

Clodolë, staring unseeingly down the dark attic corridor of her past, began slowly to walk away. A fitful wind banged the doors of the rooms where her stillborn babies lay . . .

The road leading to the plague-stricken Memizhon barracks was barricaded and the barricade was patrolled by tarkhastars. But Ymarys had once shown Lai another way in, a treacherous scramble through thornbushes and scree.

You have to be drunk to even consider attempting it . . .

Desperation drove him; he would have clambered up the sheer rockface below the mausoleum, if need be. He had to find Azhrel.

At the top, he scanned the deserted parade ground, sucking the thorn scratches on his hand. No one was about. Where all had been bustle and military precision: drills, orders, marching feet . . . now only a few birds hopped amongst the weeds.

Lai warily pushed open the armoury door. For a moment he half-expected, half-hoped to hear Ymarys's voice drawling from the shadows, 'What time do you call this? You're late!'

But the armoury was empty . . . except for a thin vapour that wreathed its way across the floor. Lai sniffed – and pulled a face. He had not smelt that foul stink of chymicals since Mithiel's Day. His guess must be right; Azhrel was in his laboratory.

Azhrel was warming an alembic over a flame. He was so engrossed in his work he did not even notice Lai come in.

'Arlan.'

Azhrel started.

'What by all the daemons are you doing here? Suppose someone recognised you?'

'I have to speak with you.'

'In a moment,' Azhrel said distractedly, tapping the grey granules in the alembic with a glass rod.

'Haven't you heard?' Lai's voice trembled.

'Heard?' Damn him, he wasn't even paying attention.

'The proclamations have been posted all over the city. They're – they're going to try her for witchcraft.'

'Witchcraft?' Azhrel's herd jerked up. The granules had begun to sputter.

'*Djhë*, Arlan, do you have to repeat everything? Laili, my sister Laili. A public trial for witchcraft. They say she brought the plague on the city.'

'When?' Azhrel said tersely.

'The Day of the Dead. Sh'amain, you call it. They're holding some kind of rite in the arena.'

The sputtering became a violent sizzling. Azhrel, glancing around, suddenly grabbed hold of Lai and threw him to the ground.

The alembic split apart in a flash of white light. Glass fragments shattered, sprinkled down in a lethal hailstorm.

Lai's ears dinned with the after-echoes of the explosion. His sight was scored with jagged lines of whitefire. Someone was shaking him, someone was asking, 'Are you all right? Are you all right?'

He put one hand to his jangling head.

'I think so.' He could not hear the words although he knew he had spoken them aloud. 'What happened?'

Thick smoke swirled between them; Azhrel's face, smeared with firedust smuts, loomed over his. Slivers of glass powdered his hair, his leather jerkin. And in that moment Lai saw what he had never seen before: Azhrel's eyes unguarded, staring wide with fear.

'The mineral salts produced a more volatile reaction at that temperature than I had anticipated.' He began to cough on the smoke.

'In other words you nearly blew us to bits.'

Azhrel nodded between wheezing coughs.

'Now surely someone will come!'

'If you hadn't interrupted me in the middle of an experiment—'

'Oh, so it's my fault?'

'Yes, damn you. Now I'll have to start again.'

'Hold still. You're covered in glass.' Lai took out his kerchief and gently wiped the smuts from Azhrel's scarred face. A smear of blood stained the fine linen. 'Was this how it happened?'

'My father was working on a new weapon for Sardion. I was helping him, learning the secrets of the art. He . . . miscalculated.'

'An explosion?'

'I was lucky to escape with my life. He was – not so lucky.' Azhrel stood up to survey the damage; glass crunched beneath his feet. 'He did not wish to make weapons. Sardion compelled him.' He took a broom from the corner and began to sweep up the shards.

'It's not going to be ready, is it?'

'I need time. Just a little more time.'

'There isn't any more time. Not for Laili. I can't wait for Sh'amain, Arlan. I've got to do something. I've got to find her.'

'You said she's to be tried for witchcraft? That's priests' business.' Azhrel propped the broom back in its corner.

'The priests of Mithiel? You think she's being kept in the shrine? Or the temple?'

'It's possible . . .'

An idea came into Lai's mind, an idea so absurd he almost began to laugh aloud.

'How do you become a hierophant?'

Azhrel looked at him.

'The ultimate irony, yes? The adept of the Goddess becomes a servant of Mithiel.'

'A servant of Mithiel! Look – I know you're upset. But take time to think this out, Lai. If they discover you, an imposter, trying to infiltrate their mysteries—'

Lai was not listening; he was already planning how he would present himself at the temple.

'I'm obviously wasting my breath,' Azhrel said, turning away.

Lai went to him and caught hold of him by the hands.

'Whatever happens to me—'

'Whatever happens to you, I'll do my part. I'll give them a display of firedust they'll never forget. And if it doesn't destroy the moonmoths, it will distract Ophar and Clodolë just long enough for you to spirit your sister away. Just don't try to take on the brotherhood of Mithiel single-handed.' His mouth twisted into an ironic, affectionate smile. 'You'd better take this too.' He handed Lai a leathern pouch. 'It will open any door – no matter how strong the lock.'

Lai tipped the pouch open: inside were two lengths of string, a set of tinderstones and a packet of grey granules.

'Firedust?'

'Indeed. So take care and don't stand too close to any naked flames.'

'And the string?'

'Not just any common kind of string!' Azhrel said, affronted. 'These are fuses – of my own designing – to set the firedust alight. Once you've lit the fuse, you've ten seconds to take cover before the dust ignites. Understand me? Ten seconds – no more.'

CHAPTER 24

Incense cones drifted thin trails of bitter fragrance into the gilded dome of the Temple of Mithiel; the air was hazed with cinnabar smoke. An incessant muttering of prayer chants, low as a murmur of summer bees, buzzed within the heart of the incense cloud.

For a moment Lai shut his eyes and let his mind drift back with the smoke to the distant Grove and the night of his initiation. They might not worship the same deity in this temple, but the spirit of worship awakened familiar echoes in his soul. If he had been born in Ar-Khendye, he might well have found himself drawn to the service of the Undying Flame.

'Whom do you seek, brother?' A priest barred his way, his eyes suspicious, unwelcoming.

'I have come,' Lai said, 'to follow the way of Mithiel.'

'The way you seek is long and many do not complete the journey. Are you prepared to leave all trappings of your life outside behind?'

'Since the plague, I have lost all that I held dear,' Lai said. It was true, in a way.

'You will leave all your worldly possessions behind. You will wear the robe of an acolyte. And you will shave your head. Are you prepared?'

His hair. Lai swallowed. But to save Laili, he would submit to this . . . and a thousand other indignities, if need be.

'I am prepared.'

A hierophant sheared off Lai's braids and then slapped a soapy paste on his skull before setting about expertly shaving off stripe after stripe of hair.

Lai sat, head bent, ruefully watching the russet locks fall to the floor. Already his head felt cold; no wonder the hierophants wore hoods.

When the shaving was finished, the hierophant took Lai down to a small plunge room, steamy with a hot stink of sulphurous water.

'Discard your clothes and cleanse yourself.'

Lai stripped and bathed in the bubbling brown spring water.

The hierophant draped a robe of black around his naked body and then conducted him deeper below ground.

'Enter the Shrine of the Flame,' he said, reverently touching his breast as he pronounced the sacred name.

The Undying Flame burnished the shadowed rocks of the shrine to a dark, metallic glow. Lai shivered, sensing the presence of an ancient and cruel deity. There was no sense of transcendent calm here. The stones had been consecrated in blood, the blood of human sacrifice.

'The High Priest of our order, is waiting. Kneel.'

Lai found himself staring into Ophar's eyes. Eyes so devoid of human emotion they could have been chiselled from chill, grey stone.

'What is your name?'

His name. Lai hesitated only a fraction of a second.

'Mirghar.' The name of Eryl's brother; it had a suitably Arkendym ring to it.

'Your face is – familiar . . .'

Don't let him recognise me. Not now. Not now I have come so far.

'And this mark – the mark of the Flame.' He touched Lai's forehead.

'I was a brandslave. I fought for my freedom – and to honour the god – in the arena.'

This answer seemed to please Ophar though he still stared piercingly at Lai.

'Welcome to our order, brother. You will serve a long apprentice-ship until we judge you are ready to take your vows. You will fast and study the holy texts. You will serve the brothers as a servant. And you will obey – whatever you are commanded to do. Do you understand?'

'I understand.' Lai bowed to the High Priest.

'Obedience is all.'

'I will obey.'

'Then plunge your right hand into the flame.'

'Into the flame?' Why had no one warned him that this would be part of his initiation?

'Obedience, brother,' Ophar said softly. 'Fail to obey and your apprenticeship ends here.'

Lai walked slowly towards the flame. As he drew nearer he could feel the heat, strong as a furnace. This flame was no illusion; whether natural gas from the rocks or slow-burning sea-coal, it was searingly hot.

He rolled back the wide sleeve of his robe. The heat burned his face, dazzled his eyes until he could see nothing but the white heart of the flame.

To turn away now would be to fail Laili. He must see this through. He had endured the tattooing in the donjon. Would this be any worse?

Gritting his teeth, he thrust his hand into the flame.

For a moment the air around him seemed to burn with an incandescent heat. Then the pain centred on his hand – his blade hand – the flesh was on fire.

A hierophant was at his side, holding a bowl of water.

'Quick. Dip your hand in here.'

Lai, eyes squeezed shut against the pain, plunged his hand into the bowl; the water was icy cold.

'Why did no one warn me?' he heard his own voice whispering.

'Would it be a true test of your faith if you knew what to expect?'

As Azhrel approached the dye works he heard a bizarre commotion: orders barked out, the cracking of whips, chains and shackles clinking.

Tarkhastars of the Tarkhas Zhudiciar were marshalling a column of chained brandslaves out of the dye works and away up the hill.

'What's going on?' He hurried over to the nearest tarkhastar. 'Where are you taking them?'

'None of your business.' The tarkhastar elbowed him out of the way.

'But these are patients of mine.'

The tarkhastar ignored him. Azhrel strode up to the gates and, catching hold of the overseer, spun him around to face him.

'I demand to know what is going on!'

'Haven't you heard, doctor? It's for the rites. The Arkhys has ordered it. Seems there aren't enough left alive in the donjon to train for the arena.'

Azhrel could see the brandslaves, shivering in the raw morning's damp, making their halting, painful way towards Myn-Dhiel. Most were bare-footed; the shackles they wore slowed their pace to an awkward, limping shuffle. His heart sank as he recognised Mirghar – and Eryl – in the line.

'To honour the god? You mean they're going to fight? The women too?'

'That's what we were told.'

'But they can barely walk!'

'Since they closed the ports, there's been no call for silk. The looms are idle and funds have run low. I've too many mouths to feed here. A few less'll suit me fine.'

'What by Mithiel's balls d'you expect me to do with this pathetic crew?'

Before he had even reached the slave compound, Azhrel heard Orthandor's bellow of indignation.

'Look at them! They're half-dead already!'

'Arkhys's orders. Any complaints – and you take them to her.'

'Arlan.' Orthandor caught sight of Azhrel. 'What are we coming to? The world's turned upside-down. First the Arkhan bans the duel rites. Then the Arkhys reinstates them.' Orthandor threw his hands high in a gesture of utter incomprehension. 'I'm ashamed to be associated with this. And where the devil's the Razhirrakh when we need him? Have you seen him?'

Azhrel hesitated.

'He's dead.'

'What d'you mean, dead?'

'Dead of the plague.'

'But he was here only a few days ago, he borrowed one of my jackets, damn him. Now I'll never get it back.'

In spite of Orthandor's blustering, Azhrel could see that he was genuinely shaken. He decided to risk everything on a hunch.

'Would you like to see Melmeth restored to power?'

'Anything would be better than this shambles.'

'Before he died, Ymarys hinted that Melmeth was imprisoned in the mausoleum.'

'Then let's round up the Tarkhas Memizhon and break him out!'

'The mausoleum's crawling with the Tarkhas Zhudiciar. I'll wager they have orders to kill Melmeth at the first sign of a rescue – and then blame it on the rescuers.'

'Hmm.' Orthandor stroked his bearded chin. 'So what do you suggest?'

'Wait till Sh'amain. Lai and I are planning a little "diversion".'

'Oho! I like the sound of this.' Orthandor rubbed his hands enthusiastically.

'And I'll need access to the arena.'

'You can have whatever you want, Arlan! Just tell me what to do – and I'll stand by you. You have my word of honour as Tarrakh on it.'

All day Lai had shadowed the High Priest, keeping just out of sight as he followed him from temple to the shrine and back again.

At dusk Lai's vigilance was rewarded; he noticed Ophar making his way purposefully towards the shrine where two of the brotherhood respectfully placed a flame-embroidered cope about his shoulders and presented him with a cruse of crimson oil. Ophar then took the stair downwards past the doors to the shine. Downwards, Lai guessed, into the tunnels. Lai waited until the two attendant hierophants had gone and slipped after the High Priest.

As Lai's eyes became accustomed to the gloom, he caught the phosphorescent glimmer of the thylz trail stones. Even in the darkest, deepest tunnels, they would show the way: crossed razhirs for the arena, rippling water lines for the Adriel Gate, a skull for the mausoleum . . .

Did Ophar sense he was being followed? Once he stopped stock still, as though listening – and Lai froze to the side of the tunnel.

Lai brushed clinging dirt from the trail stones with his fingertips. This was the way Ymarys had said he must go to find Melmeth, the way of the dead. But here there were no guards; this must be the priests' secret route known only to the chosen few.

The tunnel ended in a stone portal; Lai followed the High Priest up into the mausoleum – and stopped on the threshold. The inner chamber was full of figures – life-size figures dressed in ancient and tattered finery. He had the horrible intuition that the figures were not merely effigies – but that beneath the yellowing wax flesh were the grinning skulls and bones of the Memizhon dead.

'My lady. How fares the Arkhan today?'

Lai shrank back behind one of the leering effigies.

'No better, no worse . . .'

Clodolë's voice. She was coming this way.

'Why have you been avoiding me, lady?'

Lai detected a vivid note of emotion in the High Priest's question; his words would have better suited a rejected lover than a spiritual adviser.

'I – I haven't been avoiding you.' She walked on; she came so close now to Lai that he felt the breeze from her floating veils. 'There has been so much to do . . .'

'Please.' Ophar put one hand out to stop her. 'If anything is troubling you, you know you can always confide in me.'

'Nothing is troubling me, Ophar.' She brushed past him and vanished into the tunnels.

Lai watched the High Priest sigh and make obeisance to the flame which guttered in its niche as he returned to his duty. Ophar muttered ritual words in the old tongue as he replenished the oil. At last he completed his task and after making three solemn ritual bows, retreated.

Lai waited a while longer, fearing that he might return. But the mausoleum was silent.

At the far end of the chamber was a door; peering through the grille, Lai could just make out a figure lying on a bed, a man whose hair glinted red-gold in the gloom.

At first he wondered if this gaunt, haggard man could really be Melmeth – and then he caught the glint of the dark ruby on his finger; the ring of the flame.

'My lord Melmeth,' he called softly.

'Who's there?' Melmeth's eyes blinked open.

'Lai Dhar, zhan.'

'No . . . This must be a dream. Just another boskh-dream.'

A hand came groping out towards him through the grille, caught hold of him by the shoulder and pulled him closer, fingers moving over Lai's face. 'Lai. It really is you.'

Then to Lai's distress he began to cry.

'You haven't deserted me. Only you – a foreign slave—'

'We have to get out of here, zhan. Can you walk?'

'I d–don't know.'

'If not for your sake, then for Laili's.'

'Laili?' Melmeth's drooping head jerked up. 'Is she with you?'

'Laili is under arrest. The priests of Mithiel have accused her of witchcraft.'

'But Clodolë said—'

'You have to save her, zhan. No one else can.'

'How can I save her? Look what your Goddess did to punish me. I'm blind, Lai.'

'The Goddess? No.' Lai kept glancing behind him, listening for any stir of movement in the tunnels.

'I deserved punishment. I was presumptuous. I – I believed She had

257

chosen me. I believed She had given me healing powers – and She struck me blind.'

'Listen to me.' Lai caught hold of the Arkhan's hand and pressed it firmly between his own. 'Whatever caused your blindness – it was not the Goddess.'

'B–but I saw Her. Clothed in brilliant light. She was too bright for mortal eyes to look upon. Yet I presumed. And She – She seared away my sight.'

'Whatever you saw,' Lai said, 'was not the Goddess of Ael Lahi.'

'You speak with such certainty.'

'Later we will talk about this, zhan. But now, right now, we have to get out of here before we are discovered.'

Lai dug into the pouch Azhrel had given him and brought out the little charge of firedust. It was now so dark he could hardly see the lock as he packed the dust into the keyhole around the fuse.

'Keep your head well down, zhan.'

Lai fumbled with the tinderstones; blue sparks fizzed and died on the cold flagstones. His fingers were so slippery with sweat now he could hardly hold the stones steady. Suppose the blast blew inwards and injured Melmeth? Suppose they were discovered before the fuse ignited?

At last he struck a flame and held it to the fuse until a tongue of fire caught light and went streaking upwards. Lai dived for the floor as sparks sheared off the sizzling metal – and the steaming lock suddenly burst with a crack.

A thin, acrid smoke filled the air as the door swung slowly inwards.

Lai hurried across the chamber to where Melmeth lay cowering, his hands over his head.

'The door's open, zhan. Now's our moment.'

Lai slipped his arm under Melmeth's shoulders and heaved him to his feet. Melmeth staggered like a drunken man.

'It's no good. My legs – wasted—'

'Try, zhan. Please try.'

'*Intruder!*'

Tarkhastars came running into the inner chamber, Rho Jhan at their head.

'Go,' Melmeth murmured. 'Save yourself, Lai.'

The tarkhastars seized hold of Melmeth; Lai was flung to the floor.

'My lord Arkhan! Are you all right?' cried Rho Jhan.

Lai tried to struggle up but Rho Jhan's booted foot caught him in the face. Blood spurting from his nose, he collapsed again.

'Let go of me!' cried Melmeth. 'How dare you lay hands on your Arkhan!'

'It's for your own protection, zhan. This man is a dangerous fanatic. Take the Arkhan to a place of safety whilst I deal with the intruder. Quickly!'

Rough hands seized Lai by the collar and hauled him up; Rho Jhan's face jutted into his.

'Why, this is no renegade hierophant. It's the Aelahim.'

'What's happening, Rho?'

Clodolë's voice.

'It's as well I came when I did, Arkhys! We were just in time to restrain the assassin before he killed the Arkhan.' Rho Jhan flung Lai down again and planted his foot on his throat.

'Not – assassin—' Lai whispered, choking.

'I'll despatch him now.' Steel rasped close to his ear.

'No!'

Through the bloodhaze clouding his eyes, Lai saw a white hand reach out to stay Rho Jhan's blade.

'He knows too much, Arkhys.'

'I want to interrogate him. Myself.'

'You're making a mistake,' Rho Jhan said.

'I have my reasons.'

'Reasons!'

'He has information. Kill him now – and you'll never find out who his accomplices are in this plot. I want him taken to the donjon.'

There was a pause – then the sound of breath expelled in a snort of exasperation.

'Take him to the donjon.'

CHAPTER 25

The mills from which the bakers of Perysse bought their flour had not been replenished from the autumn's harvest. The farmers who usually shipped their flour to the granaries on the Yssil by barge had taken their grain harvests to sell elsewhere. Many bakery ovens remained cold now; the moonmoths had infested every community within the city from the eminent silk guilds down to the humblest bakers and brewers.

Queues grew outside bakeries; queues that soon formed themselves into arguing knots of discontent. They had welcomed Clodolë back to Perysse in the belief that, reunited, the Arkhan and Arkhys would work together to alleviate the city's suffering. But there seemed no end to the tribulations they were forced to endure. Was there some truth in the hierophants' warnings? Were they bearing the brunt of the excesses of the House of Memizhon?

Mutterings grew to cries of dissent. People joined together, spilling out onto the streets in one great crowd, surging up the hill towards the citadel.

A distant roar penetrated the audience chamber at Myn-Dhiel. The Haute Zhudiciar glanced uncomfortably at Rho Jhan.

'Mel–meth! Mel–meth! Mel–meth!'

Clodolë slammed the shutters and stood, her back up against the gilded panels, as though to block out the shouting of the crowd.

'Are they never satisfied?'

'They're hungry,' Rho Jhan said bluntly.

'There seems to be a general belief,' the Haute Zhudiciar added, choosing his words with care, 'that until you and Melmeth are reconciled, Arkhys, there will be no end to the plague.'

'Oh, please!' Clodolë let out a cry of irritation. 'If your men had enforced the edicts more rigorously, there would be no plague at all by now.'

'These moonmoths are impossible to exterminate. What are my men supposed to do? The city streets stink of burning mothherbs . . . and still the damned creatures multiply.'

'Mel–meth! Mel–meth! Mel–meth!'

'I'll send out the guard,' Rho Jhan said.

'Wait.' Clodolë put out one hand to stop him. 'We must humour them. Let them shout themselves hoarse. Then distribute fresh bread from the palace bakery. A gift from the Arkhys, rewarding her people for their fortitude. There will be more – and wine – at Sh'amain.'

Rho Jhan clicked his heels together in salute and left the chamber.

'They are dangerously close to insurrection,' Jhafir said. 'Will they be satisfied with a few loaves of bread? The hierophants have stirred them up, they want their blood-sacrifice.'

'And they shall have it.' She smiled at him and he noticed that beneath her veil, the red stain on her lips was dark and glossy as fresh-spilt blood. 'At Sh'amain.'

Rho Jhan brushed a smear of dust off the rich crimson cloth of his tarrakh's tunic as he waited to be admitted to the Arkhys's presence. He was pleased enough with his promotion to the command of the Tarkhas Zhudiciar, but this private audience made him wonder whether higher honours were imminent.

A dhamzel appeared in the doorway and beckoned him to follow her. So he was to attend her in her bedchamber – a privilege he had not been accorded in a long while.

Dark-spangled gauzes hid the windows, swathed the bed; the room was dim, a perpetual twilight. He blinked as his eyes strained to become accustomed to the shadowy light.

'You wanted to see me, Arkhys,' he said.

'Yes.' He glimpsed a pale figure behind the cloudy gauzes hung about the bed. Was she naked behind the drifting veils? The thought was curiously stimulating.

'Rho . . .'

'What?'

'Am I still . . . desirable?'

'You are the Arkhys. You are the most desirable woman in all Ar-Khendye.'

'You mean that my power is desirable.'

He fidgeted with the hilt of his razhir. Where was this leading?

'I've served you well, Arkhys.'

261

'Nobody could have served me more faithfully than you, Rho.'

'And would you agree that such faithful service deserves a reward?'

'Of course you deserve a reward.'

'And you deserve a consort.'

'What are you hinting at?' She moved closer until only a single gauze floated between them.

'Melmeth's blind, half-crazed with drugs. Addicts tend to be prone to accidents. An overdose . . . found choked on his own vomit . . . ?'

'But I still need him. He is useful to me. Besides, I might not want to take another consort.'

The gauze twitched. In the darkness her skin seemed to give off a faint luminescence.

'Or you might change your mind . . .' And she suddenly pressed her mouth to his, sliding her tongue deep into his mouth and it was no human tongue any more, it was long and narrow and probing, an insect sucking nectar from a flower—

'Nnnnno!' He squirmed free, holding her at arm's length, staring at her with revulsion. 'You're – you're Changing.'

She suddenly began to weep, crouching down on the bed, her long, pale hair falling like a veil over her nakedness.

'How long can you go on hiding it from the palace? From the people? When they see you – they'll try to destroy you.'

'I'm still Arkhys—'

'In their eyes you're a freak. A monstrosity that must be destroyed to put it out of its misery.'

'And in your eyes too, Rho. Oh, don't try to pretend otherwise—'

Distant shouting, like the ominous buzzing of an angry swarm, dried her words to silence.

'Firemobs,' she whispered.

He watched her drift towards the window and gaze out over the darkened city. A burst of flame lit the night sky and died away.

'Go on,' she said, whirling around, her dark eyes wild, challenging. 'Do your duty as a citizen. Call the hierophants here. Give me over to them.'

He stared at her, the feel of that alien tongue still tainting his mouth. He wondered if she knew what he was thinking, how much his eyes betrayed.

'Go. Leave me.'

He hesitated a moment – then bowed abruptly and turned for the door.

'That brief, cruel flowering of fire . . .' he heard her say, 'and then the dark.'

A trickle of damp, dark and viscous, stained the cell wall, oozing out as if the lifeblood of the rough stone were slowly haemorrhaging away.

Lai sat glazedly staring at the slow-spreading stain. His face was stiff with caked blood and his mouth fouled with the rank salt taste of it. He wanted to wipe the blood away but they had chained his hands so tightly behind his back that he could hardly move. Breathing was difficult enough through his battered nose; the cartilage felt pulpily sore and swollen. Broken, probably . . .

Not that it mattered now. What mattered was that he had failed. And failure meant death – his first, then Laili's. Bitter knowledge, more bitter than the taste of dried blood in his mouth. That there was no hope any more.

He heard the metallic scrape of the cell key turning in the lock. Had they come for him already? He had wanted a time, just a little time to prepare himself, to steel himself for the Torquistar and his machines of torment.

He slowly raised his eyes and saw Clodolë.

'Lai.'

'I've nothing more to say . . .' The words came out clumsily, almost drunkenly; his mouth seemed swollen out of shape.

'Look at me, Lai.'

'I had no – accomplices.' Such an effort to get the words out. 'I was alone. And now I'm tired. So very tired.'

'Please, Lai.'

Please? His drooping eyelids opened again. She had said please?

'Keep looking at me.'

She lifted her silvergauze veil, slowly revealing her face. Now he saw what she had been concealing from him – and from the rest of Myn-Dhiel.

Her tawny brows had vanished and in their place sprouted slender wisps as fine as the pale hair that cascaded about her shoulders, spidersilk strands that were whiter than moonlight. Huge, dark-slanted eyes stared at him from a bone-white face as though through a forest of silver-frosted fronds.

'Go on,' she said. 'Say it. I'm hideous.'

'No,' he said, still gazing at her. 'Not hideous.'

'I'm a freak. A monster.'

She came closer now, bending over him, her Changed face floating above his, a moon illuminating the darkness.

'Look more closely, Lai.'

He looked directly into her eyes.

'Why don't you turn away? Why don't you recoil from me like all the others?'

'Because . . . I find you strangely – beautiful.'

'You're lying. Lying to save your skin. You think I'm grotesque.

'I'm too tired to lie. I only say what I see . . .'

The wailing – thin and desolate – came from behind the nailed-up shutters of a silk merchant's house. Azhrel pushed the door; the lock was broken and it swung slowly inwards. A miasmic stench of decay enveloped him; he took out his kerchief and clapped it over his nose.

The wailing stopped.

'Anyone there?'

Thieves had already been in and stripped the place; the furniture, the hangings had gone, even the lucernae had been tugged from the ceiling by their chains, leaving gaping holes in the plaster.

He looked into the downstairs room: in the checkered light filtering in from the shuttered window he saw the body of a woman sprawled on the floor, head-down. Even the balsam-impregnated kerchief could not block out the all-pervading smell of death.

The wailing began again – but softer, weaker this time.

He ventured up the stairs; a covering of moth carcases muted his footsteps. On the first floor landing he stopped, blinking back tears. Children lay dead; two dark-haired boys and a little girl of no more than four or five years . . .

Looking upwards he saw newly hatched moths clinging to the ceiling, clustering in the corners of the room; the walls seemed papered with new-drying moth-wings.

A stir of movement in the far corner caught his eye. He had not seen the crib till then. He hurried across – and saw cowering inside a thin, emaciated child, a babe who stared at him with dark, terrified eyes.

'Don't be afraid.' He gently lifted the child; she was soaked in filthy rags, half-starved, a featherweight in his arms. How long had she been left there alone, untended, whilst the rest of her household lay dead?

He stared up at the quivering whitewings – then down at the dark-tousled head drooping against his chest. It took but a few seconds to scoop some of the live moths into his jar. For his purposes, he must keep them alive . . . even if for just a few days longer.

The child whimpered at the sight of the crawling creatures.

'Don't be afraid, sweetheart. I won't let them harm you. You're coming home with me to Mirali. She'll look after you.'

The Grove was lit with shafts of lemon-luminous sun; Lai wandered amongst the blackened stumps, feet scuffing through the thick cinder piles, the charred smell of burned wood in his nostrils.

Far in the mist-drifted distance, a bird called, long and low, a curling note, an unanswered question.

Such desolation. Such emptiness.

A single pearl of water dripped onto his face. He looked upwards.

Rain was falling; cool, spring rain, drop by still drop onto his head, onto the barren, cinder-choked ground. And as it fell, he saw the new green begin to push its way through the ash. Vines uncurled before his eyes, branches put out buds, freshly verdant leaves opened . . .

And still the rain fell—

Lai opened his eyes to see Clodolë leaning over him. She was silently weeping; tears dripping like spring rain onto his face.

'Clodolë?' he said dazedly, floating between dreaming and waking.

'Stop it,' she said in a stifled voice. 'Stop it happening, Lai. You can make it stop.'

'Stop – what?' He was still dizzy with sleep, disorientated.

'This.' She clutched at her pallid face, her fine white hair. 'The Changing.'

'Don't you realise yet? It's irreversible. I can do nothing to help you.'

'Don't say that, don't say that!' She clapped her hands over her ears, rocking her body to and fro in grief. 'You're an Aelahim. If anyone can do something, you can. Listen, I will save your sister from the hierophants if only you can stop this happening to me. I promise I will restore her to you, Lai. Please, please help me.'

Lai swallowed. He could lie to her – to save Laili. He could pretend powers he did not possess. But somehow he could not bring himself to lie to her. She was so distressed – so genuinely distressed. He sensed that maybe she was changing in other ways . . .

The dream image haunted him.

Her tears.

'Clodolë,' he said more gently this time. 'I can do nothing to help you.'

'Don't say that, don't say that!' She clapped her hands over her ears. 'You were my last, my only hope.'

'No one can stop it now. It is irreversible.'

She turned her head away, the fine pale hair shimmering like a silken cloak about her white shoulders; she was weaving her slender fingers agitatedly together, in and out, in and out.

'You see this Changing as a punishment – but perhaps it is something else.'

'What else could it possibly be?'

'A transfiguration . . .' he murmured, still wreathed in the mists of his dream. What had it meant? Out of her grief . . . could come a new beginning? Out of the tears of the Changed would come renewal?

Damp air, chill with the earthy fragrance of autumn rain, penetrated Melmeth's cell. But a deeper, more pervasive cold chilled his mind as he huddled, wrapped in a blanket, on his bed. The last, lingering effects of the drug had left him weak in body, but his powers of reasoning were returning, his thoughts were less confused. He could distinguish now between reality and boskh-induced hallucination.

What day was it? Lai had told him Laili was to be tried on Sh'amain, the Day of the Dead. And whilst he had been lying here in the grip of the drug, his city had fallen into the hands of fanatics.

The door grated open; he glanced up, half in fear, half in hope of release.

'I've brought your son.'

'Clodolë – is that you?' He peered into the shadows. There was a faint brightness there, a glimmer of white in the darkness.

'Your son, Melmeth.' Her speech seemed stilted, as though she were having difficulty enunciating the words clearly.

'My son,' Melmeth repeated in awe. He lifted his arms – and felt a warm, wriggling bundle placed in them. The bundle gave off a sweet milky smell: a nursery smell. His hand gingerly explored the contours of the baby . . . The soft, silky down on his head, the button nose . . . And then a small fist gripped his finger – hard.

'What a grip!' he said, unutterably delighted. 'And I don't even know your name, little one.'

'*She* named him Dion. After your father.'

'Where is she?' he said, suddenly sobered. 'And why have you brought him here now?'

He heard her hesitate.

'I thought you might like to be together for a while.'

Clodolë's fingers brushed his head. The brief touch evoked a pin-prickle of white light. Shivering, Melmeth closed his eyes – then opened them again.

For a moment he saw her. Imperfectly, but the essence of vision was there. She seemed to radiate a star-glimmer, ephemeral as evaporating mist.

'What's . . . happened to you, Clodolë? You're—'

But she had already gone, leaving him alone with his son.

Suddenly he felt a drowning wave of fear for Laili wash over him. Overwhelmed, he hugged the baby to him, murmuring into his soft hair.

'Oh, Dion, Dion, what a bitter inheritance your father bequeathes you.'

Tread of distant footsteps in the unlit passageway outside Lai's cell, coming steadily nearer—

They were coming to interrogate him again. Sweet Goddess, he couldn't take any more; he had come to the end of his endurance . . .

The footsteps stopped outside his cell door – he held his breath, awaiting the inevitable.

The key clicked and turned in the lock. The door swung slowly open. The footsteps receded down the passageway. Lai waited. No one came in.

It must be a trap. *The prisoner was killed as he attempted to escape* . . .

He crawled slowly towards the open door and looked out into the passageway. There was no one there.

He followed the high-walled passageway until it led out into the donjon courtyard; blinking in the daylight, Lai stared around, waiting to be challenged.

No one seemed to notice him. He began to wonder if he had become invisible.

He pulled the cowl down to hide his bruised face and limped across towards the gate. Now, surely, they would stop him.

The tarkhastars on duty hardly glanced at him.

'Pass, brother.'

The day was drab and a thin, cold wind blew over the city from the east. Lai walked out onto the bridge and crossed the Yssil, waiting all the time for the sudden cries, the rasp of drawn blades, the feet pounding after him. Once he glanced back uneasily over his shoulder – but no one had followed him.

On the quay, he stopped at a pump and, cranking the handle till the water gushed out, tried to wash off the clotted blood from his face, grimacing as he did so. The cold of the pump water was real, at any rate, as was the dull stinging ache of the half-healed lacerations.

What day was it? How long had he been in the donjon? Day had merged into night in an endless ordeal of interrogation. Had they set him free too late to save Laili? Or was there still a chance?

As he raised his wet face, he became aware that there were people about on the quay. People moving, as if with one purpose, venturing out of their boarded-up houses, clutching spice balls stuffed with acrid-scented moth herbs. Everywhere Lai saw pinched faces, hungry faces. Many coughed as they shuffled onwards up the hill.

He drifted in amongst them, letting himself be carried onwards, flotsam on the tide.

'Where are you going?' he asked.

'Haven't you heard, brother? They're trying the witch. The witch who caused the plague.'

It must be Sh'amain. The Day of the Dead.

A long line of hierophants was wending its way towards the arena, chanting, purifying the streets with incense herbs; some whipped themselves in their frenzy with knotted flails until the blood ran down their backs.

Lai bowed his head and followed in their wake, gradually merging in amongst the brotherhood, one dun-coloured robe amongst the many.

Blue, bitter incense fumes wafted into the subterranean laboratory.

Azhrel sniffed the air, frowning. Sh'amain funerary smoke here, beneath the armoury? He had heard the chanting, he had seen the processions of flagellants and penitents, the crowds surging towards the arena. The Tarkhas House was deserted, all the tarkhastars drafted to guard the Arkhys as she made her way to the arena to attend Laili's trial.

And no word from Lai.

Azhrel forced himself to concentrate on the task in hand; setting up the slow-burning fuse that – if his calculations were correct – would trigger off a series of firedust artifices more complex than any devised by any other Memizhon Artificiar. It was vital to ensure that a suitable time lapse occurred between the moment of fuse-ignition – and the moment of combustion.

His mind wandered again from his final calculations . . .

Had they caught Lai? Had they slit his throat and thrown his body into one of the plague pits? Or had they handed him over to the Torquistar for interrogation?

The thought nagged like a deep-festering sore. He could not bear to think of it. If they had put Lai to the question, the Torquistar would have tortured the truth from him by now. Everyone broke – sooner or later. Azhrel knew their methods. He had tried to repair the damage inflicted on political prisoners – but all died in agony, broken and mutilated beyond his healing skills.

The smell of incense wafted in again . . .

He looked up, suddenly uneasy. So little time to finish.

Even if Lai was dead, he must keep his part of their agreement. He must try to save Laili. He could only hope that his artifices would cause enough of a distraction to enable him to get to the girl in the confusion. Orthandor was primed in his part as well. There was just this final length of fuse—

The door was kicked open. The stink of incense billowed in from their Sh'amain lanterns. Suddenly the laboratory was swarming with dun-robed men.

'Arlan Azhrel!'

Azhrel grabbed his lantern in one hand, the fuses in the other and began to back towards the tunnel door.

One hierophant swept his hand along the rows of glass alembics and pipes, sending them crashing to the floor.

'The work of Ar'Zhoth! What vile heresy have you been practising here?'

Azhrel fumbled for the catch of the tunnel door; the fuses hampered his shaking fingers. They came towards him, smashing jars of iron filings and saltpetre, lacquered granules and metallic salts until a cloud of dry chymical powders clogged the air.

'You'll burn for this!'

'Be careful – ' he begged them. Why wouldn't the damned catch click open?

'Heretic!'

The door gave way and he half-tumbled into the darkness, kicking the door shut against them. Carefully setting the lantern down, he rolled one of the empty barrels against the door as the hierophants battered their fists against it.

The door timbers juddered; they must have picked up a bench to use as a battering ram. The barrel would not hold for long against such an assault.

And if they caught him – what help would he be to Laili then?

Fingers sweating, he forced the end of one of the fuses into the nearest barrel of firedust. Then, bringing the other end of the fuse to the lantern flame, he waited as the thuds of the ram shook the door timbers, each blow setting his heart thudding in sympathy.

'Light, curse you, light . . .' he muttered.

Why wouldn't it catch fire? His sweat must have dampened the fuse-cord.

A tiny flame caught – and began to travel slowly along the thick cord.

The timbers splintered and faces appeared behind the broken door. Hands tore at the wood as the hierophants began to clamber through the jagged hole.

'There he is! Take him!'

Azhrel snatched the lantern and made off into the darkness, offering up a silent prayer as he ran to any god or goddess who happened to be listening.

If his calculations were wrong, they'd all go up together.

'Help build the pyre, brother.'

A log was thrust into Lai's arms; staggering under its weight, he carried it across the arena sand to where the other hierophants were stacking logs and branches about a central stake. He handed it to them and watched as the pyre-builders poured oil onto each fresh log. This pyre would flame like a pitch-torch when it was lit.

Shading his eyes, he looked about him, searching for a glimpse of Azhrel's dark, scarred face.

It was nearly dark; the dull light of day fast fading to a dismal twilight. Guttering torches illuminated every tier of the arena, fast filling with spectators. Lai could sense the tension in the air; the mood of the crowd was sombre and dangerous.

Individual shouts rang out.

'Show us the Aelahim woman!'

'Show us Melmeth's whore!'

Clodolë and Jhafir entered and took their places on the Arkhan's dais, the Haute Zhudiciar, in his crimson robes of office, Clodolë in her ivory gown, both figures as stiff and monumental as the effigies in the mausoleum.

The shouts of the crowd suddenly became more frenzied.

'Witch! *Witch!*'

A slender figure was being led across the white sand; her russet hair was loose about her shoulders, her feet bare, her coarse prison gown tied about the waist with a length of twine.

The tarkhastars on the lower tiers linked arms, struggling to keep the spectators from bursting into the arena.

Lai felt as though a feversweat had chilled his body; now hot, now cold, he struggled to master his anger. She looked so frail, so defenceless – and yet she bore herself with utter self-composure as if she were oblivious to the shouts and threats of the crowd.

I'm here, Laili. You're not alone.

A brazen clamour of gongs dinned out, drowning the roars of the crowd.

The High Priest of Mithiel entered the arena. He was robed in his full ceremonial attire and the splendour of his gold-embroidered vermilion and scarlet vestments dazzled the eye. He stopped before Laili.

'Why have you brought me here?' Laili fought to keep her voice low and steady, determined not to show them how afraid she was.

'You are here to answer the charges put to you by the people of Perysse.'

'Charges?' Laili said. 'If this is a trial – then why is there no one here to speak on my behalf?'

Ophar turned away and climbed the stair onto the dais to take his place beside the Arkhys; two other priests, dressed almost as splendidly as he, followed. Gradually, other hierophants filed in, lining the walls until the arena was ringed with dark-robed men. Ophar raised his hand and the tarkhastars stepped back, leaving Laili standing alone, wrists and ankles shackled, before her judges.

'Our first charge is that you did summon the moonmoths by means of chants and sorceries.' The priest on Ophar's right read the accusations from a parchment. 'Our second charge is that you did seek by use of the drug boskh carried by the moonmoths on their wings to enchant the Arkhan and to bend him to your will.'

'Our third and most serious charge,' Ophar said, 'is that you did

271

then persuade the Arkhan to renounce the faith of his fathers and adopt the pagan ways of your Goddess – an act which has had grievous consequences for the Arkhan and the city of Perysse. How do you answer these charges?'

'Grievous consequences?' Laili forgot her own plight in her fear for Melmeth – what could have become of him?

'How do you answer?' repeated Ophar in a voice of stone.

'I deny them all,' she said, raising her head and staring him directly in the eyes.

A derisive murmur ran through the crowd; they were against her already, they would not take any notice of what she said.

'Let us proceed to the first charge.' Ophar sat back in his chair, folding his hands together. 'Bring in the witness.'

Lerillys was ushered into the arena. She glanced once at Laili and then, with a demure expression, declared her name and her position in the Memizhon household.

'Describe to us what you saw the night of the feast last Mithiel's Day.'

'I was passing through the courtyard below the Torella Sarilla's apartments when I heard singing. Strange singing . . . It made my flesh creep. The moon was rising and as I looked up, I saw that woman,' and she pointed accusingly at Laili, 'at her open window. She had stretched her hands out to the moon – like so – and was murmuring words in a tongue I did not recognise. Magical words. And then she brought out a flute – and began to play. Such weird music . . .'

The muttering of the crowd grew louder.

'Is this true? Did you sing at your open window the night of the feast?' Ophar asked.

'It is true,' Laili said softly. They were going to twist the truth their way, no matter what she said.

'Summoning the moonmoths?'

'On my island we sing to greet the moon in spring. And yes, we of the adept, do try to charm the moonmoths to dance in the Grove—'

'We of the adept!' Ophar interrupted. 'What does that mean?'

'I am – was – a priestess. On Ael Lahi both men and women serve the Goddess. And I served the Goddess of the Grove.'

'Make sure every word is set down,' Ophar said to the priest at his side who was scribbling busily in a ledger. 'And for what purposes do you summon these moonmoths?'

'To celebrate the Goddess.'

'And to take the dust from their wings?'

Ophar's eyes narrowed almost imperceptibly; Laili knew she must phrase her reply with infinite care.

'Only the Elder Ones know how to use the dust. I have not been instructed in its secrets.' Her milk-heavy breasts had begun to ache; Dion would need feeding soon. She wished she could ask to sit down – and yet she wanted to appear strong before her accusers. She wanted them to know that they did not frighten her.

'Even though you deny summoning these moonmoths, nevertheless they appeared in Perysse the very next night! I put it to you that this must be more than coincidence.'

'I don't understand how they could have crossed the seas in a night and a day,' Laili said, beginning to falter.

'Yet they came! And with them came blindness, plague and death. Worse than death! And meanwhile you worked your spells upon the Arkhan, inducing him to divorce his lawful consort Clodolë and banish her.'

'What proof do you have that I was in any way involved in that?' Laili cried. 'Where is the Arkhan? Only he can answer that accusation!'

Ophar rose from his chair, one finger pointing at her.

'The Arkhan does not have to answer any accusations. He is beyond inquisition. He *is* the law.'

'Then why is he not here to judge me?' Laili gazed imploringly around the arena at the impassive faces; nowhere could she see the slightest flicker of compassion or even concern. They had judged her already; this trial was merely a formality. She was guilty.

'This is an ecclesiastical court. Here we deal with matters of the soul.'

'Who saw me plying the Arkhan with boskh? Who heard me persuading him to take the drug?'

'Our proof is that the Arkhan is blind!'

'Blind!' Laili dug her nails into her hands, willing herself not to break down. Her dreams. Sweet Goddess, all her dreams had been true—

'And we are still in the midst of this devastating plague. The looms are silent, the ships are held in port to prevent the spread of the illness. The city is dying. And these cursed moths breed and multiply in the flesh of our citizens—'

The mutterings became a rumble of discontent. A single voice rose above the others.

'Burn the witch!'

'Tell us how we may end this plague. You summoned the moonmoths – now you will send them away.'

'But I can't. I don't know how.'

'Oh come now, a powerful witch who can call these creatures from across the seas can just as surely send them away again.'

Laili felt the milk leak out from one breast, staining her dark prison gown.

'I – I'm just an ordinary woman.' She turned to the blur of faces in the tiered seats. 'I gave birth a few weeks ago. I have not caused this plague. And I cannot stop it. Believe me – I would, if only I knew how!'

Ophar was not even listening; he was conferring with the two priests who sat beside him.

She let her mind wander far from the arena, longing to hold Dion in her arms again, to feel his soft cheek against hers; he was the only constant left to her in this crazily shifting world. And how long would she be allowed to keep him with her?

Ophar rose to his feet.

'Laili Dhar. You have been accused of grievous crimes. This court finds you guilty.' Laili felt her legs begin to tremble; she willed herself to stay upright. 'In order to appease the god whose anger you have incurred in bringing these creatures to our city, you are to face the fate of those found guilty of witchcraft. Death by fire.'

'Death!' arose the echo from the watching crowd.

Faces staring at her; impassive faces, triumphant faces; Lerillys, a little smirk of a smile playing at the corners of her lips.

'Death by fire.' Laili repeated without expression. She had gone numb, she felt nothing. Her mind was a blank. Any moment now she might begin to shout, to rage at the injustice of this farce of a trial – but for now she could only think of Dion.

Had they expected her to shriek, to faint? They seemed a little disappointed at her apparent lack of reaction, these venerable priests. She would not give them the satisfaction of seeing her despair. She would walk to her pyre, her head held high.

CHAPTER 26

Lai positioned himself at the foot of the pyre, his head bowed, the hierophant's hood covering his face.

Gongs dinned; the shouts of the crowd grew louder, more frenzied.

Laili was coming towards him. She walked steadily, almost unseeingly onwards, her head still held high, her blue eyes fixed on some distant horizon.

Her courage in the face of imminent death brought stinging tears to his eyes. But tears would not help her. He must stay alert. And pray that Azhrel's plan would still work.

As she began to climb the rickety ladder, she slipped and lost her footing.

He put his arms out to steady her. She glanced around – and recognised him.

'Lai?' she murmured.

'Hush.' He pushed her up the last rungs towards the stake.

'Burn! Burn! Burn!'

Lai looped a rope around Laili's waist and pretended to secure it. All the time he was speaking to her in their own language.

'When the pyre goes up – jump. I'll be here to catch you. Or you'll be suffocated by the smoke. Understand?'

She nodded.

He climbed back down from the pyre, offering one last, fervent prayer to the Goddess, lips soundlessly moving.

Hierophants surged forwards. Their bright torches dripped flaming pitch onto the oil-soaked timbers.

Ymarys's pyre rekindled in Lai's mind, the pungency of the terebinth and pine oils, disguising the reek of burning flesh—

The pyre blazed up into the night; flames began to crackle and roar.

'Jump, Laili!' Lai cried.

In the sudden billowing of smoke, he saw a swirl of movement as she threw herself towards him, the hem of her crude gown already afire. The gust of heat almost burned his breath away.

They collapsed onto the sand together, Lai smothering the flames with his body.

Torches in the Grove . . .

'Quick!' He pulled her to her feet. Once before they had fled from these barbarians. But this time they would escape. This time—

Ophar barred their way with his torch. Lai fell back, his eyes seared, half-blinded by the brightness.

'You will not stop it now,' Ophar snarled. 'She must burn—'

A thunderous explosion cracked the air asunder; the earth shook underfoot, even the stones of the arena trembled. Ophar lost his balance; his torch dropped into the sand.

An incandescent bursting of sizzling, blinding lightning followed, setting the air crackling with whitefire. Fountains of dazzling stars erupted around the perimeter of the arena, until the sand seemed awash with silver light.

Azhrel had kept his word.

The crowd seemed bemused, distracted by Azhrel's artifices, uncertain whether the brilliant display was part of the ceremony – or divine intervention.

'Over here, Lai!' a strong, dark voice cried. Azhrel came into the arena, pushing through the ranks of hierophants as they broke up in confusion.

'Sarafin's Gate. Quick.' Azhrel put his arm around Laili's shoulders and, between them, he and Lai began to hurry her through the milling hierophants. As they ran, white flakes began to spiral down, snowflakes falling from a clear, star-studded sky.

'Snow – so early?' Ophar whispered. 'Impossible . . .'

They came, a blizzard of whitewings, tumbling out of the black sky, drift upon drift of moonmoths, falling like wintersnow onto the arena.

'Not snow—' someone cried. 'Moonmoths!'

Panic broke out on the tiers and terraces.

Jhafir signalled to the tarkhastars to sound the tarkenhorns; the fanfares rolled across the arena but still the moths swirled about the torchlights, settling in women's hair, swarming over the clothes and bodies of the spectators, filling the air with the beating of their velvet wings.

Lai pushed open Sarafin's heavy fang-toothed gate; Azhrel looked back at Lai as the last of his artifices sputtered and died, his eyes burning with a wild elation.

'It's worked. Look – it's worked, Lai.'

Down they fluttered, a ghostly leaf fall blown by an invisible wind straight towards the pyre flames. Alight, moonmoths dropped like fiery hail-stones as their wings burned to ash; the hot air whirred with the last frenetic beating of their singed wings.

'Down with Memizhon!'

Lai hesitated on the threshold of the gate, glancing back over his shoulder into the arena. Just below the dais a group had overpowered one of the Tarkhas Zhudiciar and were hacking at his bleeding body with his own blade. Fighting broke out amongst rival clan groups.

'Down with Memizhon! Down with Memizhon!' The chant grew ever louder.

'For god's sake, Lai!' Azhrel cried. 'Come on!'

Lai . . . help me . . .

He saw Clodolë raise her skeletal hands to protect her eyes, the flameglow colouring the pale veins red, like fiery blood.

They cannot resist the flames . . .

And in that instant he knew in his heart he could not let her die.

Amidst the comet-hail of burning moths, Clodolë was drifting helplessly towards the pyre, a frost-rimed skeleton leaf, sucked inexorably by the fire's hot breath towards the heart of the flames.

'Help me . . .'

'Lai!' Azhrel was holding him back. 'They'll cut you to pieces!'

'I've got to go back.' Lai wrenched himself free from Azhrel's restraining grip. Running into the mêlée, he almost tripped over the body of one of the Tarkhas Zhudiciar; bending down, he seized the man's razhir.

'There's the Arkhys!' A hoarse howl of triumph arose.

All those around stopped to stare.

'*Djhë*! Look at her!'

'Obscene!'

'A freak!'

Lai struggled back through the crowd towards Clodolë – but Ophar reached her the first. He saw Ophar put his hands about her shoulders as though to protect her, he saw her turn her head to face him, he heard Ophar cry out as he saw what she had striven to hide from him for so long.

'Not you, Arkhys – not you—'

Clodolë's eyes, fireglazed, stared into his.

'One with the Undying Flame, Ophar.'

Ophar seemed to steel himself; he took her hand in his own.

'One with the flame,' he repeated. 'Yes. I see it now.'

'NO!' Lai shouted above the cries of the stampeding crowd.

'Ultimate oblivion of fire,' Ophar said, his eyes fixed on hers. Together they moved forward as one. 'Ultimate consummation . . .'

Lai grabbed hold of Clodolë's arm as the fire caught Ophar's robes alight and dragged her back from the pyre.

'Clodolë!' cried Ophar, a howl at once crazed – and ecstatic.

And then the fires roared up, whiter than molten metal. Clutching at his fire-seared face, the High Priest toppled forwards into the pyre – and the flames devoured him.

Lai could see nothing but smoke swirling about a world peopled with milling shadows.

'This way, Lai!' Other voices were calling him, urging him away from the flames, Orthandor's stentorian parade ground voice bellowing over the rest. 'Hurry! Hurry!'

Arms reached out through the smoke, hands caught hold of him, caught hold of Clodolë.

Dank air, moist and chill, on his hot face. They were winding deeper into the hill, slowly going down, down – and the angry roar of voices was diminishing, fading to a distant ominous rumble until there was no sound but their halting breathing.

Rho Jhan paused in the tunnels, listening to the distant screams and cries in the arena.

He had not abandoned his men, leaving them to the mercy of the mob. No, he had taken it on himself to end matters his own way.

The people had risen against the House of Memizhon. Clodolë had gone to the flames. Now only Melmeth remained; weak, half-crazed and blind.

It made sense.

He would be hailed as the hero of the revolution, the man who had freed the city from the tyranny of the House of Memizhon.

He drew his razhir in the dark and tested the keenness of the blade against his thumb.

It would be a clean, swift kill. A Razhirrakh's deathstroke.

Dion had fallen asleep at last in Melmeth's arms. Melmeth laid the baby gently down on the bed and moved to the window.

'Goddess,' he whispered. 'What's happening?'

He had heard that wild roar the night he had lost his sight. Then it had led to riot – and his imprisonment. This time imprisonment would not be enough; they would be hungering for his blood.

'We've got to get you out of here, Dion.'

He fumbled his way to the door. Suppose . . . just suppose Clodolë had left it open? He tugged at the handle – but it was securely locked.

If only there were some implement with which he could try to pick the lock. His fingers moved across the table, searching in vain for a spoon, a comb even . . .

His sharp ears caught the sound of footsteps outside. He stopped, listening. His tarkhastars come to protect him, or the mob, intent on assassination?

'Who's there?' He had no weapon with which to defend himself – or the baby. They could kill him if they must – but Dion, they must not find Dion.

He heard someone insert the key in the lock, the key begin to turn.

Even here, so deep below ground, the smell of the fires singed the moist air, a taste of ashes that clogged the mouth and stung the eyes like flakes of windblown sea-salt.

Lai put his arms around Laili and hugged her close.

'Where's Dion, Lai?' Laili said in the darkness. 'Where's my baby?'

'The baby,' Lai repeated, stricken. In the chaos of the arena he had forgotten Dion altogether.

Lai threaded his way through the ranks of silent, staring effigies; the baleful glitter of jewelled eyes seemed to follow his progress across the drifting charneldust on the floor.

And then he heard a cry – saw a splash of light from Melmeth's open door. Someone had reached the Arkhan before him.

He shifted his grip on the razhir hilt as he crept forwards; his flame-blistered hand was still sore and the unfamiliar blade felt unwieldy and awkward.

Melmeth was on his knees, arms flung up to protect his head; Rho Jhan loomed over him, razhir in hand.

Even in the dusty darkness, Lai could see the gleam of Rho Jhan's white teeth, bared in a predatory, feral grin. And the glint of a blade upraised to strike.

'Hold!' he cried with all the strength of his smoke-choked lungs.

Rho Jhan spun around – and his blade came shrieking down out of the darkness.

Lai parried. Sparks, brighter than firedust, spiralled into the shadows.

'Lai Dhar,' Rho Jhan said with a hint of dry laughter. 'Well, well . . . I've waited a long time for this.'

A thud shook the ancient timbers of the mausoleum door. Lai heard a buzz of voices outside, angry as wasps swarming from an overturned nest.

'You have visitors, lord Arkhan,' Rho Jhan said, still smiling. 'Shall I let them in?'

The mausoleum juddered again as axes and blades hacked at the door.

'Stay where you are!' Lai lunged at Rho Jhan, but the Enhirran neatly sidestepped the thrust, leaving Lai's blade slicing empty air.

The curved blade slashed at him again, he felt the steel sizzle past his cheek.

A baby's yell, loud and terrified, shivered through the chamber. Caught off guard, Lai glanced round—

And Rho Jhan uncurled like a snake rearing to strike; his razhir tip slashed Lai even as he vainly, exhaustedly parried, scoring his shoulder open.

The mausoleum door burst open and the mob came tearing inside, torches held high.

'Where's the Arkhan?'

'Here,' Rho Jhan said, gesturing with his razhir. 'Here's your Arkhan. This pathetic, shambling wreck of a man.'

Lai narrowed his eyes in the torchlight; there was something familiar about the leader of the rioters . . .

'Mirghar?'

'Lai Dhar? What are you doing here?'

'I'm here to defend the Arkhan.' Lai clutched at his shoulder; blood trickled out from between his fingers, hot and stickily wet.

'What do you want of me?' Melmeth came forwards into the torchlight, carrying the sobbing Dion.

'We want justice. And we want our freedom.'

'Who are you?'

'Slaves. Brandslaves.'

'But – but I gave orders that the slaves should be freed!' Melmeth shook his head. 'Were all my orders countermanded? All my reforms?'

'What are you waiting for? Kill the tyrant!' yelled one of the crowd and the slaves surged forwards.

'Wait!' Lai cried, shifting the blade to his left hand. 'Listen to Melmeth. Did you hear what he said? He gave orders that you should all be freed. And for that, Ophar and his hierophants have kept him prisoner—'

'Of course Melmeth says he intended to free you.' Rho Jhan's jeering voice drowned out Lai's. 'He'll say anything you want to hear if you'll spare his life. Is that what you want from your Arkhan? Weakness, craven cowardice? Let me kill him now – and be done with it.'

'Proof,' Mirghar said. 'Where is the proof?' His face was strained, taut.

'There is no proof,' Lai said. 'Who do you believe? Melmeth – or Rho Jhan? You have a choice.' He looked Mirghar directly in the eyes. 'I've made my choice. And to kill Melmeth, you'll have to kill me first.'

Another slave came pushing through the throng to stand beside Mirghar, blade in hand.

'How do we know you won't renege on your promise, Melmeth?'

It was Eryl: lithe and muscular, her shaven head gleaming in the torchlight, she had altered almost beyond recognition from the frail girl Lai remembered from the dye works.

'Look around you.' Melmeth's gesture encompassed the moth-eaten effigies that silently stared down at them. 'Half the wealth of the House of Memizhon is concealed in this chamber. It is yours to buy passage home to your countries or to do with as you will.'

'And will you let yourselves be bribed?' Rho Jhan said, sneering. 'It's a trick. Another Memizhon trick.'

'Look closely at the effigies,' Melmeth said. 'The eyes are sapphires, emeralds, topazes, all precious stones.'

'Doesn't it wring your hearts?' cried Rho Jhan. 'It suits my lord Arkhan to be charitable now – now that his life hangs by a thread. How can you be sure he won't set his Tarkhas on your trail, accusing you of stealing his treasure?'

Eryl dug her fingers into the yellowing wax face of a grey-bearded effigy, its dusty hair a nest of cobwebs, and plucked out an eye. Holding its jewelled facets up to the torchlight, she let out a soft whistle of amazement.

'This isn't paste – it's genuine.'

'There's only one man here whose opinion I trust – Lai Dhar.' Mirghar turned to face the other slaves. 'Let them go – and kill the

Enhirran.'

'No—' Lai began but the brandslaves had already launched themselves upon Rho Jhan, dragging him down, tearing the razhir from his hand even as he tried to beat them off.

'*Aiiii!*' Rho Jhan screamed once, a terrible, grating scream. And then there was no noise but the sound of rending and hacking. Lai, sickened and faint, looked away.

'Go now,' Mirghar said. 'Take Melmeth with you. While you can.'

Lai nodded.

'I'll never forget this.'

Mirghar briefly touched his forehead in salutation; Eryl rose on tiptoes and kissed his cheek.

'A life for a life. Now the debt is paid.'

Dawn on the banks of the Yssil. A wind stirred the willows on the far bank; a pall of rising smoke besmirched the clear sky.

Lai gazed out over the mist-wreathed water meadows. The last hours had passed as in a drear dream. Weak from Rho Jhan's blade-slash, he had doggedly led his charges through the dank unlit subterranean passages beneath the city, struggling onwards through the darkness until they reached the Adriel Gate.

'Sunrise,' Lai said dazedly.

'That red glow isn't the sunrise.' Azhrel came to stand beside him, steadying him. 'The citadel's on fire.'

'Myn-Dhiel – in flames?' Melmeth cried. Laili, Dion clasped tight in her arms, turned to look back at the city.

'It must have spread from the arena,' she said.

Lai's teeth juddered together; the world around him seemed bleak and chill.

'You're shivering with fever.' Azhrel eased Lai down onto the bank. With gentle fingers he eased away the makeshift pad he had fixed over Lai's shoulder to staunch the blood. 'Hm. This wound needs cleansing and dressing.'

Lai shook his head.

'Must – get them to safety first—' He tried to sit up; the slightest movement sent stabs of fire shooting through his body.

Lie back, Lai . . . Her voice so soft in his mind, so different from the Clodolë he had first known. The breeze stirred her floating hair, it brushed against his skin, strands of spidersilk.

Tentatively, she reached out to touch the jagged gash. Lai

flinched . . . but where her fingertips brushed the wound only a cool, numbing sensation seeped into the skin, easing the pain. Touch of silvered lips, pressed to his forehead, his shoulder . . .

'Clodolë?' he said in quiet amazement.

A drop of water splashed onto Lai's upturned face then a regular pattering began.

The dream.

'Is it raining . . . ?'

But in his dream the rain had fallen on the Sacred Grove . . . and here it was falling on the city, dampening the fires, quenching the flames.

Clodolë's hand touched his.

Yes. It's raining.

The rain fell steadily from a cloud-palled sky onto the city. The cobbles were puddled with muddy waters, rivulets ran down the steep alleyways, churning grey with sodden ashes.

Smoke still hung everywhere, the damp, fizzling smoke that lingers like yellow wintersmog long after fire has been damped out.

High on the brow of the hill, the seven harkentowers of the ancient citadel smouldered, a jagged-spined, fire-blackened crown, a row of broken teeth, snarling their defiance at the city below.

No one took much notice of the bedraggled, dirt-smeared figures slowly stumbling through the rain-drenched streets. Galingal Lane was deserted, the peeling plaster walls stained grey by the driving rain.

'Just a little further,' Azhrel said, feeling Lai's steps slacken.

Rain dripped onto their heads from the tamarisk trees. Rain poured down the slate roofs and spouted from broken gutters. Azhrel tugged at the bell-pull. The bell jangled far away inside the house.

No sound of approaching footsteps resulted, only the monotonous spatter of pelting raindrops.

'Mirali! It's me! Open up!'

Lai began to sway on his feet.

'Hold up there, Lai!' Azhrel muttered. 'We're not beaten yet. Now . . . if I'd survived a riot, would I open my door to anyone who rang the bell?'

'No, Maistre Arlan,' came an irate voice from the other side of the wall, 'and neither would I alert the whole street to my arrival home!'

The weathered timbers creaked open a crack; Lai began to slide slowly to his knees on the muddy cobbles.

'Help me, Mirali—'

Azhrel caught Lai as he fainted and dragged him over the doorstep.

Lai heard Azhrel's voice as if from the far end of a long, dusty corridor. Someone was touching his shoulder, probing it, fingers moving nimbly, expertly across the jagged wound. He winced, anticipating the scarlet pain of razhir-torn flesh . . . and felt nothing.

Azhrel must have dosed him with black poppy-juice, nepenthe to dull the pain. There should be pain. Rho Jhan had slashed his shoulder open, there had been blood—

'He's stirring. Lai. Can you hear me?'

Light penetrated his closed lids, the yellowed light of an oil lamp. He must be lying in the tiring room at the arena. Mithiel had spared him, the deathstones had fallen in his favour . . . how else could he be here?

Azhrel was peering quizzically into his face. Behind him stood Laili, her freckled face pale and drawn, her eyes dark-rimmed with fatigue.

Dull stirring of memory, transient as a pale sunshaft piercing rainclouds . . .

'My shoulder—'

'Look for yourself.' Azhrel eased back the dressing.

Lai slowly turned his head, expecting a raw, oozing gash . . . and saw that beneath the bandages the jagged edges had already begun to knit cleanly together.

'But . . . how?'

'*She* touched you. *She* healed you.'

'So you were right, Arlan,' Lai whispered, letting his head drop back on the pillow. 'The Changed . . . are healers . . .'

Laili stroked his head, the soft stubble of regrowth.

'Your hair. Your beautiful hair. You had it shaved off – to save me.'

'It'll . . . grow again . . .'

Fluttering of wings – what was that flicker of white behind Laili? Lai's hand rose, pointing accusingly.

'But – but we destroyed them all—'

In a glass nectarium, moonmoths clustered close to the light.

'These are the last,' Azhrel said.

'But you gave your word—'

'They won't escape. Trust me. I know what I'm doing.'

*

284

Melmeth and Laili sat in silence in Azhrel's kitchen. Dion lay curled contentedly in his father's arms.

'Laili. We must talk.'

She said nothing.

'You're angry with me. You thought I had abandoned you. And you have been through a terrible ordeal. But we must try to put these things behind us—'

His voice was like a caress, soothing away all the bitterness of the past months, smoothing away the pain—

'Wait!' she cried. Dion started, whimpering against his father's breast. 'What are you saying? That I should forget everything that has happened? The long months alone? The betrayal? The fear? I have endured all these things and more, Melmeth my lord, to bear your son. And in the enduring I have become what I am today. Don't just – lull them away, as if they had never been. I don't want palliatives. I want somewhere to raise my – our – child in peace.'

Dion opened his eyes. A sad, low grizzling sound began in his throat. She wanted to stop shouting, she had no wish to upset the babe but the anger still burned on, bright as the hierophants' pyre.

'What are you saying?'

'I have Dion to think of. Don't you understand? Right now all I want for us is a place of safety.'

He raised his face towards her and she saw that he was weeping.

'Don't leave me, Laili,' he whispered. 'We need to give this time. Time together – healing time.'

'Tell me the truth,' she said after a while. 'How much can you see?'

'I can hear your voice,' he said. There was no point in lying; she would know if he was trying to deceive her. 'But all I can see of you is a vague shadowblur . . .'

'Oh, love . . .' She placed her hands on his forehead, gentle pressure of fingertips as soft as flower petals.

'I need you, Laili.'

Tears trickled from his damaged eyes down his cheeks, slowly dropping one by one onto Laili's face. He reached out to brush the wetness away – and Laili's fingers closed around his fingers, slowly, tightly.

CHAPTER 27

The smell of burning still charred the air as Lai clambered up the rocky scree, clothes tearing on the black zylthorns. There was a gap in the brown rock just wide enough for a man to squeeze through . . .

The parade ground was deserted; the Tarkhas House, its wings extending around three sides of the courtyard, looked as though the fires that had ravaged Myn-Dhiel had raged through its august walls as well. Shutters dangled at crazed angles from their hinges, the cobbles were littered with shards of broken glass.

He pushed open the armoury doors; the explosion Azhrel had set off in the powder room deep underground might have destroyed a section of the tunnels but it had left the barrel-vaulted roof and sturdy walls undamaged. Spacious and airy, it was ideal for his present purpose. What better place to set up a healing house than here? It was a pleasing irony that the walls which had resounded to the clash of blades would now shelter the wounded and the homeless.

The massive door to the Tarkhas House had been left ajar; as Lai pushed it open he saw that its paintwork was blistered and scarred as though repeatedly hacked with axes.

Within, the fine stone staircase was the only vestige left of the grand apartments he remembered. The tapestries of azure and blue were gone, the Tarkhas trophies, the antique weapons on the walls. And yet if he closed his eyes, he could see the stairs crowded with tarkhastars, he could see Ymarys come swaggering out of his rooms, to show off his latest outrageously expensive outfit, his pale hair perfumed, his silver eyes glinting maliciously with the latest court gossip . . .

Echo of laughter, fey and mocking . . .

'Is anyone there?'

His voice echoed in the empty stairwell; high above where the roof was open to the sky, startled pigeons flapped away.

He was not sure what drove him to climb the stair to Ymarys's rooms; only that he found himself opening the door and staring forlornly at the wreckage the looters had left.

Maybe he had hoped to find some trace of Ymarys's presence, some memento. Anything worth stealing had been stolen. Wisps of torn silks clung to broken panels, the gorgeous cushions and luxurious couches had been ripped open; mice were nesting in the exposed springs, amidst the shredded horsehair and kapok.

Lai knelt down and sifted through the debris; pages from folios of exquisite verse, smashed goblets of Yrildian glass . . .

And then something caught his eye. He dug deeper, sending spiders scuttling away. It lay half-hidden beneath a sticky tangle of webs, almost as if it were waiting for him to find it.

Ymarys's rosewood flute.

Lai carefully lifted it out and, wiping the spiderdust off against his jacket, examined it to see if it were cracked.

Moistening his lips, he lifted it to his lips and blew a few exploratory notes.

The notes hung in the air, a little breathy – he was out of practice – but true.

He hugged the flute to him.

Perysse was burying her dead. As Lai made his way through the city back to Galingal Lane, the stark sight of the gaping mass graves wrung his heart with pity. Tarkhastars from both Houses, Zhudiciar and Memizhon, worked side by side, dragging bodies from the burned buildings, tipping them into the lime pits. The last smouldering fires were out . . . and with the fires, the anger had died. Now Lai sensed only a numbness and a feeling of loss, of purposelessness. The people who had been howling for Memizhon blood now wandered past him aimlessly, or sat amidst the rubble, listless and lost.

The instant Lai entered Azhrel's garden, he felt as if he had crossed the bourne of another world. The rainwashed air smelt sharp and sweet, tinged with a taint of winter woodsmoke. A mistle-thrush sang in the bare branches of the ancient orchard trees above a carpet of fallen russet leaves.

Lai caught sight of Melmeth sitting beneath the trees.

'Who's there?' Melmeth called as Lai drew near.

'Lai, zhan.'

'So. Tell me how it is in my city.'

'The storm has raged itself out.' Lai faltered. 'But . . . there are many dead, many more sick and wounded.'

'Do they still call out against my House?'

'They are too exhausted to call out. They need—'

Lai stopped, hearing voices in the lane. The garden door creaked open and Azhrel came in, followed by another man, well-shrouded in a hooded cape.

'I'll take you to him.' Azhrel led the visitor across the dew-soaked grass towards them; Lai tensed, recognising the face shadowed beneath the hood.

'My lord Zhudiciar?'

'The same.' Beneath the hood, Lai saw the Zhudiciar's eyes were red-rimmed with sleeplessness, his usually immaculate grey beard untrimmed, unkempt.

'Why did you bring him here?' Lai blazed at Azhrel.

'*I* asked Azhrel to bring him,' Melmeth said, raising one hand as if to quell Lai's outburst.

'Zhan.' Jhafir fell to his knees on the wet grass and seizing Melmeth's hand, kissed it. 'You are safe. Maybe there is hope for us, after all . . .'

Melmeth reached out and placed his hands on Jhafir's shoulders to raise him to his feet.

'What's happening?' Laili came running out of the house. She stared accusingly at Jhafir – and then at Lai.

'I can make plans to escort you to the summer palace at Shandaïra, my lord, until we have set everything to rights in the city.'

'Run away? How will that look? "When the city most needed him, the Arkhan retired to the safety of his summer palace." No. I'm staying here.' Melmeth had clenched his fists as if he were ready to combat anyone who gainsaid him.

'But what of Laili and Dion?' Lai burst out. 'Don't you think they deserve a safe haven? After all they've been through—'

'I can speak for myself, Lai,' Laili said. The long weeks of incarceration had wrought more than a physical change in her; Lai sensed a new toughness, a determination that she would fight her own corner against all odds. 'If Melmeth wishes to stay then I will stay too.'

'And the brotherhood of Mithiel?' Lai cried. 'In their eyes you are still a witch!'

'You did not see what happened in the arena, then?' Jhafir could not suppress a shudder. 'After Ophar went to the flames, many of his

288

brotherhood followed him, crying, "One with the Flame." Those that survived wander around the ruins like lost souls now that their leader is dead. They have even let the sacred temple fires burn out. You have little to fear from the brotherhood.'

'When Ophar hid me away in the mausoleum I felt as if I had been buried alive.' Melmeth was looking in Lai's direction as he spoke and for one eerie moment Lai felt as if those dulled sightless eyes could see into his soul. 'And then you came to me, Lai. Perhaps this is a second chance. A rebirth. A new life from the dust of the Memizhon dead.'

'Even though Myn-Dhiel is a shell, the Tarkhas Memizhon ransacked—'

'It's not going to be easy.' Melmeth's mouth curved in a sad smile. 'These are dangerous times. But I've got to help to try to put things to rights. Do you understand me, Lai?'

Laili went to Melmeth's side and slipped her hand around his. Together they faced Lai, fingers tightly interlinked.

'If I must die, I had rather die knowing I tried,' Melmeth said, 'than run away and have to live with the guilt for the rest of my life.'

Jhafir gave permission for Lai and Azhrel to set up a makeshift hospice in the ruins of the armoury. The wounded of both clans, Tarkhas and Zhudiciar, Blues and Reds, were lain side by side where once the bladesmen had practised their deadly art in training for the arena.

Word soon spread of the work of the healing house. The last surviving victims of the plague left their homes, many blind, some shuffling along; others too sick to walk were carried on improvised stretchers, a sorry, straggling procession.

Lai walked amongst the sick, stopping to touch a forehead here, hold a hand there. He was stricken to the heart by the shrunken, withered limbs he saw, the listless, lacklustre eyes staring at him so imploringly.

Azhrel drew him to one side. 'We can't do this alone, Lai.' His face was pale, drawn with fatigue. 'We need Clodolë's help.'

'She's terrified to show herself – after what happened in the arena—'

'With so little boskh left now, she's our only hope. Can't you persuade her?'

Lai nodded. 'I can try. But I make no promises.'

Laili had left Dion sleeping in Azhrel's spare room whilst she went to wash his clothes at the well.

Clodolë heard a sleepy cry. She crept to the door of Laili's room and looked in. Dion lay in one of Azhrel's chests; he had kicked himself free of the blanket Laili had wrapped around him. Clodolë glanced over her shoulder – but no one was about. Dion's face crumpled up, his mouth opened in a loud, desolate wail.

Hush, now.

She leaned over and gently touched his cheek with her fingers, fully expecting him to roar even louder as he had done before. But Dion stopped in mid-wail and stared up at her, wide-eyed.

You remember me now, little one . . .

That intense, blue stare was fixed on her. Clodolë stared back, enchanted. He was not frightened of her any more. Or perhaps she was no longer frightened of him—

'Keep away from him!'

Laili snatched up Dion, clutching him protectively to her.

'How dare you! You've no right—'

I meant no harm.

Dion began to grizzle.

'No harm? You – who took Dion for yourself, telling the world that he was your son? You – who wanted me burned as a witch?'

I wanted a child of my own. You can understand that, can you?

Laili glared at her, evidently unconvinced.

Clodolë began to drift towards the door.

I know you can never forgive me. I just wanted . . . I wanted to say goodbye to him . . .

'Goodbye? So you're going?'

There's no place for me here . . .

She would go to take one last look at the ruins of her palace, to walk in the night gardens one last time. And then she would follow the call of the dark. Never to have to endure the scorn and pity of others again, never to have to see the revulsion in their eyes . . .

'Clodolë! Clodolë!' Lai called up the stairs.

Laili came out of the kitchen, holding Dion in her arms.

'She's gone.'

'Gone? Where?'

'We – we had words. My fault. I – I couldn't trust her yet, Lai. Not after what she did to me – and to Dion. I'm sorry.'

Lai ran out into the lane; there was no sign of her. Had she gone back to Myn-Dhiel? He climbed the hill and wandered through the ruins, calling her name; but if she was there, she did not answer.

The sun dipped behind the distant hills; he sat down on a marble bench in the neglected gardens and let his head sink into his hands.

Maybe he had tried to accomplish too much too soon. His dream – the Grove built anew amidst the ruins of the city – she had been a part of it. He knew now he could not achieve the dream without her help. All the other Changed Ones had gone to the fires . . . only she had survived with her unique gift of healing.

And she had run away from him.

The twilit sky was so pale that the first wash of night had stained it purple. A single star rose, a child's wishing star, duskstar . . . and beside it, the swelling moon, a crescent of pearl, mark of the Goddess.

In Ala Sassistri's grove, the windharps whispered a faint tremor of notes.

He took Ymarys's flute from his belt and raised it to his lips, echoing the notes of the windharps . . . then wreathing a melody around them, translucent as running snowwater, the trickle of melting icicles, a song to the winter moon.

Lost in the music, it was some while before he became aware he was not alone. She was standing in the shifting shadows of the myrrh trees, listening. He laid down the flute.

Don't stop. .

'Is this where you've been hiding? In the gardens?'

Where else can I go? If I show my face by day, they'll only try to destroy me. You should have let me go to the flames. What use am I to anyone now? I'm just a freak, a dumb thing to be pointed at, a monster to frighten children—

'Is that what you think?'

She shook her head – but he knew she was listening to him.

'You haven't yet learned how to use your gift; perhaps you are not yet aware of its potential. Trapped in this Changed body, you see only your limitations.'

My gift?

'Your gift to heal. You healed me. And now there are others who need healing. They need your help, Clodolë.'

I healed you because I – because I care for you. I don't know if I can do it again.

He reached out his hand towards her.

'We can work together.'

Is that what you really want? The two of us – together?

291

'Yes.'

I . . . I need time . . .

'Time is running out for the people in the healing house.' So clumsy! The words were out of his mouth before he could stop them; he could have bitten his tongue. If she were to help them, then she must do so not because he had taken advantage of her vulnerability, not because he had made her feel guilty – but of her own volition.

I still haven't come to terms with this . . . Changing, Lai. I was Arkhys, controlled all the Seven Cantons – and just at that moment when I held all Ar-Khendye in the palm of my hand – I lost it. I lost everything. Sometimes I feel it would be better if I just . . . faded away . . .

'Clodolë – wait—'

She was drawing away from him, blending into the silver-leaved shadows of the myrrh grove.

Farewell, Lai . . . A silvered kiss, borne on the nightbreeze.

'I didn't mean – Clodolë—'

The moon vanished behind the clouds and the Sassistri's grove was plunged into sudden darkness.

The face of the winter moon illuminated the healing house, as white as pearlmilk, ancient and enigmatic.

Lai, keeping the night vigil, tried to keep awake. But his drooping eyelids seemed so heavy he could scarcely keep them open; he had been working since dawn and now . . .

As he slept, he dreamed that a veiled woman moved like a moonsilvered spectre amongst the wounded. Her cool touch drew the gnawing pain from burned flesh and broken bones; those who shook with fever were calmed into tranquil sleep.

By the morning, a transformation had taken place. No miracle cures . . . but all around Lai saw clear eyes.

'You're feeling better?' he asked again and again and each time was rewarded with the affirmation, 'Much better.'

And several spoke of vivid dreams in which a dark-eyed healer had visited them, a woman whose skin was paler than the moon.

Today I was able to assure the Arkhan that all the moonmoths had finally been eradicated and, given that assurance, he has ordered the Haute Zhudiciar to reopen the ports. If I was not strictly truthful, it was only in the interests of scientific research, as I shall now set down . . .

Azhrel checked that all the windows and the door were tight shut.

292

Then, opening his robe, he took the lid off the glass nectarium and sat down, waiting, pen in hand.

In the grey dawn, the moonmoths' glitter had dulled, their wings seemed to drag behind them, leaving a trail of powdery scales. They settled on his skin, soft as the first fall of snow. Azhrel brushed them away again and again until only a few remained, clinging tenaciously on to his flesh.

Khaldar's emaciated body, an empty husk, eaten away from the inside . . .

Azhrel gazed down at his right arm, his right breast. One . . . no, two, three, four, five puncture marks, angry and swollen, marring the tawny-smooth skin. No more. And all about him lay dead moths, their papery wings drying in the dawnlight. He began to note down his observations in his journal . . .

The secret is to nurture only a few. A very few. Just enough to ensure the survival of the species . . . and without jeopardising the host's survival.

The ache of his swollen arm nagged. The moth-eggs lay deep inside his body, waiting for the moment to hatch . . .

They are the seeds of a better world, a world where disease and decay can be controlled.

But this work cannot be done in Perysse. I have to go to Ael Lahi to consult the remaining adepts of the Grove to fully understand the potential of the Goddess's gift. And if that means nurturing the moths within my own flesh, I must endure it. If I die, others will learn from my mistakes . . . but this time the gift will not be needlessly, ignorantly squandered..

The pen dropped from his hand, leaving a blot on the journal. He lay back drained, exhausted, beached on a bare and empty shore.

Lai opened the door to Azhrel's study and then stopped as his feet crunched on the dead moonmoth carcases littering the floor. The nectarium was empty.

Azhrel lay slumped over his open journal.

'Arlan!' Lai touched his shoulder. Azhrel winced. 'The moonmoths—'

'I know, I know.' As Azhrel tried to push himself up the loose brocade robe gaped open, exposing the dark puncture wounds.

'Those marks.' Just to look at the punctured flesh, dark-swollen like the bruises left by the kisses of a passionate lover, made Lai's stomach crawl. 'You said – you assured the Haute Zhudiciar—'

'So I lied a little. No one's been harmed. They're all dead now.'

'Why have you done this to yourself? Why have you let them

invade your body, pollute your flesh?'

'Because . . . because I'm an eccentric scholar whose scientific curiosity outweighs his better judgement.'

'But we agreed to destroy them. We agreed it was the best – the only way.'

'And I wanted to prove a theory. You told me that for years without number the adepts on Ael Lahi have been nurturing these moonmoths. I think I may have discovered how: selective hosting.'

'But this – this hosting.' Lai struck the open page of Azhrel's journal with his hand. 'You're carrying the eggs of these parasites in your own body. No one has done this – and lived. You're like to *die* when they hatch—'

'Dying was not my intention. No; I'm taking them back to Ael Lahi where they belong. And if your adepts will accept me into their Sacred Grove, I hope to learn some of their healing skills.'

'Ael Lahi,' Lai echoed. 'You're going to Ael Lahi.'

'The *El'Jharradh* is leaving next week for the Spice Islands. You—' and Azhrel hesitated. 'You could come with me.'

The lure was so strong. To return home at last.

'If only I could,' Lai said quietly, his voice aching with longing. 'And – one day I will. But there's so much to be done here.'

The troubled sky showed rents and rifts in the louring cloud through which the first light was leaking.

'I understand,' Azhrel said quietly. His eyes were dark as smoke in the dawnlight and as impenetrable. 'I understand.'

The quay had come back to life. Foreign sailors from ships newly arrived in port strolled arm-in-arm with laughing Arkendym girls; children chattered and played, clambering all over the coils of ropes, dogs pranced and barked.

Barques rocked at anchor on the rivertide, dwarfing the smaller fishing craft, their great striped sails furled.

Merchants strode along the quay to inspect their cargoes. Bales were unloaded, precious woods, casks . . .

A team of workmen were hard at work demolishing the burned-out shell of the Pleasure House of Ysmodai; the giant of a foreman put down his pickaxe to wipe the sweat from his eyes and bellowed out a greeting to Lai.

'A fine morning, Orthandor!' Lai called back.

People came running up to touch Lai, to stroke his bright hair. Men whom he had first met lying wounded in the healing house, shook him firmly by the hand, fervently thanking him.

Lai smiled, laughed with them. But his eyes sought out a gilded barque; the *El'Jharradh*, Azhrel had said she was called, Swift Hunter, her figurehead a scarlet hawk—

She was already pulling away from the quay! Lai ran to the edge.

A sombre-robed figure stood at the rail, the wind tousling his glossy black hair.

'Arlan!' Lai cried. 'Why didn't you wait to say goodbye?'

'Better – this way—' Arlan's voice carried to him faintly on the river breeze.

'What do you mean?'

'One day I'll . . .' But the wind caught his last words and carried them away. Lai was left alone on the quay, watching until the *El'Jharradh* dwindled to a shadow on the horizon.

Lai rose through waves of ultramarine, translucent waters, blue as the night sky, drifting to the surface of sleep. Someone was gently stroking his forehead, his hair, his head was pillowed on a soft lap.

'Mmm . . . that's good . . .'

Lai's eyes opened to see two slanted, moondark eyes looking down into his, framed by a veil of translucent hair. A face from beyond the sea of dreams. The face of a wraith, hauntingly, weirdly beautiful.

'Clodolë?' he whispered.

Her lips brushed his cheek. He could hear the lapping of dark waters . . . and as if from very far away, he heard her speaking to him.

What I said to you in the grove . . . it wasn't wholly true. I thought I had everything as Arkhys, but it was all empty, meaningless . . . you weren't there beside me . . .

The dark pool drew them down, they were drowning in its moonlit waters, drowning deep in each other . . .

No need for words now. They understood each other perfectly.

ENVOI

The morning was misty, clear skies and pale water shimmering beneath a heat haze.

Dr Arlan Azhrel leaned over the rail, straining his eyes for a first glimpse of the island.

Wreathing mists began to melt in the sun's heat, parting veils, revealing the secret verdant island they had been shielding. Azhrel's heart danced like the gilded light on the water.

Ael Lahi. White Island.

'I've done as you wished, Lai,' he said softly. 'I've brought them home.'